WINGED HUSSARS

BOOK THREE OF THE REVELATIONS CYCLE

Mark Wandrey

Seventh Seal Press
Virginia Beach, VA

Chris Kennedy/Seventh Seal Press
2052 Bierce Dr.
Virginia Beach, VA 23454
http://chriskennedypublishing.com/

Ordering Information:
Quantity sales. Special discounts are available on quantity purchases by corporations, associations, and others. For details, contact the "Special Sales Department" at the address above.

Cartwright's Cavaliers/ Mark Wandrey. -- 1st ed.
ISBN 978-1942936725

For Fafherd, the best cat I've ever known. I hope you forgive me.
Rest and hunt in the halls of the All Father. Good journeys.

For Kim Sommer, Robert Dean, and Rich Weyland.
Thanks for the celestial calculations!

And to my wife and son, always.

"I looked, and behold, a black horse; and he who sat on it had a pair of scales in his hand."

— *Revelation 6:5*

Earth Mercenary Ship *Pegasus*

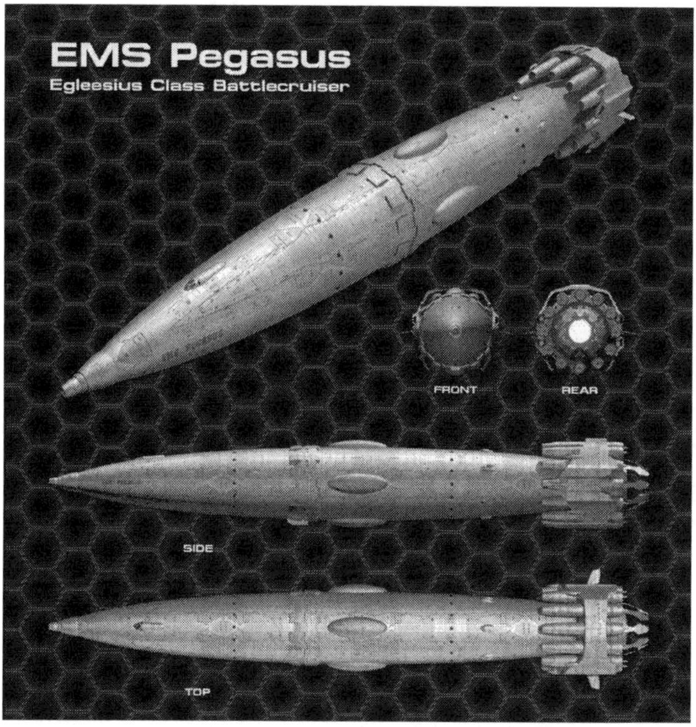

Part I

"More than three months after the last mercenary company returned from what many are calling the Alpha Contracts, we'd given up all hope of any more survivors making their way home. Needless to say, it was a complete surprise when the only company sent from the tiny state of Poland, the Winged Hussars, arrived one day. Like the other companies who made their way back to Earth, the Winged Hussars had suffered terrible casualties while completing their contract.

The only company which ventured off-world to serve as a space navy unit, Poland sold all its strategic reserves of rare earth and precious metals, as well as its ancient nuclear weapons, for a used military ship in order to qualify for what the Galactic Union's Mercenary Guild representative termed a 'fleet escort contract,' one of the highest-paying contracts taken by an Earth mercenary company. They spent months making the ship combat-worthy before leaving with the other 100 companies to find their fortune in the galaxy.

The Winged Hussars not only managed to come home alive, unlike 96 other companies, but they also came home in a different ship than they'd left with. Successfully executing part of their contract, they earned a 50 percent payout. The exact amounts of contract payments are confidential, but it was the biggest of the Alpha Contracts, and likely exceeded the GDP of most of the world's governments.

With four surviving companies back, and little chance of more, the survivors met in Houston to discuss the future. After the meeting, they noted the similar themes of their companies and logo designs, and they began calling themselves the Four Horsemen. The four companies, Winged Hussars, Asbaran Solutions, Cartwright's Cavaliers, and the Golden Horde proclaimed that this was not the end of Human mercenary service, but only the beginning."

Excerpt from "In Our Own Time – Dawning of the Horsemen"
by Jimmy Cartwright, Sr.

* * * * *

Chapter One

Obiya 199 System
Way Station *Abyss*
Inner Crapti Rift

The transport was roughly a mile across and twice that long, and shaped somewhat like a dowel. It maintained a steady spin to provide gravity for its occupants, even under acceleration, of which it had precious little. Built in a shipyard of a race that no longer existed, the UTS, or Union Trade Ship, *Topul's Pride* had plied the space lanes of the galaxy for more than a thousand years. She'd changed hands hundreds of times, and always for a few more credits than the time before.

Known affectionately as 'Heavy Haulers,' her class of ships was officially labeled *Behemoth*-class, and it was a class whose existence was absolutely necessary for interstellar commerce to function. *Topul's Pride* carried out many duties. She hauled massive bulk cargoes in bays ranging from a few dozen yards on a side to hundreds of yards. She carried as many as 25,000 passengers at a time, many more if they were packed in. A half dozen times, she'd served to evacuate refugees from war-ravaged worlds. She could also act as a transit rider, docking as many as 100 smaller ships either incapable of making the transition through hyperspace by themselves, or merely riding along for economy.

Displacing several million tons, the *Topul's Pride* was one of the cheapest ships to operate in hyperspace, thanks to the inverse square rule that made huge ships cheaper and tiny ones more power-hungry. Her only downside was the glacial pace she maintained between a system's emergence point and its stargate. She could manage, at best, a stately 0.5 gravities of constant ion-driven thrust, which meant as much as a 30-day transit between the LaGrange points in some systems. Her crew tried to transit through stargates at the highest possible speed to save travel time in the destination system, as you emerged from hyperspace at the velocity with which you entered it.

It was this which, more than anything else, determined the course the *Topul's Pride* took as it moved about the galaxy. Her master endeavored to pick star systems which possessed emergence points closest to their stargates, and to arrive at them when their geometry was the most favorable, greatly reducing her transit times.

This was why the crew found itself in the Obiya 199 star system—the transit time between the emergence point and the stargate was only six days. Unfortunately, that was also plenty of time for the ship to fall prey to pirates.

"We have hyperspace emergence," chittered the sensor operator of the pirate cruiser *Opportunity*. At least, that would have been the ship's name if it were translated into English from SleSha. The ship had once belonged to the Oogar, who'd called it by an entirely different name, before the crew had been brutally murdered by the SleSha boarding team.

"Excellent," the *Opportunity's* queen said. Both the ship's master, commander of the fighting contingent, and queen of the brood, she was best described as the mother of every being on the ship. She ran her multifaceted eyes around the bridge to verify all stations were manned and ready, then extended her awareness to the boarding teams in their shuttles. Everything was as it should be. "Helm, accelerate toward the prey, full power."

The *Opportunity* had been quite speedy before it fell into the pirates' hands. However, the Oogar were only moderately G-tolerant, while the insectoid SleSha were extremely so. They'd recalibrated many of the safety features of the cruiser which now groaned under a tremendous 11 gravities of sustained acceleration, more than 10 times the emergency power of the hapless *Topul's Pride*.

"Any signs of ships coming from the way station?" the queen asked.

"None," the sensor operator confirmed. The consortium which operated the way station maintained regular patrols of the stargate, but only intermittent patrols of the emergence point. They'd been hovering near the emergence point for two weeks now, waiting for this target to come by.

The crew stood up well to the acceleration. The ship was capable of more, though not much, as using this much power further stressed the already tortured superstructure. The Oogar were giant purple ursoids who built their ships with massive open areas. The SleSha had placed reinforcing beams everywhere, but the ship was still developing structural cracks.

"We're on intercept," the navigator announced after 100 seconds of acceleration, "closing at 30,000 feet per second!"

"Initiate coast!" the queen ordered, and the ship's thrust was instantly cut. The multitude that was the ship's brood rocked from the sudden cessation of thrust, hanging on with the hooks on their four sets of legs.

"Eleven thousand miles," the sensor operator said.

"Effective laser range," the tactical coordinator said. "We have a firing solution on their weapons' arrays."

"Have they targeted us yet?" the queen asked. The sensor operator worked at the instruments for a moment.

"No," it answered at last.

"Hold while we coast," she finally pronounced. A display, one of the efficient single subject Oogar models, showed the *Opportunity*'s closing vector and range to the *Topul's Pride*. The range decreased at over 6 miles per second. In under half an hour, they'd be on top of them.

"Range now eight thousand miles," the sensor operator said.

"Get a firing solution on their facing defensive arrays," the queen ordered, "and plot for the others. They will roll once we engage. Navigation, prepare to match their rotation. Order the boarding pod pilots to prepare for launch." She didn't have to order the boarding drones ready, she could feel their minor intelligences in her mind. They would fight until their bodies were destroyed, or she ordered them to stop.

"Firing solution ready," the tactical coordinator pronounced. The weapons operators prepared to fire.

"Launch the boarding pods," she ordered and gave them a few seconds to thrust away. She was an instant from ordering her ship to open fire when the sensor operator screamed, "New contact!"

Even though she didn't have to, the queen turned her head to look at the sensor operator's screen. It showed another ship, behind them.

"Identify it!" she chittered.

"Battlecruiser-sized," the operator said; "range 5,000 miles and closing!"

"How?" the queen demanded. Their angle of approach was completely out of alignment with the emergence point. For the new ship to be where it was, it would have had to have been lying in wait. And how long? Also, they were going far too fast! The *Opportunity's* sensors were powerful, there was no way they would have missed a battlecruiser accelerating behind them.

"We are being hailed," the comms operator chirped.

"Let me hear it," the queen ordered. A moment later the grunts and guttural growl of a mammalian race came over the bridge's speakers, rendered into SleSha by the ship's computer translator.

"Vessel *Opportunity*, this is the *EMS Pegasus*, flagship of the registered merc company Winged Hussars. Your weapons lock on the heavy hauler *Topul's Pride* has been logged and recorded as an act of piracy. By the regulations of the Galactic Union's Mercenary Guild, you are a fair and free target. You will power down your weapons and alter course away from the *Topul's Pride* immediately, or you will be fired upon."

"Entropy!" the queen cursed. Escape was their only option. "Helm, skew turn, 90 degrees off axis from the former target. Get us away, emergency thrust!" The boarding crew and their pods were a total loss. Or were they? "Order the pods to continue with their boarding operation," she added. "Tactical, fire two salvos. Disable as many of the transport's defenses as possible."

The *Opportunity* yawed, her weapons pulsing coherent light at the still unsuspecting transport. As soon as the pirates had altered their rotation, the drive system dumped super-cooled hydrogen into the ship's dual reactors and the fusion torch channeled raw energy out of the reaction chamber. The G forces quickly climbed to past 15 Gs.

"Structural failure in Bay 11!" the damage control monitor chittered.

"Ignore it," the queen barked. "We must gain speed if we are to—"

"Drone fighters," the sensor operator said. It didn't sound excited; it sounded resigned. "At least five squadrons incoming. They anticipated our course. Intercept in five minutes."

"Skew course 90 degrees!" she ordered.

"The ship will not survive that radical maneuver at this thrust," the engineering controller said, the first comment he had made. "I'm decreasing power to twelve Gs to mitigate ongoing structural failures." The queen wanted to go over and rip his antennae off, but pressed into the bear-shaped command couch under 12 gravities, she couldn't move.

"Fine," she said. "Tactical, stand by to fire missiles at the battlecruiser." The *Opportunity* shuddered, and the lights flickered.

"Weapon impact," the tactical controller said. "Particle beam, 10-terawatt range! It only grazed our shields. We have partial shield failures in three quadrants. I'm trying to compensate."

"Return fire!"

Missiles left the bays of the *Opportunity* on all sides, spun, and accelerated away at almost a thousand Gs. At the same time, the four heavy laser cannons mounted on the ship's sword-shaped fuselage maneuvered along tracks that provided purchase and power until they were able to bear on the mercenary ship, then they opened fire.

"The battlecruiser is matching course, but not accelerating at its probable top rating," tactical said. "Why not?"

"Because they don't have to," the queen said. Four minutes later the drone fighters arrived. The *Opportunity's* close-in defensive lasers began pulsing at the drones, tiny autonomous gun platforms mounted on fusion-powered drives which danced around the pirate ship and ripped at its shields. The pirates' over-stressed tactical coordinator concentrated on trying to defend against the drones, which left them momentarily open to attack.

The *Opportunity* shuddered and moaned like a wounded animal. Primary power failed on the bridge, and all thrust ceased. Several bridge crew were sent spinning across the space. The lights and bridge controls went dead, then the backup lights came on. A greenish hue, the lights were ideal for the Oogar; unfortunately, it was a portion of the light spectrum invisible to the SleSha, and it took an agonizing minute for regular lighting and some computer control to be restored.

"Damage report," the queen said, dreading what she would hear.

"Another particle beam," damage control said; "the shot was perfectly aimed. It destroyed the main power and data conduit from engineering. I have a team trying to reroute. All weapons are down, but we still have minimal shielding."

"The drones appear to have ceased fire," tactical announced. "We destroyed two of them."

The comms station beeped for attention. The queen glanced over to see why the operator didn't answer it, only to find it impaled on a broken support, spurting bodily fluids.

"Someone take the comms operator's job," she ordered, and one of the currently unoccupied weapons crew did so.

"*Opportunity*, this is *EMS Pegasus*. Our last shot was targeted to disable. You will stand down now, or you will be destroyed. You have 10 seconds to comply."

* * * * *

Chapter Two

Alexis Cromwell, commander of the Winged Hussars and captain of the company's flagship, the *EMS Pegasus,* was strapped into her free-orienting acceleration couch in the combat information center, or CIC, quietly enduring the ship's three gravities of thrust as the battle developed. The drones had done their jobs, and when the crazy SleSha refused to give in to the inevitable, she'd pumped a shot from her ship's spinal mount through the stolen cruiser's guts.

"I need that ship in one piece," a disturbingly deep voice purred from the rear of the bridge. Alexis stole a glance at their guest and contract holder. The Equiri was humanoid, though about seven and a half feet tall. He sported a rather unexpressive horse-like face with all-black eyes, complete with upright ears, but his mouthful of razor-sharp teeth indicated he didn't chew grass. His only hair was a wild mane of crimson fur, and he wore a ship's uniform familiar to any Human. Across his shoulder was the blazing blue logo of the Peacemaker Guild, a splayed tree that always reminded Alexis of Yggdrasil from Norse legend. "The writ is not one of death, and the ship has a claim against it."

"I understand that, Enforcer," Alexis said, referring to the Peacemaker by his title; "however, if they are not stopped they can do considerable damage to my ship and possibly escape." She looked back at the tactical screen. "Besides, they're pirates, not crazies. There's no profit in death."

"They are signaling surrender," her communications officer, a Buma, said. There was a murmur of celebration on the bridge. She wasn't sold yet.

"What's their status, Flipper?" The sensor tech, an aquatic Selroth, took no offense at his nickname. He'd long become accustomed to the Human habit of nicknaming aliens with unpronounceable names. He'd watched some of the old Earth TV shows to see where his moniker came from, and he had found the being admirable.

"They are powering down both reactors," he burbled from inside his full helmet. He could wear a water mask if necessary, but at battle stations he preferred the full head bubble. Should the ship get hulled, he only had to add gloves, and he was space-ready. "They've stabilized their flight and are working to control the damage. Some secondary damage to their ship appears to be the result of over-G maneuvers."

"Noted. Helm, reduce thrust to one gravity and bring us onto an intercept course for the pirate ship."

"Your ship and tactics are…unique," the Enforcer said.

"Oh?" Alexis replied casually. "Have you studied starship combat? The Equiri aren't a merc race."

"No," the Enforcer replied, "I'm an outlier in our race. There are a surprising number of our kind who enjoy physical conflict. Prior to our joining the Union, they tended to end up in more violent sports. It was our society's way of channeling that aggression." Alexis nodded, watching her bridge team work more than listening to the alien. "However, as part of my Peacemaker training, we are instructed in all manners of warfare." Now he had her attention.

"Indeed?" she said. "Humans don't yet have any Enforcers in your guild, if I recall?" He shook his head, the huge mane of bright red hair waving back and forth.

"Not yet," he said. "Your race is about to gain full membership. At that point, you will need to begin supplying staff. Up until now, it's been voluntary." Alexis nodded again, she'd known that much. "As I mentioned, the space combat orientation is part of our training. I found it interesting because my people do not go into space travel much." He gestured to his imposing body's stature. "Most space based races tend more towards your stature. It makes it uncomfortable for us."

"I can see that."

"During this study we, of course, learned how the majority of races use their layered defensive/offensive approach. Drones are used on intermediate targets only, because they tend to not carry out orders well beyond their instructions."

"Yes," Alexis agreed, "pity our AI tech is so underdeveloped." The Enforcer's huge eyes narrowed a bit.

"Your drones are incredibly capable," he noted.

"I have good programmers."

"I see. Anyway, because drones don't improvise, races tend to only use them on clear targets that aren't exceptionally good at evading. They are not cheap, and to have them go crazy and attack meaningless targets or just wander around when the ship they were sent to engage is gone, is a waste of assets. You employed them almost immediately, rather like most use seeker drones. And your spinal mount allowed you to project power at an extreme range for that type of weapon." Alexis just listened. "I assume the drones provided hyper accurate targeting data?" She shrugged, and he showed pointed teeth.

"What would you do if you encountered one of the truly powerful space merc races? They use carriers and project hundreds of drones against your few dozen."

"Why, destroy the carrier first," she said, and showed her own teeth. The Equiri's grin faltered. "Paka?" Her Veetanho second-in-command turned from her control console, pointy nose wiggling and whiskers moving. She looked very rat-like at that moment, even with the dark goggles over her eyes.

"Ma'am?"

"Do we have an update on those boarding pods the pirates launched?"

"They are still on course for the *Topul's Pride*," Paka said. "They should intercept in fifteen minutes." They'd already tried to get the SleSha to recall them. The little wasp bastards were claiming inability, or failed communications, or some other bullshit.

"Can we get the drones to them before, or target them ourselves?" Alexis consulted Edwards, their TacCom, or tactical command officer, who was the only other Human on the bridge. A black man in his late fifties, he had a form of dwarfism which his parents couldn't afford to have treated with nanites when he was a child. He had compensated for his size by excelling in math and had become the best weapons officer Alexis had ever worked with.

"They've maneuvered so the heavy hauler is in the threat box," Edwards said. "We might pick off a couple, and punch holes in the whale too." Alexis knew he meant the transport and nodded, considering. The communications system issued a series of beeps, indicating an inbound transmission. She looked down; it was the master of the *Topul's Pride*.

"Speak of the devil," she said with a chuckle.

"Why do you speak to the devil?" the Enforcer wondered aloud. Alexis ignored him.

"Accept the call," she told the computer, which handled mundane tasks like regular communications.

"Why have you allowed my ship to be attacked?!" demanded the captain of the *Topul's Pride*, his visage appearing along with the annoying voice. He was a Sidar, rather like a bat crossed with a pteranodon, complete with long leathery wings. He snapped his long-toothed beak repeatedly in nervous annoyance. "That was not part of the contract!"

"The contract was not just with you," Alexis reminded him. "The Winged Hussars were employed by the Trade Guild to intercept pirates operating in the Inner Crapti Rift." She gestured randomly. "Those pirates look intercepted to me."

"You could have simply destroyed them the minute they made weapons lock! That is allowed."

"Yes," she agreed, "it is. However, we also have a contract with the Peacemakers Guild to take the ship intact for return to the Oogar."

"Peacemakers?" the Sidar captain asked, somewhat taken aback.

"Yes," the Enforcer said, able to stand now that the thrust was reduced to one gravity. "That vessel was taken from the Oogar in an act of piracy. We are going to take the ship back to Uuwato, their home world, and put the SleSha pirates before the Mercenary Guild tribunal. Their race is becoming a growing problem, as you certainly realize."

"What about the damage to my ship?" he asked, somewhat mulish now.

"Ask the SleSha," the Enforcer said, and the captain glowered.

"They are boarding our ship," he said, adopting a pleading tone. "What should we do?"

"You don't have defensive forces?"

"We are between merc contracts. We have a few squads of Lumar that are employees of the ship…" Alexis snorted. The Lumar were a merc species, sure enough, so they'd fight. But they were about as bright as a brown dwarf. They were as big as an Equiri and more Human in appearance, although they had four arms instead of two. Their two redeeming qualities were their generally hard-to-kill natures and their willingness to do the most boring shit-work imaginable.

"What do you want us to do?" Alexis asked. "Your guild contracted us to stop the ship. We did." She called up the contract on her slate, the small transparent computers that were nearly ubiquitous in the galaxy, and gave it a quick scan, even though she'd memorized it already. "There's no clause for shipboard action." The captain looked away and spoke to someone off camera, the mic muted. A moment later, he came back on.

"We wish to negotiate a contract rider."

Alexis grinned.

*****

Chapter Three

The SleSha leading Combat Team K didn't have a name. Drones trained to lead combat teams didn't get names; they were identified by scent and visual keys. When assigned a unit, their thoraces were laser-etched and painted with slightly radioactive paint that was easy to detect in their race's visual acuity range.

Team K's pod forcefully mated with a docking collar on the *Topul's Pride* within moments of the other nine pods. The SleSha didn't use breaching pods, as they were expendable and tended to be lost in boarding actions. Their pods more closely resembled ship-to-ship skiffs, 20-foot-long cylinders with outboard motors and a single Union-type docking collar. When fully loaded with a combat team of 10 SleSha warriors and a team leader, as well as all their weapons and armor, it was a snug fit.

The team leaders served several functions. Besides being the on-site coordinators of the non-sentient warriors, they were also the heavy weapons experts, tacticians, and pod pilots. They were almost smart enough to have been mates for their queen, but not quite, so they were neutered and trained as team leaders.

"<*Boarding successful*>" he sent to the queen on the now surrendered cruiser. "<*Awaiting orders*>" The other teams had already confirmed their statuses.

The queen replied immediately. "<*Teams G, H, I, J, and K, take the ship's engineering section and rig it for self-destruct*>" the queen responded.

"<I'm sending B and C to take the bridge, or at least neutralize it. Teams D and E will sow confusion and carnage. Team F is to find and secure a hyper-space-capable ship docked on the hauler for us to use to escape. Once we have that ship, we can use it to bargain with the mercenaries for our freedom!>"

Team Leader K sent a wordless acknowledgement of receiving and understanding the order then left the pod's controls. The warriors, almost twice the team leader's size with huge mandibles that could cut light steel, floated in microgravity along both sides of the pod as he moved toward the lock at the rear.

"*<Prepare for battle>*" he ordered, and the warriors were instantly alert and checking their weapons. Each wore light armor, which protected their softer abdomens, as well as a visored helm to protect their delicate, multifaceted eyes. In their two 'hands,' they cradled short-barreled laser carbines. Battle harnesses were hooked to each of their thoraces which held extra chemical magazines for the laser, a laser cutting torch, a simple first-aid nanite kit, and several small K bombs. A group of Humans observing the stoic scene would think they'd seen a nightmare—eight-foot-long flightless wasps in body armor, armed with laser weapons and bombs.

The team leader reached the rear lock and confirmed a good seal was in place. He activated the controls, and the thin metal door segmented and rotated into its recesses, allowing access to the ship's external door. He checked the controls; sometimes, the prey was stupid enough to leave them unlocked. This time they'd been wise.

He removed his secondary weapon, a medium-sized laser pistol and fired a single full-power shot. The gun buzzed, and a light, snapping sound indicated it had fired. The laser was in a specific wavelength that was visible to the SleSha, but not to many other species, giving them a tactical advantage. The beam sliced a half-inch wide, slightly angular hole through the lock. He waited to see if there was a hiss of escaping air, an indication the prey had decompressed the other side. That would also have been a wise move with boarding teams attacking, but this time, they hadn't proved so smart. The atmospheric pressures were nearly identical.

"*<Breach the lock>*" he ordered the two warriors nearest him, and he pushed away from the door. The two hulking warriors pivoted, selected sustained beam on their carbines, and began firing. Sustained fire made a smaller, less overall powerful beam. However, the beam was not the quarter second pulse of a normal rifle shot. This one lasted almost a second. With robotic precision, the warriors fired, aiming the weapons carefully by watching where the beams went. The tiny, one-tenth-inch pencil beams sliced through the lock like mandibles through a grub.

It took 10 shots from both warriors to complete the circuit. There was a groan of slightly stressed metal and, with the last shots, the door broke free and fell to the floor with a clang. The two breaching warriors moved aside while they replaced their nearly-spent magazines with fresh ones. At the same time, the next two warriors braced themselves against footholds in the pod, lunged, and burst into the *Topul's Pride.*

Gunfire instantly responded to their entrance as chemical weapons threw metal core ceramic pellets with considerable ballistic energy. One of the two breaching warriors was hit several times, and its bodily fluids sprayed from horrific injuries. The warrior possessed no concept of individual mortality. To it, the wounds were only an impediment to its mission. With its still-functioning arm, it swung its laser carbine forward and fired as it crashed into a wall.

A squad of five Lumar security specialists clung to the companionway. They hadn't made any attempt to use the abundant cover available to ambush the boarders, otherwise they might have held the lock for quite some time. Tactics, however, were not a specialty of the Lumar; they were better as shock troops. The SleSha warrior killed two of them before it bled out.

The second, uninjured warrior rebounded off the far wall, crossing the corridor twice as it did. It drew several shots from the Lumar, who held their shotguns with all four arms and didn't aim terribly well. None of the shots scored hits. The warrior snatched a K bomb from its belt and expertly heaved it down the corridor as it flew back to the pod.

"*<Explosion>*" it sent to its teammates and the team leader. The two closest to the lock pulled heavy shields from where they were secured to the pod walls, braced themselves, and held the shields side by side, effectively blocking most of the boarding lock. Down the hallway, the Lumar barked in surprise just before the half pound of K2 explosives inside the grenade detonated. The high order explosion tore the corridor, and the Lumar in it, to shreds, scattering them in all directions. The armor plates rang as shrapnel rebounded from them before bouncing away harmlessly.

The two warriors with armor plates moved forward, now using their shields as cover, and analyzed the results. The team leader watched through their eyes, assessing the results of the explosion. All five Lumar were dead. The ship's structure was not breached.

"*<Forward>*" the team leader ordered. "*<Establish a perimeter, find a computer terminal>*" Like a swarm of birds in flight, the seven surviving warriors swarmed out and filled the corridor. The two shield bearers led the way, while the others held laser carbines in one hand and K2 bombs in the other.

"They are spinning the ship," the team leader realized as the gravity changed. The defenders would have more of an advantage in higher gravity. It was unfortunate. The SleSha's distant ancestors had possessed flight, and still had phenomenal spatial awareness and acrobatic ability. They were hellacious fighters in lower or null gravity. But ultimately, it mattered not. If the Lumar were all the prey had, the ship was as good as theirs.

In minutes, the team had prepared defensive positions while one of the warriors located a computer terminal and began accessing the *Topul's Pride* network. The prey was just as digitally unprepared as they were tactically.

"*<Ship's schematic extracted>*" the warrior sent.

The team leader examined the map on his slate, quickly scrolling through the levels until he found the primary engineering control room. "*<I have the objective>*" he sent to their queen, who instantly shared it with the other team leaders who shared his goal. By relaying their positions through the queen, they were immediately able to coordinate their actions, as the team leaders could only directly communicate with the queen and their own warriors.

The five teams took parallel routes toward engineering control. The heavy hauler's massive interior spaces were symmetrical, intended to allow a crew to move easily with gravity or without. They were also designed to make it possible to use gravity from thrust as well as rotation. The ship was now both thrusting and rotating; for many races, that would have proven difficult to deal with. Once again, though, evolution favored the SleSha; they were unhindered. Moving with half their force on the floor and the other half on the walls, they leapfrogged toward their destination, 500 yards and dozens of decks away.

They encountered a small team of Lumar and liquidated them with no casualties, as well as a maintenance crew of Sidar. The avians panicked at the sight of the onrushing SleSha and were quickly cut down, but not before they contacted the bridge. Knowing they had been spotted, the team leader altered their route to confuse the defenders. They were within 100 yards of their objective when the situation changed. Team I, which was further outboard, encountered resistance. In the center of his warrior's formation, the team leader *listened* as the encounter played out.

The warrior on point for Team I was suddenly and instantly neutralized, without time to communicate how it had died. The team stopped immediately to assess the threat. The ship's defenders hadn't shown any weaponry capable of killing the warriors with a single shot, not even a lucky one. Then their rearguard was terminated.

"*<Move>*" the queen ordered, "*<All teams alter your directional movements and be aware heavy aggressors are in the field>*"

The leader of Team L was killed, and the Team K leader lost all sense of what was going on in that quadrant. Calling up the schematics, he moved his team laterally to their previous course. The queen noted the remaining Team L warriors were wiped out without firing a shot at their attackers.

The team leader didn't worry about his own fate. Even though he possessed a sense of mortality, unlike the warriors, he was more concerned about completing the mission his queen had assigned him before he died. Failing in death was the worst ending imaginable. When Team G was attacked, they finally got a glimpse of their enemy.

Team G had been moving at an obtuse angle to the objective, cutting through a maintenance passageway, when the point warrior emerged in a life support machinery room. The main doorway was open, and a large humanoid figure was framed in light from the outside hallway. The warrior instantly raised his laser carbine and fired a single shot at the center of the figure's mass. The target moved sideways with deceptive speed for its apparent size, simultaneously producing a shield on one overly long arm. The laser beam was deflected in a flashing arc, cutting several pipes in the space and setting off a number of blaring alarms.

The warrior crouched while two more of its team exited the maintenance passageway. An arm came around the corner and seemingly fired blindly. The air was rent by a hypersonic *Crack!* as a magnetic accelerator cannon, or MAC, round tore the emerging warrior completely in half and sent its body parts flying. The Team K leader heard the narrative from Team G's leader, and it was enough to finally understand what they faced.

"*<Human powered-armor suits>*" the queen confirmed for them, having an actual visual through the surviving warriors. "*<Order of battle has changed. You must hit them in force. Teams H, J, and K move to link up with and support Team G>*"

The team leader did as he was instructed, altering his team's course toward the besieged team. The direct route led across a largely-empty cargo bay. He and his team were racing across it when he realized his error as his point and rearguard warriors were both torn apart by laser fire.

"*<Clear the lanes of fire>*" he sent and dove toward the nearest cover, a series of three massive crates magnetically secured to the bulkhead of the hold. Laser fire just missed him, and he shot back with his pistol—two wild shots. He had no idea if they hit anything. Another of his warriors went down before they reached cover, leaving only six. His team was rapidly reaching combat ineffectiveness.

His survival likely for the next minute, he checked his link with the other teams while his warriors began firing back at their aggressors. A MAC round cracked the air above their heads. He quickly verified what he'd expected, all the teams were now engaged.

“<*Team K*>” the queen sent, “<*you are the closest to engineering control. Break off and try to reach it at all costs. You must make it there; the rest of your team is not essential*>” He made a mental nod and ordered his warriors to disengage.

The floor under their feet was very thick and meant to secure cargo. However, a bulkhead only a few yards away led to a maintenance and storage area. “<*Penetrate that bulkhead*>”

While two of the warriors fired in the direction of their attackers, the other four quickly used their carbines to cut through the wall as they had the earlier hatch. Under fire, it wasn't as neat and used a lot more ammo, but after a minute, a section of badly-mutilated wall sagged outwards.

“<*K bombs*>” he commanded the two who'd covered the others, “<*then covering fire while we egress. Take their extra ammo*>” he told the other four who deftly plucked the remaining laser carbine magazines from their comrade's belts. The two who'd been volunteered to stay behind snatched K bombs and lobbed them in the direction of the incoming fire. An instant later the hold shuddered from the detonations, and the four warriors raced for the exit, their team leader nestled amidst their armored bulks.

The two lead warriors careened into and through the hole they'd made. Part of one mangled section of steel didn't give way, and a warrior lost a leg on its sharp edge. It spun aside and raised its weapon, taking no notice of the injury except to alter its movements to compensate for the mutilation. The two warriors fired with wanton abandon as their leader came through, careful to avoid the jagged metal and the still twitching leg hanging from it. As the last two entered a MAC round blew one apart, spraying them all with blood and gore.

Behind them, in the hold, the last two warriors fired furiously. The team leader led his remaining three warriors across the maintenance section and out the door without checking to see if it was clear. There was no time, as he felt the two warriors they'd left behind cut down. Before they died, though, he received a clear view of the fight.

A huge multi-legged insectoid shot one of his warriors and then came at the last warrior who fired its laser as fast as it could. The warrior got off at least nine shots, missing with every one. Several went right between the monster's legs, or so close over the top that its thick black hair scorched. The monster crashed into the warrior. A much smaller furry mammal rode on its back, holding a disproportionately huge laser pistol in its hand. As it raced by, the little furry mammal casually shot the dying warrior through the head.

"*<At least one Tortantula and rider>*" he told his queen. He pushed himself and his warriors harder, knowing the Tortantula was racing after them. They cut a crazy path through the ship's corridors. Left, right, left, left, and then down a ladder. Being naturally arboreal, they had no need to reverse and climb down, they just ran down the ladder to their destination deck. The objective was almost in site.

As they ran, the team leader again checked on the others. He was horrified to see they were the only ones left alive—all the other teams were neutralized!

The queen urged him onward. "<*Faster, faster, faster. You must not fail*>"

At long last, they turned a final corner to see their objective ahead, and the door was open as well! The team spread out and accelerated toward the door, only to come to a skidding halt when two of the Human CASPers stepped out and to either side. Something else raced between the suits. Small and incredibly fast, it tore across the floor toward them.

The three remaining warriors lowered their bodies almost to the deck and shifted slightly as they fired, stroking the triggers of their laser carbines as fast they would cycle. The suits deployed shields that had been folded against their forearms, the shields deflecting the laser beams with ease. The warrior directly in front of the team lead held its ground, protecting the leader and firing steadily at the streaking black thing on the deck, while the other two plucked K bombs from their belts. The CASPers both pivoted MACs down over their shoulders and fired.

The warrior on the right had his head and half his thorax blown into goo before he could so much as arm the bomb. The warrior on his left flipped the bomb underhanded a millisecond before the MAC round smashed through its thorax. The explosion of the warrior's body was like a small bomb, blowing the team leader aside and into the corridor wall with a chiton-crackling crash.

The leader was conscious, but stunned. He saw one of the CASPers snatch the K bomb out of the air and slap it to the deck. At the same time, its laser shield fell from its arm, and the trooper caught it, reversed it, and slapped it down over the bomb. The trooper knelt on the shield just as the bomb exploded with a disappointing "*Phut!*" The laser shield absorbed and redirected the blast with no harm to the troopers.

He now had a perfect view of the fast-moving object. Its body was about three feet long, with six legs that propelled it at a high rate of speed. Antennae stuck out from under a shell-like carapace. Another insectoid species. His stunned mind tried to call up the name but failed. The queen spoke it for him.

"<*Goka*>" she said. The warrior continued to pour fire at it, trying desperately to hit it. When the Goka was only a few yards away, it finally succeeded. The carapace only ablated under the beam, though, and a tiny, smoking indentation was all that was left as a result of almost a megawatt of laser energy. The Goka were nearly immune to laser fire, he recalled.

The Goka launched itself at the last warrior, who fired at it but missed. The Goka didn't. It hit the warrior and produced a pair of short, curved, and serrated daggers it wielded with the same speed as it had moved. The warrior let the carbine fall and tried to grapple with the Goka; it bit down on the shell of the other being with its oversized mandibles with just as much effect as the laser—a little bit of the shell's armor flaked away. An instant later the Goka's blades flashed in opposition to each other, and the warrior's head was separated from its body.

The team leader's laser pistol was a few feet away. He scrambled for it, snatched up the weapon, and brought it around. One of the Goka's blades flashed and his arm was severed at mid-joint. The leader tried to snatch a K bomb from his harness, and that arm was fell off, too. Quite literally disarmed, he was helpless.

"*<I have failed you, my queen>*" he sent, filled with disappointment. The Goka was holding both knives at his neck now, pinning him against the wall. One of the CASPers walked over, and he could hear the operator speaking; its language translated by the distant queen.

"The captain wants that one alive. It's a combat leader. The Enforcer said it's testimony before the courts will help prosecute the SleSha." The Goka's own tiny segmented eyes regarded him under its armored carapace.

"Fine," the Goka chittered, "then it lives for now."

"*<You have one last duty>*" the queen said. He waited expectantly. "*<Die>*" Happy to finally have a task he could accomplish, he did as he was ordered.

* * * * *

Chapter Four

The Hussars' medics were still working to get the CASPer open when the Enforcer arrived. He strode down the hallway on his hoofed rear feet, his metallic-alloy shoes ringing with each step. He was in combat armor from head to hoof, the blue tree of the Peacemakers emblazoned on his breast. He held a unique quad-barrel laser cannon in both hands with a casual familiarity. A heavy laser pistol was at his belt, and a single use rocket launcher over his shoulder. He looked even more pissed than normal.

"I said I wanted it alive," he snarled and whinnied at the Goka.

"I didn't kill the fucking thing," the alien marine chittered back, kicking the dead pirate with a leg. The corpse barely moved. "I think it killed itself."

"I'm going to verify that," the Enforcer growled.

"Ask me if I give a fuck," the Goka said and backed away. He moved quickly toward the downed trooper. Their race did everything quickly. The other CASPer had its suit open, the hatch standing out straight from the body because the corridor wasn't tall enough to allow it to open all the way. A Human woman sat half-in, half-out of her cockpit, haptic leads still plugged in and pinplants engaged. "He gonna make it?" the Goka asked and pointed with a gore-dripping knife. The Human female shrugged.

The armorers finally found the problem and overrode the suit's controls. The CASPer was slumped against the doorway to engineering control. A deceptively-small burn was the only damage to his armor. As the hatch swung open with a whine of electric motors, it revealed a man slumped forward against the suit's restraints. There was a burn through the center of his chest, small and neat just like the one through the armor.

"Fuck," the woman said.

"How'd it happen?" a new arrival asked. Everyone came to attention, except the Goka, who remained on the floor. He liked to keep his armored carapace between himself and everyone else.

"Captain," the woman said and saluted, getting one in return.

"I asked what happened, Corporal."

"Lucky shot," another trooper said, coming out of the control room. A MinSha in combat armor, a heavy laser rifle cradled by her middle pair of foot-hands.

"That's it?" Captain Cromwell asked.

"That's it," Sergeant T'jto answered with a nod of her heart-shaped head. Multifaceted red-hued eyes regarded her commander without emotion. "Corporal Daniels was holding the door with Corporal Johansson here. The SleSha fired at Zit," she said and gestured at the Goka. "Zit jumped and the round tagged Daniels just under his laser shield."

"He tended to hold it too high," Johansson observed, "as if he was covering his face. We'd been working on it."

"Apparently, not hard enough," Sergeant T'jto said. Johansson sighed and nodded.

"Other casualties?" Alexis asked. T'jto snatched a slate from an armored sheath on his thorax. "Four total," he said and rattled off names. Three Humans and a Zuul. All the CASPers were salvageable. Considering they'd faced over 100 SleSha, not a bad butcher's bill.

"Where's Oort?" the captain asked. Johansson hooked a thumb down the corridor.

"Eating," she said. The captain's eyes narrowed, and she just shrugged.

"Did I hear my name?" The voice was full of scratches and hisses as the Tortantula squeezed through a pair of cross-corridor doors. SleSha-colored goo was dripping from her six-inch-long fangs. On her back, sat Jeejee, stripping and cleaning his huge laser pistol.

"I asked you to not let Oort snack on the enemy," Alexis said, addressing her comment to the Flatar riding on the Tortantula's back. The diminutive mammal, resembling nothing so much as a large chipmunk, shrugged.

"The next time I convince Oort to do something she doesn't want to do," he said, slapping the hairy torso under the saddle affectionately, "it'll be the first time."

"Next time it's a 10 percent fine," the captain said, and looked the Tortantula right in several of the eyes facing her. "Do I make myself perfectly clear?"

The Tortantula chittered and scratched the floor. "Yes."

"Good," she said and turned to the Enforcer. "The boarding craft has delivered a prize crew to the *Opportunity*. They encountered no resistance."

"Prisoners?" the Enforcer asked.

"Only the queen. All the remaining warriors were in a bay that had been purposely depressurized, and the leaders like that one," she said, pointing to the one nearby, "were just dead, with no signs of injury."

"Huh," the Enforcer whinnied.

"Told ya," Zit chittered. The Enforcer glared at the little Goka. The armored cockroach pulled out a knife and began to clean and sharpen it.

"Well?" Alexis asked the Enforcer.

"I hold your part of the contract in completion," he pronounced. She took out a slate and held it out. He pressed a finger to it and held the computer up to scan his eye. It beeped once. "The Peacemaker Guild appreciates your assistance in this matter."

"And we appreciate your credits," she said, taking the slate back. She noticed her XO coming down the corridor, the captain of the *Topul's Pride* in tow, flapping its considerable wings and squawking loudly. A pair of little reptilian elSha followed closely behind. Trailing them was a bipedal work robot carrying tools and instruments.

"What have you done to my ship?" the captain cried out. "Millions in damage! A dozen crew dead! Cargo destroyed!"

"I'm sure my XO has already been over this with you," Alexis said, giving a little bow to the Enforcer who was already leaving to complete his mission. He said he'd return the prize crew when they'd delivered *Opportunity* to Uuwato, in accordance with their agreement with the guild.

"He did, but he offered no compensation for the damage!"

"You signed the standard boarding defense contract via comms," she said, just like she'd said for decades.

"Yes…"

"Well in that contract, it clearly states that damage to the ship we are defending is not our liability if the enemy causes it. Furthermore, we are permitted reasonable collateral damage in the defense of our lives. You are free to review the gun-cameras from my troopers. We avoided heavy weapons wherever possible, as agreed, and I lost four good beings. So, unless you want to bring in a guild arbitrator, I suggest you drop it."

The captain looked around the damaged corridor and squawked once before turning and walking away.

"Thanks for doing business with us," Paka said to his back. The Sidar stiffened visibly but kept walking. The pair of elSha looked at each other, shrugged, and began cataloguing the damage to the section. They gave the still corpses of the SleSha a wide berth.

"Finish up here," Alexis ordered Sergeant T'jto. "I'll see you back on the *Pegasus*."

"Yes, ma'am," the sergeant said; "we'll get right on it."

* * * * *

Chapter Five

Mercenary Company Mickey Finn

Cadre Center

Houston, Earth

Rick Culper had never minded sweating. Hell, he liked busting his butt whenever possible! Ever since he was a little kid back in the Indianapolis suburbs, he'd discovered ways to exert himself his parents didn't approve of. They were both software engineers and had physiques to match. Both were almost five-foot-nine inches tall, and a little on the soft side. When their six-foot-four-inch, heavily-muscled only child stood next to them for senior pictures, people stopped and did double takes.

"Move your fucking ass, Culper!" screamed the drill instructor over Rick's squadnet.

"Sir, yes sir!" he barked back without hesitation and triggered the CASPer's jumpjets. The Combat Armored System, Personal was over 30 years old and showed the wear. The jets engaged a full tenth of a second after he'd squeezed both pinkies into his palm, and it resulted once again in a poorly-timed hop. *Crap,* he cursed his luck for drawing suit 898-B again. It had begun its life as a front-line Binnig Mk 7 combat suit owned by the Toussaint Irregulars. After almost a decade of service, and numerous repairs and upgrades, the Irregulars folded, and the suit was sold to the Golden Horde. It spent another 15 years there, fighting all over the galaxy, at which point the Mk 8 came out, and that was it for 898-B's combat duty. The maintenance log after that was…incomplete. One way or another it had ended up back on Earth in the possession of Mickey Finn.

Mickey Finn wasn't a person and hadn't been one in about eighty years. Back then, Mickey Finn had founded a small but well-respected merc company which specialized in spaceship boarding and defense. Basically, they were space marines. He'd died only a year later, though the company lived on. When Rick joined their cadre, he'd been assigned 898-B, thus beginning his own private hell.

Rick managed to control the jump and even gained a little on the other members of his squad. They all landed together just as a simulated rocket roared over their heads.

"You're gonna lose your fuckin' head, Culper!" the DI barked.

"Sir, yes sir!"

"Return fire," his squad leader ordered, "two guided missiles!" As the squad's designated heavy weapons carrier for this cycle, Rick was up.

"On it," he said and moved the one-thousand-pound suit forward to just behind the crumbling building they'd landed next to. Mickey Finn owned a square mile of former public housing in Missouri City, on the southwest edge of Houston. The entire district had been bought by merc companies and used as proving grounds and weapons ranges. The neighbors cried daily about the explosions and general noise level, but the six-figure monthly taxes paid by the mercs from their lucrative off-world contracts meant the government had little interest in their complaints. Every year, a few more blocks were abandoned, and the mercs snapped those up as well.

Rick slid his right hand around the corner and used the camera mounted on the wrist to get a look. Two CASPers painted light red, with flashing "ENEMY" icons, appeared on his display next to another building 100 yards away, one second before his suit buzzed an alarm and his right arm was frozen. He'd taken fire. "Operator uninjured" was the war game computer's pronouncement. The suit arms were quite a bit longer than his own, and he could lose almost a foot of the suit's lower arm and hand without personal injury. Of course, the machine gun on that arm was now out of the game.

"Two Tangos," he told the squad leader.

"Light 'em up, Culper!"

"On it," he said. Rick grabbed the rear half of a mangled ground car that lay nearby with his uninjured left hand, braced, and did a pivot throw. The partial car weighed at least 500 pounds, and he threw it easily. He hung onto it for a half a second, letting the bulk actually pull him part of the way out of cover. As he'd planned, the two troopers who'd been waiting instantly engaged the car body. Rick's computer said it was hit numerous times with machine gun and MAC fire. "Better it than me," he said as he came clear of the wall.

His suit's shoulder-mounted launcher pivoted down at his command, the reticle centered on the ground between the two troopers, and he fired. The rocket left his launcher's rail with a "Woosh!" and streaked across the intervening space. The other troopers tried to respond, but the rocket only took half a second to travel the distance. It landed on target and exploded with a huge cloud of wet paint, turning half of both troopers' suits a satisfying mottled green.

"Two kills," his suit informed him.

"Forward!" his squad leader yelled, and he leaped again. This time, Rick had the lag timed out, and it went much better.

An hour later they were out of their CASPers and running diagnostics. It was part of cadre duty, you learned the care and feeding of your suit as well as how to fight in it. These city fights were the worst on the suits. Mickey Finn was a space-based unit, after all, and Rick preferred the clean indoors combat on spaceships. They had access to three hulks in lunar orbit where they trained regularly. No artillery, no death from above. Still, he figured learning to fight dirt-side was worth the time. Ships had to land sometime.

"Culper," he heard. He spun around, coming to attention. Sergeant Alvarez, the five-foot-two-inch DI for his cadre platoon was striding up. She was tough as nails and hot as a branding iron. It was a disconcerting combination.

"Sir, yes sir!" he barked.

"That skid move with the car? Out-fucking-standing!"

"Sir, yes sir!" he barked, with the barest hint of a smile.

"Don't fucking ever do it again," she snarled, then a tiny hint of a smile came across her own face. "You will, however, show me how you did that."

"Of course, sir." She nodded.

"Good. How's the suit?"

"898-B has a few more runs in it, sir."

"Very well, carry on. We're going up to Red Hulk tomorrow." Rick nodded. The three ships were called Red Hulk, Blue Hulk, and Green Hulk. Red Hulk used to be a Union bulk ore transport. It was the hardest to train in because of the large open spaces. It did, however, explain why they'd had a day of city practice—to remind them that things could kill you from further away than the next bulkhead.

"I'll be ready, sir."

After Rick finished his maintenance cycle, refilled the suit's hydrogen fuel cells, and put it to sleep, he returned to his billeting and grabbed a shower. The Mk 7 suits, and 898-B in particular, were known as hot-running models. The fuel cells were at the small of your back, and that meant extra heat. He couldn't wait to get a Mk 8 as he'd read that a lot of the Mk 7's issues had been fixed with it.

A half-dozen of his platoon mates were already in the shower, including the two he'd blown to hell with the rocket. Their entire squad had been killed while acting as the opposing force.

"Sweet move, Culper," a guy named Prendergast said and slapped him a high-five.

"Lucky," someone else laughed.

"Culper?" Prendergast asked. "No fucking way; he's got moves." Rick just shrugged and found an unoccupied shower. While a lot of other kids in school were busy spending all their time in the weight room or studying military history, just like the MST (Mercenary Service Track) government education program dictated, he'd always found time to participate in some gymnastics and even a little ballet. That was paying high dividends now. It didn't hurt he was a natural athlete and had the body of a Greek god.

Rick ignored the shower room banter as he washed. Unlike a lot of young CASPer troopers, he'd kept his hair. It was above collar-length, within Mickey Finn regulations, and dirty blonde. It went well with his blue eyes, high cheekbones, and chiseled jaw. Once he'd gotten his adult growth and begun to really build up his body, he'd developed into a man who turned heads everywhere he went. Not all were women either, though that had never interested him. He'd never gotten into chasing girls, though, out of respect for his childhood friend, Jim Cartwright.

Where Rick was the model of what the mercenary service was looking for in a recruit, Jim was the opposite. Shorter, overweight—bordering on obese—with little physical talent, Jim had struggled with the MST. Most people wondered why he would waste his time trying, as it was obvious he would never be a merc. The only problem was he wasn't just Jim Cartwright. He was one of *the* Cartwrights. Heir to Cartwright's Cavaliers. The Cavaliers were one of only four merc companies to return from the Alpha Contracts 100 years ago.

Although Jim was the heir to one of the Four Horsemen, he was unassuming and rather embarrassed by it all. Jim and Rick had been friends since kindergarten, and Jim had promised Rick a job when they graduated. Of course, that was before the Cavaliers went bankrupt.

Rick had graduated with a nearly-perfect score on the VOWs, his Voluntary Off-World assessment tests, and he'd wanted to be a Cavalier. Only Jim had disappeared, and the company had gone bankrupt, so Rick had to find his own way.

First, he'd gone to Gitmo's Own, a very old unit from which he had a challenge coin from his school days. They wanted him, but only for cadre duty. Rick held out for a quick-track combat duty assignment, and that turned out to be a mistake. With almost a thousand mercs suddenly looking for work after the Cavaliers folded, jobs proved hard to come by. When he tried to take the earlier offer from Gitmo's Own, he found it wasn't there anymore. After a month of looking, he finally ended up at Mickey Finn.

Out of the shower, toweling off, he saw a woman from logistics checking him out. She was a tall brunette who'd been spending a lot of time in the gym when he was there; Rick had noticed her, too.

Once Jim went his own way, Rick no longer felt honor-bound to pass on girls' attentions to avoid embarrassing his friend. The intervening months had found him dating half a dozen female Mickey Finn personnel, from office staff to fellow troopers. He was beginning to regret all those years he ignored girls in school—he had a lot of catching up to do!

Rick hit his bunk and grabbed his personal slate. The little computer was crammed full of files with operational details he was trying to absorb. He was sure Jim would have had no trouble with that part of the job. Rick wasn't stupid, not by any stretch of the imagination; while the VOWs were biased heavily toward physical ability, they also had a sizeable mental capacity section. Even the greatest physique wouldn't get a top score unless it was coupled with above average intelligence, and Rick's scores had been high there, as well. But he'd never be an academic; it wasn't his natural ability.

Regardless, he was pushing hard to finish the material. Their cadre unit was coming up on rotation quickly. Mickey Finn had only two company-sized units that rotated between Earth and off-world assignments. First Company was due back in six weeks, at which time Second Company, his company, would ship out. That is, if he made the grade. He was halfway through a manual on standard Union starship power distribution systems when the communicator in his ear buzzed.

"Culper?" It was Sergeant Alvarez.

"Sir, yes sir?"

"Report to my office, ASAP." Rick was up at a trot. Her office was on the same floor as Mickey Finn's Houston cadre headquarters, a former office complex in what had been the swank business and entertainment area known as the Galleria back in the 21st Century.

Now it was home to a dozen small-to-medium-sized merc companies, like his own.

Rick found her office door open, with another trooper walking out shaking his head. He knew right away—that wasn't good. He knocked once and entered, as was protocol, standing next to the doorway at attention. Alvarez looked up and knife-handed at the chair.

"Pop a squat, Culper." He did. On her desk, a Tri-V displayed a file, Rick's half-grinning face floating there. "I've been reviewing your file," she said and glanced at him. "Don't give me the puppy dog look, kid."

"Sorry sir."

She growled, then sighed. "Culper, you're a top-notch trooper, with the makings of a fine marine. We wanted to give you a slot."

"Then why are you letting me go?" he asked. She didn't take exception to the break in proper protocol.

"First Company was serving defensive duty on a Maki ship."

"The lemurs, right?"

"Correct," Alvarez nodded. "Anyway, they're great pilots and all, but they're shit for fighting on ships. They got caught in an operation that went south. We don't know the full details, only that 75 percent of First Company was lost. The remnants are on their way home now with an incomplete contract under their belts."

"Wouldn't that mean you need me even more?" Rick asked, a little horrified so many had died. Well, they'd died weeks ago, probably. It could take months for a message to get from one side of the galaxy to the other.

"It might, except for the loss of revenue and the payouts to family members of the dead. We're standing down all of Second Company, except the veterans, and rolling them into First Company when it gets here." She slid a data chip across the table. "Your severance pay and recommendation. I really hope you get on with someone else." She stood and offered her hand. Numb with disappointment, he stood and shook it. It was the first and only time she'd offered.

* * * * *

Chapter Six

EMS Pegasus

Obiya 199 System

Way Station Abyss

Inner Crapti Rift

Alexis trudged up the ramp to the shuttle, with Paka right behind her. Even in the modest spin gravity of the huge ship, she felt all the hours she'd been awake. The *Topul's Pride* shuttle bay crew sealed them in from the outside and evacuated the bay prior to decompression.

"Take me home, Mr. Southard," she said to the pilot.

"Yes, Captain," the pilot replied from the little cockpit. The bay depressurized quickly, and the pilot lifted them off the deck. The ship was under spin, so down was out. He hovered for a moment while the doors opened under them, then gave the maneuvering thrusters a few bumps, and they were clear. The pilot steadied their trajectory, aligned their course, and engaged the drive engines. A smooth one-half gravity snugged them into their seats. Clearly, the pilot knew his captain was tired; it meant the flight would take longer, but she didn't mind.

"Four dead," she said and shook her head.

"Happens," Paka replied.

"Doesn't mean I have to like it." Paka shrugged. Watching a big rodent shrug should be disconcerting, she thought, but she'd grown up around more aliens than Humans. Most of the races even vaguely humanoid used a form of shrugging. "Between these losses and those two full pods we lost in Argyle B4V, we're short a full platoon."

Paka nodded. "We have a few months before the next contract. We can stop on Earth and hire some veterans to fill out the ranks."

"No," Alexis said right away, then glanced at Paka from under hooded eyes, "not Earth."

"Are you ever going to see your home world?" Paka asked.

Alexis pulled one of the built-in computer monitors on the shuttle's arm around and tapped on it. A view of the distant but closing *Pegasus* was centered on it—a gently tapering, almost cigar-shaped ship with retractable gravity decks near the middle. The doors for the central docking bay were near the gravity decks, while missile and weapon ports dotted the hull. The squared end, where her powerful fusion torches rested, were surrounded by a ring of external reaction mass tankage and over-powered maneuvering thrusters. The bore of her immense spinal-mounted particle cannon wasn't visible in her nose; it was currently concealed behind petal-like doors.

"That's my home," she said, almost caressing the image. *And it always has been,* she thought. "Have navigation plot for Karma. We can find fresh meat there."

A half hour later, the shuttle flipped over and began decelerating. Another half hour, and the engines cut out, leaving them in free fall. Alexis watched through the monitor as the shuttle floated slowly toward her ship. They were just forward of the bulbous engine housings. Here a large bay door stood open to reveal the hangar deck. As they glided inside she could see the magnetic handling system moving another shuttle on the opposite side of the huge removable transparent shield which divided the bay. It allowed them to operate two shuttles at one time if necessary, which it often was.

The shuttle gently nudged the floor, and the deck's magnetic grapples locked it in place. Doors slid closed, and the bay pressurized in a few moments.

"Clear to go," Southard called from the flight deck.

"Smooth flight," Alexis said. He turned and nodded to her, then went back to his checklist as the shuttle's door rotated down. She floated to the door and waited while the personnel transport ropes rose from the deck of the shuttle bay. Once they were in place, she and Paka floated down, took hold, and moved toward the bay exit. Hangar personnel were already moving about, servicing the shuttle and accessing its cargo hold.

She looked back and saw the crew removing the body bags from the fight on *Topul's Pride.* She'd hoped to get Home without any more losses. A quick stop at Karma for some new hires on the way. Should be a milk run.

A day later *Opportunity* was again able to maneuver under its own power. The former ship's pirate master, the SleSha queen, was confined to a stateroom where she was to remain until her trial. *Topul's Pride* had not slowed in its transit. The damages she'd suffered were minor compared to her incredible size. She would reach Obiya 199's stargate in three more days and transition back into hyperspace.

Pegasus lagged behind almost a day, keeping her sensors open and watching for any threats. The final clause of the contract with the Merchant Guild was making sure the *Topul's Pride* left Obiya 199 unmolested. The Enforcer, who transferred to the *Opportunity* to accompany his prisoner, contacted *Pegasus* one final time before they made the transition out of the system.

"We part ways," the Enforcer said formally; the visual transmission showed the Equiri giving a slight bow of respect. "Our business was equitable. I find you an honorable Human, and your company matches its reputation." Alexis returned the bow.

"The Winged Hussars take pride in our reputation," she said. The Enforcer seemed about to terminate the communication when he stopped and leaned close to the pickup, speaking again.

"Your ship's ability, or your navigator's perhaps? Simply amazing." When Alexis didn't reply, he added, "No doubt the Cartography Guild would pay handsomely for that talent."

"It is no concern of theirs," she said simply. "Our contract included a non-disclosure agreement in relation to any proprietary abilities my company might possess."

"It did," the Enforcer agreed, "though I thought that was regarding military techniques or perhaps some arms and armor innovations." The Enforcer cocked his long face and regarded her with one eye. "Humans are an enigmatic and secretive race," he said, then laughed. "Farewell, Commander Cromwell." He cut the communications link. Paka looked up from her console and regarded her captain with a concerned gaze.

"Our secrets are going to get out," she said. "One of these days. We'll never keep it forever."

"Maybe," Alexis said, then shrugged. "Still, we've managed to keep a few secrets for a very long time."

* * * * *

Interlude

35 Years Ago
EMS Pegasus
Hyperspace

The game would be much more fun if her damn sister wasn't so much better at it. Alex always thought of herself as the smarter of the twins, yet Kat was the uncontested master of hide and seek aboard *Pegasus*. Alex was currently crawling through a cableway access shaft between Decks Two and Three. She'd been looking for her sister now for 55 minutes, and time was almost up.

When the twins had first started playing the game, they were only four years old. Their mother had strictly forbidden them to play in the ship outside of Deck 20, where they lived with her on contract. Of course, they'd completely ignored her. When they were caught on Deck 30 hiding in a marine equipment room, she'd locked them in their cabin as punishment. Two hours later a maintenance tech opened a ventilation shaft on Deck 10 to investigate slow air flow to find the girls trying to get unstuck from an air mover.

After that, their mother decided it was worthless to forbid the game, so she got them to promise to stay between Deck 12 (the enlisted galley) and Deck 20. They had done as she wished. Mostly. Forays outside of their designated AoP, or Area of Play, were done carefully from then on to avoid detection. That plan had worked excellently.

Of course, their mother's attempt to control them wasn't helped by the fact the crew of *Pegasus* simply adored the twin girls. Born with startling white hair, the heirs to the Winged Hussars were the only children on a working mercenary ship. Their father was unknown, so every man on the ship became a surrogate father, and every woman a loving aunt.

Alex stopped in the intermix chamber and listened. The sounds of the system were intimately familiar to her after years of crawling through the ductwork. She strained her ears for any sound of her sister Katrina. After a moment of nothing, she moved onward.

Even now, at almost eight years old, she didn't find it unusual that she was spending a lot of her formative years in a battlecruiser flying around the galaxy. The ship was more home, and more fun, than the planet they called Home. Besides, they got to visit strange worlds and meet strange and interesting aliens!

Three minutes left, and Alex cut across a service-way which she was now nearly too big to fit through. She managed to wiggle her hips past the support beam and made it to the other side. When she moved past the marker to Deck Two there she was.

"Gotcha," Alex said and slapped Kat's heel.

"Shhhh!" the other girl hissed.

"I win," Alex said.

"Quiet, stupid," Kat mouthed, and gestured for her to crawl up to her level. The ship was under light acceleration, so they hardly had to use the ribs of the shaft to crawl 'up.' Kat was braced next to a vent cover. Alex knew Deck Two only contained avionics and the forward missile tubes; there wasn't anything interesting up here. But as Alex came up next to her twin, she could see through the grate—someone was there.

They were overlooking Section Two, which held the missile launcher hardware and the main avionics engineering space. Inside a crewman was sitting in a chair, alone, leaning forward over a console as if asleep.

"What is he doing?" Alex wondered.

"Quiet," Kat hissed back. They'd never seen anyone in this space except during maintenance after returning from a contract. Alex was sure it was manned during combat, but the twin's combat station was in their mom's armored cabin, in their specially-made pressure suits. That was fun too, except when the ship was damaged. That was frightening.

They watched together for several minutes. After a time, Kat noticed something and leaned close to Alex's ear to whisper.

"Look at the control console," she said. At first, Alex didn't see anything, then she slowly realized it was responding to commands. But the crewman wasn't moving. They both realized who it was at the same time.

The crewman sat up straight, only it wasn't a man. She had her hair cut super short, like most of the male crewmen preferred. She did that because of the computer links installed in her head, just behind both ears.

"It's her," Kat said with awe. Alex knew her sister liked Lt. Drake. Liked might not have been a strong enough word. Worshiped? Lt. Drake was the ship's computer expert, and one of only four members with pinlinks, special computer implants in her brain that let her control computers and interface with many machines.

Lt. Drake sat staring at the console for a long moment, then turned to look right at the girls through the grate. They both gasped, and the older woman smiled.

"You two aren't supposed to be up here," she said. The two girls remained perfectly still and silent for a long moment. Drake turned the rest of the way around and stood, hands on her hips, glaring. "You two come down here right now."

"Poop," Alex said and began unlatching the grate to push it open. Kat helped, and a minute later they dropped lightly to the deck.

"What do you have to say for yourselves?" the lieutenant asked. She looked stern, but the girls knew better. Even though Drake was a bit odd, she still loved the twins, just like every other crewman.

"We were playing and got lost," Alex tried. Drake was unmoved.

"She made me do it," Kat said, and Alex popped her on the back of the head. Kat took a swing at her in reply, and Lt. Drake moved in between them before it turned into another patented twin-brawl.

"Okay, whatever the reason, you aren't supposed to be up here. Come on, I'll take you down to your quarters. We'll be at mid-course and flipping over soon." The girls loved zero-G and were at home in it.

"What were you doing?" Kat asked as they were escorted to the lift. Drake pressed the call button and glanced at the young girl.

"I was working on the fire control computer."

"Did you see the ghost?" Alex asked.

"What ghost?" Drake asked, not looking at them.

"The one that lives in the computers," Kat said. It wasn't uncommon for the girls to answer each other's questions or to ask follow-up questions for each other. Drake laughed.

"You girls are trying to make up campfire stories."

"What's a campfire?" they both asked at the same time. Drake looked at them in surprise, then shook her head.

"I forget you two have never been to Earth." Both girls made faces; Alex stuck her finger in her mouth like she was trying to make herself puke.

"Who'd want to go there?" she asked. Kat nodded in agreement.

"Regardless, stop telling those stories. They're silly."

"We've seen it," Kat said. The lift arrived, and Drake gently moved them inside with her.

"What did you see?"

"This one time," Kat said, "I saw the computer in AuxCon running by itself. It was scrolling data and running sensors."

"And what were you doing in auxiliary control?" Drake asked. Kat's jaw fell open and Alex silently berated her sister for getting caught in such a simple trap.

"The crew talks about it too," Alex said, trying to rescue her sister. "A damage control tech told me last year that they were trapped in a section that was decompressing after a battle. The air tight door controls were busted, and no one was there to help them. Suddenly, the door opened, and they got out."

"Someone on the bridge helped them," Drake said.

"No," Alex insisted, "he said the controls to the bridge were also broken, and the cameras were out. There was no way anyone even knew they were trapped."

The lift hummed along in silence for a few moments, then arrived on Deck 20. The doors slid open and Drake led them out.

"Well, here you are," she said. "You two troublemakers stay here until your mom gets off watch, and I promise I'll tell the head cook to give you both a special cookie after dinner." They beamed and promised they'd stay put. Drake smiled, mussed their hair, and turned to go.

"Lieutenant," Kat said, and the woman turned back. "I want to have pinplants just like yours."

"Why?" Drake asked.

"So I can talk to the ghost." Alex looked askance at her sister. Lt. Drake cocked her head, then got a very strange smile on her face.

"You two remember your promise, and I'll see you at mess call." A second later, she was in the lift and gone.

"You're nuts," Alex said. "Who'd want wires in their brain?"

"What's wrong with that?" Kat asked. "You've got poop in yours!" This time, there was no one to stop the brawl.

* * * * *

Chapter Seven

EMS Pegasus

S.G. Skaa System

Hyperspace Emergence Point

"So much for going straight to Karma," Paka said as the ship rocked from a salvo of missile impacts.

"Your humor is noted," Alexis said as she held onto her command chair. "Can you get us out of this?" *Pegasus* had emerged into the S.G. Skaa system, a nowhere star system in the middle of nowhere, which is why Alexis had chosen it for their stop en route to Karma. There was no direct way to get from Obiya 199 to Karma. They would need to cross the void between the Jesc arm, where they'd been, and the Tolo arm, where Karma was located. She'd informed her helmsman and navigator to pick an out-of-the-way route to minimize any potential trouble. It obviously hadn't worked out as she'd planned.

The instant they transitioned from hyperspace, they were confronted with two ships engaged in a running battle. Both were moderately damaged, and both immediately began requesting an 'On the Spot' contract with the Winged Hussars to destroy the other ship.

"I'm sorry," Alexis had transmitted to both interested parties; "the Winged Hussars are not currently accepting any contracts." She'd set Condition One, just in case. A second later both of the other ships turned and opened fire on the *Pegasus*!

"Some people just don't take a 'no' answer very well," Flipper bubbled and laughed as he began evasive maneuvers.

"Edwards," Alexis said, "please give me an evaluation of those ships."

"Ma'am," Edwards said in his Louisiana accent. "Both ships are escort frigates. The one designated as Alpha is a Desha class, made by the Izlian, the one designated Bravo is a Catroo class of Buma design."

"Buma," Alexis noted, "I didn't know they designed warships."

"Apparently, they do," Paka said.

"Both vessels have sustained serious damage," Edwards continued, "though neither is incapable of combat." The ship shuddered again as more missiles walked across their shields. Luckily, they were all conventional, or they might have been in trouble.

"I don't want to kill them," Alexis said, "they're stupid, not dangerous."

"Rude, too," Paka added; "don't forget rude. There was no reason to open fire just because we wouldn't pick a side!"

"Maybe they don't like mercs?" Alexis said. "We don't know for sure they're mercs. It's not unheard of for some species to crew their own escort ships. I think we've stumbled into some kind of non-merc turf war. Chug, get us the hell out of here." The helmsman looked back at his captain with one of his three eyestalks.

"Understood," he said. Chug's piloting shell had multiple translator speakers so non-Bakulu crew could easily understand his speech, since most humanoid species would find it otherwise impossible. Clamped into the piloting section, the alien mollusk could manipulate many controls simultaneously and was fully-interfaced via pinplants to the ship's system. Originally the *Pegasus* required four crew to man the helm; Chug did it all by himself. The acceleration alarm chimed, and the ship performed a 3G skew turn to align itself with the system's stargate. Still more missiles came at them.

"Permission to engage?" Edwards asked. Each volley of missiles was met by dozens of point-defense lasers, which were mounted throughout the *Pegasus*.

Every few seconds the two escorts launched another flurry of almost two dozen missiles.

"Do those things carry infinite missiles?" Alexis growled.

"Both the Catroo and Desha classes are missile frigates," Edwards pointed out.

"They are trying to bracket us," the bridge crew's other Bakulu, Glick, spoke up. The ship's situational control, or SitCon, he managed battles and maintained awareness of their battlespace to allow individual systems' controllers to better concentrate on their jobs.

"Guess they've worked out their differences for now," Paka said. Glick spoke up again.

"The skew turn is bringing our baffles into alignment with the Catroo class." Like old Earth submarines, the area directly behind a fusion torch powered ship was called its baffles, and was invisible to its sensors.

"Intensify aft quarter anti-missile laser fire," Alexis ordered.

"Trying," Edwards said. He commanded through a fusion of hand and pinplant inputs honed through years of practice.

A dozen missiles arced in from the Catroo class, straight at the aft quarter of *Pegasus*. The shields weren't active directly aft when her engines were operating, even at one-quarter power, and it was an area of vulnerability. While the ship's weapons could shoot through their shields, the fusion torch of her main drive was another matter.

There were anti-missile laser pods around the engine clusters for this reason, but they took a few seconds to change orientation. In this case, those few seconds were an eternity.

Most of the twelve missiles splashed against the periphery of the aft quarter's shields. Four went through. Two were incinerated by the plasma plume of the ship's drive; the other two impacted the ship. The long hull resounded from the impacts as the high explosive missiles slammed into it and detonated.

"Report!" Paka barked.

"Two hits," the damage control coordinator, or DCC, called out in his squeaky voice. The elSha glanced back at the captain, his reptilian mouth snapping in concern. "Reactor Two suffered minor damage. Commander Long informs he has placed it in safe mode. The second missile hit Deck 30, there is extensive damage and decompression!"

"Marine country," Paka said solemnly.

"That's enough!" Alexis roared. "Guylan, deal with the damage. Edwards, one ship-killer each." The short TacCom's ebony skin was shiny with sweat as he glanced at his captain, then nodded solemnly.

"Acknowledged," he said and used his pinplants to launch the missiles. "Two missiles away."

The two escort frigates were designed to get in fast, rain missiles, and get away. They were meant to operate in cooperation with laser frigates, who could screen them from missile fire. In this case, they had no such escort. Their own point defenses were woefully inadequate for the Hussars' highly-advanced version of the Union anti-ship missiles known as ship-killers.

The two missiles flashed away at almost a thousand Gs of acceleration and reached their targets in seconds. As they approached, they shed their fairings, which acted as chaff to confuse the enemy point defense systems, then split into two weapons each. The enemy defenses fired at the harmless chaff, and both missiles reached their targets.

The two weapons were identical, and set to hit within a quarter second of each other. Both were micro-nuclear bombs the Hussars called "Squash-bombs." The first knocked down the enemy's shields, the second went off against the hull.

"Both ships destroyed," Glick said.

"Confirmed," Flipper agreed, "clean kills."

"Noted," Alexis said. "Anyone else in the system?"

Flipper worked his instruments. "There are nine other ships in the system," he announced. "Five are at the stargate waiting for transition. One is at this system's gas giant mining operation, transferring cargo. The other three are in transit to the stargate. Closest ship is more than 10 light minutes away."

"Very good," Alexis said, "secure from Condition One. Guylan, update?"

"Team One is fighting a plasma-induced fire in Reactor Two," the elSha reported. "Team Two is still trying to gain entrance to Deck 30." The intraship communication chimed.

"Is the reactor going to go critical?" Alexis asked.

"I don't believe so," the scrapping, grating voice of the chief engineer, a Jeha named Long, replied.

"Bridge, this is Sgt. T'jto."

"Captain here, go ahead, Sergeant."

"Dragon Squad suited up when you set Condition One. We're on Deck 30 in armor. The missile decompressed the entire deck. We are the only survivors."

* * * * *

Chapter Eight

The *Pegasus* limped between the emergence point and the stargate in S.G. Skaa at a nominal three-quarters gravity. They could have cut a quarter of the 62-hour travel time by thrusting at a full gravity; however, Alexis decided against it after consulting with Chief Engineer Long and Guylan. Reactor Two was offline, and would remain so for several weeks. The damage was extensive; the biggest problem was the marines usually helped fix hull damage, and there weren't many marines left.

On the third day, all crew except those needed for minimal operations mustered on the primary shuttle deck. It was the largest open space on the ship with a deck properly oriented during thrust. Thirty-seven Winged Hussar flags were spread over plastic shells holding the bodies of their dead.

"We gather here to say goodbye to our comrades," Captain Alexis Cromwell said to the gathered crew. Like the caskets, they represented many races. There were more Humans present than any other race, yet they still represented less than half the crew. "They were all, like most of us, mercenaries by trade. Even those among us who do not fight, still understand the risk. We stand on our home, *Pegasus,* knowing that every time the bell sounds, we could all be cast into the black." Some of the beings bowed heads, others whispered words. Some Human men and women quietly wept. A few of the other races also visibly grieved. "Yet we face it together, all Hussars, all family." They all stood silently while several crewmen went among the caskets and gathered the flags, respectfully folding each one, before returning to the other side of the bay to stand with the rest of the crew.

"Prepare for burial in the black," Paka pronounced. The shuttle bay's divider came down and the half with the caskets partially depressurized. The surviving marines came forward with laser weapons, standing ready. Alexis looked down at the deck and spoke again.

"When it comes your time to die, be not like those whose hearts are filled with fear of death, so that when their time comes they weep and pray for a little more time to live their lives over again in a different way. Sing your death song and die like a hero going home." She turned to Paka and nodded.

On the other side, the big bay door slid open. The residual atmosphere was expelled, taking the 37 caskets with it.

"Squad…*ready!*" Sergeant T'jto ordered. The surviving marines all aimed specially tuned laser weapons and fired them at the barrier. The beams were low power—for visual effect only—to salute their lost and didn't cause any damage to the barrier.

Afterwards, back in her wardroom behind the bridge, Alexis looked at the damage reports, both material and personnel, and sighed. Paka sat in a chair on the other side of the desk. They'd been discussing the rest of the cruise. Suddenly Alexis tossed the slate on her desk and growled.

"Seventeen months."

"Ma'am?" Paka asked, her whiskers twitching in curiosity.

"That's how long we've been out, seventeen months. Four contracts fulfilled. I just looked up the details. Eleven combat actions in total. We've lost two crewmen to injuries related to combat action and one to an accident. Three crewmen killed, in total, from all those combat actions, including that running fight on the *Topul's Pride*, and a little piece of shit frigate fires a couple of damned conventional rockets up our ass, and we lose 22 marines and 15 crew. On a fucking non-paying combat action, of all things."

Her rage spent, she sat back and sighed. Paka, long used to her captain's moods, just waited. After a time, Alexis picked up the slate and went back to the matter at hand. Sometime later, Paka looked up and spoke.

"Captain?"

"What's on your mind?"

"That last line you spoke? At the service? It wasn't religious, at least not from your race. What was it from?"

Alexis gave her XO a sardonic smile that might or might not have been wasted on the Veetanho. "That? It's from an ancient Earth warrior."

"What was the warrior's name?" Paka asked.

"Tecumseh."

* * * * *

Chapter Nine

A1 Super Deluxe Inn
Startown – Houston Starport
Houston, Earth

Rick tossed his two duffels onto the bed in the hotel room, the takeout box on the decrepit dresser, and fell into the tiny office chair. It promptly broke in half and spilled him onto the floor with a crash.

"Fuck my life," he said and rolled to his feet. He shoved the remnants of the Fedmart office furniture aside, put the duffels there instead, and sat dejectedly on the bed. A pair of mating cockroaches skittered away. He wondered if the tub worked so he could drown himself. He pulled out his Universal Account Access Card, or yack, and touched the little display embedded in the plastic. It lit up with 13.2 CRU. Thirteen union credits might seem like a lot to some. It was the equivalent of about thirteen hundred US dollars, after all. The problem was the economy around a starport was fed by off-world commerce and mercs, which consumed credits like hungry vampires. He could probably have gotten a room for a month back in Indianapolis with that; here, he'd paid 5 credits for this shithole for one night. Five hundred dollars a night. Cockroaches, no extra charge.

The smell of food drew him to the dresser, where he retrieved the takeout box. A small squadron of roaches fled at his approach, already checking out what he'd brought them. He held onto the box while taking both duffels into the bathroom. After verifying that the tub appeared to have been cleaned, he dropped them in and went back into the main room. At least he wouldn't get bedbugs in his bags that way. He hoped.

Rick pulled out his slate, sat on the bed, and ate medium-quality Chinese food as he checked his email. He had an official mail from the mercenary guild informing him that since he wasn't employed by a merc unit, he would have to pay his own dues next year (that will be 100 CRU please). He glanced at the little calendar icon in the corner that showed Union dates and their Earth equivalents. At least he had four months to worry about it. There was one offer of a credit card from OWBA, the Off-World Banking Alliance. They were affiliated with the Union Credit Exchange, which was part of the Trade Guild.

He thought about that for a second, but quickly tossed away the idea. Without a job, or any prospect of one, he'd never make the payments. He knew their interest rates started at 20 percent and went up from there. No, he wasn't going to make a bad situation worse. The remainder of the messages were spam, and he deleted them.

The food mostly gone, he resigned himself to scanning the local hiring boards. Luckily, the roach motel included free Aethernet access, although the connection was crappy. He began looking for work. The first thing he noticed was that most jobs were computer-related; in particular, they wanted pinned operators. The implants inserted into your brain let you directly access the Aethernet and help you program computers. They were expensive as hell, too. Thinking about having pinplants got him thinking about his old friend Jim, and that made him set his own situation in perspective.

Jim was the heir to Cartwright's Cavaliers, one of the greatest merc units ever, but his mother had blown it all in shady credit swaps and off-world real estate deals. Even though he was unemployed, Rick reminded himself that his friend was much worse off.

On the spur of the moment, Rick pulled out his phone and thumbed Jim's number. It went instantly to voicemail.

"This is Jim Cartwright," the familiar voice said, "I'll be unavailable for a few months. Leave a message, and I'll get back to you as soon as I can."

Rick hung up before leaving a message. Hard to say what it meant. Unavailable was about as ambiguous as you could get. With nothing else to distract him, he went back to looking for a job.

It was around 11:00 p.m. when he finally gave up and admitted defeat. The facts were impossible to ignore. He couldn't make money quickly enough to allow himself to stay even in the shithole hotel room, as well as feed himself and save enough to get an apartment. His phone was still sitting on the nightstand. Rick brushed a roach away, selected a number from the list, and dialed.

"Rick?" the voice answered on the first ring. "This is unexpected."

"Hi mom," he said with a sigh. "I'm sorry I haven't returned your calls." There was silence for a long moment, and Rick wondered if she'd hung up.

"You should be," she said, but he didn't think she sounded as angry as he'd expected. "Are you about to be deployed?"

"No," he said, not sure how to proceed.

"You're still with those Mickey Fingers?"

"Mickey Finn, mom," he corrected with a chuckle. "No, they let me go."

"I'm sorry," she said, though it didn't sound very sincere. "You have another job then?"

"No," he admitted. "The Cavaliers going down flooded the market."

"Your friend Jim's outfit. I saw that on the Tri-V." She sounded almost satisfied. That wouldn't have surprised him. She'd never approved of Jim. In her mind, it was Jim that made her only son take up the mercenary life. Their family had been military pilots going back to WWI, when a long-dead ancestor had flown a Sopwith Camel. *Your ancestors would be offended at the very thought of you becoming a mercenary!* She never understood that he did it because he had to. Earth hardly had any militaries anymore. It was a calling.

"Yes, that's the one."

"So, what are you going to do now?" she asked. He didn't know what to say. "You're broke, aren't you?" How did parents know stuff like that?

"Almost," he admitted.

"Ricky, come home." He bristled at her use of his childhood name, but didn't say anything about it.

"I can't," he said instead.

"Why not?"

"I don't have enough money." That wasn't entirely true. He could probably take a maglev to Indianapolis for around 10 CRU. Once more she was quiet for some time, and he was wondering if she was going to leave him to his own devices. It would be no more than he deserved. Then he heard a '*Ping!*' from the nightstand and turned his head. His yack was glowing with a notice.

Rick picked up the card and looked at it. The "Receive Funds" green button was glowing. Surprised, he touched it without really realizing what it meant. The balance went from 13.2 CRU to 113.2 CRU.

"Mom, why? That's like ten-thousand dollars."

"We have it," she said. "Don't take the train, there was an accident just the other day." He'd heard; it was a freight train not a passenger maglev. The maglevs were safer than cars or planes. "Grab a shuttle, be home tomorrow. We'll talk then. Buy some clothes so I don't have to see you in that mercenary garb."

"I don't know what to say."

"Say good night; it's late."

After he'd said goodbye and thanked her about a dozen times, he chased the roaches off the nightstand and turned off the light. Outside the lights and sounds of Houston Startown reminded him of the old movie *5th Element* he'd watched with Jim one Saturday. Flying cars mixed with horns, sirens, and a heavy overtone of technology. Somewhere nearby, music was playing so loudly the bass rattled his windows. It was serene compared to the Mickey Finn compound. He was asleep in minutes.

The next morning, duffel bags carefully inspected for unauthorized travelers and showered with lots of the chemical-based soap the merc supply room gave out, Rick took public transportation to the starport. It cost a half a credit to ride as far as the line went, which dropped him about half a mile from his destination. He walked the rest of the way.

The sprawling starport took up a large part of what had once been the eastern Houston industrial district. Now it was hundreds of ferroconcrete bays for ships of all shapes and sizes to land and lift off from. On both sides were runways for air breathers. Some were suborbital shuttles you could hop that would deposit you halfway around the world in a couple hours. The others were regular jets, usually unpiloted. Union robotic technology didn't have a bad day and kill two hundred business travelers.

Rick walked into the main concourse and past the first level of security. A squad of SPD, the Starport Police Department, were in light armor with battle rifles held on cross-body slings. Their helmets concealed their faces and likely held all kinds of scanners to examine those going by. As if to confirm his suspicion, one of them turned as he approached the security station and looked him up and down before looking away.

"Business?" ask the screener.

"Flight," he said.

"Ticket?"

"Don't have one yet."

"Yeah? Let's see some ID and proof of ability to pay." He grunted and produced his yack. The screener interfaced the card with his slate and examined a Tri-V display. "Merc, huh?" Rick nodded. "Thought you guys were all rich."

"Can I go?" Rick asked, holding out his hand.

"Not far on that," the man said, then almost grudgingly handed it back. Rick ground his teeth, took the card, and walked through the big tube-like scanner. He knew somewhere they were examining everything about him, probably down to the nanite modifications of his skeletal system. The weapon and armor in his bag would be noted and recorded. Earth had a love-hate relationship with mercs (mostly hate), and the weapons they used.

After security, the main entrance broadened out into a wide concourse. The roof was easily 100 feet overhead, and shops lined both sides. Most sported flowing three-dimensional, Tri-V signs claiming the best duty-free off-world gizmos, or wetware upgrades for your pinplants (no questions asked). He saw at least four shops specializing in morphagenic tattoos before he got to the first branching of the concourse.

At the intersection, the concourse split in three directions. To the right was domestic and local jet travel, to the left was international and sub-orbital shuttles, and straight ahead was off-world travel and access to the myriads of starship docking bays. He examined the flight boards, noting which were going to Indianapolis, then looked down the corridor toward the starships.

There might not be any merc companies hiring on Earth, but he knew where there were. Only it would take a lot more than 100 credits to get there. And he wasn't being honest with himself. He didn't want to give up and go home. He'd wanted to be a merc since he and Jim were kids. Without another thought, he went straight ahead.

Later that afternoon, Rick was aboard ECS *Coronado*, a *Comal*-class tramp freighter riding a launch laser into orbit. Captain Edgar Holland had offered him two hundred credits a week for manual labor and security, should it become necessary. In exchange Rick got a trip to Karma, though there would be multiple stops before they got there. *Coronado* was more than 70 years old, the second class of hyperspace-capable freighter ever produced by Humans. Holland assured him there were much older ships made by aliens. He didn't worry, it felt right. He was following his dream.

They refueled in orbit. While there, Rick used the ship's Aethernet access to return his mom's 100 credits, and to email her a letter apologizing and explaining where he was going. She didn't reply before they left orbit.

*****

Chapter Ten

EMS Pegasus

Galactic Void Between Jesc and Tolo Arms

Hyperspace

The vast, unending nothingness of hyperspace was outside the two-foot-thick synthetic, transparent, ruby glass of Captain Alexis Cromwell's wardroom. She stood by the window, observing. Many found looking at hyperspace to be disconcerting at best and disturbing at worst. She'd once heard of a small minority who were driven insane from spending endless hours staring at it. Scientists said there was nothing there, an absence of all light, sound, and energy. Humans weren't equipped to see nothing, so your mind put something there. A pure white nothing.

Hyperspace was four dimensions crushed to a pinpoint, then expanded to the infinite. Calculations suggested it should be possible to enter hyperspace and emerge on the other side of the universe; however, it didn't work that way in practice. It didn't work in any way Human scientists understood. Hyperspace navigation computers would take you to any star system within the ship's range, and that range varied depending on what the Cartography Guild called hyperspatial conditions. Supposedly, the physics of normal space played a factor in how easy it was to travel through hyperspace, and the limit tended to be around 20,000 light years, with a few exceptions.

The time spent in hyperspace, exactly 170 hours each transition, was usually a quiet time on ships where the crew conducted routine maintenance; there was always plenty to do on a starship. Things broke regularly and needed repair. When in hyperspace, one duty station was always manned, though—the reactor watch. The power had to stay on to operate the hyperspace generators. If they failed, the great unknown would swallow them whole, and they would never be heard from again.

The reactor watch was kept on all shifts while in hyperspace. It was even more important on this transition, as Reactor Two was still down. Normal hyperspace procedure was to operate two reactors at 50 percent output each to run the hyperspace generators. Each reactor had enough energy at full power to keep the generators operating and the ship in hyperspace. If one began to fail or show strain, a third reactor would be powered up, the load shifted, and the questionable unit powered down. As it was now, there was no backup. If one of the two operational plants developed problems, they'd only have one left, and staying in hyperspace would take everything it had, with little left over. If that happened, the crew would finish the transition in space suits to save power, praying.

Because of the inverse square law of power required to stay in hyperspace once there, the bigger the ship, the less power you needed. Ships like the heavy haulers required a shockingly small amount of juice, only a couple of terawatts. A medium-sized warship like *Pegasus* took more than 20 terawatts of reactor power to stay in hyperspace. Little frigates like the two she'd destroyed in the S.G. Skaa system probably took twice the power *Pegasus* needed to enter hyperspace. It continued to get worse until most of your ship was reactor space, consuming massive amounts of hydrogen fuel and needing

F11 replenishment more and more often. That calculation of economy drove space travel. Most escort ships didn't even have hyperspace generators. It was simpler to clamp the smaller ship to the side of a bigger ship and hitch a ride; the increased mass even made it less costly for the bigger ship!

As Alexis stared out at the nothingness, she thought of the untold millions of spaceships sharing hyperspace at that moment across their galaxy. Were they thousands of light years away, or close enough to touch? It took incredible amounts of energy to shunt into hyperspace, and that energy was gone; it disappeared from the universe. Where did it go? Were they responsible for a white hole feeding a new universe somewhere else?

"*<The Nowhere always makes you think like this>*" Alexis grinned and shrugged.

"It isn't a natural thing."

"*<No, you just do not understand it>*"

"Who can?" Alexis floated back and caught the edge of her desk. She could feel the vibration of the fusion reactors hundreds of feet away, transferred through the steel and composites of the ship's spine. She felt the air of the life support system brush her face gently, stirring some of her white hair. The slates locked to her desk scrolled data on the ship's operation, as well as ongoing repairs from the last fight. Sitting there, she could feel the ship breathing; its heart beating through the living thing which was *Pegasus*. It was comforting. There was a knock on the door.

"Come!" she called. The door slid open, and Paka came in.

"Captain?"

"What can I do for you?"

"There's a problem in marine country."

The two floated into the lift in Section One, currently set for down, and headed aft. They hung onto the handholds as the lift began to move so they weren't pushed against one end. The interior decks were oriented like slices of the shaft of a tree so that gravity was useful during thrust. The gravity decks extended from the spinning hull to provide some gravity during transition and non-powered flight. Since they were in hyperspace, two of the four gravity decks were deployed on their spokes and the ship spun up to give a half G on the decks. Alexis seldom found the need to visit them.

They got off the lift on Deck 22, one of the shuttle/dropship maintenance and service decks. The lifts each only ran half the length of the ship to minimize secondary damage in the event of combat losses. They crossed a bay to reach the lift in Section Three. The space was mostly devoid of maintenance work, with most of the crew en route to the two gravity deck entrances. Crew morale was good. Despite the casualties, they were finally going Home.

"Is it bad?" she asked as they again began to descend.

"Problematic," Paka said.

Alexis was used to her XO's restrained nature. When the situation called for it, she'd quickly relay whatever information Alexis needed. But in situations like this, the Veetanho's nature took over, and she would draw it out to a dramatic reveal. Alexis didn't fight it; you left a good dynamic in place, even if it had a few issues.

The lift stopped on Deck 29, currently its lowest location. The missile damage had played hell with secondary systems down here, the lifts among them. They left the lift and floated toward Section Two. Deck 29 was a missile magazine, and the bulkhead was segmented to allow blowout on each section in case of accidental detonation. Each section was fifteen feet, top to bottom, filled with racks holding missiles of all types. Automatic feed mechanisms moved the missiles up to the rear missile launchers on Deck 28.

At the gangway, a Tri-V flashed across the downward ramp. "Caution – Pressure Maintenance Underway!" Alexis nodded her approval, glad Guylan was doing his job. They floated through the warning and down to Deck 30, the marines' deck.

This deck was double the normal size at 30 feet high. The extra space allowed the marines ample room for their billeting as well as a separate mess, armory, CASPer ready room, and maintenance shops. It was also home to another set of docking collars, one in each of the pie-shaped sections. These facilitated easy egress for maintenance and the loading of dropships or assault pods for combat. The damage was apparent the moment they entered.

Alexis looked at the torn wall, the blackened decks and ceilings, and the scattered maintenance equipment used to bring basic function back to the holed deck. The bulkhead between Sections One and Two had blown into Two as if someone had lit a firecracker and dropped it into a soda can.

The missile had slammed into the hull by the collar on Section One, punched through the exterior armor, and detonated inside. Several hundred pounds of K2 in a shaped charge had struck the interior like a wrecking ball. Section One was mostly marine barracks and sanitary facilities. Most of the marines not on alert had been sealed in their staterooms. They never knew what hit them.

The explosion tore through the section and blew out the bulkheads between Section One and Sections Two and Four. Section Four held office space, officers' staterooms, and training and equipment spaces. Section Two contained the marines' small mess hall,

CASPer storage, and one of their three armories. All three sections were completely destroyed.

The explosion didn't have quite enough force to breach the central spine, or continue into Section Three opposite the impact point. The lack of damage to the spine was particularly good as it held the main power, data, and fluid transfer lines for the entire ship. Section Three was home to two additional armories, a small weapons testing range, and the marines' ready room where their troopers geared up. Their only surviving members had been there, ready for action when she'd set Condition One.

Alexis moved toward Section One, but Paka put a clawed hand on her leg.

"They're in Section Three, ma'am."

"I know," she said. "I just want to see the impact point." Paka let her go, and she drifted to the blown-out bulkhead. She touched the bent metal almost gingerly, as if part of her mind expected it to still be hot. The metal felt rough to the touch, the aftereffect of the incredible explosive forces. She pulled herself through into Section One. All the individual rooms and other spaces were gone, the force of the blast had compressed them like a stack of potato chips. Seeing an interior section like this blown open reminded her of the shuttle deck. It was unnatural.

The hole in the exterior pressure wall was small, less than five feet across and 10 feet long. The missile had hit at an oblique angle from far aft; its impact hole was almost oblong. Striking at several thousand feet per second, its armored tip penetrated the hull like a bullet, then triggered the warhead a millisecond later. The hole was patched with several steel plates welded in place. A typical field expedient repair, the entire affair was sprayed with a layer of super-crete sealant. It wasn't as strong as the actual hull, but if another missile hit the same point, it wouldn't make any difference anyway.

Only five feet from the plated-over wound was the bulge of a secondary cableway. Loss of life aside, the hit had done very little actual damage to *Pegasus'* combat capabilities. The crazy bastards in the escort frigates could have thrown missiles at *Pegasus'* shields until their magazines ran empty and she'd still have had more than enough defenses to continue on.

"Lucky, and unlucky," she said as she surveyed the damage. Paka let her be. After a minute, she floated back out and around to Section Three. The bulkhead doorway was gone, the blast wave had blown it off its hinges. As she floated in she could see it, embedded in the opposite bulkhead. There was conversation on the other side.

"Captain on deck," Paka called ahead, and the conversation died out.

"At ease," she said as she drifted in. The ready room was a bit worse for wear, though not as bad as the other three sections by far. It was difficult to imagine the squad all strapped into their armor and holding onto handholds here as the missile blew apart three-quarters of the deck. She looked at the scene and immediately wondered what the fuck was wrong. "Explain?"

The squad leader, Sergeant T'jto, was hovering to one side of the room on her rear legs, the middle and top set crossed over her thorax, her multifaceted eyes taking in everything. Zit clung to a bulkhead, its eyestalks moving this way and that. It appeared to have been working on a laser carbine, though now the pieces just floated nearby, ignored. The only surviving Human member, Corporal Johansson, was sitting on a bench, anchoring herself to it with a leg bent back underneath. Like Zit, she'd been doing some maintenance on a piece of equipment from her CASPer. Unlike the Goka, she was using a sticky-mat to keep the parts from floating away—the downside of only having two manipulative limbs. She pretended to continue her work.

The last two members of the team were the creatures of interest. Private Jeejee was floating next to the wall, whiskers twitching in an obviously agitated state, eyes fixed on the point of his anger. That point was their heavy weapons and general mayhem specialist, Oort.

The Tortantula was a hulking 10 feet across from tip to tip of her nine legs. She currently was somewhat curled where she'd wrapped around a bench in a posture Alexis had never seen one of her kind assume.

"She's being an idiot," Jeejee barked and jabbed a finger in the spider's side. It didn't react.

"She looks ill to me," Alexis said.

"Mentally," Jeejee grumbled.

"Maybe one of you can tell me what's going on?"

"Captain?" the MinSha sergeant said.

"Please, Sergeant T'jto," Alexis said.

"Private Oort," she said, gesturing with a mid-hand, "is having a crisis of conscience." Alexis looked from the MinSha sergeant to the Tortantula who was curled up on the bench and cocked an eyebrow.

"A Tortantula? Conscience?" The sergeant gave a shrug. "Jeejee, maybe you can explain?" She hoped someone could.

"It started with the fight on that heavy hauler. One of the SleSha shot at her with a laser rifle. I mean, mag dump, hosed it all away at her." He looked at his partner. "Didn't score a single hit."

"Happens in combat all the time," Johansson said and snorted.

"Not when you're the size of a tank," Jeejee pointed out. The Tortantula was a huge target. Maybe not as big as a tank—perhaps just a small car. "Then when we were attacked after entering the system here, it was our squad on ready-alert rotation. Our squad, not any of the others. Call it 25 percent odds that we're the ones in the only part of Deck 30 to survive. The other three squads, instant death.

"We scuttle in and start getting geared up. Oort hates her vacuum armor. Tortantula don't like armor that covers their entire body. She takes her time. She's still finishing as you start juking us all over the place." Sergeant T'jto nodded, managing to make it look disapproving. Not an easy feat for an insect.

"I kept yelling to hurry up," the NCO said.

"She finally got her armor on, and I mean, just finished, and *ka-boom!*" The Flatar made an explosion sound and waved his hands around. "The whole fucking deck, blown to shit. The shockwave blew the damn hatch off and launched it across the deck like a stone skipping on water." He floated along the deck, pointing to two scuffs between the hatch way and where the hatch was embedded in the bulkhead. "And, where was she?" he asked, and pointed a couple feet away, directly in front of the hatch he perched on. "She was standing right there. Right fucking there, squatted down and holding the deck plates with her claws. The hatch went over her body so close it threw sparks off the armor!"

"Lucky fucker," Zit chittered from the wall.

"It was not luck," the giant Tortantula grumbled. Everyone turned and looked at her.

"Then what was it?" Jeejee asked.

"I…don't…know," she admitted slowly. For a time, no one knew what to say.

"Private Oort," Alexis address her.

"Captain?"

"I need you to get your shit straight."

"I'm trying, sir."

"No, you're curled up in a ball like a house spider someone sprayed with pesticide. A few hours ago I lost almost all my marines. You five are all I have left to defend this ship. A large portion of the crew isn't from a merc race, and if we get boarded, you're it. In a fight, you are a black goddess of unholy death, and that's how I want you." The alien didn't respond. "Can I count on you, marine?" Jeejee looked from the captain to his companion and back again, as nervous as Alexis had ever seen the Flatar.

No one completely understood that relationship, and it was a common one. The Flatars were probably the least imposing physical specimens in all the merc races. Only around one foot tall, they looked like chipmunks with rather long arms and sharp eyes, and they had a propensity for violence only equaled by the Tortantula. Some even said they were cruel by nature. Maybe it had been fated from the beginning that Flatar would ride Tortantulas in battle, relatively safe with an armored seat and a big fucking gun. They were great at picking off stragglers their partners might miss and watching behind them in tight quarters. They were basically living close-in defense systems.

"I need an answer," Alexis said, crossing her arms and hooking a foot into a handhold. Her bearing was the 'Captain ain't happy' one the crew constantly strove to avoid at all costs.

"I am here for a reason," Oort said.

"Yeah, to kill shit," Jeejee growled. Alexis motioned him to silence, and Oort continued.

"I do not know what that reason is, but clearly, my being spared the beyond three times in such a short period is a sign. I have to think on this." *Think?* Alexis thought. *Entropy, a thinking Tortantula? What next?*

"Think all you want, marine," she said, "but if that alarm claxon sounds will you fight?"

"I will fight," the Tortantula replied without hesitation.

"Good enough for me," Alexis said with a nod. If it were a Human she'd given a pep talk to, she would have patted them on the shoulder, looked them in the eye, and added a respectful nod. Oort wasn't a physical-touching being. Her skin was covered in black fur tough enough to tear a Human's skin, she had no shoulders to speak of, and there were 10 eyes all around her head. She settled on a nod for Oort, and turned to Sergeant T'jto. "Carry on, sergeant."

"Captain," the MinSha said, and gave her a brisk, insectile salute.

"Jeejee, a word?" Alexis asked. The Flatar glanced at his partner before holstering his huge laser pistol (cross body, it was too big for a belt holster), and followed her as she floated out the shattered hatchway. Paka followed a respectful distance behind. "I'd like your opinion, private," she said once they were back in Section Two and out of hearing range.

"She's fucking nuts," Jeejee snorted. "I'd say she was done, except…"

"Go on," Alexis prompted.

"Except she said she'd fight."

"Anyone can say they'll fight."

"If a Tortantula says something, you'd better believe it. I've dealt with them my whole life. Our races have intertwined fates. We go to school together as children! Flatar parents put their kids with hatching Tortantula to teach them we aren't food. The little bastards still bite sometimes. We're somewhat naturally immune to their neurotoxin, and the occasional nip at that age just strengthens the resistance. Anyway, there's two things you learn growing up around the big brutes. One is they don't know how to say quit. Ever."

"And the second?"

"A Tortantula can't lie. I don't think they know how. Just like they don't understand humor, and barely understand metaphorical statements. The ones who are too small or weak to go to war end up going into other trades, but they still pair off with a Flatar as an assistant. We guide them through interactions that are difficult for them to handle. Most Tortantula would rather eat a Human than talk to one."

"We're a very humorous race," Alexis agreed.

"You're a race of assholes," Jeejee said, then looked at her. "No offense, sir."

"None taken," she said. "So, you're saying she's all messed up, but she'll still fight?"

"Correct on both accounts," Jeejee agreed.

"You'll keep an eye on her, then?"

"Of course; it's my job."

"Let me ask something else?" Jeejee nodded in his no-neck version of a nod. "Has she always been off like that, in other ways?"

"I have no idea."

"What? You mean you aren't sure?"

"No, I mean I have no idea. We'd only been together a few weeks before we signed on with the Hussars."

Alexis grunted and nodded. "Huh, I just assumed you two had always been together."

"Lots of other races think that. You should see some of the porn that gets published." Alexis looked askance, and he laughed. "See, we do understand humor. The truth is, though, we often *do* spend our lives with them. We both get killing and violence; it comes naturally to us. Unlike Humans, we've embraced that side of our being. You hairless monkeys seem to spend more time trying to explain away your bloodthirsty side than you do embracing it."

"So how did you two end up together?" They'd stopped at the gangway up to Deck 30. The three moved aside to make room for an elSha maintenance team that came bounding down, the little reptilians as comfortable in zero-gravity as fish in water.

"We met on Telka in a merc pit. It's a shit world over in the Jesc arm." He made a dismissive gesture. "Kinda place you end up in when you're low on options. Oort had just been dropped from her company. They'd done an assault with a Besquith company, and as usual the spiders had soaked up most of the fire and casualties. Only a couple of her teammates survived, and her rider wasn't one of them. Ever notice part of one arm is missing?" The captain nodded. "Lost it in that fight. A Tortantula can lose one or two and keep going. Hell, I've heard of a few with cybernetic arms, but never met one. They're almost spiritual about it. Once you lose a limb, you're done. No unit will take you. Some shit about 'being chosen, but not going.'"

"Going where?" Alexis asked. Jeejee made a twirling motion with one hand above his head.

"The great beyond? How the hell should I know? Anyway, they're damaged goods. A lot of them end up with non-Tortantula units as hired guns. Problem is, most are bat shit crazy because they're not with their own kind. They're communal, you see? I met her there, trying to broker a pit fighting deal. She didn't realize they were trying to get her to fight five Oogar at the same time. Not actually sure she would have cared if she did. I helped her out, we teamed up, and here we are."

Alexis nodded her head. It was an interesting story and explained a lot about the enigmatic pair. She found it interesting that she'd just learned more about the Tortantula and Flatar in five minutes than in all her previous decades.

"Thank you for your insight, Private." The little Flatar shrugged.

"Her ass is my ass," he said; "if she goes limp in a fight, I'm as easy a target as she is."

"You have a good point. Please let me know if you need anything."

"Or if I notice she's gone over the edge?" Alexis gave him a nod. "Will do."

"Dismissed." He caught a handhold and pushed back toward what remained of the marine's area, and she floated up the gangway. Paka fell in next to her. As they reached the top, the all hands' warning sounded.

"All hands, prepare for spin." The two stopped and held onto the wall as the horn sounded twice, and *Pegasus* began to rotate on her axis. After a minute it reached five RPM and stabilized. "Gravity Decks One and Four are now open," the voice said. "All off duty crew are at liberty until we reach the stargate. That is all."

Now that the ship was spinning, there was gravity as they worked their way upwards. Both experienced spacers, Paka and Alexis merely took advantage of it and walked up the ramps at an angle, hopping between steps.

"Aren't you concerned about the Tortantula?" Paka eventually asked as they rode the lift up toward the ship's control room.

"Of course," she said, "but a Tortantula is going to do what a Tortantula is going to do." It was quiet for a bit as she thought. "I figure we can't get in much more trouble before we pick up additional crew. Two more jumps and we're at Karma."

* * * * *

Chapter Eleven

Mars Station Varley
Mars Orbit – Sol System

Rick floated down the docking collar and expertly caught one of the yellow/black-striped handholds that surrounded the passageway, locked a leg under another, and leaned over backward just in time to intercept the cargo container. It had far too much mass to stop, but using all of his upper body strength, he redirected it toward the rear of the cargo module.

He turned and inspected his work. The module sailed across the hold with nearly zero spin and perfectly on target to where two other cargo handlers waited for it. Both strong men like himself, they braced and used their bodies like biological springs, bringing it to a stop.

"Good bounce, Rick!" one of them called. He waved and shoved back down the docking collar. He grabbed a handhold at the edge, stopping himself and checking for the next cargo container. They were still maneuvering it out of the station storage area. With a minute to kill, Rick enjoyed the view.

The receiving area of the Martian Transfer Station was a huge plastic dome that afforded an incredible view of the planet 300 miles below. At the relatively low orbit, the landscape whisked by quite quickly. He'd spent some of the three days' transit to Mars studying the planet's geography. Unless he was wrong, they were currently passing over the Acidalia Planitia. Its landscape had a distinctively blacker appearance than most of the rest of the planet. A moment later the edge of the massive Lloyt crater came into view, confirming his guess.

"Heads up!" called the station crew, and Rick prepared for the next container. Two hours and 30 containers later, they'd finished loading *Coronado*. Captain Holland floated among the dozens of cargo containers inside the inflatable hold linked to his ship and examined the rigging with a critical eye. Rick and the two other loaders floated nearby, holding on with a foot or a hand, waiting on his pronouncement.

He'd mumble something, pull on a polyrope here, or pretend to tighten a strap there, but the truth was, he didn't find anything to criticize.

"Not bad," he finally said. The loaders all smiled and nodded to each other. Rick thought it was an excellent job, considering all he did was move containers. The other two men did all the stowage. He took his clue from their reactions and smiled too. He already knew from his short time on the *Coronado* that Holland was not liberal with his praise. "Now secure all those unused straps and gear; I want to get underway in an hour."

"We finished ahead of schedule," one of the loaders said, a question hinted in his voice. Holland glanced at his watch.

"Huh, so you did." The other two men grinned hugely. "Fine, go over and take two hours."

"Yea!" they both cheered and leaped toward the docking collar. Rick watched them go and shook his head.

"What about you?"

Rick looked at the captain. "Me, sir?"

"Yeah. You're half their age. You don't want to go drink Martian rot gut and act like a fool?"

"No sir, I'd rather just stay aboard."

"A merc? Bullshit, get off my ship and don't come back for two hours."

"I don't have any money, sir."

"Oh, for the love of…" Holland growled and reached into his pocket, then floated over to Rick and held out his hand. Rick took what was offered. There were 20 plastic coins.

"Real Union credits," Rick said in amazement. They were pressed with the symbol of the Union Credit Exchange inside the symbol for the Trade Guild. But in the center, set in the plastic, was a tiny red gem. Rick held it up so the light shown through to cast a red spot on his eye. "I've never seen a red diamond before!"

"They're in all the Union's hard credits," Holland explained. "Bigger the denomination, bigger the diamond. It's never quite as big a diamond as the credit's value, keeps people from chopping up the chit for the gem. Still, idiots on Earth do it all the time." Holland shook his head. "I saw a million-credit chit once. They're slightly oblong and have a five-carat red diamond in them!" Rick looked at the pile in his hand. Around the edge was about 100 tiny symbols, none of which he recognized. The captain saw him examining them. "Oh, that's the denomination. Five credits, in all the most common languages."

"I don't see English," Rick said.

The captain chuckled. "Son, we ain't common. Many thousand races in the galaxy, and we're one of the newest. Maybe we'll be on there some day, if we live that long."

"Huh?"

The captain laughed and closed Rick's hand around the credits. "That's 100 credits, advance on your next pay. Won't buy too much here, but you can get a few drinks and maybe some pussy." Rick's face turned red, and the captain roared with laughter. "Shit, you are as green as the summer grass! Go on, git."

The Mars station served several purposes. It was a sprawling affair, unlike the big double wheel of Heinlein station in Earth orbit, which was mainly habitat and orbit-to-ground transfer. Varley station sat in low Martian orbit because it wore so many hats—cargo transfer, research in a dozen fields, hub of the Beanstalk Project, and Earth Defense military base. It was a huge ball, with a single ring orbiting on tracks to serve as its gravity deck.

Through the center of the ball was the tether which would maybe someday be a space elevator to the surface of Mars. The bottom would be anchored to the surface at the equator, the other end on Deimos. If the project ever got past the concept stage, both the station and the moon would need to be relocated.

Rick spent a few minutes visiting the Martian Elevator Project office and watching a Tri-V show on what they hoped to do. He'd learned about it two years ago in high school, though, so this was nothing new. He wandered to the gravity ring where he could see through the floor and watch Mars rotate by every 92 seconds.

There were a few shops along one section. He got a burrito and a bulb of fruit juice for three credits (be sure to put the empty in the marked bins) and ate as he walked. Several of the shops sold handmade items, all crafted in the settlement of Bradbury, below, or one of the outlying settlements. He did find an interesting bracelet in a tiny shop full of hand-crafted jewelry. It was silver and Martian malachite. He liked it and payed the exorbitant price of 5 credits.

Rick re-boarded *Coronado* at the appointed time. His fellow cargo handlers were well laid and thoroughly intoxicated. Captain Holland pushed them toward their bunks as he signed off for the last of the hydrogen and other consumables being loaded aboard. He glanced at Rick and frowned.

"You at least get a drink or a souvenir?" he asked. "God knows when you'll be back in-system."

"Yeah," he said and touched the bracelet, "I got something."

"What is it?" the ship's master asked. "Hope you didn't buy some line about ancient Martian alien artifacts to clean out your pockets."

"No," he said, "just something to remember Mars by." Ten minutes later, *Coronado* pushed away from Varley station and began building speed to break orbit. Rick got to watch on the monitor from his acceleration station in enlisted country. As they moved around Mars, he got a great look at the shipyards on the far side of the planet from Varley; it was a vast gossamer web of struts and supports surrounding numerous nearly-complete and partial ships. He knew from school it had taken humanity decades to get to where they could build their own capital ships, and the Martian yard was only capable of cruiser-sized ships and smaller.

Coronado steadily picked up velocity and on the next orbit the shipyard was so far below it was nearly lost against the red of Mars. In only one more trip around the planet, the ship broke orbit and headed for her next stop, Jupiter.

*****

Chapter Twelve

EMS Pegasus

Approaching the Sulaadar System

Hyperspace

"Transition in T-minus one minute," the computer announced throughout the ship. The crew rushed to complete final preparations before emerging into normal space.

"Paka," Captain Cromwell addressed her XO, "set Condition One throughout the ship."

"Aye-aye, sir," the Veetanho said and entered the command on her control board. The alarm for battle stations sounded, a harsh alien whistle that went up and down in intensity, and the CIC's lighting changed from yellow to red. Some things, like the alarm, had been left unchanged since the ship's creation, while the lighting had been altered to a more Human norm.

"Ship reports Condition One set," Glick, the SitCon, reported after less than 20 seconds.

"Thirty seconds to transition," the computer updated. Sulaadar was a major star system, and a hub of commerce and industry in the Tolo arm. Situated near the void between it and the Jesc arm, it was as natural a place for intergalactic commerce to be located as Egypt had been on ancient Earth. Alexis and Paka had decided on it after the near disaster in S.G. Skaa. If a nowhere system hadn't proved safe, maybe a huge hub world would.

"Ten seconds," the computer said. The ship thrummed with power, though with one reactor down, not as much as her crew was accustomed to feeling.

"I'd really like to have that power from Reactor Two," Alexis said, aiming her comment at the screen which showed the waving antennae of Long, her chief engineer.

"I'm sorry, ma'am," Long said; "we can't risk a containment loss." Alexis grunted as the holographic clock counted down. Loss of containment on a fusion plant wasn't as catastrophic as old science fiction used to make it out to be. However, it also wasn't something one would hope for, even on a good day. The computer began final countdown.

"Transition in three…two…one…"

A quick sensation of falling, and the wrap-around monitors which displayed the ship's camera views went from pure white to black with pinpoints of light. One screen (dimmed for easy viewing) showed a blue-white star, and another a circle of brownish light, the closest planet.

"Status?" Paka called.

"Running sensor sweeps," Flipper said as he operated the ship's various passive sensors. As was standard procedure when transitioning under Condition One, only passive sensors were used to decrease their visible signature to possible hostiles. Suddenly he issued a snapping, bubbly word that wasn't immediately translated. His tiny hand danced on the holographic controls and a trio of red triangles appeared on the display. "We have three unidentified ships," he chittered, "marking Bogey One, Two, and Three. Distance two light-seconds. They were all running hot and active and have altered course for intercept."

"You have got to be kidding me," Alexis said. "Hoot," she said to the comms officer.

"Ma'am?" the Buma replied.

"Would you please contact those vessels and inform them we are not hostile?"

"Right away."

"What are we dealing with, Edwards?"

"Running it," the tiny man replied. He was manipulating sensor data through his pinplants so fast it was impossible to read on his monitors.

"There appears to be a conflict underway in the system," Hoot said.

"You think?" Alexis asked.

"So it would seem," Hoot replied, displaying the typical humorless Buma attitude. He put one of the current transmissions up on the CIC speaker.

"To all ships entering the Sulaadar system," the alien voice was translated by the computer or the individual crew member's translator. "This system is under interdiction by the Transki Syndicate. All merchant ships will stand by to be boarded and searched for contraband. All private vessels will be escorted to the stargate for immediate transition out-system. All mercenary vessels will immediately accept employment with Transki or be declared enemy combatants."

"Well that explains a lot," Alexis said, and sighed. Transki was one of the biggest pains in the galaxy's ass. They were the living embodiment of why the libertarian form of government the Galactic Union used wasn't the best, just what worked. They'd started as a consortium of industrial and trade concerns more than a thousand years ago, and quickly grew in power and wealth. But as the Union provided no promise of assistance or restriction by a government entity, competition became ever more powerful. They began to fight that competition with a creative use of innovation and violence. Eventually it became mostly violence. Although not all mercs were willing to take contracts that involved extortion, enough did.

"I have probable identifications on the bogies," Edwards announced. Alexis turned her full attention to the TacCom's screen in the semi-circular CIC. "Bogies One and Two are *Sheek*-class laser frigates." Alexis nodded, she was familiar with the class. They were a reliable old design with good firepower and shields, although they weren't very fast or maneuverable, despite their size. "Bogey Three appears to be a *Pakatol*-class cruiser." That was worse. The Pakatol was as venerable as the Sheek, but while the frigates were common and less than top-of-the-line, the Pakatol were made by the Izlian who had been known for making powerful, flexible warships for thousands of years.

"I have the cruiser on comms," Hoot said. Alexis gestured, and the transmission replaced the repeating statement.

"Unidentified warship," the voice was translated, "this is the cruiser *Yushispa.* Per the terms of the broadcast you are receiving on system-wide transmission, you must declare your intentions." Alexis touched the control on her pinplant and saw she was linked into the transmitter.

"This is the unidentified warship," Alexis sent, "what company do you work for, *Yushispa*?"

"We are with Quigg du Snoo, unidentified ship." On one of the screens, Glick instantly put up data on Quigg du Snoo. Alexis glanced from it to her helmsman, Chug, and SitCon, Glick. Both had one eyestalk focused on the display, while the others looked at her. Since Quigg du Snoo and the two crewmen were all Bakulu, it was no surprise they would be interested. The situation kept getting worse—the Bakulu produced good ships and good crews, and the snails were naturals at space combat. "And whom are we addressing?"

"You are addressing Alexis Cromwell, commander of the Winged Hussars, aboard our flagship *Pegasus.*"

"I see," the reply came. It would seem to be difficult for a snail to be taken aback, but you would have been convinced otherwise listening to the master of *Yushispa.* "I am Geshakooka, captain of this vessel, and commander of this squadron. It is an honor to meet one of the famous Human Four Horsemen I've heard so much about. A truly fortuitous day."

"The honor is all mine, Captain Geshakooka. As to it being fortuitous, that would depend on where we go from here. I see two options."

"I am listening."

"Bogies have ceased acceleration," Glick informed her over her pinlink; "however, the frigates have altered course to spread out. I estimate weapons range in 10 minutes."

"Expected," Alexis sent back. "Update if they show targeting profiles or begin maneuvering again." She switched back to comms with the *Yushispa.* "One, you simply let us transit to the stargate and we go on our way. I know it's against your blockade rules of engagement, but it's your best option."

"What is the other option?"

"I kill your entire squadron," Alexis said calmly.

"Those are interesting options," the opposing captain replied, "and worthy of consideration."

"Glick, Chug," she sent to her two Bakulu command crew, "I assume you are listening to their un-translated speech." Both indicated they were. "I need to know if Captain Geshakooka is displaying any emotions." The two Bakulu swiveled an eyestalk at each other, then back to her. Although they had three eyestalks, they could use different numbers independently, depending on their mood. As was common, on the *Pegasus* bridge, it was the more communicative of the two who replied.

"Not that I can tell, Captain," Glick said. "If we were to hazard an opinion, we would say the captain is conflicted."

"I see," Alexis said and chewed her lip. After a moment with no reply, she transmitted again. "Captain, I don't know why you are working for the Transki in the first place. They're little better than thieves with a thin layer of moral justification. I wouldn't take a contract with them on a dare."

"It is a complicated arrangement," the other captain replied. "I do not want to fight you," it added; "it would be easier if you would just take the retainer and work for the Transki for the duration of this embargo."

"I'd rather transition to hyperspace with a failing fusion reactor."

"Weapons range in seven minutes," Glick informed her.

"Captain, I do not wish to fight you either," Alexis said, "but if you do not alter course in two minutes, you give me little choice." Throughout the ship, her crew stood at combat stations and awaited their fates. Space combat was often composed of long waits, followed by moments of intense violence.

"Then I guess we have no choice," Captain Geshakooka replied. "We must fight."

Alexis bowed her head and sighed. "Very well. I am sorry."

"As am I." The transmission ended.

"Paka, bring us to full combat footing!" Alexis snapped.

"Reactors to full power," Paka ordered. "Shields up; launch drone fighters!"

"Charge the spinal mount," Alexis commanded, "and bring us around to face the *Yushispa*."

Pegasus fired her oversized maneuvering thrusters and came about to face the enemy ships, which were only just beginning to power their drivers. On the blunt nose of the *Pegasus*, a multi-segmented door opened like the petals on a flower, exposing the bore of her spinal particle accelerator cannon. Already its channel was sparkling and glowing slightly as the super-dense metal was preheated to reduce stress.

"Main gun charged," Edwards reported. "I have a firing solution on Bogey Three."

"Match bearings and fire," Alexis ordered.

The *Pegasus'* two operational fusion plants were fed dense streams of hydrogen through microscopic discontinuities in their magnetic bottles. The tiny suns inside flared with immense power, which was captured by radio-thermocouples and translated into energy that was fed to the ship's main weapon. In the front quarter of the ship, banks of massive capacitors received the power from the reactors, and in seconds they were fully energized. On Edwards' status panel, the spinal mount status blinked 'charged.'

"Firing," he said. After a quick check through his pinlinks to verify the target was in the anticipated strike window, he touched the release button.

Terawatts of power surged into the densely-stacked lines of accelerator coils. One after another they discharged into the next coil, and the next, and onward. This progression took less than a microsecond. Exactly one-quarter of a second after Edwards' stubby finger touched the button, *Pegasus'* spinal-mounted gun discharged a one second long, 40-terawatt pulse of coherent energy which traveled to the *Yushispa* at the speed of light. It stuck a glancing blow off the cruiser's shields.

"They anticipated the shot and had their shields up," Glick said, "although one of their shields was overloaded."

Damn, Alexis cursed inwardly. Although she hadn't wanted to destroy the other ship, she'd hoped for a quick disabling shot to take them out of the fight. The other two escorts might then have rethought the entire engagement.

"Noted," she said. "Standard recharge. Power to secondary weapons and shields, 20-percent reserve."

"I have missile launch," Glick said, "tracking 20 inbound missiles from Bogey Three; target is now maneuvering evasively."

"Drone status?" Paka called out.

"Drone Control," a ghostly voice said over the intercom, "First Squadron is away. Second Squadron in 20 seconds."

"Enemy missiles' time to impact, 39 seconds," Glick said.

Alexis hissed. Too damned close.

"Load aft tubes with anti-missile missiles and fire."

Paka glanced at Alexis as Edwards executed the order. It took a little more than 10 seconds to change from offensive to defensive missiles. Once the aft tubes, half their complement of launchers, were loaded with defensive missiles, it would severely limit their offensive punch. The clock clicked down until Edwards spoke again.

"Firing anti-missile missiles," he said, and the status board showed the green specks flying away. Outside the ship, twelve missiles left their tubes like the spokes of a wheel. A split second after inert gas expelled them into space, they spun to face forward, ignited their engines, and accelerated away at 1,000 gravities.

Pegasus was ringed with a squadron of 10 drone fighters, and the second squadron had just finished exiting the landing bay when the defensive missiles reached their targets. The two flights of missiles approached each other at hundreds of miles per second, far too fast for a Human to react. Their computer brains analyzed data they'd been preprogramed with before launch and sensor data gathered during their flight. The inbound missiles tried to evade anything that kept them from reaching their objective; the outbound ones strove to kill the first.

The anti-missile missiles were relatively simple. They used terminal guidance to place themselves in the path of an oncoming missile, and when less than a mile away they detonated a pair of charges. The first turned the carefully crafted nose cone into a near wall of high density shrapnel. The enemy missile would have to fly through the debris. No matter how tough the anti-ship missile might be, hitting a piece of hardened-alloy steel with a combined closing velocity of several hundred miles per second would end it. The second charge turned the booster into similar junk, thus increasing the odds of a kill, if only by a tiny amount. At so close a range, the detonation window was less than a picosecond.

"Fifteen of the incoming missiles destroyed," Glick said, "and one more is wild."

"Reloads won't be available in time," Edwards said.

"Drone Control, get those drones away so I can maneuver to shoot, god damn it!" Alexis ordered.

"Clear," the passionless voice announced.

"Paka!"

"Roll the ship, engage with all lasers!" the Veetanho snarled. The two squadrons of 10 drone fighters shot away from their mothership at high acceleration, clearing the battlecruiser's threat box.

Spaced along the *Pegasus'* cylindrical hull were three rings of eight laser emitters. As soon as the fight went hot, their covers slid aside, and the emitters rose on short projections to give them a wider area of fire. The maneuvering thruster fired again, the ship spun to afford the lasers more targeting opportunities, and the lasers began firing.

Each emitter was a complicated series of mirrors and a camera. Depending on the power needed, each could generate a single 100-megawatt beam, or be split into four 20-megawatt beams, which were ideal for missile and fighter intercept. In an instant, a deadly light-show of 96 lasers was flashing out at the surviving missiles.

Sensors locked onto the five rapidly approaching missiles and guided the laser fire. The intercepting beams crisscrossed in a complicated algorithm designed to cover as much space as possible in the missiles' flight paths. It was extremely effective. All five were vaporized in seconds, the last one less than 50 miles out.

"All missiles intercepted," Edwards confirmed.

"High-G maneuver," Alexis ordered, "widen their target box!"

"Four Gs of thrust," Paka ordered, "skew turn, bring her about to 165-mark-210!"

As the maneuver began, a Tri-V globe formed in the center of the CIC. A miniature *Pegasus* was in the center of the sphere, oriented so it's nose pointed at the nose of the actual ship. Flashing red points showed the bearings to the three enemy ships, and steady blue dots showed the ship's drone fighters, now racing away nearly as fast as missiles in two groups of 10.

In the center of the ship, the CIC felt little of the turn. Centrifugal forces were minimized there, one of the many reasons why the CIC was located where it was. Most of the officers were strapped into self-orienting chairs, or locked in place (for the aliens). The only one who preferred to just wing it was Paka. The somewhat rodent-like Veetanho would simply cling to whatever console she was currently using.

As the ship spun and built thrust, the CIC crew were shifted sideways and pressed into their seats. Outside, the ship pointed to the new bearing, and its fusion torch flared with blinding power, altering the ship's course in a wide skew turn.

"New course and bearing set," Chug reported. His piloting station had a series of suction points that locked his shell in place against the forces the ship experienced.

"Forward missile batteries target the cruiser," Alexis ordered. "Fire!"

Twelve missiles left the forward tubes. Just like the defensive missiles, these were fired straight out from the hull; they aligned on their targets and shot away under high acceleration. Only these were ship-killers, larger and slower than their anti-missile counterparts, but infinitely more dangerous.

"Missiles away," Edwards confirmed.

"Configure laser batteries for ship-to-ship fire," Alexis ordered. Outside the ship, the mirrors on the laser pylons shifted to fire single beams while the smaller point defense lasers prepared to take up the slack.

"The frigates are intercepting the missiles," Glick said.

"Good," Alexis said. "Edwards, target Bogey Two, all bearing lasers, and fire."

Fifteen of the 24 laser emitters had clear bearing on the intended target. Each laser only consumed a tiny fraction of the power used by the spinal mount; fifteen lasers burned 1,500 megawatts per pulse. Only fifteen ten-thousandths the output of the spinal mount. However, they weren't powered by the spinal mount's capacitor banks, they drew directly from their own power feeds. They fired constantly in 100 millisecond bursts while the spinal mount slowly charged.

The enemy frigate was slightly over a light second away. *Pegasus* fired 10 bursts from each laser before the first hit its target. The 100-megawatt pulses tracked along the anticipated course of the frigate, peppering the target box with coherent beams of laser energy. One in five had its wavelength modulated slightly to make the beam more visible to the ship's sensors.

Fighting a battle hundreds of thousands of miles from your enemy, when both ships are moving, sometimes at extreme angles and speeds to each other, is a duel of prediction and guessing. In some ways, it was like old Earth WWII anti-aircraft gunners trying to predict the flight paths of incoming fighter planes. Computers analyzed the enemy ship's flight path, then added its drive characteristics and any details available about its commander to come up with a probable targeting solution.

The intermittently visible shots acted like tracers for targeting, helping the gunnery computers and tactical team fine tune their follow-up shots. The first several dozen pulses hit nothing; the next were on target. The frigate was concentrating its fire on the flight of missiles targeted at their cruiser, the job of an escort. To be effective, they were not evading. The ship was a nice, steady target.

The frigate's shields lit up as thousands of megawatts of energy poured into them. The ship's commander realized his peril too late, as the entire might of the battlecruiser *Pegasus'* bearing laser batteries unloaded fifteen gigawatts of energy into his vessel's shields in one shuddering second of violence. Hole after foot-wide hole was punched into the ship, penetrating armor, burning through bulkheads, and destroying vital interior spaces.

"Multiple hits," Flipper confirmed.

"They're hurt," Glick said as he analyzed the ship's energy profile in the data fed by Flipper.

"Finish it," Paka ordered. Another second of laser fire shredded the smaller ship. A series of bright flashes were visible across the many thousands of miles separating them.

"Their reactors are hit," Flipper said. "They're adrift."

Without the benefit of both its frigates providing defensive laser fire, the cruiser was no longer in a favorable position. One of the *Pegasus'* missiles made it through and detonated against its shields with a spectacular flash.

"Cruiser took one," Flipper said.

"Their forward shields are down," Glick said excitedly.

"Redirect lasers to the cruiser," Alexis said.

The lasers stabbed out at the cruiser, and missed as it performed its own skew turn. Follow-up shots hit, but on the still-powered flanking and aft shields. Alexis grunted and nodded; Geshakooka was an accomplished combat ship's master.

"Hits on port forward quarter shields," Edwards announced. "Multiple hits, 100-megawatt range. Shields down 10%." Then a second later. "Additional hits, ventral forward quarter shields. These are 20-megawatt, but rapid fire. Shields are down five percent, 10, now 15!"

"Roll the ship," Paka ordered.

"Drone Control," Alexis said, "time on target?"

"Approximately 20 seconds," the voice replied. "Target?"

"Take out the other escort." She knew the cruiser was the bigger threat, but the drone fighters didn't carry missiles. Each was a 12-foot-long flattened cylinder with a miniature fusion reactor, a tiny fusion torch drive, electronic brain, sensors, and a small shield generator. They were armed with a single, two-megawatt high-pulse-rate laser, and could carry a single ship-killer missile in place of the laser. Individually, they weren't a threat to a capital ship, but in squadron-sized formations, they were a serious problem.

"Acknowledged," Drone Control replied.

A light second away, the two squadrons of drones turned like a flock of birds toward the second frigate in a complex and well-orchestrated attack pattern. The frigate maneuvered and fired at the drones with its main lasers as well as its smaller defensive lasers. The ship's larger lasers couldn't come close to the darting fighters, and the point-defense lasers were stopped by the drone's shields. Several of the frigate's little one-megawatt point lasers scored enough hits, though, that two drones lost their shields, and one was destroyed. Then the drones struck.

Acting as one, the two squadrons suddenly came together in a pin-wheeling formation and fired. The frigate's commander gasped in surprise at the coordinated attack. Drones didn't work together with that level of intelligence! The impact area on the frigate's shields was only 20 feet across. Almost 40 megawatts of laser energy slashed into the shield 20 times per second. The shield failed in a second and a half, and the drones altered their aim points and spread their fire along the entire length of the unshielded hull. The 19 drone fighters shredded the frigate.

"Second frigate is down," Flipper informed. "Cruiser is disengaging."

"Pursuit?" Paka asked her commander. Alexis considered having the drones finish the job. But did Captain Geshakooka and his crew deserve to die because they took a shit contract from a shit syndicate?

"High probability of new aggressors in our threat box," Glick warned. "Based on the direction of retreat and posture of Bogey One." Alexis cursed under her breath. Of course, with as big an operation as Transki had mounted here, they wouldn't have left emergence interdiction to a single cruiser squadron. Captain Geshakooka had just been buying time.

"Very well, Paka, disengage."

"Recover drones," the XO ordered. "Chug, come about to course 45-mark-160, three gravities." *Pegasus* spun, though without the urgency of earlier maneuvers, and began to boost away from the area of engagement. Her drone fighters changed course to match for intercept. Five minutes later, their sensors picked up exactly what Glick had predicted.

"Drones relay multiple new targets," Flipper reported. "I have at least two cruisers, one battlecruiser, nine escorts…" he paused to examine the data, "and there is a high probability of a battleship."

"Continue present course," Alexis ordered, "increase power to five gravities, and deploy decoy drones." Paka gave the orders. "Drone Control, bring your fighters back cold." The alarm sounded and the warship groaned under the huge acceleration.

"Acknowledged." The order would cause the drones to split up and go dark for several minutes, which kept the enemy from getting a clear heading to the *Pegasus*. Once *Pegasus* had time to pull away, the drones would rendezvous with her. The fusion torch poured on the power as the ship launched decoys, cylindrical canisters with radioactive debris whose signature, from a distance, resembled a fusion torch under thrust. "Once we have some space between us and our pursuers," Alexis grunted under five times her normal weight, "launch a message drone to the stargate and schedule a dedicated transition."

Paka's long neck craned around from where she'd been clinging to the sensor operator's position. Her XO knew only too well how expensive such a stargate activation would be. She also knew it was all but impossible for them to come in and make it through the stargate at any of the scheduled windows. Transki would be sure to be waiting for them.

"Decrease thrust to one gravity in five minutes," Alexis said, struggling to breath. "Expected time of arrival at the stargate?"

"Approximately eleven hours if we flip at midpoint," Chug said.

"And if we don't?" Alexis asked. Now she had the attention of everyone on the bridge.

"Seven hours," he replied. "We'd arrive at the stargate going approximately 150 miles per second." The CIC was quiet except for the background chatter of crew relaying information as five minutes passed. Everyone struggled under the ship's power, quietly bearing it. Then the fusion torch throttled back to a smooth one G. Alexis breathed a sigh, her chest aching from five long minutes of breathing in high gravity.

"I'll have additional orders in three hours," she said as she released her restraints and headed for her wardroom adjacent to the CIC. "XO, would you join me?"

Paka followed her captain. "What do you need, Captain?" she asked once inside the small office.

"This situation sucks," Alexis said, dropping into her chair. Paka stood next to one of two seats in the wardroom.

"So how is this different from any other day?" The line was delivered completely deadpan. Alexis looked at her XO for a long moment, then shook her head and laughed. Paka gave a few chipping laughs herself.

"All joking aside," the captain said, "this is the second system in a row where we blundered into a," she lifted her fingers like quotation marks, "'combat situation.' That's ridiculous."

Paka nodded in agreement. The statement was accurate. "It's a dangerous universe."

"From now on, I want our drone fighters locked on the hull for combat deployment at all times. Go crack the whip on Long and find a damned way to get that reactor back on line."

"Yes, ma'am," Paka said. She gave a little bow before leaving. Alexis stared at the door long after the Veetanho was gone. Finally, she put her hands on her desk and closed her eyes.

<*You are right to be concerned*>

"Do you know anything that can help?" Alexis asked.

<*I sense something. But nothing certain, yet*> Silence for a few moments. <*Remember the Morphut system?*>

"Yes," Alexis said. Their last contract before the current one had been to travel to the Morphut system and provide space defenses for the Wathayat trader syndicate. When they'd arrived, they found nothing but death and destruction. No signs of a raid, only carnage. There were no survivors, and inconceivable amounts of damage to the planet.

<*Somehow that event is part of a chain of events we are being drawn into*>

"Okay, but how does that affect us here, now?"

<*I am uncertain how this all draws together…*> The voice seemed to drift in and out.

"Damn it, I need certainty." She sat for at least a minute. "Are the Hussars in danger?"

<*Yes*>

"Here, in Sulaadar?"

<*Yes, that much is certain*>

Alexis nodded. She stood, brushed pure white hair out of her eyes, straightened her uniform and headed back to the CIC. Heads, tentacles, and eyestalks turned as she entered, the command crew waiting expectantly for her orders. She moved across the armored command center and took her seat. Paka finished issuing an order to the engineering staff and looked up at her.

"Chug," she said, "increase acceleration to two gravities and get us a solution for a high velocity transition through the stargate." Several of the command staff exchanged worried looks. "We're getting out of here, now."

* * * * *

Chapter Thirteen

ECS Coronado

Approaching Jupiter Orbit

Sol

The *Coronado's* departure from Martian orbit had been set to make the transit from Mars to Jupiter at an optimal time. As the orbital velocities of all the planets were different, matching orbit could take vastly different amounts of thrust depending on when you made the trip. In this case, Jupiter had been a quarter of the way around the sun from Earth when the ship pushed away. After the days in transit to Mars, and the time to unload and top off fuel, Jupiter had moved closer, and *Coronado* had less distance to travel.

Rick was much more interested in the view as they decelerated toward the Jovian system than he had been in the approach to Mars. The massive reddish gas giant was also visible to the naked eye much, much sooner than the proportionally tiny disk Mars had been, as Jupiter was 21 times the size of Mars. The timeless swirling mass of sublime gas clouds, all mixing and racing around the equator at different speeds, was a visual lure that drew the crew to the big Tri-V display in the mess hall at all hours of the ship's day.

Coronado finished braking into the complex, interconnected orbits of the planet Jupiter. With 63 moons and four not-quite moons, it was the busiest planet in the system after Earth. With the tech boost provided by joining the Union, and the funneling of millions of credits from merc taxes, the various governments and corporations had raced out from Earth to find riches and opportunities in the solar system, and Jupiter's moons teemed with all manner of enterprises.

Even with fusion torch-powered ships, travel back and forth between Earth and Jupiter took time, fuel, and most importantly, F11. Ganymede, as the largest and most stable of the Jovian moons, became the center of operations for the sub-system. Despite the size of the moon, it only possessed a gravity one seventh of Earth's, equating to an escape velocity of just 1.7 miles per second. Captain Holland joked you could throw a baseball into orbit.

A dozen starships were tied up next to the main orbital transfer station at Ganymede. *Coronado* only spent an hour in orbit waiting for its flight assignment before descending to the moon's surface. The descent was managed vertically, using the ship's less powerful but cleaner ion engine until they approached the settlements, then via its hydrogen thrusters. It was so gradual, and the gravity so light, Rick didn't feel the touchdown. The ship sat on her tail, just as she had before boarding in Houston.

Once cargo was transferred and his work done, Rick went to Kubrick City. Captain Holland gave him his first weeks' pay, minus the advance he got on Mars. Unlike Mars, there was no shortage of things to do on Ganymede. The city sported a permanent population of more than a quarter million. Several times that amount went through each week, to other Jovian satellites as well as to the rest of the solar system.

In Kubrick City, he spent time walking through various domes, saw a low-gravity ballet (which he found beautiful), and took a hopper out for an excursion on the moon's surface. After returning, he found himself in the city's entertainment dome and spent the evening club-hopping. Quite a few people his age had found their way to Ganymede for opportunities and freedom. Unlike Earth, the laws in space more closely resembled those of the Union. That is to say, there were very few laws to speak of.

Rick returned to *Coronado* well before the planned time for liftoff. He'd taken a room for a few credits late in the morning and gotten a few hours' sleep before returning. The captain greeted his returning crew, as was his policy.

"Glad you had some fun," he said as Rick bounced down the hallway in the low gravity.

"I did," he admitted. "Kubrick is a neat place."

"The rest of the stops are boring. Now I'd like to leave, so get to your station so we can get out of here."

Coronado lifted off the surface of Ganymede and back into orbit using her ion drive, something impossible on most worlds. Kubrick's traffic control carefully monitored their progress. From orbit, they headed deeper into Jupiter's gravity well, down toward Europa. Once there, they transferred still more cargo. The moon was home to a research station and tourist stop, and rich people would come from Earth and travel miles down through the ice to spend days in submerged habitats. Microbial life swarmed in the water, one of the rare non-Earth life forms found in their star system.

The next stop, Io, was to service another station. This one was a naval installation operated by Earth's government. It provided a base for patrol ships as well as sensor visibility outside of Earth's orbit. A small facility was maintained by Earth's mercs for training, as it helped defer costs.

The last stop in the Jupiter system was at a space station orbiting the gas giant. Like one of the sixty-three moons, the station had its own orbit, deep down where it skimmed the outer edge of the planet's atmosphere. *Coronado's* nominal shields were massively taxed as the ship rode its fusion torch down, braking to drop into an ever-lower orbit, until it finally matched that of the station. The station's shields then protected both craft.

"She's actually an old freighter," the facility administrator, Francisco, explained to Rick during a tour. Once offloading was completed, they were allowed to poke around. The man looked like he enjoyed the chance to talk to a new face. "A consortium led by the Winged Hussars purchased it as scrap, moved it here, and refit it to act as a proof of concept. They also do other special research."

"What concept?" Rick asked.

"Why, F11 mining, of course."

"I thought you only found F11 near black holes and systems where a supernova had occurred."

"Yes," Francisco said with a smile, "but F11 isn't there because of the supernova. It accumulates naturally in the cores of gas giants, a molecule at a time. Only, you can't get it out very easily while there's thousands of miles of atmosphere in the way." He gestured out the synthetic clear-ruby window to the incredibly close clouds of Jupiter. Their low orbit made the planet fill half the sky, stretching out in all directions. The ex-starship, not station, had a rotating gravity deck around its cylindrical center, which allowed the main station to remain weightless. The observation area was in the weightless zone. "We dip a tube down and suck up gas from the lower layers. We extend it a few miles a year. Slow work building material that tough."

"How low?"

"We're not even one percent of the way to the surface. Just over two thousand miles long, so far." Stretching out from the end of the station was a thick line, extending down toward the planet. It thinned until it was swallowed up by the multicolored depths of Jupiter.

"How long before it's low enough to reach the F11?"

"Oh," the administrator laughed, "we already have." Rick blinked. Francisco nodded.

"Wow, how much?"

"We get exactly one ten-thousandth of an ounce per 10 million gallons of atmosphere we pull up."

"I'm sorry, did you say one ten-thousandth of an ounce?"

"Yes, amazing, isn't it?" Francisco beamed like a new father.

"I'm sorry," Rick said, "I don't understand. That's such a tiny amount."

"Tiny? Well, yeah."

"Then why is it amazing? It can't possibly be profitable."

"No, of course not. We burn almost a gallon of F11 through the fusion plant every week just in station-keeping and sucking up and filtering raw atmosphere. Even more for running the shields!"

"Then why?" Rick asked, the confusion clear on his face. The administrator laughed yet again. He was obviously a jovial man.

"Because we're less than one percent of the way down!" Rick's expression must have looked bewildered because the administrator continued. "In a decade or two, we'll be far enough down to get into the serious gravity flux zones." Rick just stared. "Don't you see?" Francisco asked. Rick shook his head. "Finding this much here means there must be *lots* of F11 in flux zones; that's why they find it in deposits in the cores of gas giants where the atmosphere is blown away. If we can get to the lowest levels, the density is probably more than one part per million!" Rick still didn't really get it, so he changed the subject.

"You mentioned some other special research?"

"Uhm…" Francisco said. He looked at Rick's uniform, merc standard with his name on the breast, but no logo on the arm. "I figure it's okay to tell a merc." Rick didn't mention he wasn't currently assigned to any unit.

"They have a lab here researching AI."

"Artificial intelligence?"

"Yeah," Francisco said.

"Don't we have that all over the place?" Rick asked.

"No, what we have are just fancy decision trees. Computers can't really think. They don't make up songs, or do anything out of the box. Here, they're working on the real deal."

"You mean like a sci-fi, alive computer?" Rick asked.

"Yeah, sort of. Independent thought. They can think for themselves."

Rick scratched his head and mulled it over. Sounded like something his friend Jim Cartwright would like. "Okay, so why do it out here in the darkest corner of the solar system?" As soon as he said it, he was afraid the man would be offended. "I mean, isn't Earth a better place? Or even Mars?"

The other man laughed. "Well, it's sort of illegal."

"On Earth?"

"No, in the Union." Rick looked skeptical. "I know, there isn't much illegal in the Union." The man ticked off some points on his fingers. "Space ships can't shoot at planets from more than 10 miles up; no nuking civilians, even if military are hiding among them; no bio weapons; and no genetically-manipulated life forms." Rick nodded, he was familiar with all that, both from merc training and his Union civics class in school. "However," Francisco continued, "apparently AI are illegal according to a clause which states you can't turn weapons over to a computer. AI are considered computers, and since most Union laws are about blowing each other up..."

"The researchers are afraid of crossing a line," Rick finished. Francisco grunted and pointed at him for successfully figuring it out.

"They have some huge computer processing power, Union built, all set up and running. They bought a couple of junked warships from the Maki and the Bakulu, just to get the tactical computers. Apparently, those races have the best prediction combat computers. Borderline AI, I guess. Anyway, they're running with it. I've heard they're making progress too!"

Rick wondered if the AI researchers knew that Francisco was this chatty with random visitors. If they did, it would likely make them reconsider just how much they told him. Then a thought struck him.

"That sounds expensive. Who's paying for it?"

"It's a joint venture," Francisco said, "between the universities on Earth and the Winged Hussars."

"The F11 mining *and* the AI research?" Rick said incredulously. Francisco nodded.

"Yep, they apparently spend millions on all kinds of research. I hear the other horsemen do as well. You know it was the Cavaliers and the Horde that funded the development of the mecha, right?" Rick hadn't known that. He'd always thought it was the Japanese doing what they do. The conversation drifted into other areas, and eventually Rick had to head back to his ship.

Coronado clawed its way back to a higher orbit. All the way, Rick thought about the interesting, and pricey, operation they'd left behind. That the Winged Hussars were funding it was curious to him. What kind of forward-thinking outfit paid for such an experiment? He knew F11 was expensive. Like 10,000 or 20,000 credits per gallon expensive. That ten-thousandth of an ounce they'd harvested at a cost of 20,000 credits (plus basic facility operation costs), was itself worth only about an eighth of a credit! Yet the Winged Hussars were dumping a fortune into an operation that was light-years from yielding a profit. Then there was the AI project. Forward-thinking and dangerous. Fascinating.

After refueling at Ganymede station, *Coronado* left Jupiter behind and fell back toward Earth's orbit. During the trip, Rick did research on the Winged Hussars via the ship's Aethernet node. It was a fascinating history, both from their position as one of the storied Four Horsemen and the fact so little was known about them. They were, by far, the richest of all the Horsemen; they were also the only one with a large number of aliens in their employ, which was rare among *any* Human merc unit. For a Human merc company, they also had little presence on Earth and no bases.

Four days later they decelerated to Earth's 5th Lagrange point, or L5. The *Coronado* came to a stop within a mile of the stargate, a huge ring of satellites interconnected by cables, with miles of solar arrays drinking in the sun's power and storing it in massive capacitor banks. Nearby, four other starships waited with *Coronado* for the appointed hour.

As the clock ticked down, Rick borrowed the ship's high-powered navigation targeting scope (not in current use) to look at the planet of his birth. Earth was huge and blue with swirling storm patterns. The moon was a tiny white spot almost behind it. He felt a strange sensation of completion watching the planet as transition stations were called.

"All personnel, prepare for stargate transition." The ship's fusion power plant spun up to full output, pumping terawatts of energy into the hyperspace nodes placed all along the hull. *Coronado's* thrusters pushed the ship toward the stargate as the giant hyperspace shunt used all the accumulated power it had stored over the last two days to twist space and make a discontinuity. Minutes later, *Coronado* and the other four ships which had been waiting moved as one into that discontinuity.

Rick felt like he'd been utterly obliterated for a split second, then he was back. The image of Earth and all reality was gone, replaced with a featureless whiteness in all directions. There was no sign of the other four ships. They were in hyperspace.

The ship's power plant throttled back to the output levels needed to keep them in hyperspace, while the navigation system automatically began to draw them toward their destination. In 170 hours, they would arrive at their destination, more than 1,000 light-years from Earth.

* * * * *

Chapter Fourteen

Ardent Grove

Sulaadar System

Stargate Highguard

The embargo of the Sulaadar system by the Transki Syndicate had proven a profitable endeavor for the Guardian Forest mercenary company. An entirely Maki-owned and operated space-based merc outfit, they were the preeminent assault company in the guild with more than 100 starships at their disposal. They commanded everything from battleships and carriers to squadrons of patrol boats. As a merc, it could all be yours, for a price.

"Courier outbound from Sulaadar 3," the SitCon announced. Captain Yackyl looked up from his command station, his delicate lemur-like face examining the main status board. The commander of the *Ardent Grove*, a *Thrush*-class battleship, and its squadron, he was responsible for the system's highguard on the stargate, which meant he held the system and kept anything from leaving without Transki's approval.

"Do they have the day-code?" Yackyl asked the comms operator. The captain shifted for a better look, his bifurcated tail instinctively grasping one of his command station's many holds.

"Yes, captain," the tech confirmed.

"Very well, inform the picket to allow them through."

Yackyl had hoped to have overall command of the combat operations part of the contract in Sulaadar. Unfortunately, that had gone to his brother, Syshkyl. At least Syshkyl didn't have anything bigger than a battleship. Now that the system was in hand, Yackyl commanded more ships! Syshkyl only had a battleship and its escort of two battlecruisers and a flight of five escort frigates. Yackyl had the same arrangement in his battleship's task force, but he also commanded five squadrons of 10 interceptors. They weren't hyperspace-capable vessels, but they were incredibly fast and heavily-armed, as their fusion plants only had to power weapons and shields.

They'd held the system for over a week now, and only an occasional merchant craft had come in to be taken by the blockade. One merc frigate yesterday had tried to shoot its way out of the blockade at emergence. The Bakulu company assigned to watch the emergence point had dealt with that handily. Yackyl would rather Guardian Forest handle all the work in the black, however Sulaadar was a massive operation by the Transki.

The syndicate had been trying to get the Sulaad to accept their help in developing several new technologies involving drone cargo haulers. The Sulaad weren't interested; their society emphasized individual jobs for everyone, and robots took away valuable work. The Transki decided to up the ante, but Sulaadar was a massive system with thousands of ships transitioning through it every year. It was all but certain someone got away before the stargate was properly interdicted, and a major merc unit or 20 would show up. That was the other reason they let the Bakulu watch the emergence point. Let them die, if necessary. Should more throw weight arrive than Guardian Forest could handle, their control of the stargate would allow them to easily escape. To entropy with Transki.

"The courier has been cleared through," the comms operator confirmed.

"Any more traffic scheduled?" Yackyl asked.

"No sir," SitCon replied.

"Very well." Yackyl released his hold on the command station and shoved himself toward one of the CIC's exits. "I'll be in my wardroom. Klakys, you have command."

"Yes sir," his XO said. He floated over to grasp the commander's station like his captain had. Several of the other bridge crew looked after the departed captain, then at the XO.

"Why is he so angry?" the most senior staff member asked.

"He's upset he didn't get overall command."

"Still?" someone else asked. The XO shrugged. The crew worked at their duties for a while, each doing their best to make the contract successful and profitable.

A short time later a message drone arrived at high speed. They were common and since the message wasn't for the picket fleet, it wasn't interfered with. The sensor tech did notice its high speed, and it beamed a secure message to the stargate before shooting by into deep space. Its purpose complete, its fuel spent, it would be just another piece of space junk for eternity.

Hours passed. Watch on picket duty was tedious. The sensor tech thought he picked up a fusion torch drive plume. He directed more intense sensor readings to that quadrant of space, but only got tiny intermittent bursts. More like electromagnetic bursts from attitude motors, though far more powerful than he'd ever seen before. He watched the phenomenon and began to wonder if it could have a natural cause. It seemed to be getting closer.

The radio operator received a dispatch from fleet command. It was the scheduled update, which came through four times per solar cycle. But as the tech was scanning through the messages, he found one that was out of place. A ship had arrived in system some hours ago, a warship which had blown through the defending Bakulu squadron like they weren't there. One frigate had been destroyed, another put out of action. The dispatch said it was a single cruiser of unknown design. Why hadn't this message been sent flash traffic to the rest of the fleet? He activated the intercom.

"Captain?"

"What is it?"

"There is something in the hourly dispatch you should see." The tech sent the data to his captain's personal slate.

"More of my brother's grandstanding?" Yackyl mumbled as he picked up his slate. He'd been reviewing communications from the company command on a possible follow-up mission, and he planned to find out what the radio operator thought was so important, reprimand him when it turned out to be nothing, and get back to important business. After reading for a few seconds, he fairly shot out of his wardroom and back into the CIC. The crew spun around in surprise. "Inform the fleet there was an incursion at the transition point almost five hours ago!"

SitCon shook his head in consternation. What idiot wouldn't consider that important? "What happened?" he asked the captain.

"A single cruiser shot its way through the Bakulu squadron on defensive overwatch," the captain said. "It destroyed a frigate and disabled a second." The SitCon laughed.

"Were they incompetent? I thought the Bakulu were a good naval race."

"Data indicates it was the Human ship *Pegasus,* of the mercenary company Winged Hussars."

The SitCon stopped laughing and looked back at his board. Now it made more sense; the Winged Hussars were an elite unit. Even though they possessed no ships bigger than a battlecruiser, he'd heard stories that strained all credibility. Most of those stories were of this *Pegasus,* and they all ended in disaster for whoever faced her. What had seemed humorous a moment ago had quickly taken on a deadly edge.

The sensor tech turned back and looked at his board. His already wide eyes nearly bugged out of his head in shock.

"Ship in the threat box!" he barked.

"How?" the captain demanded. "Nothing was noted from the planet or any of the outlying escorts!"

"Unknown," the tech said and fed his data to the SitCon.

"Confirmed," SitCon said. "It's a single ship. Entropy, it is moving *fast!* Heading straight toward the picket. Range one seventh of a light second!"

"How did they get so close?" the captain wondered in amazement.

"Battle stations!" Klakys, the XO yelled. "Crew to battle stations! Scramble drones, inform the fleet!"

The picket had guarded the stargate without incident for more than a week. Until now, every time they'd had an incident, the crew had had an hour or more to prepare. During that time, the commander of *Ardent Grove,* bored and unhappy with his assignment, never once ran any drills. Now, with the battle claxons sounding on the flag ship and the rest of the squadron, the crews mostly took their time preparing for what they thought would be another boring encounter with a defiant merchant trying to escape the embargo.

"Identity confirmed," SitCon said, turning to the captain, "it's the *Pegasus*."

* * *

"What do we have, Glick?" Alexis asked. The CIC's massive Tri-V displays all showed forward views as *Pegasus* fell toward the stargate at a phenomenal speed. The SitCon replied instantly.

"Defense of the stargate is presented in a typical denial formation," he bubbled. "There is a single *Thrush*-class battleship, two *Petal*-class battlecruisers, five *Bloom*-class frigates, and at least fifty interceptors. I can't tell what models those are."

Sections of the Tri-V showed the various classes of Maki-designed ships and capabilities. The battleship was, of course, a monster compared to *Pegasus.* The beast was five times their size, with 10 times the firepower. They were more than a match for any two of the battlecruisers, or even all the frigates. But as a combined squadron, especially with the interceptors, *Pegasus* would be no more than a passing annoyance. Alexis had known a formidable force would be on highguard, and that's why she had elected to thread the needle.

"What's your confidence on the stargate, Chug?"

"We're on course," the helmsman confirmed. We'll pass through the center with an error of plus/minus 1,000 feet."

"What size gate is this?" Paka asked.

"One mile across," the Bakulu helmsman replied. They'd performed final course corrections while more than a million miles away, to avoid detection. The final hour they came in cold. "I can correct in the last 10 seconds if I have attitude control."

"No," Alexis said, "I want weapons and defense to have it." She scrunched up her brow in consternation. A thousand feet either way was way too close for comfort with only five thousand feet total to deal with. This was where you trusted your crew.

"Distance to stargate is 26,000 miles," Chug said. "Velocity stable at 217 miles per second. Eta to stargate T-minus two minutes."

"Prepare for combat," Alexis ordered, "battle stations." The ship-wide claxon sounded. "Status on the picket ships, Edwards?"

"They are not maneuvering," the small man replied, "and I show no signs of shield emissions."

"Got them flat-footed," Paka snarled, her teeth glinting in the red-tinged light.

"Charge the main gun," Alexis ordered.

"Target?" Edwards asked.

"Whatever is closest to our bearing to the stargate. Avoid hitting the stargate at all costs. You may fire at will."

Edwards' grin became feral, while on the Tri-V, the mile-wide stargate was growing fast.

* * *

"What is taking so long?" Captain Yackyl roared. Of all the stations on the battleship *Ardent Grove,* only shields had responded. Of course, it was the easiest to answer the call, taking the least crew and preparation to operate. As he watched the sluggish response of not only his flagship, but the entire squadron, he suddenly realized just floating here and chewing his anger was probably not the best decision of his career.

The huge Tri-V that wrapped around the battleship's CIC showed all the capital ships in his squadron. The frigates were hundreds of miles away, arrayed in a circle around *Ardent Grove.* The battlecruisers were only a dozen miles away, one to either side. As luck would have it, he was glaring at the one to port when a flash of light made him blink his sensitive eyes. It had been a pencil thin beam of pure crackling energy cutting across the entire screen, and through the battlecruiser. A split second later, the warship exploded into a ball of expanding fire, debris, and gas.

"Shields full!" Yackyl screamed, "Get us maneuvering power now…*now* you entropy-cursed tail hangers, *NOW!*" He was almost in full panic mode as he cried out the last. It was only five seconds after the first battlecruiser died that another flash cut the screen. This one was moving slightly, so it didn't score a direct center of mass hit on the second battlecruiser. Instead the 40-terawatt beam cut the battlecruiser into two almost equal halves. A split second later the crippled ship's shields flashed to life, too late, then almost immediately went out as secondary explosions played along the scalpel-precise cut.

Erratic and uncontrolled, the battleship's engines lit and she began to maneuver. Her shields began to come on, but not in any coordinated manner. The captain kept up a constant litany of chittering curses, certain his ship would be the victim of the powerful energy weapon any second. What cursed right did a cruiser, a *cruiser,* have to possess such a powerful weapon? The biggest guns he had were a pair of bay mounted 20-terawatt particle cannons designed for use against battleships.

"Enemy cruiser entering point blank range!" the SitCon barked. "Point defenses are coming on line."

"Array all defenses against potential missile-" The sensor tech cut him off.

"Incoming missile storm!"

"Engage the missiles," the captain yelled, "where are my main guns?"

"One main gunnery station has reported," the SitCon said. "However, it's on the port side, opposite the incoming enemy."

"Shoot something at that ship! Fire the turrets on automatic if necessary, but fire!"

"The stargate has been activated," the navigator said, confused. "Who ordered it?"

"That message drone," the SitCon moaned.

"*What message drone?!*" the captain bellowed, nearly incoherent with rage. The SitCon grasped his station with a death's grip and shook in fear and anger, then saw something new.

"We can't engage the missiles," he reported.

"Why?" the captain demanded.

"Because we're not the target."

* * *

The frigates were barely under power, but at least they were maneuvering. It didn't help as a storm of 48 ship-killers in two waves of 24 flashed down on them at hundreds of miles per second. Their defensive lasers engaged, but thanks to the incoming speed of the missiles, it was at a much closer range than normal. Nuclear fire flashed in a rippling wave of destruction across the entire squadron. Many of the missiles in the second wave had no target because all the frigates were severely damaged, or simply gone. As they'd been programmed, the second wave of missiles sought alternate targets. Fifteen of the unshielded interceptors were annihilated by nuclear explosions in a display of epic overkill. In just seconds, *Pegasus* had swept all the Maki frigates from the black.

Pegasus flashed into the midst of the shattered remains of the once proud squadron of Guardian Forest merc warships, which was now reduced to a single battleship and 35 terrified and scattering interceptors.

The SitCon on the *Ardent Grove* saw a green light appear on the starboard particle pulse-battery. Without waiting to inform the nearly apoplectic captain, he transferred fire control to the TacCom who'd been plotting the inbound enemy ship helplessly. The battery of five two-terawatt particle guns blazed fire at the streaking *Pegasus.*

Broadsides just didn't happen in space combat. It wasn't like old sailing ships, because you never knew what side would be facing the enemy. Weapons emplacements were uniformly distributed on larger warships to allow them to fight in any direction. Only smaller ships and specialized capital ships had weapons which faced just one direction. Even the ancient designers of the Winged Hussars flagship had given her formidable omnidirectional weapons, as well as her main forward-facing punch. But this battle, brief as it was, wasn't normal.

As the *Pegasus* flashed by, the two capital ships were within a dozen miles of each other, and side by side, as well. *Pegasus* had been waiting for the pass and unleashed all her lasers and missiles as she went by. The *Ardent Grove* had only partially succeeded in getting her shields up. Fifteen of *Pegasus'* 24 laser turrets pulsed 100-megawatt bursts of energy into the battleship in a strobing line as they passed.

Even at a 20-millisecond pulse, each turret only got two shots on target before the ship flashed past.

Twenty-one laser pulses passed through the battleship's inactive shields. Eleven splashed against armor or were deflected off more reflective points. The remaining 10 penetrated *Ardent Grove's* primary hull. Three tore through non-essential spaces. Four punched through the battleship's number two reaction mass tank, causing multiple geysers of fluid to flow into space. The remaining three hit a sensor array, a shield generator, and a hyperspace node. The latter caused a chain reaction which disabled all the nodes on that quadrant of the ship and overloaded the computer which controlled them.

Ardent Grove's fire was much less timed, or coordinated. Her particle cannon only pulsed four times a second, which meant each of the five cannons with a bearing on *Pegasus* only got one chance to hit the target before the cruiser flashed by. Of the five, two hit the ship. One went almost squarely through Deck 10, only missing the ship's all-important spine by feet. The two-foot-wide energy beam destroyed a dozen enlisted quarters and killed one young rating who was in bed recovering from an illness. He and his quarters were destroyed, and it would take days for anyone to realize he was vaporized with the room. The last took a chunk out of Deck Two, wrecking one of the forward missile tubes.

Alexis held on as the ship shuddered from the impacts. The final moments of their flight had passed in what felt like two quick heartbeats. The weapons fired automatically, as Edwards had programmed. One moment the stargate was a spot on the Tri-V, the next it grew like a stone thrown at her face. She unconsciously gritted her teeth and fought to keep from flinching. If the stargate didn't activate as she'd requested via that message drone…

The timing was insane. If they'd requested the stargate to open a minute sooner it would have cycled and shut down before they got there. A minute later and they'd have already flashed through its aperture without going anywhere. As it was, Alexis saw space distort five second before they reached the ring of asteroids which held the massive hyperspace shunts. She knew her ship was firing at the battleship as it went by, hoping for a lucky shot, but all she could do was watch the approaching stargate. Death loomed. Quick, final, and brutal death. Then in the blink of an eye they were annihilated, and recreated in hyperspace.

"We're through," Chug confirmed. He examined a readout. "Cleared the stargate with 322 feet to spare."

"We have damage," Guylan, the DCC said.

"Report," Paka said.

"Two impacts," he said and described the results. "The shields blunted them, a little."

"Two terawatts packs quite a punch," Edwards remarked.

"Tell that to those Maki battlecruisers!" Flipper bubbled. Everyone looked at each other, and the bridge erupted in laughter and a few cheers. It had worked spectacularly.

"What's the kill count?" Alexis asked Flipper who was playing the final seconds repeatedly on a series of small Tri-V monitors, his sharp eyes looking for details.

"Both battlecruisers were hit. The first exploded; the second was cut in half. They might be able to salvage that one; I don't know. The missile waves took out all five frigates and a handful of interceptors. We also strafed the battleship with laser fire on the way by, as planned." An image froze on his Tri-V. The battleship's side, the image blurred by their velocity, despite the high-speed, high-resolution camera. It was hard to get a good picture when passing at several hundred miles per second, especially when the camera only had the ship in frame for 0.002 seconds. Despite this, the picture showed several clear penetrations of the battleship's shields and hull. "I can't believe they were that unprepared."

Alexis shook her head in amazement. It was one of the most one-sided battles she'd ever commanded. The Maki were much better than that, and they'd just gotten their asses handed to them. If she'd known they were that ineffective, she didn't think she would have hit them quite that hard. There could be some blowback.

"Dispatch damage control teams," she ordered Guylan. "Stand down from battle stations." The damage control coordinator hissed his ascent and went to work.

"Chug, try to find a way to slow our velocity after emergence."

"Will do, Captain." Alexis looked up at the clock, 169:58:12 remained.

"At least we don't have to worry about trouble in Karma," Paka quipped.

"Why is that?" Alexis asked.

"Because if there's fighting in a guild hub like that, we're all dead, anyway."

* * *

"Can we maneuver or not?" Captain Yackyl demanded.

The harried DCC was sweeping his hand back and forth, trying to make sense out of some of the mixed signals his system was sending. It looked like they'd taken nine hits from the Earth ship's lasers as it went by. The targeting accuracy had to be insane to get off that many shots as they went by. A fraction of a second was all they had, and dozens of laser beams stuck home. Luckily, most were absorbed by *Ardent Grove's* powerful shields…except that some of those shields hadn't been up at the time.

"I'm still checking, sir," he said to his increasingly erratic and impatient commander. He could tell several of the lasers only hit work spaces or other non-essential internal structures. One of the reaction mass tanks was hulled and leaking. Space was freezing the escaping water, though it wasn't an effective solution so he'd begun transferring as much as he could to the other two tanks. The loss of reaction mass was a potential problem because it was becoming obvious the captain meant to pursue the entropy-cursed Humans into hyperspace!

"They'll run for Karma," the captain mumbled to himself. "They'll think it's safe there. Well, I'll show them. You don't shoot up a Maki squadron and jump into the high branches without expecting Guardian Forest to come after you for payback!" The XO clung to his command console and watched the captain nervously. "Hundreds dead, the very idea!"

The DCC tried to finish his evaluation. A shield generator was down, he noted, destroyed. They could overlap the field, so that wasn't a problem. However, hull damage was registered in Section Nine, Deck 11, but there were no internal indications of secondary damage, and that was troubling. There was almost no armor there. The Human's damnable 100-megawatt lasers should have punched right through. What was he missing?

"Your determination?" the XO requested of him.

"I cannot be sure all vital systems are functioning," the DCC replied. "I need to get a damage control party to Deck 11 to evaluate a hull impact."

"There isn't anything essential on that deck," the XO commented.

The DCC agreed, in principle, but why wasn't the internal system reporting the damage? "No, but—"

"Enough," the captain snapped. "If nothing is damaged, order an emergency gate activation and take us to Karma!" The helmsman programmed the course and engineers spun up all five power plants in preparation. As power flowed, nothing went red on the DCC's status board. He slid his incisors against each other, yet remained silent. "Helm," the captain ordered, "get us underway!"

Five minutes later the *Ardent Grove* came about and ignited her fusion torches, pushing her nearly half million-ton bulk toward the stargate. As they maneuvered, the surviving interceptors raced to attach to the hull. One was damaged by a stray laser shot and couldn't join up. Its five-man crew watched as their mothership prepared to leave the system.

"A trio of frigates from the main fleet are in route to take over our duties here," the *Ardent Grove's* XO told the interceptor's crew. "You will be picked up in a day. We must pursue these treacherous Winged Hussars and enact revenge for our comrades!"

The commander of the interceptor wished them well as the stargate activated, and the battleship pushed through the event horizon.

Less than a second after entering hyperspace, the DCC knew the transition had been a terrible mistake. Power feeds which ran the energy hungry hyperspace nodes should have drawn their expected power load upon entering. Before the ship entered hyperspace via a stargate, the power was just a potential and was not being consumed. As soon as the ship transitioned, the load hit the system to keep them in hyperspace. One entire bank of shunts showed no load, and the rest of the banks drew much more than expected.

"Oh, elder gods," he hissed in despair.

"Hyperspace field is unstable!" the navigator screeched.

"What?" the commander asked.

"Nodes are overloaded," the DCC said, "a bank was damaged during the battle." It was the weapons damage he couldn't account for. One of the nodes must have been hit, and the energy caused a chain reaction. Somehow it took out the monitoring computer too. What were the odds?

"Emergency power to all other nodes," the navigator pleaded, and power was routed.

The hyperspace nodes functioned as a web of hyperspatial anchors, keeping the ship in hyperspace as it was drawn toward its destination. It was like sliding down a zipline, only you had to have each hand and foot hooked to the line or you risked falling off. Without almost a quarter of their hyperspace nodes, the strain on the remaining banks was immense. In seconds, the extreme power demand caused the electrical bus overtemp alarms to sound. The power feeds were overloading.

"Attempting to route power through backup—" the DCC started to say, but the emergency overload breakers on another bank of nodes tripped. There was a sickening moment of acceleration—acceleration with no direction—and he felt like he was being torn apart in every direction. He started to scream, and *Ardent Grove's* hyperspace generators failed. The ship fell out of hyperspace only 20 seconds after entering it, and the huge Maki battleship went…elsewhere.

*****

Chapter Fifteen

ECS Coronado

82 Eridani System

After 170 hours in hyperspace, the clock ran down to zero, and the *Coronado* transitioned to normal space. It wasn't as bad as going into hyperspace; instead, it was more like a moment of disorientation and a feeling of falling, and they were surrounded by stars again.

"Welcome to 82 Eridani," Captain Holland said over the intercom.

The star system of 82 Eridani was found to have planets that might be inhabitable by Humans back in 2011, well over 100 years ago. Shortly after Earth joined the Galactic Union and got access to the Cartography Guild's catalog of stars, it was found to have a stargate but was not inhabited. Humans had long thought it was the closest, best world for Human habitation, so a ship was sent there when one became available. They quickly found out why no aliens ever settled the world.

Rick's first visit to another star system was less than fun. A lot less than fun, truth be told. 82 Eridani was home to one habitable world, though it was only barely habitable. The weather was like being in a perpetual hurricane, and sunlight never completely reached the surface. It had been colonized 80 years ago by Muslims using the remnants of their once vast oil wealth. The world lease from the

Cartography Guild had been a steal. Though almost uninhabitable, it provided an abundance of metals and petrochemicals.

They'd spent four days on New Mecca, as the planet was called, but Rick only went to town once. The city observed strict Sharia law, which meant no tobacco, no alcohol, and no women. You couldn't even look at them. The hotel he stayed in had walls ten feet tall, and only men could work there. He had heard stories from other visitors that the New Meccan's were building an army to ensure they would be left alone. He indulged their desire and returned to the ship the next morning.

Once away from New Mecca, the captain obtained a departure window for hyperspace at the stargate and accelerated to three quarters of a G. The crew worked to finish the last necessary maintenance prior to transition, and Rick helped one of the two ship's mechanical engineers with a hatch that kept sticking closed. Ships often warped and shifted over their lives, and the big airtight hatches the older Earth ships used could be temperamental.

"We usually heat them a little with a laser cutter," the old mechanic cackled as he ran the laser along the hatch seam. "Once it's good and hot, we slam the door…" he handed the torch to Rick and slammed the hatch, hard. "And that should do it," he said. He pulled it back open, and they waited for the metal to cool. The mechanic tested the hatch; it worked perfectly.

"Will it leak?" Rick asked.

"Ship this old, everything leaks. But a tiny air leak on this bulkhead hatch is the least of our worries, if one of the compartments is hulled." Rick nodded. That made sense. Suddenly a shudder reverberated through the hull, and the thrust faltered.

"What was that?" Rick asked. The ship rocked a bit, indicating the fusion torch thrust angle was varying. The old mechanic's eyes darted back and forth, his decades of experience in space speaking to his instincts.

"Something hit us," he said.

"You mean we hit something?" Rick asked.

"No, it hit us. From behind."

Rick considered. Ships got hit by things in space all the time. Space was big, but with thousands of ships moving around star systems, it was simply a matter of odds. Older spacers joked about it, saying sooner or later everyone caught a rock. But ships also had sensors to watch for things in their paths. They watched ahead because the chance of something hitting them from behind was effectively zero. The ship had an engine and accelerated, rocks didn't. He shook his head, trying to clear the thought. It wasn't a hard impact. He thought it through again and came to the same conclusion. Without another thought, Rick ran for the ladder to his quarters.

"Where you goin', kid?" the mechanic yelled after him. Rick was already up the ladder to the next level of the freighter. He climbed as fast as he could. Two decks up, he passed the loadmaster smoking a cigarette in the airlock, a serious breach of shipboard rules. He'd been wondering where the chronic smoker was getting his fix.

"Call the captain!" Rick said as he ran by and leaped to the next ladder.

"Why?" the loadmaster asked, trying to hide the incriminating butt.

"We're being boarded!" Rick yelled as he cleared the next hatch.

He finally reached the crew compartment and dove inside. It took him a minute to drag his duffle bag from the tight little locker he'd been given, more time than he wanted to spend. Finally, it popped free, and Rick tore the zipper open and began yanking out articles. He'd just started to put them on when the alarm sounded.

"Everyone to their emergency stations!" Captain Holland yelled over the PA. "Close all airtight doors." Even as he finished the order, Rick heard the unmistakable sound of a laser weapon firing. A high-pitched snapping whine, the combination of the charging coils, and the chemical cycling system. Damn, he hated to be right. He ran for the ladder again, but went down this time. He almost collided with the loadmaster coming up.

"Where the hell you going now, boy?" he asked. He'd been about to dog the hatch. "We're under attack!"

"I know," Rick said, pushing past him. "They'll empty the hold of the high value freight and then come for us," Rick said.

"Who is it?"

"Pirates." Another laser shot, and a grunting scream from down the hatch. "Move," Rick said and pushed the old man toward the next ladder up. Two levels above them was the bridge. "When you get to the bridge, tell the captain I need him to do something!" The loadmaster listened to him, eyes wide.

"But," the loadmaster complained, looking at Rick's armor and holstered gun.

"No time!" Rick said. He grabbed the side of the ladder in both hands and let go, sliding down to the next level with a squeal of metal against his gloves.

He went past the galley and down to an amidships engineering deck, where he stopped and listened at the hatchway. He heard the sounds of things being broken and a strange growling, purring speech. Confused, he looked down at his ever-present translator, which looked like a small pendant around his neck. An advanced computer, it could translate hundreds of common languages from races all over the Union into English. A tiny red light was flashing on its side. Unrecognized language. *Well that's a pain*, he thought. Rick glanced at his watch; he was almost out of time.

He laid down on the deck next to the hatch and slowly poked his head over the side so one eye could see. This was the hatch into the ship's offices. The purser, who served as the *Coronado's* business manager, worked there. He spotted four beings in the room. Holy shit, he thought, we've been invaded by Bengal tigers! They wore space combat armor and would have been at home on any battlefield. Their helmets were open, and they spoke to each other. Two of them held efficient-looking laser carbines; the other two were attacking the ship's safe, which was welded to a structural beam, with a small laser cutter. A few feet away lay the ship's purser, his body twisted in death, with two smoking holes in his chest. The way he lay, it looked like he was staring right at Rick. It made a shiver go up his spine. One of the aliens with a laser started to turn and check the hatchways. Rick quickly slid back away from the hatch, making sure none of the metal on his combat armor scraped the metal deck.

Rick checked his watch. Damn, no time. Quickly, he drew his Ctech HP-4 and removed the magazine. He reached around to back and pulled another out of his magazine pouch. This one had a flange on the plate that he could feel, even in combat gloves. The pouch held six spares, though only two had the flange. He slid the new magazine into the pistol, put the other special mag into a chest pouch on his left side, and put the one he'd removed from the gun back in the pouch. It was time.

Rick slid back to the hatch, pulled himself over and lowered his right side through. Fighting wasn't like in the movies. You didn't yell to get the bad guys' attention, or give them a sporting chance. His hand engaged the gun's safety points and the laser sight came alive as he aimed. A pulsing spot appeared on the back of the neck of the first cat. He let his breath out and pulled the trigger.

The Ctech HP-4, or high power, was a favorite among Human mercs. It was a relatively-light spun-carbon ceramic which fired a caseless 13mm high velocity bullet. Rick had put thousands of rounds through the weapon since he bought it the day after signing with Mickey Finn. It was a good gun, reliable. Despite being in business for only 50 years, Ctech had become the preeminent firearms manufacturer for mercs on Earth, and exported thousands of guns off-world.

Rick had set the gun for three round bursts. Like all the Ctech caseless series, it loaded propellant a split second before it fired. *Bang, bang, bang!* The gun barked, and he managed the recoil. The bullets left the barrel at just over 2,500 feet per second. About five inches from the barrel, their three petals discarded and the tiny tungsten-chromium penetrator dart, or sabot, flew free. The penetrators were unspectacular on impact, the specially formed tip punched through the weak neck joint of the combat armor and into the alien's neck, where the dart flared into a diamond shape. Still traveling almost 1,000 fps, the projectile did massive trauma to a nearly two-inch-wide wound channel before smashing against the inside of the front neck armor and stopping. The penetrators were designed that way, and as such, ideal for shipboard use.

His second shot went high and ricocheted off the base of the helmet, the third punched through a quarter inch below the first and did even more damage. Both penetrating rounds were killing shots, but he'd had no way of knowing that before firing. "Never take just one shot at a target," his handgun instructor had told him, "when three will make sure."

Without knowing the results of his first burst, he turned to the second laser-wielding cat and fired again. The alien was already turning and bringing its gun up, uncertain where the threat was, but the booming of the big 13mm Ctech was deafening in the hatchway. Rick's second burst of three rounds was not nearly as well placed. One sparked off the cat's helmet, the next was simply absorbed by its shoulder armor, and the last missed the intended target entirely and hit one of the pirates with a laser cutter in the small of the back, penetrating its armor. It yowled like a wounded housecat.

The logical thing to do would have been to pull back under cover. Rick had other plans. Instead, he fell face first through the hatch and prayed his timing was right. There was the snapping whine of a laser being fired, and he glimpsed a beam flash between his legs.

Rick fired another three-round burst as he fell, upside down, gathering speed through the eight-foot-tall deck on his way to the next hatch. He used both hands, not bothering to reach up to cushion his impact. All three shots flashed sparks as the surviving laser wielder spun, bouncing the little darts harmlessly off the heavier front and side armor of his suit.

There was another snapping whine, and he felt agony sear his left thigh a split second before he plummeted through the lower hatchway. He looked up (down) and saw the hatch to the next deck was closed; he was hurtling toward it at breakneck speed.

"Well fuck," he snarled through teeth clenched against the pain. The entire leg was quivering from the shock of the wound. For some reason, he didn't think getting shot with a laser would hurt this badly. He looked up and cursed again as he realized the hatch wasn't coming at him as fast as he thought. In fact, his fall quickly slowed to a stop, and reversed.

"Yes," he hissed, "way to go Captain Holland!" In those frantic seconds with the loadmaster, Rick had asked him to tell the captain to kill all thrust in exactly two minutes, and then hit the braking rockets for all he was worth. He'd prayed the captain would follow the instructions of the young merc he'd hired as a cargo monkey, and that he would time it right.

As he began to fall back upwards, Rick called on his hours of training and flipped himself so he was facing upright and took the HP-4 in both hands. The injured leg didn't want to tuck properly, so he compensated as he arrested the spin. He'd fired three bursts of three, which meant he only had eleven rounds left. He needed to make them count. A second later he soared back through the hatch he'd just fallen through.

The aliens weren't strangers to micro-gravity, but the sudden reverse had caught them off guard. With one dead and another wounded, they were both pissed and surprised. The wounded cat had landed on the roof and was looking right at him when Rick reappeared. It was holding a paw against the small of its back, and when it saw him, it screeched and pointed. Rick wasn't falling as fast this time, so he took his time and did it right. He put a three-round burst into the alien's face. The high velocity sabots pulped its head. Eight rounds left. Rick shifted aim as the gun's recoil bounced his back against the ladder he was falling along.

The laser wielder was rolling on the roof, trying to bring its out of position carbine in line with Rick. The barrel flashed and a beam went somewhere. He was halfway through the room when he fired at the laser-wielding cat. Although Rick's pistol pointed at the target, he waited until his laser aiming dot tracked up its chest before stroking the trigger. The first two rounds bounced off the chest armor, and the final one went right in the alien's nose and out the back of its head. Five rounds left.

He looked for the last pirate as he sailed toward the hatch. He found the alien; it shot him in the chest with a laser pistol it had drawn. The snapping whine of the much-smaller weapon seemed almost muffled—the only thing that told him he'd been shot was the searing pain of the melted armor on his right pec.

Only three feet from the alien, he could see its eyes were wide with anger and fear as it followed him and tried to take another shot, its weapon held in both hands. With only two feet left before the hatch, Rick pulled the trigger and hosed the last alien with all five-remaining rounds. It screeched as it fired, as well. The last thing Rick remembered was a splash of blood and a cool slashing against the side of his face.

* * * * *

Chapter Sixteen

EMS Pegasus

Approaching Karma System

Hyperspace

They'd used the week in hyperspace to make as many repairs as possible. They'd also buried Specialist Ja-klie, a young Cochkala who'd signed on just before the cruise. The casket was empty except for a commendation from the Hussars; the particle beam from the enemy battleship hadn't left any actual remains.

Alexis said some words, but her mood was too dark to put the same level of feeling into them as she'd done the last time. She was getting damned tired of burying her crew for nothing. Dying on a contract was different. Even the non-merc races understood the risks. The pay overrode their species' natural fear of putting themselves in harm's way. They were finally about to arrive at Karma.

"Prepare for transition in one minute," the computer announced.

"Set Condition One," Alexis ordered. Paka and Glick looked at her, but the order was carried out. Everyone was thinking the same thing. Would there be a fight here, too? "Drone Control, stand by for combat launch."

"Standing by."

"Transition in five, four, three, two, one..." A moment of falling, and the stars were back.

"We're in the Karma system," Chug confirmed. Flipper looked at his sensors, searching for targets.

"I have the expected squadron of system patrol craft," he bubbled.

"I have radio contact," Hoot said, and a translated voice came over the PA system.

"*EMS Pegasus,* this is Karma traffic control, we have your transponder. Welcome back."

It took several hours for *Pegasus* to lose the considerable velocity she'd had when entering hyperspace. Even though there weren't any signs of trouble, the crew remained on edge, even after the captain secured from Condition One. As the multiple spinning wheels of the station loomed closer, though, everyone finally relaxed. At last, they could stand down.

A dozen other mercenary cruisers floated nearby, or were docked with the station. Among them, Alexis noted, was the *Bucephalus*, flagship of Cartwright's Cavaliers, which helped alleviate some of her concern. While fighting between Human units was rare, it had happened. The Four Horsemen, however, had never gone to war against each other; they had a special bond.

Pegasus stood off about a mile from the spinning station and waited for a parking assignment. As she did, other ships came and went, and shuttles flitted about on unknown missions. Many of the shuttles slowed as they passed to get a better look. Alexis imagined her ship was quite a sight. She had a huge section of torn hull on one of the reactor pods, and two ugly holes burned through her hull by the Maki battleship's particle cannons. It was rare enough to see the flagship of the Winged Hussars in person, rarer still to see it shot to hell.

"Shore leave?" Paka asked once a parking location was assigned.

Alexis considered before answering. "I was going to say no, but we've been out for longer than planned. Give them 24 hours." Paka nodded and gave the order. "I need to go over to the station and do some business."

She'd already showered, so Alexis was ready to go. She and Paka traveled down to Deck 21 where a shuttle was waiting for her, magnetically secured to the deck. The marines were already floating over to the shuttle when she arrived with the XO.

"Southard," she said as she entered the shuttle. The pilot saluted her, and she returned it.

"Captain," he greeted her.

"You seem to keep ending up as my pilot."

"Chief decided I could handle you, ma'am." She lifted an eyebrow, and he laughed. "His words, ma'am."

"Okay," she said, "I'm kind of hard on pilots." She'd been a pilot since she was a teenager and had no patience for a less-than-perfect pilot. "Everyone aboard?"

He confirmed they were, so she went to her seat. The marines were already securing themselves. Sergeant T'jto was forward with his second, Corporal Johansson. The MinSha and Human made strange partners, but that's what they were. Behind them were Privates Zit and Jeejee chatting about something that amused them. Behind them, taking up the entire next row, was the Tortantula Oort.

Alexis slowed as she went by. The huge spider had a slate held in one of its manipulators and was focusing several eyes on the display. As Alexis strapped herself in, she tried to decide if she'd seen what she thought she'd seen.

"Something wrong?" Paka asked, strapping in next to her. The shuttle pilot, Lt. Southard, was scanning his passengers to make sure they were all properly secured. Another dozen crewmembers going on leave filled in the remaining spaces.

"I'm not sure," she said, shaking her head.

"Want to share?" She could just see Paka's eyes through the goggles she always wore. The Veetanho had a curious expression on her face.

"I think my Tortantula heavy assault specialist is reading Beyond Good and Evil by Friedrich Nietzsche." Lacking a point of reference, the XO could only wonder what that meant. A minute later, the shuttle buttoned up, and the hangar deck decompressed. In vacuum, the shuttle detached from the floor and carefully exited the bay with tiny puffs of its maneuvering jets. Alexis again admired Lt. Southard's control. She still wished they'd let her fly herself around, though, at least occasionally.

The flight to the station only took a few minutes. Alexis passed it scrolling through procurement requisitions, crew reports, and repair orders. In addition to hiring replacements for the lost troopers and crewmen, seven crewmembers' contracts had expired, and they had elected to separate on Karma. The Hussars usually maintained a high level of retention. By her records, the company employed more than 27,000 personnel, and even with combat losses, they averaged less than a one percent yearly turnover; so the 41 casualties plus the seven terminating contracts constituted a large number.

"Is T'jto handling the trooper screening?" she asked Paka, glancing up and out a window to check their progress.

"She's on top of it," Paka said.

"And what about Oort?" The Veetanho looked at her boss and gave an all-too-Human sigh. Shortly before they arrived in system, Alexis had sent a recommendation to the trooper commander to terminate Oort's contract. That would also mean Jeejee would go. She believed the Tortantula was becoming unbalanced, and an unbalanced ten-foot-wide, seven-hundred-pound spider that enjoyed using energy weapons and explosives was not a good combination. Especially considering Oort's job was shipboard defense and assault.

"Sergeant T'jto has elected to not take your advice."

"I expected as much," Alexis said.

"If you did, why did you even suggest it?"

"Because that's my job."

"You can simply make a command decision and terminate the spider's contract."

"I could," Alexis agreed, "but I won't."

Paka's looked at Alexis in confusion. "You Humans," she said, "I don't understand you, sometimes."

"You were a marine commander on *Alicorn*, and then the XO aboard *American Pharaoh* under my mom. Did you understand her any better?"

Paka grumbled and then gave a few of her kind's yipping laughs. "No, not at all."

"I decided that, as badly as the troopers got creamed on this cruise, cohesion was more important than the risk of a meltdown. Even a Tortantula meltdown." She wondered quietly if the few remaining troopers would be enough to put a unit back together. She hoped she wouldn't be forced to start from complete scratch.

Karma Station was chaotic, at best, most days. Besides being the closest trading world to Earth, it was also a mercenary hub for the area, and held the largest merc pits in the Tolo arm of the galaxy. Alexis' ancestors had said that on Karma a thousand fortunes were made and a thousand lives lost every day.

Alexis was dropped off by Lt. Southard at one of the many central hub docking points, the center of the spinning wheels of the station. The hubs were zero gravity and the ideal place for small to medium ships to dock. *Pegasus* was too big and would undergo repairs floating nearby in her own orbit.

Alexis floated out as soon as the pilot opened the hatch. Outside was one of the huge promenades which ran the length of the hub. Thousands of beings from hundreds of races floated back and forth.

The planet Karma was below, providing a breathtaking vista for the first-time visitor. Alexis had first seen it when she was five, but planets had never been all that fascinating to her. Sergeant T'jto and his squad headed off in one direction immediately. She knew they were making for the station's merc guild office to file their request for personnel. Most companies would need to go to the planet to meet potential mercs, but they were the Winged Hussars. They didn't go looking for personnel, personnel came looking for them.

"Hey, Captain Cromwell!" she heard as she walked through the departure gate, and a Jivool stutter-slid over to her. The Jivool was huge, ursoid, and from a merc race like her own.

"Commander Gukkal?" she asked. It was a guess, but she only knew a handful of Jivool by name, and only one who was white.

"None other," he said. The floor of the promenade had grated floors and a gentle overhead airflow. You could jump and soar, but the current always pushed you back down. A few of the flight-capable races flew along, wholly in their element. "Are you here looking for work?"

"No," she said as she made room for more of her crew exiting the shuttle. Over the lock, the programmable display said "*Pegasus* – Winged Hussars" in several changing texts. English rotated through every few minutes. "We're hiring some personnel and doing some repairs."

"I heard you had a ruckus," he growled and grinned, showing long razor-sharp canines. Fuck, Alexis thought, a ship must have come through from Sulaadar right behind them. They'd only been in Karma a little more than a day.

"Just a second," she said to the grinning bear and touched her pinplant. "Edwards," she transmitted without speaking aloud.

"Here, Captain," he replied instantly. He'd been left in command while she was away.

"The word about Sulaadar has already reached Karma."

"That was fast," the TacCom replied.

"My thoughts exactly. Best keep an eye out for any Maki ships. Keep a shield watch on duty and the sensors hot until repairs begin. No one would be crazy enough to risk damaging the repair ships, so we should be safe then."

"Aye, aye, Commander," he said, and she turned off the pinlink. Commander Gukkal was waiting patiently. "What did you hear about us?" she asked.

"That you shot up a bunch of Maki ships and ran like hell." Not too far from the truth, she thought.

"They had a blockade on Sulaadar," Alexis explained; "they thought they could war prize or press gang any mercs who came through."

"Weren't bargaining for that flying kill stick of yours, were they?" He was still smiling, and Alexis wondered what he was getting at. "You want to consider hiring Kaashu Baaku?" he asked. Now she was even more curious.

Five years ago, she'd done a deal with the Jivool that involved a hot extraction of several companies of mercs trapped after an op went south. By the time the Hussars arrived, it was a total Zuul screw. Kaashu Baaku were the only ones still alive. The Hussars shot their way in and extracted the survivors, minus all their equipment. Most mercs would be grateful for having their asses pulled out of the fire, especially big furry, flammable asses. That wasn't the Jivool way. They tried to file a grievance against the Hussars with the guild. Breach of contract for not arriving in time (they arrived 5 days ahead of schedule), and disregard for company equipment and essentials (nothing in the contract stipulated the Hussars were required to get their junk off the planet, only their personnel). The guild sided with Alexis, and ever since, they'd been on the bears' shit-list. Having the Jivool company suddenly offer to sign was not normal.

"We're putting out a hiring notice to fill our personnel roster. Any extra personnel you have are welcome to apply," she said.

"No," he said, shaking his huge muzzle from side to side. "Why not just hire us instead? We'll take care of it all for you! Simpler, faster, and we all win." His tiny black eyes were like ink spots on a pure white piece of paper. They regarded her intently.

"I'm sorry, but I'm going to have to pass," Alexis said, shaking her head and smiling. "We prefer to hire directly. Subcontracting is too complicated."

"What, you no trust Jivool?"

Alexis hesitated the barest heartbeat. "Actually? No, I don't."

The tiny black eyes narrowed, and Alexis flipped her long white ponytail over her shoulder so she could casually put her right hand on the butt of the GP-90 compact assault pistol. Behind her, Paka had a hand in a shoulder bag she was carrying, but nothing had come out yet.

"You insult us," Gukkal grumbled.

"You've tried to cause us grief a number of times since we saved your bacon five years ago."

"That was unfair—"

"I think it's about time for you to move along," a voice said in clicks and chirps. Gukkal turned his head slightly to observe Sergeant T'jto standing a few feet away, a laser carbine slung cross body and two foot-hands resting on its stock. The Winged Hussars logo was clearly painted on her thorax.

"You leave us to our business, crunchy bug," Gukkal said.

"Who you calling bug, meat sack?" His head turned again, and he found Private Zit almost behind him. The Goka had no evident weapon, but an unarmed Goka was just as scary as an armed Goka.

"Yeah," another voice grumbled and scratched. Oort was only a few feet away on the other side. Jeejee was in his saddle, and, unlike the others, he already had his massive hand-cannon out. Alexis didn't see Johansson, but she knew the sharpshooter would be nearby.

"Your fate is your own," the Tortantula said. "What you do here is not written in stone. Choose a wise path. I do not wish to kill you." Everyone turned to look at the massive, hairy black spider. Gukkal stared at Oort, his jaw falling open slightly.

"Y-you are trying to provoke me," Gukkal managed to stammer as he moved sideways, out the only exit left to him by the encircled mercs. "I will not forget this."

As he turned he almost walked right into Johansson, who was tall for a Human female. "Neither will we. Bye, now." She tried to push him away, but the Jivool shrugged her off and stormed away. Johansson joined the others. "Well that was fun," she said to her commander.

"Yes," T'jto agreed; "what was that about?"

"I don't know," Alexis said, eyeing the Tortantula suspiciously. If this had been a few weeks ago, the spider would have been sucking out Gukkal's bodily juices by now. What the fuck was going on in that little brain? She regretted not ordering her to be let go. "Everyone needs to be on guard." She turned to Paka. "Send a message to all crew on leave. Only go about in pairs. Watch out for Jivool in particular."

Paka nodded.

"Go and deliver the recruiting notice to the merc guild," Alexis ordered T'jto. "We'll see you shortly."

Now much warier, Alexis and her XO moved down the promenade to a glideway and slid along it out to the 3rd ring. The ring was mostly full of offices, including the Karma offices of the Winged Hussars. A Human secretary greeted her as she entered.

"Welcome back, Commander."

"Good to be back, Wendy." The woman was in her thirties, blonde, and extremely attractive. Like Alexis, she was not native to Earth. She'd been born on a Human freighter plying its way through the galaxy. She'd left to find her own path a few years ago, and, low on funds, had responded to an ad Alexis ran for an office manager at the station. She'd learned bookkeeping and other clerical work on her home ship and liked the idea of staying at Karma for a few years. That was five years ago. "Anything urgent?" The woman indicated the waiting room in the adjoining office.

"There's a representative of the Cartography Guild to see you," Wendy explained. "He requested a meeting before I even knew *Pegasus* had transitioned to Karma."

"I was expecting this," Alexis said. Wendy looked confused, but didn't push her boss. "Give me five minutes to get settled and show him in. Have you heard from the maintenance contractors yet?"

"Yes," the woman said and handed Alexis a slate.

"Excellent. Paka, go ahead and work with this and coordinate with T'jto for interviews while I deal with the Lord of the Rings." Paka snorted at Alexis' favorite nickname for a leader of the Cartography Guild.

Alexis walked to her office, passing the small employee lounge on the way. A Human male was inside, looking ghostly white and holding a dripping towel against his head. He wore a Hussars uniform with a logistics patch, the name "Sommerkorn" on the chest. She wondered what that was about as she entered her office and closed the door with a sigh. When was the last time she'd been here? Six months ago? A year? She'd lost track. The office was simple, with a desk of polished metal, a comfortable chair behind it, and four for guests. On the other side of the office was a conference table with 12 chairs. There was also a small bathroom and an autochef for late nights. It was sufficient.

She set her shoulder bag down and sat in her chair. Entering a code into the slate built into the desk unlocked all its functions and the multiple Tri-V came alive. There were messages from Home waiting. She decided to wait on those for now, and instead touched her pinplants and spoke.

"That Jivool was trying to infiltrate."

"<*Yes, he was*>"

"Okay, but why."

"*<I am working on that>*"

"Any sign of threats in the system?" Alexis asked.

"*<Not at this moment. However, the probability increases by the hour>*"

"How long do we have?"

"*<Four days, maybe a week>*"

"Surely, no one will attack us here." Silence. "Would they?"

"*<That is not a safe assumption>*"

Fuck, she thought. What in entropy had they gotten themselves into? The office intercom chimed.

"Master Gevastopal from the Cartography Guild to see you," Wendy said.

"Show the master in," Alexis said, and clicked off her pinplant. She rose just as the door opened, and a massive form stooped, and slid sideways through the door. "Welcome, Guild Master," she said as she bowed.

"I greet you, Commander Cromwell of the Winged Hussars," Gevastopal said, bowing in return. He was just under nine feet tall. A member of the Sumatozou race, he resembled an upright elephant with stubby-fingered hands, and a bifurcated trunk. Their race was usually a gray or brown, and they took to wearing elaborately-wrapped robes around their somewhat rotund bodies. Their faces had natural red and green mottled striping that had something to do with their sexual maturity and herd status. Sumatozou had striking red stripes that ran along his trunk to curve back under his eyes.

"To what do I owe the pleasure?"

"We received an info packet from your ship as soon as it made transition from Sulaadar," he said. Alexis gestured him to one of the four chairs in front of her desk, the one that was a simple bench and would support him. He nodded congenially and took the seat. "Your use of the stargate was non-scheduled."

"And expensive," she said, nodding. "Sadly, as you probably are aware of the combat conditions there, it was also necessary." His trunk waved in the air over his head, a shrug in his race.

"Yes, of course, yet this doesn't negate the cost of an unscheduled transition."

Alexis grunted. No one was using the stargate in that system much, so it wasn't like they'd needed to use the fusion plant to recharge. There was no real cost involved. Yet, here he was. "I understand. You can add it to our quarterly fee."

"Yes, well," he said, "I'm going to have to request cash payment of your current fees."

Alexis straightened up, her eyes narrowing. "*What?*"

"I said I'm going to have to request cash—"

"I heard you just fine, master. What I don't understand is why. The Winged Hussars have been a registered merc company for over 100 years, and we've never failed to pay on time."

"Yes, I know, but the fee for that unscheduled operation is quite…"

"Expensive," she finished for him, and he nodded his head, more of a bow since the Sumatozou didn't really have necks. "We've paid it with the rest of the fees every time we've done an unscheduled transition, and that has to be at least fifty times!" She was starting to get upset. It wasn't the cost, even though it was high; it was the principle of the thing! The guild master made an expansive, helpless gesture.

"I have my instructions."

Alexis' mouth set in a thin line of disapproval. This had never happened before! "What prompted this change?"

"I'm not at liberty to say."

"Then I'm not at liberty to pay!"

"Commander, please, this is difficult enough as it is."

Alexis snorted. "Our credit has always been good until now. What happened?"

"Cartwright's Cavaliers," he finally blurted.

"They're one of our Four Horsemen, sure, but what does that have to do with us?"

"They are insolvent. Out of business."

"Impossible; their ship is here at Karma." That same frustrating shrug. She clicked her intercom. "Wendy, what's up with Cartwright's?"

"Better check your email, ma'am." Alexis grumbled and pulled her email back up. It only took a second to find it. Cartwright's had been temporarily off the active contract list. Something had gone south, something involving the wife of Thaddeus Cartwright, the deceased commander. His son was too young to take control, and his wife had been running the financials until he was old enough. She ran it alright; she ran it right into the ground. So why was the *Bucephalus,* the Cavaliers' merc cruiser, here? She found that in another email. Company lawyers had bought the ship from the Cavaliers out of bankruptcy to keep it in the Horsemen. They'd bought the half billion credit ship for 5 credits. The Horsemen protected their own.

According to records, Jim Cartwright had assumed command only recently and had begun running limited missions. They were a mere shadow of their former selves.

"Okay, I see now." The Sumatozou nodded again. "What I fail to see is how this affects my company's credit."

"You are a Four Horseman, yes?" This time she was the one to nod. "Now there are only two left."

"What?!" That expansive gesture. Dumbo was really starting to piss her off. She was about to call Wendy again, but decided to check her email once more. The next news item she was looking for was even more recent. Asbaran Solutions, the smallest, but always the most tenacious of the three ground-centric horsemen, had been devastated in a series of miscalculations during costly contracts. Apparently the fourth in line, a previously disinherited heir, was now in charge and running around the galaxy on a personal vendetta. What the hell was going on?

The guild master was waiting patiently, so she did a quick check on the Golden Horde, the last of the Four Horsemen. Nope, no problems there. Good, she was beginning to think there was a conspiracy against them.

"You think we're next? Guild Master, I can assure you, we are financially sound." He waited, staring at her. "I'm tempted to tell you get your sizeable ass out of my office."

"That is, of course, your right, Commander Cromwell. However, I will be forced to revoke your stargate access."

"You wouldn't dare." Expansive gesture. "I'll file a grievance with the mercenary guild if you do." Shrug. With a growl, she accessed her desk controls. It didn't make sense to argue any further. Sure, she could file a grievance, and she might well win. But it could take months to work its way through the system, all the while her company would be grounded. Grounded, and unable to get Home. "Exactly how much was that unscheduled gate access?"

"Unscheduled gate access from a Level Two stargate is one hundred thousand credits."

"Thief," she said. It looked like he was smiling now, though it was admittedly difficult to tell if an elephant was smiling. She keyed in her cypher code, touched a finger to the locking plate, and drew a symbol. The safe popped with a click. Alexis reached inside, dug around and pulled out a credit chit. It was round, about twice the size and thickness of a regular denomination, and had a one carat red diamond in the center. Laser-etched on the diamond was 100,000 GCU in several languages, none of them English. She tossed it on her desk. It bounced twice and the guild master caught it deftly with his trunk. He examined it, almost curiously, for a few seconds. Just as she was starting to wonder if the bastard was going to pull out one of the little pocket validators some merchants carried, he set it back on the desk. "Yes?" she demanded.

"I believe I said all your current fees."

Alexis blanched. "Are you serious?"

"Deadly serious," he said.

"Is this in place across all my company's ships?"

"I'm afraid so," he said, "at least for the foreseeable future. I'm so terribly sorry." Alexis snorted again. He wasn't sorry in the least.

"How much?"

"One million, one hundred seventy-five thousand, two hundred credits." She tapped the slate dedicated to company finances and accessed the last quarter's bill. Just under a million. The number he'd given wasn't far outside the norm.

"That includes the hundred thousand there?" An elephantine nod. "Very well," she said and dug into the safe. This time she produced an unusual credit chit. It wasn't round, like all the others, it was more oblong but flat on top and bottom with little indents along the flat point. It was obviously made to be stacked. The center was transparent and held a five carat red diamond of exquisite quality with a tiny built-in light source that made it glow slightly. On this one was printed 'One Million Credits.' The guild master's eyes got wider. Then she added another.

"Surely, you don't expect me to make change." He picked up the two million-credit chits and rubbed them together with the digits of his trunk.

"No," she said, "and it's not a tip. That's credit for continued operations." She typed in another slate. "If we exceed that, come see my assistant. Wendy is authorized to pay you in the future."

"Wonderful," the guild master said. He stood. "I believe our business is complete."

"Yes," she smiled savagely, "once you give me a receipt it is."

When the annoying pachyderm was gone, she grumbled and closed the safe. The stack of million credit chits wasn't noticeably smaller. It would take a lot more than a two million credit shakedown to affect the safe. The one in *Pegasus* was much bigger, and much fuller. Every ship's captain in the Winged Hussars had a small stack of those oblong chits as well. In the Galactic Union, one never knew when cold hard red diamonds would get you out of a pinch. As she'd just been reminded, cash often trumped credit.

Other business needed her attention, and soon. She'd probably have a few less of those fat chits after the Karma maintenance crews finished the rush job she wanted. But instead of turning to that work, she sat and thought about all the events swirling around. Cartwright's Cavaliers badly damaged, Asbaran Solutions in a death spiral, and her own ship in fight after fight. Only, her Hussars were a lot more than just this one ship.

"Shit," she said and got back on her slate. She'd been so wrapped up in her own issues she'd forgotten about her other ships. Task Force Two was her concern. The Hussars had a contract pending, and she'd intended to attach *Pegasus* to that task force to assist. She scrolled through her email and found what she was looking for. Relay from Home, Task Force Two was dispatched on contractual commitment four weeks ago.

She'd expected as much. It was a high-value contract, and when her job for the Peacemakers ran long, it only made sense that Operations sent the task force ahead without her. Captain Kowalczy was in command of Task Force Two. It was a powerful group of ships, after all, and though *Pegasus* was the most powerful ship in the fleet, it wasn't the only powerful ship. He'd be in command of *Alicorn*, a damned fine ship. She wouldn't normally have given it a second thought, until now. Were her own events tied to those of the other Horsemen?

The Four Horsemen had faced innumerable challenges over the century since they came into being. "Born of dire battle and desperate necessity," was a phrase Jimmy Cartwright, founder of Cartwright's Cavaliers, had used in his silly autobiography. He'd spent a lot of words to paint his Cavaliers as the reason any of them had survived. Alexis snorted. He had no fucking idea.

Outside, the world of Karma spun by lazily. Blue bodies of water, green continents full of life. So much like Earth, the world of her people's birth. Why did she hate it so much? Maybe because the only place she considered home was parked a few miles away while her crew desperately worked on it. *Now you're being sentimental,* she chided herself.

On her financial slate, a glowing deduction was at the top of the debits column. The credits she'd taken from her safe to pay the extortion to the damned guild master. A computer in the safe had dutifully noted the cash removal in their balance log. It wasn't much, in the grand scheme of things; the Hussars had always been wealthy, but few knew just how wealthy they actually were. Those 2.1 million credits were all but invisible on the bottom line—that's how wealthy. And that was part of her anxiety. Maybe a realization that despite their wealth and prominence, the history of the Winged Hussars was no more than a historical footnote in the annals of the Mercenary Guild. Here today, gone tomorrow. Tomorrow was only a day away.

*****

Chapter Seventeen

ECS Coronado

Approaching Karma System

Hyperspace

Rick came back to consciousness slowly, with a feeling of deep disorientation. Something was beeping loudly, and he wished it would stop. He'd been dead and found he rather liked it. It was better than all the pain he'd suffered shortly before he died. The beeping continued to intrude on his happy afterlife, and worse, the lights came on and seared his brain, even through his closed eye lids.

"What the hell?" he mumbled. It came out as "Wha eh ell?" He realized something was down his throat, and he almost panicked.

"Woah, son," someone said. His eyes didn't want to focus entirely. It was like looking through a yellow, murky haze. He shook his head and immediately regretted it. Whatever was down his throat didn't give him a lot of room to move, and it jerked in his mouth. He felt sick. "Damn it, if you don't hold still I'm going to tranquilize you!" The voice was slightly familiar. The ship's cook? He was in the galley? What the fuck happened?

Still, the pain from his throat was enough to make him follow directions, and he forced himself to calm down.

"That's better," the cook said. "Are you breathing okay? Just a little nod is enough." He nodded his head fractionally. "Excellent.

Are you in pain?" A tiny shake this time. "Good," the cook said, and Rick heard the artificial clicks of keys on a slate. "Rick, I'm Brad, the *Coronado's* medical officer." Rick was still confused, because he'd been right; Brad was the cook. "Yes, I'm also the cook. But I was a medic back on Earth years ago before robots and nanites started making the job redundant. I did a tour in the Earth Defense Service when I was a kid. The only job they had was cook. Got cross-trained as a medic, and it gave me a job I could sell in space."

Rick's head was beginning to clear. Things were starting to make sense. He began to remember the harried fight against the alien raiders. He'd been shot. Several times. So maybe he had been dead.

"Glad you're up. Hold on a minute while I have the autodoc run a few tests, and I call the captain."

Sure, Rick thought, not like I'm going anywhere with this thing down my throat. While he waited, he tried his body out and found nothing worked. That concerned him a little, but not as much as he'd thought it would. Ever since he was young and decided he wanted to be a merc, he'd known deep down he might die. Even kids knew it wasn't safe being a merc, when the news was full of stories of merc companies taking huge losses, and the history books began with the Alpha Contracts. One hundred merc companies accepted the first contracts, and only four returned. The Four Horsemen. He finally decided he must have been given some drug that kept him from moving, and settled down to wait.

Brad the cook/medic continued to work on his devices. Rick still couldn't focus through the strange yellow haze, so he tried to recall how he ended up drugged, with a big tube down his throat. He didn't have any memory of what happened after he made his reverse-G pass. Finally, he heard the captain's familiar gravelly voice.

"So, our savior is awake at last?" Rick turned his head as much as he could and was just able to make out the captain's rotund form through the yellow haze. He gave a little nod. "How's he doing, Brad?"

"Everything looks good," the other man said, showing the captain the slate. "Autodoc says we can unplug him."

"Excellent," Holland said. "Let's do it."

The two went to work; apparently Holland knew a bit about medical procedures as well. Rick had never been in an autodoc. He'd been to the hospital once as a child, but they didn't use the computer-controlled automatic medical systems known as autodocs. Earth doctors used all kinds of advanced Union tech these days, but largely relied on their own medical knowledge, along with a healthy dose of nanites thrown in.

After a minute, he felt himself buffeted like a wind was blowing and heard a sucking sound. The yellow haze began to go away, and he realized he was surrounded by a fog, inside a bubble. It only took a few seconds for his vision to clear, and the two men to unlatch the bubble and open it.

"Doing okay?" Brad asked. Rick nodded. "Good. We're going to remove the breathing tube. It's going to hurt a bit." He was about to nod when the man did something out of Rick's view, and there was a sudden, painful pulling sensation inside his chest. He tried to gasp but couldn't breathe. For a second he felt panic, but then he felt something slide over his tongue, and he saw Brad taking something off his face. He could breathe again!

"Holy shit," he gasped through an incredibly dry, scratchy throat.

"Yeah," Brad laughed. "I hear it's not fun."

"How you feel, kid?" Holland asked.

"I still can't move," Rick said.

"Oh, duh," Brad said, and he examined the slate one more time. He finally tapped a control and Rick felt a moment of pain in his neck, right at the base of his skull. Like a wave, full feeling and movement returned. He was sitting in a chair, slightly reclined, with pads under his arms to hold them out and away from his body.

"How long?" Rick croaked. It felt like they were under light acceleration. Brad handed him a cup of water before answering.

"Eight days," the older man said, consulting his slate. "We need to go through a series of mobility tests. Okay, raise your right hand and make a fist with one finger at a time until they are all clenched."

"But I want—" Rick started to complain.

"Do as he says, son," Holland said gently, but insistently. Rick sighed and followed the instructions.

The series of tests took almost a quarter of an hour. During that time, many of the crew came through and nodded or waved to him. Most seemed curious; they all looked at him differently. Rick was a little disturbed; he'd been in the galley for over a week, on display like a freak show.

"All right," Brad finally said, "you're 100 percent. You can get up."

Rick was glad gravity was light, because he felt unsteady on his feet. He was dressed only in a pair of boxers, his skin covered in a light dusting of yellowish material.

"Come on lad," Brad said, and the two men took him, one by each arm, and helped him into the deck's bathroom where they waited while he stripped and showered. He'd long gotten used to nudity in groups, so that didn't bother him. As the slow-falling water washed away the yellow dust in lines down his body, he felt steadily better.

When he was drying, he noticed the first of his souvenirs from the battle. Just above his left nipple was an almost perfectly shaped rectangular scar of pink tissue. There were numerous little pink flecks all around it. He reached over his left shoulder and found another, similarly shaped scar on his scapula.

"Other than some lung damage," Brad said, "that was the least of them. The little marks are from melted armor." One of the other crewmen came in with some clothes from Rick's locker. As Rick dressed, he saw the second scar on his right thigh. Shaped like the first, it penetrated mid-thigh, toward his inseam, and exited directly opposite on the back of his thigh.

"Penetrated your femoral artery," Brad said. "Luckily, the frequency of the alien's lasers cauterized the damage. You still bled heavily, but you survived." Rick shook his head at his luck. He didn't see the last scar until he looked in the bathroom's mirror after wiping away the fog.

"Oh, shit," he said.

"I couldn't do anything about the scarring," Brad said, with remorse in his voice. The left side of Rick's face had a line of pink scar tissue running from his nose to over his left ear. The hair that should have grown over his ear was gone, and he could feel the scarring on the back of his head. It looked like someone had tried to cut his fucking head in half. "It penetrated your cranium. But the extreme angle and speed of the trauma, coupled with the fact that it was a pistol and not one of those big rifles, means the damage was minimal."

"How minimal?" Rick asked.

"It can't say. It's an alien-made autodoc, reprogrammed on Earth for Humans. It does a pretty good job, as you can tell. But the cerebral programming is the most complicated." The other man shrugged. "None of your motor functions were affected; we confirmed that when you woke up. It says language, cognitive functions, and memory could be issues."

Rick sighed and bent over the sink. He hadn't even been fighting for a merc company. It was just some kind of a damned pirate raid, or something. It wasn't fair. He felt a strong hand on his shoulder.

"You saved our bacon, son," Captain Holland said.

"Just leave me alone for a few minutes. Okay?"

"Sure," Holland said.

"But—" Brad started to say.

"Give the man some time," Holland said and pulled his cook/medic out, closing the door on the small bathroom as they went. The ship was obviously under spin. Rick guessed they were in hyperspace. If they were between emergence point and stargate, they'd be under thrust. He looked back up at himself in the mirror. He'd always been good looking, he knew that. Girls in school chased him constantly, and he'd never had trouble finding a companion from the moment he joined Mickey Finn. The image that looked back at him was like something from a war film. What had happened to his brain? Everything seemed to be working, but a laser had burned through his skull. That had to have left *some* side effects. But there was no emotion. None. He didn't feel mad, disappointed, upset, nothing. He just felt empty. He'd felt that way since waking up.

He wanted to yell, to rage, to cry, something. However, nothing was there. It was like opening the door on a burning building, expecting to find an inferno, and finding a normal room. It didn't seem right, or normal. He grunted and thought about an old friend. What would he think of him now? Who would think…wait. The scarred visage in the mirror crinkled its eyebrows in concentration trying to remember a name. He had a few scattered flickers of a fat kid laughing, of a Tri-V action movie, buckets of popcorn, watching spaceships taking off and cheering. But no name came to him, and he couldn't focus on the face. Oh no, he thought, what else can't I remember?

Eventually he exited the bathroom, fully dressed in an undamaged pair of his merc camo BDU, his camouflage battle dress uniform. Whoever had brought them hadn't picked a pair at the top of his duffle bag; these were the ones stuffed in the side. As he exited he saw it still had a Mickey Finn patch on it, a cartoon Irish man riding a dropship with a bottle of beer in one hand, while making a menacing fist with the other. As he came out, he tore the patch from its Velcro backing and stuffed it in a pocket.

The galley was empty except for Captain Holland, who watched him with a critical, expectant look.

"You okay, Rick?"

"Yes sir," Rick said and went to sit next to the captain. The older man pushed a steaming cup of coffee over, and Rick took a grateful taste. It was good, made with cream and two sugars, just as Rick liked. It gave him no real pleasure. "Tell me what happened?"

Holland nodded and began his tale.

The raiders had been terrorizing 82 Eridani for some time. Because New Mecca only had a couple of antiquated patrol boats, the raiders were difficult to catch. Of course, the planetary government was keeping it mostly quiet. Tramp freighters like the *Coronado* might well reconsider coming if they knew raiders were hitting ships regularly.

The raiders' MO was simple. Slip in close with a blacked-out ship's boat and quietly board. Then neutralize any resistance, take anything valuable they found, disable the ship, and escape. So far only a few lives had been lost.

"Who were they?" Rick asked. "I've never seen that race before." Holland tapped on a slate and handed it to him. A picture of a felinoid just like the ones he'd battled appeared.

"Pushtal," Rick said, reading aloud. They were listed in the Galnet as a registered merc race. Sometime in the past they'd made the wrong enemies and lost their planet in a vendetta with the MinSha. Rick nodded, the praying mantis-looking aliens were major players and didn't take insults or slights lightly. You could ask any Iranian about that, if you could find one still alive.

Now the Pushtal survived largely by odd-job merc contracts, or out-right piracy. They didn't own any worlds or colonies of record anymore.

"You killed all four of the boarding party," Holland said with a nod. "The survivor in the shuttle tried to detach and run. I dealt with that one."

"But you don't have any weapons," Rick said, then eyed the old captain, "do you?"

"I'd love to, but the old girl doesn't have the power output or surplus space." He grunted. "I might have to just suck it up and add a missile launcher. Anyway, I might not have a weapon, but we fly with the next best thing." Rick gave him a confused look. "The torch, son." Rick's eyes got wide. "Yeah. It's why the raiders always disabled their victims. As soon as the shuttle detached, I could see it on the screen. I fired the torch and gimbaled *Coronado* so the plume was aimed right at him. It was like watching a plastic toy hit with a laser." Rick nodded. Served him right.

"What about their mothership?"

"Never picked it up on the sensors. It was probably a few light seconds away. I'm guessing it's a freighter too, or they'd have splashed us after losing the shuttle. After we'd made them, they couldn't risk us getting sensor data and transmitting it. They just crawled away to lick their wounds."

"So, that was it?" Rick asked. "You just let them get away?"

"Son, this is no warship. My sensors are second rate and older than sin. Even if I did find the bloody Pushtal ship, what could I do? Try that trick with the torch? They probably had at least a few small lasers. No, we killed five of them and destroyed their shuttle. We lost Link, the purser, and you were wounded. Discretion was the better part of valor."

"I would have liked to get some payback," Rick said.

"You gunned down four." Rick only nodded and felt the unfamiliar scar on his face. "There isn't much more we can do for you on the ship," the captain continued. "I used almost every nanite we had on board to save you and fix the head wound." Rick nodded again. That would probably have cost the captain quite a bit. Nanite treatments weren't cheap. The yellow fog had been nanites. Trillions of them. He'd probably washed fifty thousand credits down the drain.

"Thanks for saving me," Rick said.

"What was I going to do, blow you out the lock?"

"Some would have," Rick said. "It would have been cheaper and easier."

The other man reached across the table and put a hand on Rick's shoulder. "I'd be lying if I didn't say you were right. But that isn't how the *Coronado* operates."

Rick smiled a little. "Where are we now?" Rick sipped some more coffee. "And can I get some chow? I'm starving."

"We're about a day out of Karma," Holland said, taking Rick's mug and getting up. He went over to the autochef and tapped on the screen to see what options Brad had cooked and stored. The machine took cooked ingredients kept in a freezer and mixed, reheated, and served them. Expensive models could start with raw meats and vegetables, or even protein cubes, and produce meals. This was a much cheaper model. He came back with more coffee for them and a plate of steaming chili for Rick, who dug in with a zeal. Like the coffee, the chili was good, but gave no pleasure. He frowned. "I'm going to transfer cargo, hit another colony, and go back to Earth. You're welcome to stay on, or get off at Karma like we agreed." Rick chewed the food and thought. Eventually, he told the captain he'd decide when they docked.

Rick had to admire Karma Station as the *Coronado* braked with her ion drive. Compared to all the stations and habitats he'd seen in his home star system, it was tremendous. Three huge rings rotating around a stable central zero-gravity hub. Dozens of starships were parked around the station, many of them warships, with some freighters and a few ships of unknown utility. The planet looked a bit like Earth with huge oceans, white icecaps, brown/green land masses, and swirling cotton candy clouds. It was the most interesting place he'd seen since leaving home.

"It's quite the site," Captain Holland said, coming down to the mess where the non-essential crew stayed during close approaches and docking operations.

"Our first stop after the Alpha Contracts," Rick said. A lot of Human history for mercs centered around this station and the city under its geosynchronous orbit. One of more unusual ships near the station caught Rick's attention. He looked closer. It was a long tapering cylinder dotted with obvious weapons points. At the blunt point of her stern was a ring of modules, probably engines or fuel tanks. Several recent battle wounds marred its simple lines. "What's that ship?" Rick wondered and pointed.

"That ship?" Holland asked. "That ship is famous."

"For what?" Rick asked. "Surplus junk?" He'd seen images of lots of warships of both Human and alien design. They tended to be graceful looking affairs, with disks near the rear to provide stability and gravity decks, and extended booms for weapons. All of them were on the long side, and narrow, because it made for harder targets and thrust forces moved along straight lines. A spherical warship was a huge target, so only the biggest were that shape.

"That is the *Pegasus,*" the captain said; "it's the flagship of the Winged Hussars. One of the Four Horsemen."

Rick observed the wounded ship as they slowed into their parking orbit. The Winged Hussars, one of the Four Horsemen, was here, now. What were the odds? He knew what he was going to do.

* * * * *

Chapter Eighteen

Silent Meadow

Sulaadar 3

Sulaadar System

Captain Geshakooka was stuck to a wall with his XO listening patiently as fleet commander Syshkyl vented in rage. The Maki clung to the office desk with its split tail, which allowed the little mammal to gesticulate wildly as it screamed in a most mammalian fashion.

"The entire highguard squadron, devastated!" Syshkyl screamed and hit his desk, making him swing around by his tail in a most amusing manner. Geshakooka enjoyed the reaction openly, although only another Bakulu would realize he was grinning ear to ear. "My own sibling, Yackyl, is missing. His battleship, *Ardent Grove,* never reported in. After two weeks, it has been assumed lost."

"No debris was located at the stargate," a tactical advisor said, "and the commander of the lone surviving interceptor reported seeing them make transition, but with an unusual visual distortion." Syshkyl looked over at his chief engineer who sighed and shrugged.

"We can only assume *Ardent Grove* was so severely damaged in the skirmish it suffered a hyperspatial failure after transition." Every being in the room cringed or shuddered. No one liked to contemplate that great unknown. Many a grisly tale had been invented to explain what happened to starships whose hyperspatial nodes failed in hyperspace.

"Thusly," Syshkyl continued, "this entropy-causing Human merc ship *Pegasus* has cost us eight capital ships and forty-nine escorts."

"That doesn't include my two frigates," Geshakooka added.

"To entropy with your pathetic frigates," the fleet commander snarled. "I want your cruiser to assist in finding this Human ship."

"Personal vendettas are not our way," Geshakooka said, then continued before the enraged Maki could interrupt. "In addition, our contract is over, and we have no intention of extending it. We're expecting full payment plus the combat loss contingency of our frigates." It would never replace the losses of the ships and crews, but it would blunt the blow. The fleet commander considered Geshakooka for a long moment. The Bakulu commander weighed the possibility the angered mammal would try to steal their ship or do him harm. But instead Syshkyl just made a dismissive gesture.

"You are released," he said.

As if I need your permission, Geshakooka thought as he unstuck his foothold on the wall and fired a jet of air from his breathing vent precisely aimed to take him toward the exit. Back aboard his ship, *Yushispa,* Geshakooka was surprised to find he had a visitor waiting in the wardroom. He was even more surprised by whom the visitor was.

"To what do I owe the honor of your visit?" Geshakooka asked after greeting the esteemed guest.

"We are interested in your encounter with the Human warship, *Pegasus.*"

"It possesses power and speed you would not expect from such an ancient design," Geshakooka admitted. "And the drone fighters it employs…"

"Yes?" the other asked. Geshakooka considered his answer for a time.

"They are unremarkable in appearance, though of a design no one else employs. They are unique to the Winged Hussars. Their performance is within Union norms, but like so many things about those Humans, they have many little advantages."

"Can you explain?" the visitor asked. Geshakooka put his thoughts in order, then continued.

"The drones operated as if they were manned fighters. Yes, I am aware of how this sounds, but my TacCom can show you the recordings. They act like they're hive-minded. It reminds me of how the SleSha work, in what some call telepathy. They respond faster than a remote teleoperator would be capable of. Even if they were teleoperated, their tactical awareness is in the upper one-thousandth of a percent in both prediction, response options, and validity of action. It is as if all the drones were being operated by a pilot with many lifetimes of experience, and they work together in unimaginable concert! It is like watching a school of Glnsheel in the surf, darting around a predator in prefect formation."

"Anything else?"

"The warheads on their ship-killer missiles are elegant. The missiles are standard affairs, produced by a dozen different races with little variation; they are made to be fired from standard launchers. However, the warheads are special, even unique. I have heard rumor the Winged Hussars call them 'Squash-bombs,' and they are a hybrid micro-sized nuclear device."

"Is that it?"

"I hesitate on the last."

The visitor considered Geshakooka for a moment. "Please, share with me."

"It is, like the bombs, only a rumor. But on multiple occasions, adversaries of the Winged Hussars have claimed their ship can appear in a star system anywhere it chooses."

"Indeed?"

"Yes, a strange, fanciful tale! While some warships do possess their own hyperspace shunts, despite the great cost and limited use on such a ship, it isn't unheard of. However, to be able to appear at a place other than an emergence point? The very idea is outrageous. Only, it would account for much of their martial prowess, especially since they do not employ any ships larger than battlecruisers."

The visitor absorbed all of this in silence; Geshakooka observed the other being at the same time, allowing one of his three eyes to study her in detail. The visitor stared back with shaded eyes, whiskers twitching as she considered Geshakooka's words. He was beginning to wonder what his visitor wanted, besides information. His ship's repairs weren't quite complete, and a fleet courier was due to deliver him new escorts any day.

"These questions aside, may I inquire why you have come to me today?" Geshakooka finally asked.

"Yes," the being finally said. "We'd like to hire your company, Quigg du Snoo, to pursue and destroy *Pegasus.*"

* * * * *

Part II

"The Winged Hussars, even from the beginning, were the most enigmatic of us. My Cavaliers, Asbaran, and the Horde were all less than thrilled with our treatment at the hands of aliens during the Alpha Contracts. It was more than the fact that we'd gotten our collective assess kicked. A good ass kicking is what it is—usually deserved and completely avoidable. No, I'm talking about the atrocities many of the damned aliens committed. From Besquith executing surrendering soldiers, to Tortantula feeding on the dead, it seemed the aliens had none of the morals we did. They acted like…well, like aliens!

Now, the Hussars were different. They only survived because of their luck in finding that derelict ship. That, and they linked up with dozens of alien survivors from other merc companies caught up in the same disastrous contracts we were. Yeah, it's a little-known fact we Humans weren't the only ones who got our butts handed to us. A lot of the aliens blamed their losses on our inability to provide the support we were hired to give. They might have had a point. But the Hussars not only turned lemons into lemonade, they made a lemon meringue pie and put a slice on the glass of tequila, too! None of us are surprised they're still the richest of us, and maybe the most arrogant."

Excerpt from "In Our Own Time – Dawning of the Horsemen"

by Jimmy Cartwright, Sr.

* * * * *

Chapter Nineteen

Karma Station
Karma System

Being on Karma Station was almost like being in a large habitat over Earth. It was so large the only way to notice the curve of the rings was in one of the huge malls or numerous parks and promenades scattered about. Standing on the floor level, you could look into the distance and notice the slight upwards curve of the floor moving toward the roof. On the tiny Human habitats, that curve was profound. The other thing you noticed was the gravity was a bit heavier, about 1.1 gravities.

Rick spent his first night playing tourist around the district where his hotel was located. Each district represented a pie-shaped slice of a ring, or about forty-five degrees. Each ring also had several stories, with the outer floor having the highest gravity (1.1 G) and the inner less (0.2 G).

He visited a dozen casinos, saw hundreds of shops, private businesses, vendors selling all manner of goods, and even what looked like a small zoo. Six hours later, he gave up and returned to his hotel without ever leaving the floor of his district. The station was that big. The GalNet said it had a constant population of several million, but fluctuated greatly. In the hub were thousands of warehouses, industrial operations, and ship maintenance firms. He was further stunned when he considered that Karma was kind of a backwater location.

There were trading stations coreward of Earth, in the highly-populated Gresht region, that were 20 times the size of Karma.

Returning to his hotel, a modest affair with 120 rooms and a restaurant catering to Humans and similar humanoids, he had a nice meal of Chicago-style pizza and a reasonable imitation of Dr. Pepper. The food was made by a well-programmed autochef, and only cost him 2 credits, less than it would have on Earth. For that matter, the room was only 5 credits a day. He'd paid that much for the dump back in Houston. His room here was rather bare by Earth standards, but nicely accommodated. It included a large bathroom with programmable shower (no water limit, a luxury after weeks of shipboard life), a nice sitting area with a full-wall Tri-V, and a bed big enough for a merc company. There was even a programmable beverage dispenser (unlimited access included).

The crew and Captain Holland had said their good byes at the hub where the *Coronado* docked. As Holland was shaking his hand, he pressed a small bag into Rick's.

"It's from me and the crew, son. God only knows what would have happened to us without you." Inside was his pay, just over 500 credits, but also a 2,000 credit chit.

"Sir," he complained, "that's too much." Rick tried to hand back the chit.

"No," Holland said sternly, "it sure isn't. I would have lost 100 times that if they'd gotten away with the safe and wrecked our fusion drive. You take that and be careful. It's enough to keep you fed and housed for a lot longer than your pay would have." He looked Rick in the eye. "Don't go signing with some nefarious sort. You sign on with a good company, or use the last to go home."

"Thank you," Rick said. He wasn't emotional about it. He was becoming increasingly convinced his emotions had been damaged along with some of his childhood memories.

After spending a few dozen credits, he still had better than 2,000 credits to his name. When he'd checked in, Rick had inquired about long-term housing. The owner said it was 30 credits a week, or he could pay 50, and that included meals at the hotel restaurant and late-night access to the autochef. If he used the autochef, he had enough to live here for almost a year, if he wanted to. But he didn't.

The second morning on Karma Station Rick made his way to Ring Two, taking a transfer shuttle instead of travelling all the way to the hub, and riding a glideway back out. The shuttle cost a credit, the other way would have been free. Ring Two held commercial office space and permanent housing. He'd looked up his destination before leaving.

On the fourth floor of the ring in District Four of Ring Two were a series of offices. After exiting the lift to that floor, he walked along the lines of offices until he found one with a simple circular logo of a winged helmet, the motto below; 'Plan, Prepare, Strike.' He pressed the announcement button and waited.

"Can I help you?" asked a feminine voice in English.

"I'm looking for work."

"Registered merc?"

"Yes, ma'am." He took out his UAAC and held it up for the scanner to register. There was a moment while the woman on the other end read it, then the door slid aside. Rick walked in.

It wasn't at all what he'd expected from a Four Horsemen office. He'd visited the Golden Horde's office in the merc tower back in Houston, and it was enormous. The Horsemen all had entire floors near the top. The smallest had been the Hussars, and that seemed to hold true here. There was a reception area with a single desk, with a woman sitting behind it. To either side were four exits, presumably to other offices, and a waiting area with room for about 10 people. There was no artwork or other decorations.

"Welcome to the office of the Winged Hussars. My name is Jennifer."

"Nice to meet you ma'am, Rick Culper."

She gave him a patient, congenial smile and held out a small slate. "Please complete the questionnaire. Be sure to okay the authorization to access your merc guild records."

He thanked her and went to the waiting area. The space was almost full. To his surprise, a lot of them were aliens. There were only six, but two were Oogar. They were the size of a CASPer, almost eight feet tall, and they loosely resembled grizzly bears. The biggest differences were their smaller mouths, bigger eyes, longer arms…and their striking purple coloring. They also didn't have what Human parents called indoor voices. They were whispering to each other—low shouts to everyone else—and held their slates in hands so big the devices looked like decks of playing cards.

Besides the Oogar, there was a Zuul, a pair of little elSha sharing one seat, and something else. Rick almost tripped over one of the Oogar's feet when he got a good look at the other being. It was as tall as a man, wore strange loose-fitting clothes, and sat hunched over a slate. Its hands were as dark as space, and when it looked up he saw two glowing red eyes and the glint of sparkling silver teeth. Rick half sat, half fell into an empty seat next to one of the pair of Humans.

"Something got you spooked, kid?" asked a Human voice. He turned and saw a man in his forties grinning at him. Rick looked confusedly at the strange humanoid again. It looked at him and showed more teeth. Rick felt a shudder race up his spine.

"Not really," Rick said, trying to shake it off. "Just confused by that," he stopped in mid-sentence. The strange black-skinned alien was gone. "Did you see a dark-skinned alien?" The other man looked where Rick was gesturing, and shook his head. "Weird," Rick whispered. The other man shrugged and held out his hand.

"Stan Jones," he said by way of introduction.

"Rick Culper."

"Good to meet you. Right out of cadre?" Rick nodded dejectedly. "Don't worry about it, we all start somewhere."

"Thanks. Are you as intimidated by the possibility of working for a Horsemen as I am?"

"Naw," Stan said, though his face had a strange expression. "I worked for the Horde before they went crazy."

"Mr. Jones?" the receptionist called, "Room Four, please."

"Good luck," Rick said as the older man got up, nodded to him, and headed for his interview.

It didn't take Rick long to complete the questionnaire. Mostly details he couldn't provide, such as deployments, bonuses, and awards given. Then it got to questions on familiarities, and he felt better. One of the first questions was zero-G operations and dropship operations. He clicked off on both of those. Then one he wasn't surprised to see. 'Are you comfortable working with aliens?' He checked 'Yes.' It was the last question, so he pressed 'Send.'

"Your name will be called shortly," the slate informed him. He put it back on Jennifer's desk. She smiled and thanked him. The

Oogar were still arguing over their own slates. One by one the others were called. When Rick's name was called, the Oogar still hadn't finished, and there was still no sign of the strange, black-skinned humanoid.

"Mr. Culper?" Rick looked up. "Door One, please."

Rick went to the door and opened it. Inside was a small, unadorned office with a desk and a woman sitting behind it. She looked up from a slate and gestured for him to come in.

"Mr. Culper?"

"That's me," Rick said as he came over to the desk. She stood, and he was surprised by how tall she was, at least six-two. She had super-short, dark brown hair and matching eyes.

"I'm Corporal Eva Johansson, Winged Hussars marine, and I understand you want a job."

"Yes, ma'am."

She smirked. "Corporal is good enough, or Johansson."

"Call me Rick."

She nodded, and she looked down at her slate. "I see you haven't done any combat deployments yet."

Rick gave a mental sigh. "That's correct, Corporal."

"It's okay, Rick, it's not a requirement. In fact, we've found less experience can be a bonus. The Hussars are a non-standard sort of unit."

"After that crowd in the waiting room, I see what you mean," Rick said.

"Yes, we hire aliens." She glanced at the slate. "You said that doesn't bother you. Were you being honest?"

"To be completely honest, I've never worked with them." She grunted and made a note. "I have killed a few." She looked back up at him, then at his face, cocking her head.

"You know, I've lived with people with scars, so it didn't even occur to me that you might have seen action without being active." She pointed at the scar, almost casually. "Care to tell?"

"The merchant ship I was on was attacked by pirates." She set the slate down and sat up, gesturing for him to continue, so Rick told the whole story. She became increasingly interested as his tale unfolded.

"Pushtal, eh?" she asked when he was finished.

"Yes, Corporal."

"And you killed four of them."

He nodded, and put a hand up to the scar on the side of his face. "Got shot three times for my efforts."

She put the slate down and leaned back in her chair. "Any lasting effects from the head wound?"

"Some long-term memory," he said. She looked expectantly, but he didn't add his concern about his emotionless state.

"A condition of employment with the Winged Hussars is that you have to be pinned," she said and turned her head slightly so he could see the pinlink behind her ear.

"I don't have that much cash," he admitted.

"We'd front the cost against your salary. Plus, we have our own medics, so it isn't as much as you'd pay on Earth."

"That's fine," Rick said. "I'd be okay with it."

She nodded and looked him in the eye. "Are you ready to meet one of our sergeants?"

"Sure," he said. Johansson touched a control on her desk, and a side door appeared where there hadn't been one before. It slid out of the way, and he heard the distinctive clicking gait of an insectoid race. The shining carapace of a MinSha walked in on its rear four legs. She, he remembered—nearly all the MinSha who served as mercs were female—was big for their race. She had double cross-body bandoliers holding laser rifle magazines, and the weapon they fit hung on a two-point sling. An equipment vest was also fit around her upper body, which held a slate and some other gear. On the vest was the winged helmet logo of their outfit.

"Rick, this is Sergeant T'jto." The sergeant's huge multifaceted eyes glimmered as she nodded to Rick.

"Good to meet you, trooper," the MinSha sergeant's clicks and scrapes were translated into English by Rick's pendant. "Corporal Johansson says you might be a good addition to our marine contingent."

"Would I have to go back into cadre?" Rick asked hesitantly.

"No," T'jto said, "we don't really believe in taking already trained mercs and sitting on them for months. It's better to just add them to a squad so they can get up to speed." Her head cocked, and she came closer, leaning toward him a bit. "Do you hold to Asbaran's hatred of aliens, and my race, in particular?"

"No," Rick repeated. "I can see how some do, though; your people did glass an entire country."

"I wasn't involved in that, and neither was my clan."

"I understand. To answer your question, I'm not too thrilled with the Pushtal specifically, but I hold no ill feelings about aliens in general."

"In the interest of full disclosure," Sergeant T'jto said, "I know Captain Holland of the *Coronado*. He contacted me about you yesterday, just after he docked." Rick stared, his mouth agape. "He also relayed the story of your valiant efforts against the Pushtal raiders."

Rick turned to look at Johansson in confusion. "And you let me sit here and tell the entire story?"

She gave a sly smile and shrugged elegantly. "Yes, I did. You see, traders have a habit of embellishing their tales and exploits. Hearing it from the Equiri's mouth was preferable." Rick ground his teeth and narrowed his eyes. "Relax. We want to advance your application."

"Meaning?" he asked.

"Meaning," T'jto said, "come back tomorrow morning for some tests, and we'll see."

"Fair enough," Rick said. "Thanks for giving me a shot." Johansson gave him a chit with appointment information and Rick turned to leave.

The two mercs watched him leave, then Johansson spoke. "What do you think?"

"I believe he is young, but worth a try," T'jto admitted.

"I agree. What about the other Human, Jones?"

"He seems competent," T'jto said. "His records indicated employment terminated with the Horde, but not a reason."

"That's probably not good," Johansson said, "or he wouldn't have traveled to Karma to find work."

"You might well be correct." She turned her heart shaped head toward the door. "Well, we shall find out more about this Mr. Culper tomorrow."

"We already know he's tough," Johansson said, "that laser scar was a hair's breadth from being lethal."

"It takes more than an ability to soak up damage to be a merc with the Hussars," T'jto reminded her and left. Out in the reception area she spoke to Jennifer. "Are there anymore today?"

"The Oogar got in an argument over the application and left," the receptionist said. "That only leaves…wait, where did it go?"

"Who?" T'jto asked.

"I'd swear there was another applicant." She screwed up her face in concentration. T'jto was far from an expert on the expressive Human faces and their meanings, but she knew enough to know that Jennifer was confused. "I guess I was wrong. A few have come in and left without filling out an application."

"Very well," T'jto said, "we will continue tomorrow morning. Corporal Johansson will handle primary interviews. The rest of my squad and I will be conducting follow-up evaluations on the five candidates who are not experienced."

"I understand," Jennifer said and made some notes as T'jto left. A short time later as she was working to secure the office for the afternoon, she found one of the questionnaire slates sitting on a chair. Her mind tried to come to grips with a memory of someone sitting there with the slate, but as she thought about it the memory fell apart. When she thought about it, all she saw was a hole where that person had been, as if there was nothing at all there. A true nothing. She felt dizzy.

"I'm working too hard," she grumbled and picked up the slate to return it to her desk. She was so busy trying to figure out why she felt so strange, Jennifer never noticed the extra ID card disappearing from her desk drawer.

* * * * *

Chapter Twenty

The next morning Rick rose early, showered, and headed for his meeting with the Winged Hussars. Unlike the offices in the high gravity area of the 2nd ring, this appointment took place in the more industrial 1st ring. It turned out the Winged Hussars had a small complex there, including several warehouses, maintenance shops, and a small training area down by the central shaft in zero gravity.

Rick arrived at the office right on time and was met by Sergeant T'jto. It reminded him of an office that had been thrown up on top of a warehouse, and, once inside, he saw he was right. The windows overlooked a floor filled with rack after rack of goods of all kinds.

"Right on time," T'jto said and nodded her head.

"That's a lot of stuff," Rick said and gestured out the window.

"We like to keep supply caches in various places. This is a small one, but serviceable." Rick shook his head.

"How many are there like that?"

"In the galaxy?" T'jto asked, and Rick nodded. "I don't know, maybe 20 or more? They're strategically located so a Hussars' ship is never more than a transition away."

"You people like to be prepared."

"It's a central tenet of the Winged Hussars, going back to the beginning. Plan, prepare, strike! That's the company motto. You can't exactly prepare if you don't have supplies around." Rick thought about how expensive it must be to have dozens of such caches around the galaxy. "Shall we proceed with your evaluations?"

Rick spent the morning with four other Humans going through a series of physical tests, which varied from simple dexterity and strength, to familiarity and comfort with Union technology. He only struggled with the physical endurance part of the test. He figured it was the combination of spending so much time in space and an incomplete recovery from his injuries.

Sergeant T'jto and two Human assistants reviewed the data and then provided them with lunch, a selection of roast beef, turkey, and tuna sandwiches. They were even offered Earth-manufactured sodas or beer.

During lunch, Rick chatted with the other four applicants. Three were men, one from the United States, like himself, one from France, and another from Australia. The final one was a Canadian woman named Lynn Jordan. He hadn't run into many female mercs since his time with Mickey Finn. They all had deployment experience. He was the only one who'd never fought as a merc; however, none of the others had marine training like he had.

"How'd you end up here?" Jordan asked when the other three men left to use the restrooms. "I mean, we're here because we stayed here after we left our companies. But you've never been out on a contract. It's not cheap to fly here from Earth."

Rick nodded and shrugged. "I worked my way here on a freighter." She looked at him with an appraising eye. "There were no jobs for inexperienced mercs on Earth—a down time, I guess—so I came here." He shrugged.

"Resourceful," Lynn said.

"Desperate," Rick countered. Sergeant T'jto skittered into the room to see the two of them laughing. They both stopped when they saw her.

"Did I interrupt some sort of Human mating ritual?" she asked. Both Rick and Lynn blushed, then laughed. T'jto cocked her head and regarded them with her huge eyes. "Please report for the next step of evaluation," she said and instructed them where to go.

They went together and rode a glideway down to the hub and into a zero-G work area. When they arrived at the Hussars facility, they found six CASPers waiting for them. Rick blinked when he saw them, gleaming in silver and gold paint, with the Winged Hussars logo on their shoulders.

"Mark 8 suits," he said as he floated over to examine one. There wasn't a nick in the paint, a ding in the armor, or any signs of repairs. "They look new," he said.

"That is because they are." Rick looked over and saw a small reptilian elSha perched on one of the CASPers, a slate sized to his race's use held in one dexterous hand. "I'm Kleena, chief armorer and development specialist for the Hussars." Rick and Lynn both said hello. "My two assistants here are T1 and T2." A pair of red chitinous heads poked out of the armor suit Kleena was perched on. They had dangerous looking pinchers, tiny black eyes, and waving antenna. Rick had never seen Jeha before. One slithered its entire long length out, gripping the suit with a multitude of tiny legs that each ended with a pointy pincher. They resembled millipedes, but ones that were four feet long. "And Sato is the Human genius that keeps us busy."

"I prefer evil genius," the man said. He floated amidst a swarm of mechanical parts and tools. He was young, and Rick guessed no more than 20 or so, probably Japanese based on the name and appearance. His head was shaved, and he had pinlinks clearly visible. Only, he had a third one over his left eye in addition to the ones above and behind his ear. That was something Rick had never seen before. He was dressed in rather common-looking coveralls, except they were covered in dozens of pockets. "Are you the new recruits?" he asked.

"That's us," Lynn said. Rick nodded.

"Want me to add some special modifications to these suits for you?"

"Say no," Kleena said without looking up from his work. Sato looked askance at the reptile and started assembling the parts. Rick leaned closer and whispered to Lynn.

"He can't be any older than I am."

"You'd be surprised how old I am," Sato said without looking. "I'm older than Captain Cromwell." Rick thought the Hussars commander was at least forty. "I know, doesn't make sense, does it?"

"Can you read minds?" Rick asked. Sato stopped in mid-assembly of his device and his eyebrows furrowed.

"I've never tried," he said. "Let me think about that." And he went back to work.

"Don't forget the evil part," Kleena said. A moment later Corporal Johansson floated in. She immediately noticed Sato floating in the middle of his constellation of parts and tools.

"What are you doing here?" she asked, then addressed Kleena. "You didn't let him fuck with the suits, did you?"

"No," the elSha said. "We don't want to kill the fresh meat before it's had a chance to sign on the dotted line." Both Rick's and Lynn's eyes got wide.

"Don't listen to our armorer," Johansson said. "We call this crew the Geek Squad. A necessary evil, to keep us ahead of the game in the merc world."

"Is that what we're doing?" Sato asked. He'd finished assembling the device and Rick was surprised to see it was just a little maintenance robot. They were everywhere in Karma Station. They could move along on four legs, had a pair of arms for repair and cleaning functions, and a set of ducted fans for maneuvering in zero-gravity areas. Sato deftly reached out, touched the robot, and it came alive. Its fans whined as it oriented, spun about, and shot away. In a moment, it was gone.

"Sato," Johansson said, "what did you do to that robot?"

"Oh, nothing much," Sato said as he stowed his tools in his pockets. Johansson looked from Sato in the direction of the departed robot, and her mouth became a thin line.

"We don't own any of those," she said. Sato didn't respond. Having finished putting away his tools, he now had a slate out and was doing something with it. Johansson sighed and floated over next to Rick and Lynn. "Are you two ready for your next tests?"

Rick and Lynn were quickly fitted into two of the CASPers. Lynn did hers faster, while Rick struggled a bit. He'd never worn a MK 8 before. It was a tighter fit, and some of the connections were different. The biggest advantage he realized immediately was that the MK 8 had sensors built into the machine's limbs and torso that took direct readings, and the helmet had a sensory halo that could read many of the Human nervous system's muscular control impulse commands. This worked in concert with the haptic suit to provide much more precise, and dependable feedback. It was possible to operate the unit without a haptic suit at all if necessary, at least somewhat. He was immediately impressed with how much more advanced it was than the Mk 7 he'd trained on.

Once they were suited up, Johansson donned one as well. Hers was obviously used, though in top condition. 'Corporal Johansson' was stenciled in green paint on the suit's torso. Rick and Lynn went through a few minutes of orientation in the suits, then Johansson led them into the next room, where they found a large, empty, million-cubic-foot warehouse. A few crates were locked to points on the wall, and a few more floated around.

"Okay," Johansson said as she moved to the center of the space using her CASPer's maneuvering jets with expert control. "Let's see how fast you get to the other side. GO!" she yelled.

Rick was a bit surprised when the corporal yelled, and he hesitated. Lynn didn't, and she shot away on a short blast of her main jumpjets. Rick ground his teeth together and did the same, though with less of a push. He knew she'd beat him, but suspected it might not work out in her favor. Besides, the Mk 8 felt like it massed about 200 pounds less than the Mk 7. He wanted to be careful until he got the feel of the lighter, more maneuverable suit.

When Rick was halfway across the room, he used the little maneuvering jets to flip. On marine equipped suits, they were basically compressed-gas nozzles. His was equipped with 24 of them, scattered around limbs and torso. He reoriented and used the suit's variable HUD, its heads-up display, to check his position and proximity to the wall in time to see Lynn not brake in time and smack into the wall.

Rick pulsed his jumpjet carefully, bent his knees, and landed on the wall perfectly. He engaged his suit's magnetic grapples as soon as he made contact and expertly caught the flailing Lynn by a leg and pulled her back down next to him.

"Thanks," she said, but he could tell she was less than thankful.

"Anytime," he replied, glad she couldn't see his ear-to-ear grin.

Over the next hour, Johansson ran them through drills. Rebounding jumps, sliding along walls, simulated weapons' fire while flying and dodging moving crates, running along a wall/floor/ceiling using the controls of the magnetic grapples. She finished with a little hand-to-hand. The only time Rick came up short was in the hand-to-hand portion. Corporal Johansson was way more familiar with the smaller, lighter suits. Rick kept trying to use the suit's mass as an advantage, only to be beaten by judo-style throws and redirects. He had to admit, Johansson was a master with the Mk 8.

"You have to get used to the fact that the Mk 8 isn't the powerhouse the Mk 7 was," she said as they were climbing out of the suits. Lynn was quiet, obviously chaffing under the fact that the much-younger Rick had shown her up time and time again. "And Jordan, you're doing fine, considering you aren't marine-qualified like Culper here." The other woman nodded, though she still looked upset. "I'm going to put you two in the same squad so you can learn from each other's strengths."

"That's fine with me," Lynn said.

"What?" Rick asked.

"You don't want to work with her?" Johansson said.

"No, I mean, that's it? I'm in?"

"Of course," the corporal said. "Do you think you'd get to play with brand new suits if it was just a test?" Rick scratched his head, a big grin breaking out on his face. "Rookie," Johansson said, then laughed. Rick blushed but laughed anyway. "Yeah," she added; "we want to offer you a two-year contract. Welcome to the Winged Hussars."

* * *

Alexis cursed and dropped the slate onto her desk. She was in the Hussars office in the 2nd ring, where she'd been stuck for three weeks since their arrival in Karma. It was supposed to have been a couple days' stop to resupply, hire new personnel, and conduct a few repairs. Most of those objectives had turned to shit in rapid order. The reactor servicing facilities of the station were booked for the next month, minimum. Even the mechanics to help finish refitting the marine compartments were overbooked. Guylan and his DC teams had some help, but not enough. Everything was taking three times longer than it should.

As for hiring, there weren't nearly as many employable personnel as she'd like to have seen. Her encounter with Gukkal shortly after arriving had critically altered her thoughts on hiring people quickly and getting out of there. They needed to choose carefully. That meant more time to review candidates. Instead of waiting for the reactor-servicing contractors on Karma to come loose, she'd cleared Commander Long to take Reactor Two down to see if he could repair it. She'd just finished reading his preliminary report when her pinplant chirped for her attention.

"Cromwell," she said/thought.

"Captain, it's Breta from stores."

"Go ahead, Breta," she said. She only knew the Cochkala by name because earlier that morning she'd set him to figuring out why the needed parts to finish repairs on the marines' decks weren't aboard yet.

"I found the problem," he said. "Logistics screwed the Zuul. Four pallets of interior fittings should have been put on a transfer shuttle to *Pegasus* yesterday, instead I found them in Warehouse Three down in Bartertown."

"What the fuck?" Alexis growled.

"It was our Karma Station logistics head of staff," Breta explained. "A specialist named Sommerkorn." Alexis frowned. *Now where had she heard that name before?*

"You're certain?" she asked.

"The orders were logged with his access ID," Breta confirmed. "I'll unscrew it," he promised.

"You do that," Alexis said and immediately called Wendy on the intercom.

"Yes, Captain?"

"Can you come in here for a moment?"

Wendy appeared in a couple of seconds. "Yes, ma'am?"

"Who the fuck is this Sommerkorn?"

Wendy sighed and bowed her head before replying. "I hired him, ma'am," she said dejectedly. "About a week before you got back. We needed a new logistics head after another company hired ours. Sommerkorn turned up on Karma looking for work."

"You just hired some moron? Wendy, that doesn't sound like you."

"I ran him through the guild, Captain," she said, her cheeks coloring. "He's worked for Cartwright's and Asbaran, with letters of recommendation from both. I'm sorry, I didn't notice at the time he only had a few weeks with each."

Shit, Alexis thought; one of those perpetual fuckups who kept getting passed around. "I'd be lying if I said I wasn't disappointed," Alexis said, and told Wendy about the misplaced shipment. She'd been digging with her pinplants ever since talking with Breta. She was finding Sommerkorn's ID all over transfers that went the wrong way, or never arrived. Her eyes narrowed as she wondered if he was working for someone else. "Is he incompetent?" Alexis asked.

"No, he's pretty good, but too detail-oriented. That and he's been space sick since he got here. The logistics office is in the hub." Space sick, Alexis thought. Then she remembered where she'd seen him. He'd been in the employee lounge, looking like warmed-over shit. "No excuse, ma'am. I'm sorry." Though she wasn't in the Hussar's combat arm, the girl stood almost at attention, ready for whatever her boss decided to do.

"It's okay, Wendy. Even the best of us screws up occasionally. Terminate him. Note the mistakes in his permanent file, and specifically note he is not suitable for space duty."

"Yes, ma'am." She could tell Wendy felt sorry for him.

"Give him an extra month's pay."

"I will, and thanks." Wendy left again, and Alexis moved on to other work. She only got a few minutes before her communicator buzzed again.

"Captain," Sergeant T'jto said. "We have filled out all three squads. I'm sending you the info now." She felt the data arrive in her pinplant and with a thought, sent it to her slate. She'd never been a natural at sorting and reviewing lists in her mind. Her sister, on the other hand...she squelched that line of thought and began reviewing the new marines.

"Wow," she said after a moment. "After three weeks, this is the best you could do? Out of fourteen new hires, five have never been in a combat unit or seen action."

"Yes ma'am," her command sergeant replied.

"I'm not filled with confidence, Sergeant."

"It gets better, Captain, read on." She scanned beyond service stars and noted races.

"Good grief," she moaned. "*Two* Oogar?"

"They've veterans," the sergeant said, "and they both have marine experience."

"Two Zuul, one a rookie. And you put them both in Raptor Squad?" The Zuul were like big fluffy dogs, but they were easy to get riled up and hard to reason with.

"Their race works better in groups. I put them under Sergeant Jones. We got him after the Horde let him go." That might or might not be a good point, Alexis thought, remembering Sommerkorn.

"And where in the hell did you dig up a Lumar?" While the huge, seven-foot-tall humanoids were immensely strong and notoriously difficult to kill, they were also about as smart as a malfunctioning missile.

"He's got a service record from several freelance companies. It's the first time he's worked for Humans, but I did his interview myself. He'll make a good heavy entrance specialist. I put him under our new Zenith Squad commander, Sergeant Leshto." A Veetanho, Alexis noted. Paka would be glad to hear that. There were no others of her kind aboard the *Pegasus*. She kept looking and found more gems.

"A Pushtal? Did you run his records thoroughly?"

"Yes," the sergeant replied, "twice actually. No recorded instances of piracy and no accusations of wrongdoing. He's one of the most experienced marines I hired, so I put him as corporal under Leshto."

"And an elSha. I don't think I've ever seen more than a few in a combat arm."

"She's an interesting type," T'jto admitted. "Not much for weaponry, but cool under fire and one of the best code breakers and encryption specialists I've seen. I had Afeeko go over her qualifications, and he said she was top shelf." Alexis shrugged. If Afeeko thought someone was good at something, she was more than willing to listen.

"I see you spread out the inexperienced personnel among all three squads, except for Dragon, where you only put one."

"I didn't want to slot in more than one with my squad because of Oort," the MinSha sergeant admitted. Alexis could see that. She looked at the list one last time. To think, a few minutes ago, all she was worried about was one slightly-unbalanced Tortantula. The Oogar, Pushtal, and a pair of Zuul ought to make things quite interesting down on Deck 30.

"Okay," she said finally, "it is what it is. Guylan informs me the repairs on your deck are effectively completed, minus those misplaced fixtures. You won't have a lot of privacy yet. Go ahead and move your new people aboard and start getting them familiar with *Pegasus*. I want them ready to rock and roll ASAP. We've been here too long already."

"You're expecting trouble, ma'am?"

"What have we had the last few months, except trouble?" She cut the connection and sighed. Transferring the new personnel list to her master, she added it to the message update going to Home that afternoon via courier and turned back to other matters. Just in time to get called again.

"What," she grumbled over her pinlink.

"It's Long," her chief engineer said. The Jeha was blunt, as usual.

"Go ahead, chief."

"We finished the reactor survey. Transmitting results." She sent the new file to her slate and examined it. More bad news. "As you can see, nine of the 70 containment buffers have been damaged. They still work, or we would possibly have lost containment, but I don't know how two of them are. In addition, the main pressure vessel is compromised."

"How long for repairs?" she asked.

"Without assistance from the reactor specialists here, forever. I can replace some of the buffers, but I'd have to open up the engineering section to get at all of them. I can't fix the pressure vessel. It might be possible to do it here, or back in the yard at Home, but not by myself. It's a one-piece woven carbon/nanobond. That missile detonation screwed up the release mechanisms for the buffers, and severely stressed the pressure vessel. Another few feet inboard, and it would have punched right into the reactor, and you'd have had a 40-foot-wide hole in the side of the ship where Reactor Two used to be. The Karma specialist companies keep saying they'll be available in another week."

"They've been saying that for more than two weeks already," Alexis grumbled. "Okay," she said, "replace the buffers you can get to."

"Why bother?" he asked, the clicks audible over the translation. "The two buffers I can't fix are working through an act of deity alone."

"Because we don't have a choice. Is the pressure vessel intact?"

"It leaks," he said, and Alexis flinched. A leaking pressure vessel meant loose plasma. "On standby, just a trace amount. Under power, who knows? It might be a trickle; it might be a geyser! Shit, the vessel could just rupture under power and—"

"Yeah, I know," Alexis interrupted, "that same 40-foot hole you mentioned earlier. Still, a questionable reactor is better than a collection of strapped-down parts. Get to it."

"Yes, Captain." Once more, she went back to work, and just like before, she was interrupted after only a few minutes.

"Captain?" It was Paka, onboard the *Pegasus.*

"Go," she said impatiently.

"A Bakulu scout just arrived in-system."

She sat up as her XO sent the data feed. The Bakulu had plenty of ships around the galaxy; however, as she reviewed the sensor logs Paka sent, what caught her attention was quickly evident. The ship wasn't approaching the planet, the station, or heading for the stargate to move on. It was hovering near the emergence point. Damn, Alexis thought; that's not good.

"Call the senior staff together tomorrow morning," she said. "I want a meeting to discuss our options for departing Karma in the next 72 hours. Maybe as soon as 48."

She began to work out a detailed plan, but after a few minutes she gave up and decided to go for a drink. She needed to get out of the office for a few hours. She called Paka and a shuttle arrived with a few marine guards and Paka herself. Several hours later, she was riding back to the ship, chewing over further developments.

She'd met the new commander of Cartwright's Cavaliers, just returned from an assault contract. Jim Cartwright was barely 19 years old. She'd met him years ago when he was a young boy accompanying his charismatic father, Thaddeus, on a contract. The Cavaliers had taken heavy losses, including their older model ship, captained by Reginald Winslow. Winslow was well known in the space-based merc community. She'd tried to pry him away from Cartwright's a decade ago and failed; that was unfortunate. It wasn't the losses, in particular, that interested her, but rather what they'd encountered on the contract.

"A Canavar," she thought. Monsters of legend no one had seen in thousands of years. And the Cavaliers had managed to acquire a couple of working Raknar, the giant robots used against the Canavars in that cataclysmic war of destruction which gave birth to the Union eons ago. They'd been the only weapons known to be effective against Canavars...besides orbital nuclear bombardment, of course. And somehow, that 19-year-old kid had figured out what no one had been able to do in thousands of years—he'd used a Raknar in combat, and won.

Alexis had sent Jim Cartwright and the other Horsemen a message weeks ago, before the whole incident with the Peacemaker, warning them that something strange was going on. An outpost she'd encountered in a contract had been destroyed, despite seriously reinforced defenses. The damage was too convenient, too extensive. None of them had apparently gotten the message. Her suspicions were even greater now.

She'd sold Jim Cartwright the *Bucephalus* back at twice what the Hussars paid for it, 10 credits. What need did she have for an *Akaga*-class cruiser stripped of most of its offensive capabilities anyway? Canavar, Raknar, conveniently-timed contracts, mounting losses; they were all pieces of a puzzle.

She considered sending yet another message to the Horde and Asbaran, then decided against it. The first message never reached the other Horsemen. *Someone is intercepting our communications*—it was the only reason possible.

When a message was sent, it often took a dozen different paths to get to its destination. Lacking direct faster-than-light communications, messages were given to a number of ships heading in the same direction. When one finally reached the destination, the computers that handled those messages noted its arrival, and all other versions were deleted as they arrived. Otherwise, you'd get the same message a dozen times as ships arrived at different times, having taken different routes. News and GalNet updates propagated in similar ways. All of this was handled by the Information Guild.

Many never gave the Information Guild a second thought. They were as ubiquitous as the old Post Office of Earth. Drop a letter in the slot and forget about it. Their charter from the Union kept messages and data flowing in an uninterruptable form across the galaxy. Even when regional conflicts broke out, messages would still reach their destinations, often carried by the combatants. You could blockade ship traffic in a system, but not data.

Ships arriving in a system instantly transmitted data packets to the stargate which then relayed them onwards to outbound ships and through every GalNet node installed on the system's worlds. The Information Guild saw to that, and the Cartography Guild did its part. The fine print of passage through a stargate included your consent to move data packets. Data packets which were massively encrypted and said to contain gigabytes of false data as well. Yet despite all of this, her messages had somehow never reached their destinations.

She'd typed up an inquiry to send to the Information Guild and had almost sent it when she stopped. How could a message like hers have been stopped? Only one entity could interfere with messages, but their charter with the Union stated they were never do that. Ever.

If the Information Guild was *stopping that communication, it must mean there is something in it they don't want to go out. And that means they're reading them,* she thought. *And if they've read that message, they've read them all.* The algorithms used by the Information Guild were the standard encryption key used on messages. Sure, the Hussars had their own encryptions, but any encryption can be broken, with enough computing cycles. And who had more computing cycles than the Information Guild? They had the proverbial keys to the kingdom, and apparently were using them. *That's a hell of a risk they're taking,* she continued thinking; *if word ever got out that the Information Guild was intercepting and decrypting messages from the Mercenary Guild, the shit would hit the fan in a most spectacular manner.*

Would the Union revoke a guild's charter? She wondered if that had ever happened and didn't know the answer. What was the Union, except the guilds? Seven powerful guilds held the balance of power within the Union, none more powerful than the other, at least on paper. Sure, the mercenary guild had armies at its beck and call, but the Cartography Guild could just deny them the use of the stargates. Or the Information Guild could refuse to move messages. The Trade Guild could refuse to move your goods, and the Merchant Guild might not allow you to manufacture those goods. It went on and on, a mutually-assured cooperation pact. *Mutually-assured,* she thought. *One guild wouldn't do something that could bring about retribution from another guild unless they were in agreement.*

Her mind kept circling back to that undelivered message. Months had passed. Months that should have taken that message from one end of the galaxy and back again more than once. Months that meant whoever had gotten her messages knew everything that was happening within the Hussars, from their organization to contracts.

Alexis came to a decision. She didn't know what was going on, but something was. Something dire enough for one or more guilds to conspire against her. If they'd intercepted her messages, they could do much, much worse. Maybe send killers to get her. Or to get her people. Task Force Two.

She didn't immediately share any of this with Paka. After the XO returned to *Pegasus,* Alexis went to her office and accessed the desk's built-in, standalone computer. Using that, she prepared a message that would appear as nothing more than routine comms traffic to anyone other than a captain in the Winged Hussars or above. Once it was prepared, she saved it as a draft on her personal slate, and deleted the original. It wasn't time to send that message, yet. She wasn't sure just how far down the rabbit hole this plot went, or if it was all in her imagination. For now, she needed to concentrate on getting them out of Karma as soon as possible.

* * * * *

Interlude

27 Years Ago

Winged Hussars Prime Base

New Warsaw System

"Second born, second place!" Alex growled as she fought to make the shuttle do what she wanted it to, despite all the safety interlocks designed to stop her.

The path through the debris field was chaotic, making it an ideal place for the twins to do insane things where none of their teachers could see.

"You're going too fast," Alex yelled over the radio to Kat.

"Scared?" Kat replied. Alex was terrified. They'd played these games many times, but always at relatively low speeds. A mistake with the shuttles at slow speeds and the shields would protect the ship, but they were going more than 5,000 feet per second relative to the debris now. That gave them very little time to plot a course and make the maneuvers required to avoid it. It also meant a solid hit on a sizeable chunk of space garbage would turn them into more space garbage. On her tracking screen the other shuttle pulled a little further ahead. Alex growled and increased her speed another hundred feet per second. "That's more like it, little sister!" A second later, Kat clipped a large chunk of debris.

Alex saw the flash of discharged energy from the shuttle's shields on her screens. It would have been intense enough to be visible with the naked eye, if the shuttles had possessed windows. The flattened bullet-shaped shuttles had retractable wings and were made for efficient movement of freight and personnel in the New Warsaw system. Also, because of the nature of their private star system, they had shields to protect against all the junk.

The other ship skewed and bounced off a second hunk of garbage, spinning wildly.

"Kat!" Alex screamed. All that came back was wild laughing. The other girl fired her engines, skewed her movement at the last instant, and bounced off a third piece of trash. While it put her back on course, the delay let Alex catch up and pass her.

"Not going to stop and help your older sister?" Kat's mocking voice came over the radio.

"Fuck you," Alex snarled.

Kat pushed her shuttle, but the impacts had damaged the craft, as well as severely depleted the shields. She wasn't crazy enough to pass that invisible line. Alex soared through the huge hole in the middle of a hulking dreadnought a full second before her sister. The two pulled up and out of the debris field.

"Impressive, little sister."

"You are crazy," Alex snapped, "you almost died!"

"Almost only counts for nuclear missiles and EMPs."

"Echo One, Echo Two, report!" barked an authoritative voice over the radio.

"Good job," Kat said, "you got us in trouble again!"

"You bitch!"

"Cut the chatter," the instructor said. "I cut you two loose for 10 minutes of free flight and you go screw around in a debris field? You're grounded! Report back to base immediately."

An hour later they were standing in front of the flight academy director for the Winged Hussars. Both stared straight ahead without showing any emotion. They'd had plenty of practice at this.

"Explain yourself," the director ordered. Despite only being a little over two feet tall, and a lizard, he could be frightening.

"We got carried away," Kat said.

"You know how it is," Alex agreed.

"Jivool-shit!" the director chirped, slapping a hand on his desk. Both girls jumped a little. He pointed at Alex. "Your shuttle has impact damage!"

"That was my shuttle," Kat said. The director looked flustered and changed colors several times in his rage. The twins were hard enough to tell apart by Humans; to most aliens they might as well be the same person. It had given their instructors fits. Both girls giggled.

"Enough!" he yelled. "You two think because your mom owns the place, I won't flunk you?" Both girls thought about saying yeah, that was right, but Alex thought better of it before her sister pushed the reptile too far.

"No sir," Alex said. "Besides, you wouldn't do that, because we're the best pilots you've ever taught!" The director's eyes focused on both at the same time, a disconcerting thing for most Humans. "Would you?"

"I could ground you for a year; how would that sit? Send you back to the planet. Your mother would be thrilled to see you'd gotten thrown out of school again." Both girls flushed and looked down. They were incredibly light-skinned, and their white hair made it worse. That little mutation was rare in Humans in space, and it set the girls out instantly as space-born. "But I won't, because you're right. You are both gifted beyond reason. Thirteen-year-old Humans have no business being better pilots than their Bakulu instructors. Still, rule-breaking cannot be tolerated." They'd both started to smile. His last statement wiped the grins from their faces.

Later that night, they were mopping the floor of an abandoned hallway in the base. Prime Base was miles on a side, slowly rotating at a LaGrange point between Home and the stargate. Thousands of the Hussars' personnel and family lived there, and there was room for a thousand times more. The girls had spent years exploring the far reaches of the ancient station. Their collective knowledge of Prime Base was more extensive than anyone in the Hussars. Compared to *Pegasus,* it was a planet unto itself.

Mopping empty hallways was a common punishment for them. After the first few times escaping their punishment to explore, the teachers had assigned robots to watch over them. The girls had reprogrammed the computers to do the cleaning and had disappeared anyway. Now a senior student oversaw them. The academy only had two hundred students from among the Hussars and their dependents; the older boy was not happy to be watching the Anarchy Twins.

"How did you pull that off?" Alex asked when she was sure the senior was watching his slate and not them.

"What?"

"That maneuver, the ricochet off the piece of junk?" Her sister looked at her with a mischievous grin. "Tell me, damn it." Kat tapped her head. "Trying to say you're smarter than me? You're not." They both knew Alex tested slightly higher on mental tests, while Kat was slightly stronger and had faster reflexes.

"No, stupid." The senior glanced at them, and they shut up. He was huge compared to them, and like most of the other students, jealous as hell of the boss lady's two child prodigies. At 13, most kids weren't old enough to join the academy for another two years. He looked back at his slate and Kat brushed her hair back away from her ear and touched her pinlink.

"What did you do?" Alex asked.

"I hacked the autodoc when we got our last upgrades!"

"You didn't?" Kat grinned hugely. The girl had been absolutely fascinated with pinplants since they were little. When they'd gotten planted two years ago, it was the happiest day of her life. Alex had been ambivalent about the brain-implanted sensor leads, and she had only been excited about it because it meant they could start their flight training. Frankly, Alex was more excited about her growing bust line, and the attention it was getting her from older boys. Kat must have done it when they got their motor cortex mods a couple weeks ago. "What did you get?"

"I got a full co-processor and 100 exabytes of storage," Kat said with a proud grin. Alex was both impressed and appalled. That level of modification was restricted for medical reasons. Doing it to a child was unethical and dangerous. The locations for the implants were inside the cranium, and movement as the cranial sutures closed could cause major complications.

"Why did you do that?"

"You saw me out there," Kat bragged, "and that's just the beginning. I've been dating a boy in medical. I'm going to eventually get his access code to the implanting autodoc and do even more!"

Alex didn't know what was worse, her fooling around with some older boy in the medical section, or doing it just to trick him and then have an unauthorized medical procedure done on herself. Her conscious told her which was worse.

"I'm going to tell mom," Alex said. Kat's head snapped around, her eyes flashing dangerously.

"You wouldn't dare," she hissed.

"Kat, you're being stupid. Those procedures are limited to adults for a reason!"

"Yeah, to keep us under their control. Alex, there are only a dozen Hussars with the level of pinplants I have now. After this next round, I'll be the one with the most."

"You won't because I'll tell." Kat shot hate at her. "Okay, I won't tell about what you have now." Her sister's eyes narrowed, and she got a little, smug smile on her face. "As long as you don't get any more."

"You can't stop me."

"No, but you'll wish I did. I swear by entropy I'll tell mom if you get one more."

"You two!" the senior barked. "Shut up and mop." Kat ground her teeth in rage, but Alex just shrugged and stared back.

"Fine," Kat said after a second, and looked away. Alex could feel the rage radiating from the other girl.

"Promise."

"Screw you."

"Promise, or else." Kat looked at her, and behind the anger Alex saw betrayal. Pain and betrayal. "That's the deal."

"Okay," Kat said with a little sigh. "I promise, no more implants."

"Good," Alex said, and went back to mopping. Of course, Kat broke her word only a few weeks later, and the sisters' relationship was never quite the same.

* * * * *

Chapter Twenty-One

Karma Station

Karma System

Rick finished securing the duffel bag which held all his worldly possessions to his seat with a strap and adjusted his buckles. It was the first time he'd rode in a ship designed with the nearly infinite shapes of aliens in mind. He had the feeling it could accommodate almost any race…and none of them would feel comfortable.

"All set?" He looked up to see a Human male floating down the middle isle of the shuttle, checking the passengers as he went. He was in the regular black uniform of the Winged Hussars, with a logo on his shoulder, and a nametag that said, "Southard."

"Yes, sir," Rick said.

"Just Larry is fine," the man replied. "Pilots like me are about the same rank as a corporal in the Hussars. I might outrank you, but only technically. Behave yourself, and I won't have to boss you around." He grinned at Rick who smiled back.

"You bet," Rick said. "How long is the flight?"

"Oh, *Pegasus* is parked just a few miles away. Once we get clearance, maybe 10 minutes. You aren't bothered by free fall, are you?" Larry glanced at Rick's brand-new uniform, but it didn't have any insignia yet. "I'm guessing you're one of the new marines?"

"Right in one," Rick said. "No, I'm fine in null gravity. I'm just eager to get aboard."

"Okay," the pilot said. "Won't be long." He nodded to Rick and floated along to check others. The big purple bears, the Oogar, were struggling with straps which were barely long enough for the aliens. Further forward, a strange four-armed humanoid who looked like an advertisement against gene therapy abuse appeared to be completely confused by both the seat and the belts.

"Mind if I sit with you?" Rick looked up and saw Corporal Johansson.

"No, ma'am," he said.

"Eva is fine when we're not in suits," she said. Rick gestured to the seat, and she quickly configured it, swung around, planted herself, and belted in. It only took a couple of seconds. "Excited to see the ship?"

"I got a look at it from the outside, on the way in, aboard the *Coronado,*" he explained, "but I'm looking forward to seeing more of it."

"We have launch authority," the pilot's voice came over the PA. "Prepare to detach."

The shuttle was clamped onto an unmoving central hub section of the huge Karma Station, one of hundreds of similar docking points. It was far easier than docking on the rotating sections, and made transferring crew and cargo immensely simpler. Southard released the mechanical docking collar and floated away on maneuvering thrusters. With a bump and a slight feeling of motion through the seat, they were clear. Toward the rear, the two Zuul yipped and panted excitedly.

"Prepare for slight acceleration," the pilot added. They were pushed back a bit as he gave the shuttle some power, and they were off toward their goal.

"How long have you been with the Hussars?" Rick asked his new corporal.

"Five years now," she said. "I served with Bert's Bees before. Didn't feel like that was going anywhere, so I ended my contract with them when we landed here. I was picked up by the Hussars a few weeks later."

"Have you always been on this ship?"

"I've only served on *Pegasus* for about five months. Before that I was on the battlecruiser *Sleipner*. And before that, I was in the Hussars rapid deployment force." Rick thought for a moment.

"Sorry about all the questions."

She made a dismissive gesture. "You're one of us now," she said, "ask away."

"How big are the Hussars?"

She smiled slyly at that, for some reason. "Well, I know we have more than 100 starships, and something like 20,000 paid personnel." Rick's head came around and his eyes bugged out. "Yeah."

"That's gotta be the biggest merc unit in the galaxy!"

"Not even close," she corrected. "Biggest Human-owned unit, even though Humans only make up about half of that. Have to, by guild law, or you can't be declared by that race. Anyway, there are alien merc units with over 100,000. I know, sounds crazy. But you must remember, there are no militaries like Earth has, or used to have. Mercs keep the peace, or break it sometimes. We're the only way races have of dealing with each other once diplomacy fails. Many never even try diplomacy, for that matter." She chuckled, and he shook his head. Merc humor. "I read once that there are about 20 trillion beings in the galaxy. That's an estimate, mind you. But only about 100 million total mercs. That's only one merc for every

200,000 civilians. On Earth, before first contact, the highest ratio was 22-1. The average was somewhere around 120-1. So you see, in the Union, the number is pitifully small."

Rick said he understood, but he was still trying to come to grips with the numbers. He'd known some of this from his schooling, though not to the extent Johansson had explained. He decided to give the corporal a break and took out his slate. Using it, he linked with the shuttle and got access to an external view. The shuttle's design was no nonsense, so there were no windows in the passenger area. Using the slate, he could see they were already closing on the *Pegasus.*

The ship was just as he remembered from his arrival at Karma. A long-tapered tube with bulges of gravity decks and weapons points. Now he could see the damage was gone, covered and patched with new hull plates. Quite a few small craft hovered near those repairs, likely still completing them. Most of the small craft were near the rear, around one of three bulges which had to hold the ship's massive fusion drives. Even from 1,000 yards away, Rick could see open access panels and the internals of the drive decks.

He was still struck by the unusual look of the *Pegasus.* She had none of the retractable rings, and lacked the graceful lines of other warships. Even the hangar deck, almost directly amidships, was simple and utilitarian.

"The *Pegasus* is different, isn't she?" Johansson asked, looking down at the view Rick had of the ship.

"Very," Rick agreed. "I haven't seen many warships up close, but none look like the *Pegasus.* Where was it made?"

"We didn't have it made," she explained. "We found it."

"I don't understand."

"You know the Winged Hussars are one of the Four Horsemen, so we go back to the Alpha Contracts just after first contact." He nodded and she continued. "The people who operated the Hussars got enough money to buy a little escort frigate and managed to secure a fleet operations contract. Big bucks, even back then, but like the rest of those contracts, we were basically set up. It turned into a rout and the Hussars ran for it with a crippled ship. The official story doesn't give a lot of details, only that they found the *Pegasus* in an asteroid field while hiding from pursuit. They got it running by gutting their ship, shot their way out, rescued some of the ships they were supposed to have been protecting, and made it home." She paused and then added, "*Pegasus* looks like it does because it's a pure weapon."

"It's like a big ugly sword," Rick said. "It's designed to do a lot of damage, and no one cares what it looks like."

"Yeah," Johansson said; "I guess you're right. Ask again and I'll tell you more about her sometime. Let's just say we shot our way out of a system a few weeks ago. I didn't see the fight, of course, but I've talked to those who did. We destroyed several battlecruisers and a bunch of frigates, and tore up a battleship."

"A battleship?" Rick said incredulously. She grinned savagely and nodded. "They're like 10 times as big as the *Pegasus*, right?"

"From what I hear. But Captain Cromwell is…gifted."

"Gifted, how?"

"Gifted in fucking up other people's shit," Johansson said.

Rick was glad he was on the Hussars' team. It sounded like the last place he wanted to be in the galaxy was fighting against them.

"We're landing in a minute," she added, "and I have to take care of a few things." She leaned her head forward and closed her eyes.

Rick recognized the look of someone concentrating on their pinplants and didn't ask any more questions. He just sat and watched as the shuttle closed in on the battlecruiser's docking bay and thought about what life was going to be like as a marine aboard *EMS Pegasus.*

* * *

From the moment he floated out of the shuttle and grabbed the guide rope to pull himself to the bay's personnel doors, Rick was on a non-stop rollercoaster of challenges. First, he had to learn the layout of the warship. Compared to some of the ships docked and floating around Karma Station, *Pegasus* seemed small. Once aboard, he found out 'small' was a relative term, based on experience and perception.

Johansson took her charges in hand and moved them to the nearest of four airlocks in the corners of the bay. This one stood open as the doors were closed and the bay pressurized once they'd landed. Rick gawked at the open doors on the other side of the huge transparent divider where spacesuited figures were floating around a small, open-sided shuttle under repair. He couldn't imagine the stresses that piece of glass or plastic must be under—it had to be at least 60 feet wide and 20 feet tall!

In the room adjacent to the lock was a gangway. One side went up, or toward the nose of the ship, the other down, toward the engines.

"There are vertical access shafts in all four corners," Johansson explained, using her fingers to make quotes around the word corners. "Two are gangways, like these; two are lifts. The lifts are reserved for movement of the ship's crew, not marines. We walk or float."

Rick was watching some of the other new hires and saw a wide variety of zero-gravity familiarity. The older Zuul was bouncing around with the same level of assurance as Johansson, while the younger one was slower and more cautious, making sure he had handholds at each movement. The pair of Oogar seemed as at home in space as on the ground. Same for the strange burly four-armed humanoid.

The gangways Johansson mentioned were ramps with non-slip surfaces. In zero gravity, their hand rails provided a quick way to move forward or aft. Under acceleration, they'd be easy to walk up or down (at one gravity), but probably impossible at higher gravities. Rick thought they were likely a bit steep for Humans at one gravity, and was reminded the ship wasn't designed by Humans. That also explained why the decks were so tall. Twelve feet was almost double what most Human ships used.

Johansson took them aft as a group. As they passed through decks, she explained some of the layout.

"The bay we landed in is Deck 21. As you can see, 22 and 23 are support and storage for flight operations. Here on Deck 24 are the hyperspace electronics and control system, and 25 houses the aft laser batteries." Rick got a glimpse of several mechanisms used to raise the laser arrays through openings in the hull. They were each several feet across, with massive power cables attached. "Each laser projector can produce a beam of 100 megawatts.

"Decks 26 and 27 are engineering spaces. Life support, water processing and recycling, waste management, and shield generators are just some of the systems centralized here." Each compartment they saw was crammed full of equipment. Rick thought a lot of it looked Human-manufactured, though just as much wasn't.

"Corporal," one of the Zuul spoke up, "how do you know so much about the ship's systems?"

"I'm glad you asked that," she said, bringing them to a stop on Deck 27. It was rather loud, with running equipment and a Human/elSha team working on an open electrical panel. "On *Pegasus*, the marines double as damage control assistants. Part of your training will include familiarization with the ship's major systems, as well as welding and other skills." Some of the new recruits looked interested; others, not so much. "Don't worry, we'll be evaluating your abilities to perform these tasks. Those who show interest and aptitude will receive further training. However, marines are usually the best trained at zero-gravity spacesuit operations, so we'll be the ones to help with exterior damage control. You'll all be more adept in a suit very quickly." She got them moving again.

"This is Deck 28, the aft missile battery, and below it is the magazine." The missile magazine was rack after rack of six-foot-long missiles in a serpentine handling system that fed through to the deck above. Rick could see the floor and ceiling were heavily armored. "And below us now is Deck 30, marine country. Welcome home."

"Right below the missile magazine," Lynn said from behind him, "damn."

"I'm sure you are all thinking how awesome it is being right behind the missiles," Johansson said and many of them nodded. "Well, the magazine isn't the best place to be, but keep in mind, like all the other decks, it's split into four sections and the walls are armored. In addition, the exterior bulkhead of each section has blow-out panels. In the event of a magazine detonation, all the force should be channeled outwards."

"Should be," Sergeant Jones, the new Raptor Squad sergeant said.

"Yeah," Johansson agreed; "they should be. Remember this, marines, there are over 400 people on this ship. The marines and our support personnel are only 25 of those. If the magazine takes us with it, the ship can still fight. Our space was originally filled with more missiles before it was refit." They entered the deck and saw it was, in fact, split into four sections, like most decks, and each section had an open catwalk framework separating it into two levels. "Each squad gets a section. The fourth section houses a training/equipment area, the commander's quarters, and the galley. Under the other three sections are a small gym, an armory, and a medical bay. We also have our own life support."

"We can dock boarding pods or a shuttle here," she explained. "The only other docking point for the ship is on Deck Four." Several people noticed the heavily-armored hatch in the ceiling. "And, yes, we help load missiles aboard when they come in." Rick was beginning to get the idea his job was a lot more than fighting, and he was glad he'd done his tour on the *Coronado.* The skills he had picked up would probably prove handy.

They floated down through the gangway into the galley on the lower level. The currently-serving marines were waiting for them. Rick came to a stop when he caught sight of a massive spider clinging to a wall opposite the ramp. Several others ran into him from behind.

"Holy shit," Lynn exclaimed when she caught sight of the Tortantula.

"Some of you have already met the commanding sergeant," Johansson said, "T'jto." The MinSha she'd addressed was holding onto a seat with a pair of her rear legs and watching the new arrivals. Someone behind Rick pushed him, and he cleared the gangway.

"Everyone find a place," Sergeant T'jto said, gesturing with her hands. It was crowded, but they managed, even though most didn't want to be too close to the huge hairy spider. For its part, the Tortantula seemed indifferent to the new arrivals. "As Corporal Johansson explained, I'm your commander. Normally I'd be a lieutenant; however, marines operate a little differently, so I'm just a sergeant, or command sergeant if more than one of us is around. I run Dragon Squad with Johansson as my second. We've added privates Culper and Jordan to our squad which includes veterans Oort and Jeejee," A little chipmunk-like Flatar grunted from where it was sitting next to the Tortantula, which Rick guessed was Oort. "As well as Zhkt, who we call 'Zit.'" Rick couldn't see the last member until Lynn tapped him on his shoulder and pointed. In the corner was a huge cockroach sharpening a knife. It regarded them with tiny eyes on short stalks.

"I've placed Stan Jones," she said and gestured to the man who nodded, "in charge of Raptor Squad with Corporal Jakal as his second." The older Zuul raised a hand. "With them are privates Bill Alvarado, Eskla," the younger Zuul waved, "Alan Bacord, and L'kto." With the last name, the other MinSha's antenna waved in a friendly manner.

"Zenith Squad will be run by Sergeant Leshto, with Corporal Meeroo as her second." A dark-furred Veetanho held up her hand, and a Pushtal gestured as well. Rick wasn't sure how he felt about serving with one of the felines, and he was secretly glad they weren't in the same squad. After the incident aboard *Coronado,* he was second-guessing his commitment to serving with aliens, especially with regard to Pushtals. "Rounding out Zenith are Privates Ed O'Neal, Klon and Dron," the two purple Oogar grinned hugely, "Godor," the four-armed humanoid grunted and looked around with a confused expression, "and Ifeeka, who is a technical like Jeejee." The elSha chirped in a friendly manner from where she was hanging on the wall. Rick noticed the cockroach named Zit eyeing the elSha.

"Sergeants," T'jto said, "take your squads and show them their quarters. In your quarters, you'll find your assigned equipment, including a slate with your new duty and training roster. When we're underway, we run eight-hour rotating shifts. In port, they're twelve hours to allow down time. Combat situations will vary. All other squads, dismissed. My new Dragons, follow me."

T'jto led Rick and Lynn to their quarters in Section Two. Their rooms were next to each other. Rick looked inside and found a space configured for Human use, about eight feet by five feet with a little desk and a fold-out chair. There was a small Tri-V projector and a slate sitting on the desk. Home sweet home.

"You two are bunked next to me," T'jto explained, "so any questions, just knock."

"Everything looks new," Lynn said, feeling the smooth, shiny metal fixtures.

"That's because it is. Not too long before you came, a missile destroyed almost the entire deck."

"Oh," Rick said. "Any casualties?"

"Yes," T'jto said, "all the marines except my squad." She turned and went into her quarters/office, leaving Lynn and Rick alone to think.

*****

Chapter Twenty-Two

The beds came equipped with the choice of nets or straps. Rick had always felt fairly at home sleeping in zero gravity, so he slid a strap over his legs and one over his abdomen, and he slept like a baby. The alarm woke him six hours later.

When he felt awake enough, he floated down to his section's bathroom and used the vacuum shower to clean off. He floated past Lynn in the hallway and nodded to her. As they were both naked, she would have been a sight to enjoy, but he showed no sign of noticing. Human mercs, like Human military, were fully integrated, and you didn't get far if you couldn't ignore the fun parts when you weren't off duty.

He got dressed in his quarters then grabbed his slate. His duty shift began in two hours, so he spent part of that time going over the ship's layout and basic organization. The crew was made up of 300 enlisted and 80 officers and senior enlisted, and the ship was divided into sections, depending on assignment and duties. There was no segregation of sex or species; any race that didn't get along, didn't stay. Discipline was handled on an escalating scale, depending on the offense. Failing to carry out assigned tasks could result in fines or the termination of your contract. Insubordination got you fired. Assault or directly disobeying orders that resulted in casualties or failure to complete a contract, could get you tossed out an air lock. Most merc units had capital punishment written into their employment contracts, though he'd heard it wasn't often carried out. Per the manual here, it was, and had been. He filed that away.

An hour before his duty time, he left and went to the galley. He was surprised to find an actual cook and not an autochef.

"Morning, private," a rail-thin man in his later years said. Morphagenic tattoos of women doing lewd acts danced on both arms, and humor flashed in his eyes. "Welcome aboard. Gabriel Ponzetti is the name, grub is my game. What can I do you for?"

"Morning Mr. Ponzetti, Rick Culper. Call me Rick."

"Gabriel is fine, or Gabe," the man said and took Rick's hand in a firm shake.

"How about an omelet?"

"Sure," Gabe said. "Ain't got no real eggs, but the synthetics are pretty good. The cheese is the real deal, made by a lady here in Karma. What do you want in it?"

"Meat. Earth veggies. Surprise me." The cook gave a sly grin and nodded.

"You betcha." He turned and began cooking. Rick could see the cooking unit was designed for zero gravity or acceleration. It was simple and efficient, like almost everything else on the ship.

"I was surprised to find out we have our own galley," Rick said as the man cooked.

"Main galley is up on Deck 12," he said and pointed up toward the nose. "The spacers don't like marines all that much, and it's about 300 feet between here and there." He cackled and shrugged. "I guess someone along the line decided it was less annoying to give us marines the convenience of our own grub-hub than having to see us tromp through their pretty ship three times a day."

"You're a marine?"

"Used to be. I served with the Hussars for 30 years before retiring. Too brittle to get folded into a suit anymore. Now I play backup pilot and cook for you kids."

"You weren't here when…" Rick looked around and made an explosive gesture with his hands.

Gabe laughed again. "No, I bunk up in the enlisted spaces. You folks only need me a few times a day. I prepare lunch and store it in the cooler. The rest of the time I help out in the hangars." More redundancy of duties, Rick realized. He wondered how big the crew would be if each member only did one job. While Gabe was finishing his meal, the other Humans new to the Hussars began arriving. Rick's meal was finished and delivered to him on a plate with a cover (so it didn't float around the room). Since Gabe now had several more customers, Rick floated to a table, hooked a foot through a strap on the deck and pulled himself down.

A short time later, he was joined by Lynn, then Bill Alvarado and Alan Bacord from Raptor Squad. Ed O'Neal, the only Human from Zenith Squad, also joined them. The Hussars had hired fifteen new mercs for the marine positions, yet only six were Humans. It felt strange that he'd be fighting with aliens instead of against them.

The group chatted while they ate, each one fishing into the container that held their food for bites or, in the case of Alvarado, opening the container and shaking some out to catch with his mouth. Lynn watched him for a minute with displeasure on her face. When a piece of egg got away from him, and he caught it with his left hand and scooped it into his mouth, she couldn't contain herself anymore.

"Didn't your mother teach you it's rude to eat like an animal?"

"Mother died when I was born," Alvarado said without looking up, his mouth full. He smiled open-mouthed as he chewed. "Why?"

Lynn ground her teeth and looked away. Alvarado laughed.

"Gabe make you all some good food?" Johansson asked as she floated in. Everyone said how much they were enjoying it, except Lynn who was staring at the wall. "He keeps us fat and happy."

"I try, Corporal!" Gabe said from the little kitchen. He was busy making sandwiches and storing them in small containers. Floating ingredients were plucked and utilized as needed. Johansson consulted her slate and spoke.

"Okay, we're going to break you up into two groups. First, I want O'Neal, Bacord, and Alvarado to head over to the armory to finish getting their CASPers fit. Jordan and Culper come with me to medbay." Everyone acknowledged, quickly swallowed their last bites of breakfast, and dropped the containers into the recycler on the way out.

The medical bay was located under Zenith Squad's bunks. It was a decent-sized setup with two examination tables and three recovery units. Rick recognized a slightly more advanced medbot than the *Coronado's*, in addition to a pair of ultra-modern medical nanite fabricators. What he wasn't prepared for was the medical staff. Johansson introduced them.

"This is our assigned physician, Dr. Gorge Ramirez. He's listed as second physician for the Hussars, and if we don't have medical problems here, he's up on Deck 14." The man was handsome and fit, looked to be in his forties, and was dressed in a white-accented version of the Hussars black uniform, with a caduceus logo on the arm opposite the Winged Hussar logo. "And this is his assistant, Nemo."

What Rick had assumed was a medical device full of liquid turned out to be a temporary habitat affixed to the upper deck. A mass moved inside and tentacles slithered out. The shape that resolved itself looked surprisingly like a large octopus, complete with a bulbous mantel with a pair of blue eyes. It flashed a bright and varying pattern of lights and colors, and a Human voice came from it.

"I am pleased to meet my new crewmates."

"I don't recognize your race," Lynn said, obviously fascinated.

"We are not common," the pulsing lights were rendered into speech, not by each crewman's translators, but by a device the being wore. "My race is known as the Wrogul by your race. We are not mercenaries by career, but instead ply a valuable trade in genetic cures and surgical techniques." Dr. Ramirez smiled and spoke.

"Nemo likes to joke it is more an instrument than a person, but the truth is it is an extremely accomplished surgeon and bioengineer. It has some amazing talents that have saved many crew's lives. Nemo probably knows more about alien physiology than anyone else in the galaxy. It's rare to find a Wrogul; they tend to stay on their planet or work in the Science Guild."

"It is true," Nemo admitted, "despite our natural affinity for new species and unusual lifeforms. Our bodies are fragile and the environments we can survive in limited, so we tend to be somewhat xenophobic." Rick thought that was an interesting combination, to be both an expert in various lifeforms and xenophobic at the same time.

"You're here because you are the only Humans we have who don't have pinplants," Dr. Ramirez explained. "The good news is you have one of the best beings you could ask for to do the procedure. The bad news is it isn't Human." He was straight-faced for a moment, then chuckled at what he thought was a great joke. Lynn and Rick weren't nearly as amused. "Who would like to go first?"

"I will," Rick volunteered. Lynn didn't object. He was led to the autodoc chair where he was strapped in and the sensors attached.

"We don't want you floating away during the procedure," Ramirez explained. "The anesthesia is entirely voluntary."

"Won't it hurt?" Rick wondered.

"You will feel nothing," Nemo assured him.

"That's what I'm afraid of," Rick said, and got a sympathetic look from Lynn. The problem was, he wasn't afraid. He logically knew he was about to have his brain modified, and that didn't bother him in the least. Rick wondered just how far fearlessness would go. Could he jump into a fusion plume without fear? "I'd rather not be anesthetized, then."

"Very well," Dr. Ramirez said. He floated around behind the chair, and Rick heard it come to life and respond to his controls. After a moment, he spoke again. "Nemo, we're ready."

The Wrogul had been floating near the center of the room, its huge eyes watching Rick. Upon hearing its name, the being's tentacles gathered in a mass, and, with a "Phfft!" of expelled air, Nemo propelled itself toward Rick and the autodoc. The medical assistant caught the chair with a wet slapping sound. In a moment, it had swung around behind Rick and out of sight.

Rick was about to ask what function the Wrogul had in the surgery when he felt something brush his hair. It felt a little like someone had blown a gust of air across his head, and he felt something wet against his scalp. Lynn caught his attention. Her eyes were bugging out of her head, and her mouth had fallen open. Rick felt a sensation inside his skull. A slight pressure and a feeling like his brain was moving by itself.

"Woah," Rick said as the room swung, and he suddenly knew what the number seven tasted like. "This is weird!" He heard wet sounds, and the inside of his skull itched. He was suddenly glad they'd tied him down.

"Oh…" Lynn gasped, her hand going to her mouth, "oh god!" Dr. Ramirez launched himself toward her with a plastic bag in hand. He wasn't quite quick enough.

* * *

Alexis arrived back aboard *Pegasus* under the watchful eyes of Zit and Jeejee. Even though the Flatar didn't have his Tortantula, he was still formidable enough on his own with his huge pistol. As formidable as a foot-tall chipmunk could be, anyway. Paka had said it was better to go low key, and the Goka and Flatar were the least flashy of the experienced marines. Least flashy, but also two of the most trigger-happy when things went sideways.

The shuttle wasn't piloted; instead, it was a drone cargo shuttle with only two seats folded down from the walls. She'd shared the space with the two marines and 40 tons of various consumables. Alexis wondered if that, too, was her XO being overly protective.

The shuttle magnetically clamped to the docking bay floor of *Pegasus,* and, as the hatch slid aside, the furred face of Paka was waiting.

"Status?" Alexis asked.

"We're still not ready to push off," the Veetanho said. "The last of the engineering spaces are being secured, and the tanker bringing reaction mass is due in an hour."

"I thought we were supposed to get fuel six hours ago."

"Everything has been behind schedule," Paka said.

Alexis cursed under her breath.

"<*Haste is of the essence. Something is happening*>" Alexis jerked and almost missed her grab for the rope leading from the shuttle to the bay access. She pushed, off, letting the rope slide through her hand as she activated her pinlink.

"What's happening?"

"<*Comms traffic in the system has subtly changed. Ships are slowly moving away from* Pegasus *for no obvious reason*>"

"Paka."

"Captain?" the XO asked, sliding along behind her.

"I want us ready to move as soon as absolutely possible."

Paka's whiskers twitched as she accessed her own pinlink, contacting the engineering and materials handling teams. As Alexis reached the bay doors, she had the answer. "Three hours, ma'am."

"Damn it," Alexis said and shot for the gangway. "As soon as I'm in CIC, get me Long in engineering."

Paka grimaced, but said she would. Chief Engineer Long was going to get an earful.

*****

Chapter Twenty-Three

Alexis soared into the CIC, expertly caught the back of her command chair, and flipped into it. She didn't bother strapping in; there was too much to do.

"Report!" One at a time, sections reported they were ready until they got to engineering. "Where is Long?"

"He's directly supervising the crew finishing up on Reactor Two," Guylan told her. Alexis' mouth became a thin line. She could feel every second ticking by.

"Start spinning up the other two reactors," she ordered.

"Most of the engineering crew is seeing to Reactor Two," Guylan reminded her.

"I'm aware of that, but the computer can handle a gradual power up."

"*<I will monitor the situation>*" Alexis activated her pinplant.

"Thanks," she replied. "I'm trying to get us out of here."

"*<I know, and I will help>*" Alexis' face was a mask of concern. She usually didn't get that kind of direct help unless things were dire.

"Tanker is alongside and reaction mass is transferring," the loadmaster reported via intercom.

"About damned time," Alexis snapped. Displays showed the tankage status, and reports were relayed as she sat in her seat, fingers tapping impatiently on the arm rest. Everything in her screamed to get away from the station, to put her ship under power so it wasn't a sitting duck. The Tri-V of near space showed just what she'd been told earlier—no ships except the tanker were within a half mile. In the crowded space around Karma Station, that was crazy.

“<*We’re out of time*>” Alexis physically jerked from the voice in her head.

“Battle stations!” she barked, and the command crew, despite the unexpected command, lurched into action. As soon as sections began calling in their readiness, the first alarm went off. “Report.” It was Guylan who was responding to the signal.

“The tanker is not responding,” the elSha DCC said. “We’re nearly at capacity.”

“Shut off flow,” Alexis ordered.

Guylan worked on his control board, then shook his head. “The system is not responding.”

Alexis touched a control and a Tri-V came alive next to her with the external cameras. She pulled up the aft series and then the one that overlooked the starboard fueling point. The tanker was far enough away that only a curve of its hull was visible. A series of thick hoses curled across the space between *Pegasus* and the bulk of the tanker. They were jerking spasmodically. There was no sign of any of the tanker’s crew which should have been visible in space suits.

“Pressure now above red line,” Guylan said, “and still rising.”

“Damn it,” Alexis said, “get me someone in engineering!”

A second later a Human voice came over the PA. “This is engineering, we’re under attack!”

The voice was punctuated by an explosion.

* * *

Rick was in his little cabin, with the accordion-style door pulled closed, and his straps holding him in bed. He'd thought that horrible day in that fleabag hotel in Houston was the worst day of his life, up until now. After the implants, he'd spent a glorious hour completely disoriented, bumping around the place, as the marine armorers Gene Crenshaw and Skitee (an elSha) fit him with a CASPer. There were so many other new people getting their armor and gear that the Geek Squad was on board as well. Even Sato had been enticed to abandon his experiments and help, something Rick was led to believe was a rare event.

The implants, he thought. He hadn't even had time to get used to them yet. That procedure was just the icing on the shit sandwich. He nostalgically thought back to the day in the hotel room as he tried to get to sleep while simultaneously trying to forget the feeling of octopus tentacles in his brain.

"Oh, fuck me," he groaned and gave up. He slid sideways in zero gravity and found his bag where it was hooked onto a clip on the wall. In an outside pocket was a little plastic container with sleeping pills. Sleeping in zero gravity was easy, going to sleep was often challenging for him. He almost popped four, the maximum dosage, then thought better of it. He was aboard his duty station now, and his instructors at Mickey Finn had drilled into him; "Shit doesn't call you to schedule when it plans to go south; it just does." He took one pill. Luckily, it did the trick, and he was asleep in less than five minutes.

When his alarm went off, Rick rolled over and looked at the display next to his bunk and saw it had only been six hours. He should have had another hour. Then he realized the wheep, wheep, wheep sound wasn't his alarm, but the ship's battle stations' claxon.

"Oh, crap!" he said as he flipped out of the straps. He'd been so out of it, he'd strapped in without getting undressed so he yanked the accordion door aside and stuck his head out. No one was there, but the lighting was pulsing red. He had a moment of confusion, uncertain what to do. He hadn't had his briefing yet on where their duty stations were. "This a damn drill?" he wondered aloud. A second later, the Goka member of his squad shot by like a rocket-powered cockroach.

"Muster in the armory!" Zit yelled as he soared past.

"Move your meaty ass," Jeejee added, right behind the Goka. Rick started to flip into the passageway and was almost creamed by 500 pounds of hurtling black body and legs.

"Look out, Human," Oort, the Tortantula, clicked. Rick noticed she was wearing her saddle and, in a moment of potentially poor judgment, snagged the handhold. He almost got his shoulder dislocated as he was jerked out of his quarters and down the hall. The Tortantula didn't react to Rick grabbing onto the saddle, except to use a couple of her long legs to counter the sudden spin Rick had induced so she could keep going in the same direction. Rick could see a couple of the eyes that surrounded the arachnid's head looking at him coolly. He wished he didn't feel like a tasty bug.

With the speed boost provided by his squad-mate, Rick reached the armory at almost the same times as the rest of the marines. He arrested his momentum by bouncing off the far wall, then slid along to reach his locker. He'd only put his gear there a few hours ago, and had been shown the weapons and armor racks at the same time. The Winged Hussars believed in keeping a well-stocked armory. Sergeant T'jto came flying in from the adjacent gangway which led to the adjoining decks.

"What's the op?" Jeejee asked.

"Don't know," the MinSha said. More and more of the marines were flying in, with varying degrees of zero-G grace. "Gear up, just in case."

Rick had plenty of practice donning combat armor in zero gravity, and his light armor rig was made to be put on fast. Slide both legs in, cinch it up just below the knees, pull it up his back, get both arms in, and scrunch forward to get the arms all the way in. Even with his mind still fuzzy from the alien octopus' cranial surgery, he was in and zipped up in under 10 seconds. He pulled the helmet on and slid down the visor, ready.

He caught sight of Johansson and Lynn both pulling on more elaborate rigs as he pushed over to the light weapons rack. There was an assortment of slug throwers of various types as well as a variety of energy weapons. He already had his Ctech HP-4 in its holster and had added several magazines to the armored vest before stowing it, so he grabbed the first two weapons that came to hand, slung one cross body, and took the other in both hands. Both had multiple magazines on their slings.

"Marines," he heard in his head like someone was perched on his shoulder. He jerked and yelled, banging his head on the weapons rack and earning a laugh from several of his fellow teammates. "Alert, alert, repel boarders! Repeat, muster to repel boarders! Deck 32."

Rick didn't think. In his current state of mind, actions happened before he had time to associate a plan with them. In a flash, he spun and pushed off toward the gangway which was at the side of the armory compartment.

"Standby!" Sergeant T'jto chittered, but Rick was already in motion. Not hearing his name, he didn't respond. The sergeant watched him go in confusion. "Is that Human crazy?" she asked.

"We just got our pinplants a few hours ago," Lynn said. "He was a little out of it, after the procedure. Nemo said there was some brain damage he had to work around from that laser wound." Jeejee was laughing as he holstered a pair of huge handguns and swung into Oort's saddle.

"I think I'm going to like him!" His Tortantula partner had strapped on several pieces of armor to cover her squishy bits, as she called them, and some weaponry that mounted on her legs. By the time Jeejee landed on her back, she was ready to go.

Zit was ready. All he'd had to do was grab the laser weapon configured for his use and wait for orders. Johansson and Lynn were both zipping up their own light combat armor. T'jto noted the members of Zenith Squad were the furthest from being ready and pointed a grasping hand at their sergeant, Leshto.

"Get your squad in heavy armor," she instructed them, "and set up a static defense on our deck." The Veetanho sergeant looked ready to complain. "We don't want any risk of them getting past us to the upper decks! No one gets forward of this. Understood?"

"Yes," Leshto replied, though obviously unhappy with being ordered to be backup. Raptor was further along, but still not ready.

"Jones," T'jto said, "as soon as your team is ready, follow us down."

"We'll be ready in a few seconds."

"Don't rush!" T'jto said. She pointed, and her squad raced after Rick. "Select heavier weapons and follow, but hold at Deck 31. We don't want them sabotaging the reaction tanks."

As T'jto followed her squad down the extra-long gangway to engineering, Jones snapped at his squad. "You're making us look bad. Move it, damn it!"

Leshto took her squad into the part of the armory where the powered armor waited, including the CASPer for her Human. The Oogar in her squad would don heavy body armor, as they were close to being CASPers without them.

Rick was already heading down the long ramp that led from Deck 30. As he hit the entrance to Deck 31, he found the hatch closed and couldn't figure out how to open it. He turned at a skittering behind him and found the huge form of Oort.

"Sergeant is pissed," Jeejee told him.

"Why?" he asked as he wrenched the handle to no avail.

"You didn't hear her yelling at you to stop?"

"No," he said. He pointed at the door. "Damn hatch is stuck."

"Move, Human," Oort said. When a ten-foot-wide spider said move, you did. He floated back against the gangway wall and Oort pushed in close, examining the hatch. "It's locked on the other side," she said after a moment.

Johansson and Lynn arrived, with T'jto right behind them. Zit joined them, skittering along the wall, somehow clinging to the smooth surface. Nice trick, Rick thought.

"What do we do?" he asked the Tortantula.

"That's what I'm here for," Jeejee said. Grabbing handfuls of spider, he moved down the alien and around to her front where he could get at the hatch. He removed tools from his combat harness and went to work.

"What was that all about?" T'jto asked Rick when she was abreast of him.

"I didn't hear you," he said.

"Unlikely," she said, her huge faceted eyes examining him. "If you aren't fit for duty, I want you back up ship."

"I'm fine," he assured her. "Besides, if whoever boarded us gets at the reactors, I'm just as dead up there, as down here."

"You have a point," she said, "but disregard my orders again, and I'll have you locked up for your own safety." Rick nodded but found her concern for his safety amusing given the ongoing combat situation.

"It's spot-welded on the other side," Jeejee said. He'd slid a tiny camera through an access hole on the hatch. He held a small, Flatar-sized slate in one hand as he manipulated the camera control with the other.

"Any enemies?" T'jto asked. Jeejee flipped a control and panned around. Not finding anything, he flipped another switch and it changed to the IR spectrum. There were a lot of heat sources within view of the engineering space, and many were moving. As they watched, several bright lines slashed across the screen.

"I have multiple targets and weapons fire," he said.

"Get us in there," T'jto ordered. The little, furry alien nodded and pulled himself back to his saddle on the Tortantula. From a pouch, he extracted several explosive charges and returned to the door.

"Back a few yards," he warned.

"CIC this is Dragon Squad actual," T'jto called over the squad net.

"Go ahead," Captain Cromwell replied.

"The hatch to Deck 32 is welded closed. We have evidence of combat in the engineering spaces. I've ordered the hatch breached. Recommend you have damage control parties standing by."

"Understood," the captain said, "we have additional situations outside the ship. Be aware there could be more aggressors trying to board."

"Got it, Dragon out." She turned to the Flatar. "How are those charges coming?"

"Ready," he said.

"Zit, you're first in!" the sergeant ordered. "Oort and Jeejee second, then Johansson and me." She looked at Lynn and Rick. "You two last. If it turns bloody before you come in, secure the hatch, and hold this space."

"Yes sir," Lynn and Rick said in stereo.

T'jto nodded and turned to the Flatar. "Go."

Jeejee pushed back from the hatch, palming a tiny control. Without being instructed, Oort grabbed him with a long leg, wrapping him like she was tucking an infant under her arm, and turned away, putting her armored torso between the door and her partner. Rick was amazed at the fluid grace of the two working together. No words were needed; it was like watching a choreographed ballet. "Fire in the hole!" Jeejee barked and detonated the explosive.

The specialized breaching charges each contained an ounce of K2. The advanced, high-order explosive was like the Human's C4 plastic explosive, only about four times as powerful. Jeejee used four of the charges, the resulting blast carefully shaped into the door's hinges and mechanisms. It wasn't that loud, but Rick heard several pings of debris ricocheting off the Tortantula's armor. Oort locked several legs against the gangway walls, kicked back with a pair, and the hatch flew free into the engineering space.

"Go!" T'jto barked at Zit, and the little Goka raced forward through the hatch, strangely-formed laser pistols held in two of its hands. After all the laser fire Rick had seen flying around on Jeejee's slate, Rick figured the little bug was toast. He was curious that it would so gladly charge into the meat grinder.

Sure enough, warned of the coming assault by the breaching charges, lasers slashed out at the hurtling shape of the Hussars' insect marine. Several made contact, and Rick's eyebrows went up as the jet-black carapace of the alien seemed to sparkle and flash when laser bolts grazed its surface. There was no more effect than that; the damned bug seemed to be laser resistant! While the boarders tried to take out Zit, he returned fire.

T'jto turned to the Tortantula. "Go!" she chirped.

Jeejee locked his legs into the saddle as the huge arachnid exploded into motion. She didn't spin and go in fangs first, as Rick had expected. Her back facing the breached doorway, she pushed backward through the hatch, legs tucked in under her body. Her softer abdomen and wasp-like waist were heavily-armored and presented toward the enemy. Many times bigger and moving slower than the Goka, she instantly drew fire. Rick was again caught off guard by the tactics. This wasn't what he'd expected from the alien race which had been one of humanity's more vicious competitors in the merc business.

T'jto nodded at Johansson, and the two launched themselves through the hatch, in slightly different directions. Lynn and Rick moved forward to either side of the hatch as soon as the other two were clear, both holding laser carbines at the ready.

The lights were out in the section of engineering they were looking down into. Both Humans used their riflescopes' IR feature to see better. After a second, Lynn cursed and started fiddling with her gun.

"What are you doing?" he asked.

"Our pinplants, remember? I'm linking the gun to mine."

"Oh, right," he said. Flipping open a panel on the gun's stock revealed the controls. He'd seen how to do it in training, but lacking pinplants, he had never done it. He pressed the 'link weapon' button and held it down for a full second. 'Stand by,' it said. A little hesitantly, he reached up to do the same on the external control of his implant. He had to worm his hand in under the edge of his helmet, squeezing a finger through the padding. Luckily, it was fit to him and that space had been intentionally left less snug. The synthetic plastic appliance of the pinlink was fused with his cranium, and it felt strange beyond words to touch it instead of his skull. After the short wait, the gun control said 'linked,' and he saw a tiny gunsight appear at the edge of his peripheral vision. "How do I use the thing?" he asked.

"Concentrate on it," Lynn said. He concentrated on a better view, and instantly half his vision was filled with the gunsight! It should have been disconcerting, having one half his vision be from his eyes, and the other half from the gun's scope, but it wasn't. It seemed the most natural thing ever. "You can make it go away by sort of mentally shrugging it away." Rick did as she said, and the site shrank to where it was before.

"Wow," he said in amazement.

"Yeah," she agreed. A *shpring!* of suddenly-melting metal sounded as a laser flashed between them and cut a wedge from the hatch frame. Both snapped back to the real world.

"That was close," she said. Rick nodded and brought the gun-sight up. He immediately wished he'd had this when fighting the raiders back aboard the *Coronado.*

In the engineering space, a laser firefight was well underway. Jee-jee and Oort were crouched behind a huge machine and were firing intermittent snapshots further into the room, apparently trying to keep the boarders' heads down. T'jto and Johansson were slowly crawling along a pair of huge pipes, but were having to duck and backtrack repeatedly as lasers bounced and flashed from the next section. There was no sign of Zit.

"I see at least two groups," Lynn said. "Maybe three each?"

"Agreed," Rick said. "Only standard anti-personnel lasers. They're playing it safe."

"Check the hatch at nine o'clock," she said. Rick leaned a little forward into the hatch and swung the carbine around, the image relayed directly into his brain. The hatchway she was indicating had several laser scores around it. As he watched a head popped up for a half second and a laser beam lanced out at Corporal Johansson, missing by inches. "Did you see what it was?"

"No," Rick said, "they're wearing full suits." He watched the exchange of weapons fire between the two sides for a moment until he saw a pattern. "I think I got this," he said and set his gun's aiming point. A second later, he triggered the carbine. It gave off the typical snapping whine of a handheld laser weapon. He also felt the slight shudder as the internal mechanism cycled the chemical elements it used to create the deadly beam. He fired twice in rapid order and was rewarded with an explosion of visor glass as a laser weapon came arching through the hatchway. "Bingo."

T'jto and Johansson responded instantly by bounding out of their cover and heading for the hatchway. In a half-second, they were gone through to the next compartment.

"Hold the gangway," T'jto ordered over the squadnet, "don't let them double back on us!"

"Got it," Rick replied.

"Will do," Lynn agreed.

"And good shot," Johansson added. He was beginning to see the MinSha was rather miserly with her praise. She was an insect, after all.

Rick and Lynn pulled themselves through the hatch into engineering and took what cover they could behind machinery on either side. Because of the gangway, there was pitifully little in the way of cover.

The two discussed it and settled on covering both approaches at once. Rick continued to watch the open hatchway Johansson and T'jto had gone through, while Lynn watched further into the section where Oort and Jeejee had moved while exchanging fire with unseen foes. They sat that way for a few moments, then the machinery around them began to hum and vibrate.

"Oh crap," Lynn barked. Rick was more familiar with shipboard life. The sound was indicative of a reactor powering up. They were getting ready to do something. There was a series of loud claps and quick hums. Relays, Rick guessed. Was the ship opening fire? Then the hull sounded like a huge gong, and they felt the great ship move. Something had hit them. The lights in the engineering space went out.

"Shit," Rick hissed and concentrated, trying to cycle the riflescope enhancement to IR. After a second he gave up and raised the stock. Flipping open the cover again, he tabbed the infrared setting and swung it around, in time to see a pair of figures flying at him and his partner.

* * * * *

Chapter Twenty-Four

"Pressure's still rising," Guylan said. "It's way above red line! I'm getting status alarms from the tank regulators!"

"That's enough," Alexis said. "Edwards, bring the port aft laser online."

"Standing by," he reported.

"Sever those hoses," she ordered. "A five-megawatt pulse should do it."

"Yes ma'am," he said. "Firing!"

Outside the ship, a single laser emitter popped up from the hull, its internal mirrors aligned as laser energy was channeled. Edwards felt the firing as a pleasant tingle in his mind and saw the line of energy cutting along the hull. The hoses connecting *Pegasus* to the tanker were sliced cleanly, the tanker end flailing violently as liquid vented into space. Automatic valves inside *Pegasus* sensed the pressure drop and sealed.

The wildly spewing hoses induced yaw to the tanker, yaw that wasn't countered because the autopilot had been disengaged. The thrust wasn't huge, but it was constant. In only a moment, it was apparent the tanker was swinging around toward *Pegasus*.

"Collision alert!" Glick, the SitCon warned.

"Shields!" Paka ordered.

Edwards responded immediately, bringing the battlecruiser's defenses online. The tanker hit the shields, making them flash with absorbed energy. Both ships rebounded from each other.

"Helm, back us out!" Alexis snapped.

"Maneuvering," Chug replied, and everyone felt the ship shift away from the tanker, which was now beginning to spin faster and faster.

"Marines, update," Alexis called.

"Corporal Johansson reporting," the voice came over the PA.

"Where is Sergeant T'jto, Corporal?" the captain asked.

"She was injured, though not badly."

"Very well, report."

"We estimate the boarding party to be between six and eight in number. They came aboard through the Deck 32, Section 2 maintenance hatch. It appears they overrode the security." She stopped for a moment, and the sounds of laser fire could be heard. "Two of them are confirmed dead. Oort and Jeejee have several pinned down behind Reactor One. The sergeant and I have a couple more cornered in auxiliary engineering control. Private Zit is out hunting stragglers."

"Any sign of engineer Long and his team?"

"They are trapped in primary control, sir. It's a crossfire situation. We've exchanged hand signals with them. Most of his staff appear okay. Someone spotted the boarders, and he had his people retreat into control and barricade themselves. By the looks of the damage to the control runs, it's likely communications were severed."

"Smart bug," Paka said, to which Alexis nodded, then spoke.

"How bad is the damage down there?"

"I'm no engineer, sir." She paused to fire several times. "That said, there are some leaking pipes and a few alarms going off. No fires, and our radiation meters aren't freaking out. For the time being, I think we're okay. It's a standoff."

"Can you get a communicator to Long?" It was silent for a moment.

"I think I can get Zit to sneak one in there."

"Then do so. I need to find out our options, and only Long can give me them."

"Understood."

Alexis ground her teeth as she watched the tanker on the big Tri-V display spin faster and faster.

"Karma Control is on the radio," Hoot said. "They want to know why we're firing."

* * *

Rick had just enough warning to call on his zero-G training and roll his shoulder into the hurtling figure. Lynn wasn't that lucky. She was much newer to fighting and moving in null gravity. She tried to bring her gun up without anchoring herself; her aim went wide and induced a spin.

"Shit!" she said, and the attacker hit her at the same time Rick hit him.

Rick released the rifle, letting it fly free on its sling as the impact shoved him back into the gangway up to Deck 31. He grabbed the suited figure, which was Human in shape and had a visored helmet covering its head, and he rolled as he hit. The move was designed to throw the attacker off him, but his enemy was just as good in zero gravity, and physically stronger! Since the figure was no bulkier than him, even in his armor, that meant it probably wasn't Human. The helmet looked more elongated too.

During his training, he'd learned how to fight many different alien races; each was its own challenge. One of the hardest was the MinSha, because of all the limbs. You used joint breaking maneuvers on them. Bigger races like Besquith you used leverage and kept away from their mouths. The truly big ones like Oogar and Tortantula? The best way to win was not to fight at all.

When he tried to pull and flip the enemy, it grabbed Rick's opposite arm and punched him. Hard. All the air went out with a "Whuf!" If it weren't for the rigidity of the light combat armor, the punch would probably have broken ribs.

As they rebounded, they faced each other head to foot, so Rick punched the figure in the crotch. He didn't feel anything, and the enemy didn't react other than to the blunt force. Not Human, then. No vulnerable genitals, elongated helmet, stronger than a Human. *Gotcha,* he thought. When they bounced off the roof of the gangway, he leveraged himself sideways enough to throw an armored elbow into the other's face with his full strength, and was rewarded with smashing plastic. He got another punch to the ribs for his effort, but at least he saw his enemy's face.

"Zuul, eh?" Rick asked. The enemy barked and growled something Rick's translator didn't catch, as the Zuul rammed a knee into the side of Rick's head, perfectly timing it with the collision against the top of the gangway to Deck 31. That one made Rick see stars. He shook his head to clear it, and the Zuul tried to snatch a compact gun on his belt. Rick slapped it aside as it fired; the weapon made an unimpressive 'Pop!' and tore a sizeable chunk of metal out of the nearby bulkhead.

They floated in a tangle of limbs and bounced off bulkheads and ramps, both trying to get leverage on the other. Neither succeeded; Rick dislocated a finger, although he succeeded in getting the Zuul's helmet off and bloodying his muzzle.

Rick could hear Lynn cursing and crashing around; at least she was still alive. He'd finally managed to get a grip on one of the Zuul's arms and was trying to put it in a joint lock when his enemy snatched the laser carbine's one-point harness and jerked. Hooked around his neck armor, it jerked his face forcibly into the Zuul's knee hard enough to make him black out. When he came to, the alien had him in a headlock and was choking the life out of him.

Well, this sucks; finally get a good merc gig and won't live a week. He tried to pull his leg up and get the knife sheathed there, but the Zuul sensed the move and wrapped both its legs around his torso, effectively neutralizing him. He tried throwing elbows, kicking out, slamming his head back, but nothing fazed the Zuul. His vision started to swim, and all he could think about was the friend whose name was lost to him.

As his consciousness faded, Rick could have sworn he heard yelling. A second later, the pressure was gone from his neck, and he floated free, gasping for breath. Struggling to breathe, he grasped the rifle sling and pulled his carbine into his hands, searching for a target.

"Calm down, mammal." His vision focused on the black image of Zit. Next to him the Zuul was struggling feebly, blood flowing from several holes in its armor. It gushed in big red blobs, floating around or sticking to the walls. Zit held a pair of long, thin, red-stained blades in two of its arms.

"They…got…<cough>…the jump on us," Rick choked out.

"Rookies," Zit chittered, spun, and rebounded off the wall back into engineering. Back down the gangway Lynn was grasping a handhold and trying to catch her breath as well. She was holding a hand against her leg, the armor there stained red from a wound. The Zuul she had been fighting was also losing blood rapidly. Zit had taken both enemies out in a matter of seconds, with just his knives! They heard the Goka over the squadnet.

"Deck 32 is secure," he said. "The larvae were in trouble. I dealt with it." Rick felt his face burning and Lynn shook her head.

"Are either of you injured?" Johansson asked. Rick wondered where T'jto was.

"We're fine," Lynn said before Rick could say anything.

"Okay," Johansson said. "Continue holding the access."

"How badly are you hurt?" Rick asked, floating up next to his fellow trooper.

"Fucker stuck me with a knife like the Goka had," she explained. He gently pulled her hand away from the armor. Blood flowed, but didn't spurt.

"Yeah, I gotta get me one of those," he said and opened his medkit. "Get your carbine up and watch while I look at this."

"Sure," she said and shouldered her gun, sweeping it around to scan the area. The ship shuddered slightly, and they drifted down to thump onto the gangway. "We're under thrust," she said.

"But not much," he agreed. He pulled out the field nanite dispenser and checked the design. It was almost identical to the one he trained with on Earth. A selector let you choose the type of injury, either external or internal. Another was a severity selector, from one to five. He selected external injury, and guessed at two for the severity. "I hear these things sting a little," he said.

"Yeah, they're—ARGH!" She contorted and yelled as he sprayed the full dosage over the wound. "Next time warn me!" she snapped and banged an armored fist against the wall. "Son of a *bitch,* that hurts!"

"Sorry," he said. He turned to put away the dispenser, so she didn't see the grin on his face. By the time he turned back the bleeding had stopped. Trillions of tiny robots were busy hyper-accelerating her body's natural repair factors and knitting the flesh back together. In less than five seconds, it was done, and she sighed.

"I'd forgotten how much that hurts," she said.

"How many times have you used it before?" he asked.

"Twice," she said, "but both were more minor. That one must have nicked an artery judging by the way the blood was flowing."

"Better now?"

"Yes, thanks." Rick nodded and examined his left ring finger, bent at an odd angle. It wouldn't help his marksmanship. With a sigh, he grabbed the finger and jerked. He gasped in pain; with a *pop*, it went back into joint.

"Ouch," he said through gritted teeth.

"That was hard core," Lynn said as they resumed their posts.

They heard weapons firing from inside engineering, then footsteps came bounding down the ramp. Rick glanced back to see Sergeant Jones and Privates Bacord and L'kto of Raptor Squad approaching.

"I thought the sergeant ordered you to stay on Deck 30?" Rick asked.

"She said to come down and relieve you," Sergeant Jones said. Rick saw Sergeant Jones wasn't happy about it, either.

"What are we supposed to do?"

"Go find the MinSha sergeant," Jones grumbled and gestured with his laser carbine into engineering. "We're to hold the gangway. Corporal Jakal has the rest of the squad on the other gangway. The captain was afraid they'd try to cut through that one, even though the blast door was secured."

"We stand relieved," Rick said and saluted, following the procedures he'd learned at Mickey Finn. Jones gave a halfhearted return salute.

"You are relieved. Find Sergeant T'jto." Rick and Lynn pushed off into the maze of main engineering.

* * *

Alexis had just finished a heated conversation with Karma Station's defensive coordinator, a very annoyed Veetanho, when the intraship radio came alive. "Engineer calling CIC."

"Long, good to hear you are okay," Alexis said.

"We're glad to be well," the Jeha engineer replied. "I have four injured, but no dead. Two of my elSha techs spotted the boarders. We grabbed some guns and started shooting at them."

"Well done, Long."

"I'm not letting someone shoot up my engine room!" Alexis smiled at her chief engineer's dedication. "They managed to cut communications and control. Marine Zhkt brought us a radio, so at least we're in touch."

"Tell Private Zit, well done."

"Yes, Captain."

"What do you believe is their goal?"

"The private says they killed a pair who were installing a patch in one of the main reactor control lines. I think they were trying to cause an overload."

"A forced overload might destroy the ship," she said.

"If they managed to override enough of the safeties," the engineer agreed, "the blast could destroy the ship."

"Can we still use the maneuvering engines?" The engineer was silent for a moment before answering.

"They should answer to your commands without main power," he eventually said. "You will not get more than a tenth of a gravity on backup power."

"Understood," she said. "Helm, maneuvering engines, get us out of here!"

"Aye-aye, Captain," Chug replied. A moment later they felt a tiny amount of thrust as *Pegasus'* ion drives came online and began to move the ship.

"The tanker is falling astern," Flipper reported.

"Very good," Alexis said, "maintain maximum thrust, set course for the stargate." She changed to the marine frequency. "Sergeant T'jto," she called.

"Here, Captain."

"You are injured?"

"Just a leg," she reported. "It's serviceable at present."

"Very well," Alexis said, "you heard the conversation with Engineer Long?"

"Yes, Captain."

"We cannot allow the boarders to take control of the reactors."

"Private Culper just joined us; they held the deck exit. He says the enemy are Zuul."

"<*There are others*>" Alexis shifted her attention away from the marines.

"Who?"

"<*I do not know. They are either here already, or coming*>"

"How do we avoid it?" The answer was immediate and unambiguous.

"<*Run*>"

"Sergeant," she said, addressing her marine commander once more.

"Captain?"

"Take them out using any means short of doing irreparable harm to the drives."

"Understood," the MinSha replied. Alexis turned to her helmsman.

"I need a sliding solution to make the next transition at the stargate."

"Next transition is in seventeen hours, forty-five minutes. We won't make it on ion drive."

"I understand that," she retorted. "I need a drop-dead time for getting our reactors online, including ready solutions as that time approaches."

One eyestalk turned back to look at her as a pair of Tri-V screens appeared, and the mollusk used a combination of manipulative pseudopods and pinplants to begin working the problem faster than any Human could.

Come on marines, Alexis thought, *get me control of my ship!*

* * * * *

Chapter Twenty-Five

Rick and Lynn floated up behind a huge, robust-looking machine where Sergeant T'jto and Corporal Johansson were taking cover. A laser beam flashed against a pipe from the machine with a high pitched *shring* as they approached. Obviously, the enemy were still actively fighting back.

"Are you both well?" T'jto asked as they arrived. Rick saw their sergeant had what looked like concrete wrapped around one of her legs; the limb was folded back and immobilized against her thorax.

"We're okay," Lynn said, "what about you, Sergeant?"

"It is just a leg," she explained. "Dr. Ramirez and Nemo can repair it more permanently when time allows." Another trio of laser shots flew at them, making Rick and Lynn duck. "Oort and Jeejee are busy with the last pair further aft; we need to deal with these. The engineering staff are worried they are going to try and overload the reactor."

"Do we have any remote bombs?" Rick asked. The others all looked at him curiously. "In Mickey Finn we had these little bombs we could fly with remote control drones, designed for situations like these."

"Ah, drone charges," Johansson said. "Yes, but we don't use them on our own ship." She gestured around her at all the pipes and cables. "For obvious reasons." Rick nodded; that made sense. He hadn't been trained to defend a ship, only to assault. He reflected that those were indeed two entirely different objectives.

"We have stun grenades," he said and pulled one from his armor, suddenly thinking it was damned fortunate none of the pins had been pulled during the fight with the Zuul. Even with the Union technology, Humans had stuck with what worked when it came to grenades. A cylinder with a pin to arm it, and a spoon that flew free to start the timer. They didn't have internal burning fuses, like the old Earth weapons, and you could program the detonation via a digital input, or a simple twisting action, from one second to five minutes.

"The problem," T'jto said, "is if we start pitching stun grenades, they'll simply seal their helmets and ignore them. Combat armor can screen out the flash and the sound."

"Not if they don't know they're coming," Rick said as Zit arrived, skittering along a cable run at high speed. Everyone turned and looked at the Goka, who stopped and regarded them suspiciously, his antenna waving back and forth.

"Why are you all looking at me like that?"

A few minutes later, Rick watched as Zit moved back along the cable runs. Jeejee reported he and Oort had the last one in the rear of the compartment trapped. It couldn't get out, but they couldn't get at it either. The sergeant elected to wait until these two trying to sabotage the reactor could be dealt with. Zit continued to make slow, deliberate progress toward the nexus of several machines, where the pair of Zuul lurked.

Rick centered his scope on the Goka trooper on the other side of the compartment, waiting next to a junction of two pipes. At a word from Lynn, he turned and saw a large reddish Jeha moving along the wall. Like a massive millipede, its multitude of legs moved in coordinated waves to propel the alien toward them at a surprising speed.

"The engineer?" Rick asked.

"Ch't'kl'tk," Johansson said, struggling with the multiple guttural stops. "Captain calls him Long." Rick smirked, it was a fitting name for such a creature. The Jeha arrived and examined them with its pair of mobile eyestalks. A pair of elSha hung on its side; they dropped off and grabbed their own handholds.

Long took a device from its armored body with one of four long manipulative arms near the massive mandible-like jaws. Rick could see the engineer had a number of devices hooked to securing clamps glued to his armored body. The device turned out to be a monocular, which the engineer held in front of an eyestalk and observed where the Zuul were hidden.

"We must hurry," Long said after a moment.

"We are," Sergeant T'jto replied.

"No, we really must hurry. We had a wavering of the containment field in this reactor."

"Could there be a breach?" Johansson asked, checking the radiation meter on her armor's sleeve.

"No, they stabilized it," Long explained.

"I don't understand," the Sergeant said. "If they want to blow the reactor, why stabilize it?"

"Because they want to cause a catastrophic overload, not just blow it," Long explained. "The compartments are designed to contain a reactor failure. They will blow out and limit the damage. *Pegasus* has experienced reactor failures before with minimal loss of life, and repairs were made. My assistants have been monitoring their activity through data feeds, and we're sure they are trying to supercharge the reactor, then they'll blow the F11 containment. The reactor will run away, and the explosion will destroy the ship."

"Zit," T'jto spoke over the squadnet, "get the package in there ASAP."

"What the fuck do you think I'm doing?" the Goka asked.

"If you don't get your chitinous ass moving, the Zuul are going to blow the reactor, and the whole ship with it."

"And that's my problem, why?"

"You're on this ship, too," Johannsson barked, "you fucking psychotic cockroach."

"Mammals are always so worried about dying," Zit said. They saw it start moving again. "Death takes us all, you know. Now, later, why worry about it so much?" Zit reached the edge of the machine where the Zuul were laboring. Using one of his manipulative limbs, he removed a belt with a dozen flash-bang grenades and manipulated their controls.

"Because we don't breed as prolifically as you do," T'jto said over the squadnet, "and we'd rather not die today," she added for those nearby.

"And we haven't been paid yet," Johansson added. Everyone, even the Goka chuckled. Merc humor—dark as space and just as cold.

"Ready," Zit announced. Rick, Johansson, and Lynn prepared themselves, while T'jto moved a bit to the side and secured herself with her three good legs. Long and his assistants took cover behind a power distribution panel.

"Go," T'jto said once she verified all was in readiness. Zit grabbed a wire and yanked, pulling the pins on six of the flashbangs in quick order. Holding onto the machine with his versatile grasping feet, he swung the string of grenades overhead like a pendulum, flinging the bunch out on a short rope around the corner of the machine. When they were perpendicular, he let go, and the string of grenades flew into the space between the two machines where the Zuul were working. Zit flattened himself against the machine and all his legs and head completely disappeared. The instant Zit released the string of grenades, the three Humans launched themselves across the engineering space.

The grenades went off in rapid staccato order as the three Human marines crossed the open space. They flipped over as one and activated the grapples on their boots as they impacted the machinery above the Zuul.

The flash-bangs were designed for use on ships, and were all light and concussion, with no smoke or debris. As the three landed, they found two confused Zuul, their helmets up, with electronic gear floating around a control panel they'd taken apart. Lynn and Rick each aimed at one of the Zuul and fired three times through the aliens' heads, with Johansson on overwatch.

Rick was listening to the sergeant report when he saw Lynn get hit. A laser beam scored off her helmet, flashing the ablative covering and making her jerk to the side in surprise. She gave a strangled scream, and her rifle flew from her hands. Johansson and Rick both pivoted to see a single Zuul soaring toward them, a laser pistol in each hand, flashing death in their direction.

Johansson crouched down in the concealment which had protected the two Zuul they'd killed only moments ago, but Rick recognized the threat and felt no fear. Using the laser carbine's built-in targeting linked with his pinplants, he brought the weapon around and got a better view of the Zuul. Its combat helmet was closed, the armor was scored in several places from weapons fire, and dried blood was caked on both. It was a suicide charge. He knew he couldn't take it down with the few shots he'd get before the alien reached him, where the pistols would hold the advantage over the bulkier rifle, so he went for the harder target.

Mickey Finn had stressed the basics in their cadre program, and that started with marksmanship. Very few of their troopers had pinplants; the older owners of the company hadn't trusted 'that alien brain crap.' Thus, troopers spent many hours at the range. Rick took basic marksmanship training, then spent extra hours of personal time learning every weapon the merc company had, including most of the lasers. His instructors said he was a naturally-talented shot, and his new pinplants augmented that talent.

Rick let the pinplants guide him. It took a fraction of a second to get the shot he wanted, and he took it. There was a sputtering discharge from one of the Zuul's pistols as Rick's beam cut the gun in half. It didn't do the Zuul's hand any good either. A beam flashed by the Zuul's head, coming from where Sergeant T'jto was perched. She didn't have a very good angle, though, and the shot missed.

Instantly, Rick shifted to the other hand. The Zuul had begun to spin, letting the ruined weapon fly away, sputtering and sparking, and it aimed for Rick. The movement brought the enemy's canine-like face into view, and Rick smiled; its face shield was up.

"Bad move," Rick whispered, and shot the snarling Zuul through the nose. The beam carved through the enemy's face, lower jaw, and into his neck. The alien jerked from the trauma and crashed against the bulkhead next to Rick.

Rick grabbed the enemy to keep him from rebounding away, shoved his carbine into the helmet, and fired twice more. The body convulsed and went still. Blood began to float out of the helmet in spinning, crimson globs.

Rick turned to Lynn. "Are you okay?" he asked, bending over her. She was still hooked to the machine by her boots, but curled up in a fetal position. Some blood had pooled on her helmet, but not much.

"Fuck, fuck, fuck," she cursed repeatedly.

"Let me check," he said, using his helmet's light to examine the laser wound. It had grazed the helmet and had taken a quarter-inch chunk from her scalp, two inches above her left ear. She'd been extraordinarily lucky. "It's not bad," he said and took out a sterile dressing from his medkit. "Patching you up is becoming a hobby." She laughed a little, confirming his impression the wound was superficial.

"Oort, Jeejee," Sergeant T'jto called out. "Report."

"There were three back here," Jeejee reported. "We used your trick with the grenades and flushed them. Oort and I got two of them. The last one rushed by."

"Private Culper got the last one," the sergeant said. "Return and regroup. CIC, Dragon Squad, we're going to do a sweep, but I'm reasonably certain we got them all!"

* * *

Deck 14 held the ship's primary life support equipment and its modest medical facilities. Lynn sat on one of the couches in the ship's one-sixth of a gravity, while Sergeant T'jto clung to another. Doctor Ramirez had been forced to cut Lynn's helmet off as some of the metal had melted into her hair and scalp. Rick hadn't watched as the helmet was split and peeled away, her hair and skin tearing with it. It was a cringe-worthy moment.

At the same time, the Wrogul medic Nemo was working on Sergeant T'jto's leg. That was a much more complicated procedure, because of the MinSha's open circulatory system. Nemo used his special ability to slip his tentacles through the concrete leg bandage and treat the wound underneath.

"What was that all about?" Sergeant T'jto asked Rick as the Wrogul medic slid several tentacles in and out of the bandage.

"I don't know what you mean," Rick replied.

"In engineering, when the last Zuul rushed us." Rick looked at her, waiting. The MinSha cocked her head and regarded him, her antennae waving back and forth as if they were trying to sense his mood. "It went straight for you, and you didn't move an inch."

"Seemed the thing to do," he said coolly. Johansson was watching from nearby where she was holding Lynn's hand as Ramirez cleaned her head wound.

"That raider had you dead-to-rights," T'jto said, "and cover was just a few feet away. Instead, you stood there and calmly shot one of his pistols, then put another shot right into his face." Rick shrugged. "You weren't frightened?"

"No."

"That doesn't seem possible," Johansson chimed in. "Sure, you've been in a fight before, but not like this. Shit, kid, I've been shot at more times than I can count, and I dove clear."

"He's incapable of fear," Nemo said, and everyone turned to look at the octopus-like alien. He was removing T'jto's temporary cast to reveal a more permanent bandage.

"What do you mean?" Ramirez asked, spraying some nanites on Lynn's wound. She'd already had an analgesic applied; she only cringed and jerked slightly as the tiny robots went to work.

"The amygdala of his brain suffered damage because of the laser wound."

Dr. Ramirez shook his head slightly and looked hard at his assistant. "What? When did you find that out?"

"Why, during his pinplant procedure, of course."

"Nemo," Ramirez said with a sigh, "do you remember when I told you not to withhold information on a patient's condition?"

The Wrogul sat still for a moment before answering. "Was this one of those times?" The translator rendered his words so precisely, it was easy to forget you were talking to a squid.

"Yes," Ramirez said; "yes it was. How badly damaged is his amygdala?"

"It's the connections that are damaged," Nemo explained, "the organ itself is intact. It appears that bone shards from the laser damage were scattered through his temporal lobe. The repairs appear to have been done by an autodoc?" The question was addressed to Rick.

"Yes," Rick agreed, "it's all they had on *Coronado*. The medic was proficient, but he didn't have much to work with."

"It was sufficient to avoid serious side effects, as you see," Nemo agreed, "but also simply field expedient. Nanites are not particularly adept at fixing Human neurological damage."

"What other damage is there?" Ramirez asked. Since work on Lynn couldn't continue until her nanotherapy was complete, he took a slate and accessed Rick's file. Rick could see high resolution images of his brain through the back of the translucent computer. It looked like any of a dozen pictures of Human brains he'd seen before.

"About seven cubic inches of the temporal lobe were obliterated by the laser path. Although the symmetrical nature of a Human's brain provides a great deal of redundancy, the damage to his amygdala has caused an emotional disconnect, and he probably has some memory loss."

"Yes," Rick admitted.

"From certain time periods?"

"Mostly," Rick agreed.

"The nanites reconstructed a lot of the lost brain tissue," Ramirez said, examining zooms of Rick's brain. "However, they can't recreate the neurological connections. Like Nemo mentioned, our brains have a lot of redundancy, so there's hope."

"What do you mean?" Rick asked. "My memories might come back?"

Nemo pulsed and his tentacles waved.

Ramirez nodded slightly, then shrugged. "It's possible. I can't say for sure."

"And my emotions?" The doctor sighed and shook his head.

Rick knew he should feel something, but again, he was incapable. It was just how he was now. He only felt things in a hollow sort of way, almost like watching a movie through a fog.

"I could try to fix it," Nemo offered, obviously game to give it a go.

"I believe that would be ill-advised," Ramirez said.

The PA came alive. "All senior staff report to the Captain's wardroom," Paka announced.

"I think I'm going to be fine," Lynn said, and glanced at Rick before looking away. She was keenly aware how much worse her head wound could have been.

"Good." Sergeant T'jto turned to Johansson and added, "Corporal, verify with Raptor and Zenith Squads that the sweep of the lower decks is complete and report directly to me."

"Yes, sir," Johansson said.

"I don't want to take the chance we've missed any of the bastards." She looked at the Wrogul and flexed her damaged limb. "Will this repair hold for now?"

"It's a polyacrylic/nanotube infill," the alien said. "Until I have a chance to print a replacement piece of chiton, it will work perfectly in almost all situations."

"Very well," she said and headed for the lift. "I'll be with the captain."

* * * * *

Chapter Twenty-Six

Alexis sat in her chair and listened. In her hand was a computer chip provided by Hoot. The dispatch had arrived during the brief battle, and she'd called the meeting immediately after the last of the boarders were dispatched. As they accelerated away at a snail's pace, she nervously rolled the chip between her fingers.

Long reported from the engineering spaces and scrolled down a list much like his name. The battle in engineering only lasted a quarter of an hour, but the damage it caused was substantial. Nothing irreplaceable had been destroyed, but many subsystems, piping, electrical conduits, and control systems were damaged. A firefight in a starship's engineering spaces played hell with its systems. There was a knock and Sergeant T'jto entered the wardroom. The captain nodded, and the marine commander walk/hopped over to a chair and perched her thorax on it. She was the last of the senior staff to arrive. Long finished his report.

"Bottom line," the captain asked, "how long for repairs?"

"Complete repairs?" he asked. "At least 96 hours. Could be more. I have to tear down two of the main power relays from Reactor One."

"Just give me the fusion torch," she said. This time there was a pause. Everyone could hear banging tools and the snaps and hisses of welders as the engineering crew worked.

"Twelve hours," he said finally, "but only one engine. Give me 16 hours, and I'm reasonably certain I can give you two." Alexis narrowed her eyes.

"<*Take the one, and get us out of here*>" the voice said.

"Twelve hours," she said, and turned to her helmsman. "How does that put us for making transition?"

"Close," Chug responded. "The margin will be less than a half hour."

"Continue maximum thrust under ion drive," she ordered.

"We're stressing the ion drive," Long interjected. "It was never made for sustained full power thrust like this. It's nothing more than a glorified maneuvering thruster, and it wasn't even part of the ship's original design."

"Monitor it, but maintain full power," Alexis ordered; "we can't afford to miss the transition window." Long acknowledged her order. She looked at Guylan. "Give Long as many of your people as you can to expedite repairs."

"We still have a lot of damage to fix," the little elSha said, gesturing helplessly. "We were going to work on that en route to Home. There are open power panels and access shafts on three decks."

"Can't be helped," Alexis said.

He grumbled, but said he'd comply.

"Sergeant," Alexis said to the MinSha, "what's your troopers' status?"

"We took two casualties," T'jto replied. "Myself," she said and held up the temporarily repaired leg, "and Private Jordan. I'm fine, and she will be after she's healed. It was a superficial head wound. Luckily, you Humans have thick skulls." The Humans in the room all chuckled, and the aliens nodded their heads, or whatever sufficed for their race. "We're completing a thorough sweep of the lower decks, just to be sure we got them all."

"What were they?" the captain asked.

"A squad of Zuul mercs," she said. "Boarding specialists. But they bore no insignia, and the gear was all brand new, right out of the box."

"Sounds like a takeover team," Edwards said. He was rubbing his stubbled chin as he thought. "But you usually don't see Zuul doing that."

"They weren't here to kill us," Alexis said, "though they sure made it look like it."

"And nearly succeeded," Long agreed.

"You think they were trying to slow us down?" Paka asked. "You know something, don't you?"

"Yes," she admitted. "I haven't wanted to talk about it yet, because I'm still not sure. I figured this close to Home, I could put it off until we were safe. Apparently, we're not going to get that chance." They all looked at her expectantly. "To put it bluntly, I think that someone, or several someones, want us dead." No one looked surprised.

She took a moment to gather her thoughts then said, "This may be a move against the Four Horsemen in general, and we're just part of it. Several months ago, you probably heard Cartwright's Cavaliers went bankrupt. That, in and of itself, isn't anything spectacular. Thaddeus Cartwright, their previous commander, was killed on a mission four years ago, and control reverted to his wife because his son was too young. I believe this may have provided the window of opportunity which set the current chain of events in motion.

"Thaddeus' wife was either coerced or simply duped into making a series of highly risky, and ultimately disastrous, business decisions. The company became insolvent, and most of the assets were sold. However, we Horsemen have taken measures to make it hard for any of our companies to outright die, short of being destroyed in battle, of course." She chuckled. "Even that might not suffice.

"Anyway, Thaddeus' son is now in charge and has begun rebuilding using gear and funds his father hid from the lawyers. Cartwright's is recovering, though it is only a shadow of its former self. The next target was Asbaran Solutions. This plot was considerably more successful, and it succeeded in all but decimating their leadership and gutting their fighting force. Like Cartwright's, I understand an heir is now in charge. However, unlike Cartwright's, this heir appears to be storming around the galaxy on a personal vendetta. The jury is out on how that will end. And that's where we come in."

Alexis took a drink of water from a bottle on her desk and used the opportunity to look over her command staff. They were all paying close attention to her, a mixture of concern and fear evident on their faces. After a lifetime of dealing with all the species present, she was pretty good at reading their body languages. Even the mollusk-like Bakulu gave you clues, if you cared to look for them. It was no surprise the non-merc races on her command staff were the ones showing the most concern. She continued.

"I began to think something was amiss when the Peacemakers contacted us for the last job, and the Equiri member of their guild came on board. We were on the far side of the galaxy already, and the timing seemed too serendipitous."

"Are you suggesting the Peacemakers are involved?" Paka asked.

"No," she said quickly. "Although I haven't ruled out some sort of guild politics, I believe the Peacemakers are above this." *But they're probably the only guild above external politics.* "Whoever is pulling the strings has deep pockets and vast power, though, if they are able to manipulate the Peacemakers. Everything since that contract has been geared toward destroying us or maneuvering us into life or death situations. This has become increasingly obvious."

"And desperate," Edwards agreed.

"So, you see it, too?" Alexis asked, relief evident in her voice. Almost reluctantly, the small black man nodded his oversized head.

"The blockade of Sulaadar was too fucking convenient."

"Wait," Hoot interrupted. "You're suggesting that someone interdicted a major trade hub like Sulaadar just to get us?"

"I'm saying they manipulated the situation to their advantage to put us in harm's way. Maybe that little gig had been in the making for years, and whoever is doing this got word of it. They knew we were probably going through and pushed it ahead," Alexis said. "They knew we were going Home. Even if they don't know where Home is, they could probably have guessed Sulaadar was a logical stop."

"But not the only one," Chug pointed out.

"No," Paka agreed, "which is why I did some checking when we got here. There were incidents in the three other logical destinations we could have gone after crossing the Crapti Rift." Alexis looked at her XO, who nodded gravely. Alexis wasn't surprised Paka had been investigating, as well. Everyone was silent as they let the information sink in. "Someone wants us dead and is sparing no expense."

"What about the Golden Horde?" Flipper asked.

"I sent a message to Sansar Enkh, commander of the Horde, but they don't currently have a rep on Karma. We must assume they're either in danger, or are about to be. They have a large team working on our defenses at Home; I'll discuss this with them when we get there."

"But why is this happening?" Edwards asked. "What does it get whoever is doing this? The Hussars are just one of hundreds of Human merc units."

"I don't know yet," Alexis admitted.

"<*There is something larger in play*>" the other agreed. "<*We're just one piece in the game*>"

"You mentioned you were going to wait until we reached Home," Paka said, "but now you can't?"

"Yes," Alexis said, and held up a computer chip. "Hoot just gave me this a few minutes ago. A courier from Home brought it. We had a contract that's been waiting, a contract to provide fleet assistance on an assault. It's a big contract. I planned on leading the mission with *Pegasus*, but because of all we've been through, we're late. Commander Kowalczy followed procedure and took Task Force Two on this mission more than a month ago." She rolled the chip in her hands. "They've been ambushed and trapped in the Grkata system by a huge Maki fleet that interdicted the stargate. They're being hunted and will likely be wiped out if not relieved."

"It's a trap," Paka said with finality. "They're trying to get you to take Task Force Three and our ready reserve to rescue Task Force Two."

"Yes," Alexis agreed. A shouting match broke out as everyone tried to make their opinions known. Slowly, they stopped when they saw the look on their captain's face.

"What are you going to do?" Paka asked.

"Not what they were expecting," she said. "Not quite, anyway."

* * *

Pegasus labored along at one sixth of a G under its ion drive, while the engineering staff struggled to get her main fusion torch drives working again. The damage was spread throughout the deck, a result of the Zuuls' actions as well as weapons fire by the ship's marines. Six hours after the last of the Zuul were neutralized, the sensor techs picked up new arrivals at the system's emergence point.

"Report," Alexis said as she half-floated, half-hopped into the CIC from her wardroom.

"Two cruisers and three escort frigates just transitioned into the system," Flipper said.

"Confidence is high they are Bakulu ships," Edwards said.

"<*Time is up*>" she heard.

"Engineer Long," Alexis called on the intercom.

"Captain?"

"How are we coming?"

"Slightly ahead of schedule," he said. Alexis glanced at the clock displayed on one of the Tri-V tactical screens.

"The new ships are taking the most direct course for the stargate," Flipper said.

Chug manipulated the sensor data, inserted the planet Karma into the view, and displayed the info on one of the Tri-V screens. The emergence point was on the other side of the planet. The new ships were on as close a direct course as was possible, almost skimming the planet's atmosphere as they passed. Paka looked at the track, and her whiskers twitched.

"Add our track and probable intercept point, please," Alexis said. Chug worked and updated the displays. *Pegasus* was in green, the Bakulu ships in red. Time indexes were logged at points along the courses. The two merged in a little more than seven hours. Alexis quietly cursed.

"Long, we need power as soon as possible or we're going to have to fight our way out of here."

"In Karma?" the engineer asked incredulously.

"Yes, in Karma."

"Entropy, this is insane," the Jeha said. Alexis couldn't argue that.

Long turned to his two elSha assistants, who were looking at each other in dumbfounded concern. The ship had already been pushed past the breaking point several times in the last few weeks. Now they were testing the bounds of the possible.

"I need an assessment of the possibility of bypassing the second level safety checks and bringing Reactor Two into torch mode." His two assistants blinked their independent eyes and checked their slates. Each was handling a separate crew of repair and damage control specialists. They consulted in their own language for several minutes.

"We both estimate a seven percent chance of a failure resulting in drive damage," the senior of the two reported.

"And the chance of catastrophic failure?" A catastrophic failure of a fusion torch wouldn't destroy the ship, but would probably kill most of the engineering staff and put the ship out of commission.

"Less than one percent," they stated.

Long nodded his mandibled head and turned his eyestalks to his slate, where one of his delicate manipulative hands tapped and moved status bars. "Captain," he finally said, "I can give you a torch in two hours with an acceptable chance of secondary failure."

"Very well, please do so. Will power be available for tactical systems?"

"You have tactical power now," he said. "Reactor Two, the damaged one, is idling at five percent. That's all that is available for shields and defensive armaments."

"That should suffice for now," Alexis said. "Well done."

Long signed off and dispatched his assistants to spread the orders. They knew the risks and the crew would as well. They also knew if the ship couldn't maneuver and fight back, the risks were an order of magnitude worse. His sinuous body moved rapidly along conduits and walls toward the control room, which had just been put back into service.

* * * * *

Chapter Twenty-Seven

"Update on the quarry," Geshakooka ordered.

"They are still under less than one quarter gravity."

Geshakooka's three eyes blinked as he considered. The information transmitted by the agents on Karma said the Human mercenary ship *Pegasus* should be disabled. A special team had been inserted into the ship and should have disabled their drives, making it easy prey. That would seem to have been an overstatement, although the ship was only thrusting under ion drive. "At our nominal five gravities, we will intercept in another four hours."

"How long before they reach the stargate?" The answer only took a moment.

"Nearly three hours after intercept."

"Increase thrust to six gravities," Geshakooka ordered. His crew complied immediately. As a semi-aquatic mollusk race, they were uniquely suited for both space and high-gravity maneuvers; however, more than a few hours of acceleration in excess of four gravities was tough, even with their unique physiology. Geshakooka was taking a chance on a contract he was less than thrilled with.

"All craft complying," SitCon reported.

"Have medical monitor key crew for signs of acceleration stress," Geshakooka ordered. It wouldn't do to catch their prey, only to have his ship unable to fight. Plus, he knew all too well just how deadly that ship could be. In less than four hours, they would find out how deadly he could be.

* * *

Two hours passed. Everyone on the bridge watched the constantly updating data feeds. Suddenly the enemy intercept began to move closer. Alexis sat forward in her command chair and watched. Yes, it was definitely getting closer.

"Helm, report," Paka ordered, having seen it, as well. Chug worked his controls, tapping at instruments with his pseudopods and using his pinplants to analyze the data.

"The enemy ships have accelerated to six gravities," he reported at last.

"How long can your race tolerate that level of acceleration?" Alexis asked.

"We can do it for a little while without too much difficulty," Glick offered. It wasn't uncommon for one of the two Bakulu bridge officers to answer for the other. The track now showed intercept in less than four hours. "Still, for that long, it will be a strain."

"Bridge, this is engineering," Long's voice came over the PA.

"Go ahead, Long," Alexis said.

"Bringing a torch drive on line in two minutes."

Alexis had been juggling numbers in her head, and wasn't sure if she liked the conclusions. "Are we going to have power for the hyperspace generators when we get to the stargate?"

"Ma'am, I've been trying to get you main power without blowing up half the ship; I don't know how long it will last. When do you need hyperspace generators?"

"Depending on how much thrust you give us, in as little as three hours."

"You are kidding, right?" Long asked.

"I'm not kidding," Alexis said.

"Reactor Two is going to be pushing the torch. If I have a minute to decouple it I can power the hyperspace generators," Long replied.

"I'm going to need quite a bit more, for a few seconds at least," Alexis said.

"Oh," was Long's monosyllable reply. "Three is at least six hours from going online; it had the worst damage to its control systems. That's the one the damned Zuul were trying to use as a bomb. If Two wasn't questionable at full power, I could give you all the power we need."

"Reactor Two is operational," Alexis countered.

"Sure, if you don't push it past five percent. Every point past that increases the probability of blowing its containment."

"I only need it for 30 seconds." She could practically here the Jeha grinding his mandibles together in frustration.

"That's an unwise course of action," he said.

"Your concern is noted," Alexis said. "Prepare to use Reactor Two as we approach the stargate. Chug will provide you with the timing via real time data feed." She turned from the intraship to her pinplants. "I need your help."

"*<I know what you are planning>*"

"Will it work?"

"*<I can make it work, if the power is there>*"

"Make the calculations," Alexis said.

"Main drive is online," Chug announced. "Up to three Gs of thrust at your command."

"All of it, please."

"Aye-aye, Captain," the helmsman replied and entered commands.

"All hands," the PA blared, "prepare for high-gravity acceleration! In three…two…one." The fusion reactor's burning heart was channeled through the reaction chambers, and mass was added. The matter was subjected to plasma as hot as a star and sent out the ship's super-dense engines with incredible force. Nearly 80,000 tons of warship surged forward, dancing on a star.

* * *

"The enemy ship has begun boosting at three gravities," SitCon announced. Captain Geshakooka was not as fast in responding as he'd been a short time ago. He wasn't a young nymph, and six gravities was telling. It took him a moment to recognize the report and devise a reply.

"Predicted intercept?" he asked.

"Less than one hour before they reach the stargate." Geshakooka ground his radula in frustration, then used his pinplant to contact the ship's chief medical officer.

"Yes, Captain?" the medical officer replied.

"What is the condition of the crew?"

"They are tolerating the strain."

"Can they tolerate another G?"

"For how long?"

"Several hours," the captain said.

"That would likely be injurious to many," the doctor said.

"Understood," the captain said and severed the connection.

"Orders, Captain?" the helmsman asked.

"Maintain course and acceleration," he said.

* * *

"They have not increased their acceleration," Flipper confirmed.

"We're going to be really moving when we hit the stargate," Chug said.

"Can you thread the needle again, like in Sulaadar?" Alexis asked.

"I'm going to do my best, Captain," he said.

"*<I am augmenting the calculations>*"

"Make sure no one knows," Alexis replied through her pinplants.

"*<It is rapidly reaching the point where most of the ship will know what I am>*"

"I'm aware of that," she said, "but for now keep it under wraps." She changed to audible commands. "SitCon, will they make weapons range before we reach the stargate?"

"Affirmative," Glick replied immediately. "Edwards and I agree the lead ship is likely the *Yushispa*, the Bakulu cruiser we faced in Sulaadar."

"The Bakulu aren't ones to hold a grudge," Alexis noted. Glick and Chug each glanced at her with an eyestalk.

"Do you know what's going on?" Paka asked. "Why is a Bakulu cruiser hunting us?"

"Later," Alexis said, ending the discussion, although Paka looked at her curiously for several long moments.

"If that is the *Yushispa*," Glick continued, "it will be in weapons range an hour before we reach the stargate and make transition."

"Then we need to give them something else to shoot at," Alexis said. "Drone Control, I have a mission for you."

* * *

Rick wasn't thrilled with his tasking. *Pegasus'* crew had assigned duties they carried out during combat actions, which meant the marines covered a lot of the unassigned jobs from damage control to grunt work, like moving ordinance and parts.

"Sometimes it doesn't pay to be Human!" Private Alvarado laughed next to him. Rick grunted in reply. He was enjoying the chance to work in his new Mk 8 CASPer, sure, but with the warship under three gravities of acceleration it meant only a few races could move around and work. Only the Oogar and Humans in CASPers could do any real lifting. Right now, it was taking almost all his concentration to maneuver the crate between himself and Alvarado.

"You Humans are so puny!" one of the two Oogar from Zenith Squad said in a reasonable approximation of a snort, making his buddy who held the other half of their crate roar with laughter. Rick bit back what he was going to say. Coming from a world with more than two gravities, the big purple bears already had a huge advantage in these situations. Alvarado was less accommodating toward his alien marine comrades. As they turned the corner of the gangway between Decks 24 and 23, he freed his hand long enough to flip a middle finger at the Oogar. The two ursoids laughed even harder, confirming the aliens had worked around Humans before.

"Tell me again why we can't use the lifts?" Rick huffed. Despite the enhancements of the suit, his body was still under the assault of triple its normal weight. It hurt to breath, and he was carrying a half-ton crate up a ramp.

"Too dangerous," Kleena, head armorer and leader of the scientific Geek Squad, said. He rode on the crate, watching the Humans work. The little elSha weighed less than 50 pounds in a standard gravity; considering the bulk of the crate, the little reptilian didn't amount to much extra mass. As a species, the elSha seemed to tolerate higher gravities fairly well. "The lifts are locked above two gravities," Kleena explained. "Imagine what would happen if one failed on an upper deck under this kind of acceleration?"

Rick thought about it. The exercise gave him something to help him forget the physical strain his body was under. The elevators were in shafts that ran almost the entire length of the ship. If one broke loose up by Deck Two (its highest point), it would be going a couple hundred feet per second when it reached the end of its travel.

"Like a bomb," Rick said between panting breaths, "when it hits the bottom."

"Exactly," Kleena said. "The mechanism can handle up to five gravities, but better safe than sorry."

The two teams reached the top of the gangway where it opened into Deck 23. This deck, like the two above it, was only split into two compartments and was full of maintenance machinery, parts, work areas, and a few partial or complete small craft. This was the lower area of flight operations, and as high as they had to move their crates. A Jeha, low to the deck and moving on hundreds of legs, undulated over to them. Its carapace was painted in red and yellow stripes, a sign it worked in the drone and weapons sections.

"Are those the drones?" the Jeha asked.

"Yes," Rick huffed. He'd safed his suit after setting the crate down and was letting its fixed stance support him while he breathed. There was still a lot of pressure on his legs and groin.

"Excellent, put them on the lift, please," the technician said and pointed with one pincer-tipped arm. The two Oogar grunted an affirmation and immediately grabbed their crate. Rick and Alvarado both groaned, took their suits off safe, and picked up the other crate.

The hangar decks were split in two, just like the supporting decks below. Somewhat resembling an old Earth carrier, each side had an elevator platform which was used to move small craft and equipment between the three decks. The lift itself was a big section of deck, sized the same for all three levels, with powerful hydraulic rams to push it up and lower it down. It was currently in the lowered position, its dimensions outlined with black and yellow paint on the deck.

The Oogar quickly placed their crate on the deck and stood next to it, while the two CASPer-suited marines took a little more time. Once they'd put their crate down, the technician moved over to them, and a buzzer sounded. The lift started up a second later. Rick guessed the Jeha had triggered the mechanism via pinplants.

The lift rose at a leisurely pace, something he later found out was a courtesy to them. The Jeha was one of the most G-tolerant races in the Union, and that was apparent on each of the hangar decks. Fully half the personnel who were moving and working were the long, millipede-like race. The elSha were common as well, though they did much less of their signature wall climbing. A fall in three gravities could be deadly.

The lift stopped on Deck 22. Here there were fewer machine shops, and more craft. Around the outside walls waited the ship's complement of shuttles, while racks of drones were stored near the lift. A pair of unusual insect-like Vaga were also there. Like the Jeha, they were more adaptable to high gravity. They looked like dung beetles and used incredibly powerful pinchers to lift and move items. Rick always thought they looked like biological loader mecha. They were busy moving drones onto another lift.

As soon as the lift stopped, several Jeha and an elSha came over. The elSha was riding on the back of a Jeha like Rick had seen in engineering. They opened the crates quickly, and removed a pair of cylindrical drones. These drones had larger openings in their central section than the ones being moved on the other side of the bay.

Their main job done, Rick and the other three marines moved back while the crew got to work assembling the drones. You could tell they were incredibly experienced in the task as it only took them minutes. A hatch in the deck nearby opened, and a pair of elSha ran power cables to each drone.

As the crew finished initializing the new drones, Rick wondered why they were bothering. The floor-to-ceiling racks were full of drones already. The Vaga were only setting a couple dozen on the lift, barely a quarter of what appeared to be stored here, including a couple with the same 'unusual' payload potential. But as he was pondering that, a robot came trundling across the deck. It moved over next to one of the newly assembled drones and, without being prompted, extended a probe and linked itself with the drone.

Rick didn't know why the appearance of the robot struck him as odd, until Alvarado spoke up.

"That's the first robot I've seen on this ship," he said, and Rick realized he was correct. Robots were as common in the Union as anything else you'd see in a technological society. Although the Union's overall technology level had been more advanced than Earth's at first contact, robots were not as omnipresent as had been expected, as artificial intelligence wasn't as advanced as futurists had expected it would be. On *Pegasus*, though, this was the first robot he'd seen.

Rick looked at the other drone he'd brought up and saw another robot was linked with it. Now he was really curious, enough to temporarily forget about the misery of being stuck in a CASPer under three gravities. His curiosity was only getting warmed up, though, as first one robot, then the second jerked and fell over on the deck as if they had been shot. None of the technicians exhibited any surprise.

Lights and status indicators came alive on the drones an instant after the robots keeled over. Control thrusters moved, sensors swept, and the thrust nozzle of their tiny fusion torches gimbaled. An elSha went to each of the disabled robots and opened a little access panel. Switches were thrown and the robots, shaped a little like beetles, folded legs in on themselves to make themselves no bigger than small dogs.

"Will one of you marines take these robots up to drone control on Deck 18?" a Jeha asked.

"I'll do it," Rick said, volunteering immediately. The tech leader agreed and showed Rick how to pick them up to avoid damaging them.

"Never volunteer, rookie," Alvarado chided him as Rick took the two drones and headed for the gangway.

"I'm curious," Rick admitted over the squad net.

"You know what they said about the cat, right?" Alvarado asked.

"Not really," Rick replied, "I shoot cats in the face." As he walked toward the gangway, he watched on his rear camera as a Vaga took control of the new drones and rolled them on small built-in wheels to the elevator.

Climbing another four decks almost exhausted him, although each step brought him closer to some answers. Had those robots transferred their entire power reserves to the drones, and collapsed? That didn't make sense, because he knew the drones were fusion-powered. What were the robots doing?

Rick reached his destination, Deck 18, home of auxiliary control, the backup in case the CIC was destroyed, and drone control. He had to stop at the landing for a minute to catch his breath. He eyed the suit's stimulant reserves and considered it for a time. There was a wide variety of stimulants, but all came at a price. No one had told him how long they would be under this kind of acceleration, and there was a limit to how long you could push your body. Running out of steam was the body's self-defense mechanism against serious injury. He resisted the temptation and rested a bit.

The deck's air tight hatch responded to his touch, revealing a short corridor that ran down the center of the deck and ended with a hatch on each side of the passage. He clomped down the corridor, the hatchway closing automatically behind him, and reached the two doors. He touched the control for the one labeled "Drone Control."

"*Yes*?" a voice responded. It had an odd timber to it, as if run through a translator several times. He'd encountered that once before with an exotic alien race known as the Izlian, squids that floated in the air and spoke through a combination of radiations. He'd seen one on Karma briefly. Rick activated his external speaker.

"This is Private Culper," he said. "I was ordered to bring these robots to you." Silence followed for several seconds. "Do you just want me to leave them here?" he asked. In response, the door popped open and slid aside. "Okay," he said inside his suit, not activating the microphone. The room was dark. He slowly and carefully stepped inside, and the door immediately slid closed behind him.

He realized the room wasn't completely dark. There were panels with slowly flashing lights, a few Tri-V displays showing views outside the ship, and a data track of multiple starships. One monitor displayed an incredibly complex computer code. He could have activated a suit light or switched to infrared, but both seemed rude and inappropriate. The occupant likely had the lights turned down for a good reason. A light sensitive race, perhaps?

"*Place them on this bench,*" the same strange voice said, and a low directional light came on illuminating a long bench covered with tools. Rick walked over carefully, so he didn't crush anything—under three gravities, the suit weighed 1.5 tons—and he placed the drones on the bench.

After making sure the robots wouldn't fall off the table, Rick turned to where the suit's directional mics indicated the voice had come from. Without any of the suit's visual enhancement systems, he could only see dim, shadowy outlines from the single light shining on the work bench. There was a Human figure standing a few feet away, tall and thin, but not defined.

"*You may leave, Private Culper.*"

"May I ask who you are?"

"*Let us just say, in a game of cat and mouse, I am the cat.*"

"I thought there would be an entire crew to run the drones," he said, and looked around. The person didn't reply, so, having been dismissed, he turned and left.

On the gangway going down, Rick almost jumped out of his skin when a voice spoke over his shoulder.

"So, you met the drone controller."

Rick spun and almost fell, and his elbow hit the wall and caused an indentation in the steel. Using his pinplants, Rick spun his visual sensors to look up and behind and saw a familiar elSha clinging to his suit, just above the power supply. He took a deep breath to steady himself before speaking.

"Hello, Kleena," he said.

"You recognize me?"

"Of course," Rick said. "elSha are easier to tell apart than a lot of races. Can I ask why you are back there?"

"After the drones were activated, I noticed one of the interface panels on your CASPer wasn't properly locked shut. I hopped on to take care of it, and by the time it was secured you were halfway up the next deck." Kleena gave his race's equivalent of a shrug. "I didn't figure you'd notice the extra weight."

"And you were correct." Rick resumed his trek down the gangway to where he'd left Alvarado. "Would you explain what that was all about?"

"To what are you referring?"

"Now you're starting to sound like a Jeha." Kleena gave a couple croaking laughs. "With that drone. Since when does a robot have to die to bring a drone to life?"

"Is that what you thought you saw?"

"That's what it looked like to me," Rick said.

"What if I said you weren't far from the truth?"

"I'd want to know what the rest of the truth is." They moved silently for a time, Rick carefully taking each step. Going down the gangway was physically easier, but mentally more taxing. It was twice as easy to misstep and sprawl face first down the angled ramp, and because of the acceleration, that fall would be three times as damaging.

"Private Culper, you are brand new to the Winged Hussars, and what you have already seen and wondered at is more than many who've been with us their whole lives understand."

What the fuck? Rick wondered silently.

"Is the drone controller a Human?"

"That's also difficult to answer."

"Should I be afraid of this ship?"

"That's for you to decide," Kleena replied.

They reached the hangar deck, and Rick turned into the open space where two dozen normal drones were arrayed by the closed bay door, along with the two unusual ones he'd carried up with Alvarado. The crew was gathering equipment, lowering drone racks in the elevator, and scrambling toward the exit. Rick elected to take the express; he took several quick bounds and stepped over the edge of the elevator.

"Yikes!" Kleena chirped as they fell toward the descending elevator at three gravities. Rick expertly fired his jumpjets, timing the breaking thrust to account for the speed of the ship and the rate the elevator was descending. He hit the elevator at less than 5 miles per hour, easily absorbing the landing with a flex of his mechanically-enhanced leg muscles.

"Nice landing," Alvarado remarked. Variable gravity jumps and landings were something they practiced a lot during his cadre training. Of course, that was all simulated within the software of the CASPer. The 20-foot fall in three gravities would have been like falling off a three-story building if he'd mistimed it.

"Thanks," Rick said. A second later the elevator reached the bottom with a *thunk*, and the deck closed above them so the landing bay could be depressurized.

"All hands, set Condition One!" the intercom blared with the computer's voice, "repeat, set Condition One. Prepare for battle."

Kleena crawled down Rick's suit leg and skittered over to a tool rack. His slitted eyes regarded the two suited Humans.

"You better get down to marine country," he told them, then he turned to look at Rick. "Maybe we'll talk more about this later."

"I'd like that," Rick said, and the two marines headed for the gangway to tromp back to the marines' deck below.

* * * * *

Chapter Twenty-Eight

"Drones report ready," Glick said as the signal came in from the hangar deck. A Tri-V showed the hangar elevator closing and the usual swirl of light FOD—foreign object debris—as the atmosphere was pumped down to near vacuum.

"Enemy will be in weapons range in fifteen minutes," Flipper noted.

"Launch drones as soon as able," Alexis ordered. The big Tri-V display showed the enemy ships closing on them. They had assumed a star formation a few minutes ago, with the two cruisers at the center and the frigates slightly further out. A minute later, the drones launched.

"Fourteen drones in the black," Glick said. The Tri-V updated with the new tracks. On the display, *Pegasus* was in the center, a green miniature ship, while fourteen blue darts flowed out and away, quickly beginning to fall behind as the warship accelerated.

"Drone Control," Alexis said, "initiate the program."

The 14 drones fired their powerful micro-fusion engines. The short-lived power plants were expendable and could provide several thousand gravities of thrust, if necessary. The lifespan of the engine was rated in G-hours. Whereas the fusion power plants which drove starships contained a sustained fusion reaction, the ones which operated drones more closely resembled barely-contained fusion bombs.

Drones were the preferred way to engage in stand-off combat and could carry energy weapons, missiles, and ECM modules to distract or disable an enemy. Fighting at distances of light seconds or more made combat challenging. Missiles had long flight times, during which their targets could move considerably from where they should have been. Energy weapons required huge amounts of power, and the shot-to-hit ratio was often hundreds to one—not a great investment of power. Drones took almost as long to reach a target as missiles, but were semi-autonomous and could be sent to attack a target with a variety of engagement profiles. They had the mobility and range to pursue and fight far beyond a ship's weapons range.

Riding their micro-fusion torches, in just twelve seconds, the drones accelerated to a speed of over 750,000 feet per second relative to their mother ship. Two cut their engines while the other twelve altered their vectors and burned for another twelve seconds. Now they were shooting away from *Pegasus* at a relative speed of one and a half million feet per second, or over a million miles per hour. If their power plants had the endurance, and if it were possible under the restraints of physics, the drones could have reached the speed of light in just over four hours. The drones revised their flight paths for an additional second. Angle of attack and velocity established, they went dark.

The drones coasted toward the pursuing ships which were pushing hard toward their target, *Pegasus.*

"*Course and plot for drones set,*" Drone Control confirmed.

"Helm," Alexis said; one of Chug's eyestalks turned toward her, "prepare to maneuver."

* * *

"Possible missile launch!" SitCon called out in the *Yushispa's* CIC. Captain Geshakooka instantly became more alert. He'd been mostly retracted into his shell to minimize the stress of the G forces. He extruded his head painfully from the shell and extended his eyestalks to look at the Tri-V display. The SitCon was a backup, the main one had succumbed to the stresses of the extended boost and was in sickbay under sedation. He wasn't alone. Twenty-two crew on *Yushispa* were down so far, along with another 35 on the other cruiser and escort frigates.

Geshakooka examined the Tri-V, forcing his mind to fully understand. The sensors had picked up several electromagnetic radiation spikes from *Pegasus*. These spikes had lasted for 24 seconds, then disappeared.

"Too long a boost for missiles," he said. "Were you able to get a fix on what they were?"

"No, Captain," the sensor operator reported, acting as slow as Geshakooka felt. "The enemy ship's torch is putting out too much hard radiation. It is interfering with our sensors."

The captain evaluated the info and decided the SitCon was right; it was a launch of some kind. Only what? Missiles didn't put out strong EM spikes like that. Only ships with fusion power produced that kind of signature. Their prey didn't have any frigates attached, so that meant one thing.

"Drones," the captain said. "Notify the escorts to prepare for a drone attack."

They were still half an hour from weapons range. Geshakooka berated himself for not expecting it. They hadn't been fired on for the same reason they hadn't fired on the other ship. Karma was a busy center of commerce. Dozens of ships were behind them near the planet and Karma Station, and more were ahead of them around the stargate. Missiles were smart enough to disarm themselves if they missed their targets, but lasers did not care. A wild laser shot could hit and damage a ship a light hour away, or even further.

Responding to his orders, *Yushispa* slowed, allowing the escorts to pull slightly ahead of the two cruisers. Bakulu escort frigates specialized in screening capital ships. They had relatively light shields, but formidable close-in laser defenses and disproportionately powerful sensors. Warned, they aimed those sensors at a smaller threat box to watch for the coming attack. The ships also began jamming to block any remote drone controllers.

The drones were less than a yard across, and shaped with stealth technology. Their tiny fusion cores were wrapped in jackets of F11 which absorbed radiation. While not actively firing their power plants, they presented almost no electromagnetic signature. They were black, nearly invisible, silent killers racing toward their targets. The escorts used every trick they had to find them, and eventually they succeeded.

A target appeared on the master Tri-V display, complete with angle of approach and velocity. Geshakooka blinked all three eyes, it was coming fast. The SitCon had added probabilities of risk to the ships along the direction of counterattack. They were small, but still there. Geshakooka made a decision.

"Engage the drones," he ordered. "Spread attack on probable locations of all undetected targets." Since drones worked together to increase their potential to overwhelm a target's shields, he knew the others were likely not far away.

The escort closest to the bearing of the drone cut its acceleration and yawed. It began to fall back in formation as the other four ships continued to boost. The elongated wedge-shaped frigates had laser batteries mounted along all sides, though only a few on the nose. Coming about allowed the greatest number of weapons to bear on the target. The ship unleashed a screen of crisscrossing low-power laser fire. Centered on the identified target, the high-frequency pulse lasers created a veritable wall of coherent light. The drone was obliterated in a fraction of a second.

The other escorts used their sensors in concentrated scans, looking for the telltale flashes that indicated other drones had been destroyed. There were no other explosions. As the precious seconds ticked by, Captain Geshakooka's response went from uncertainty, to confusion, and then fear. There was no possible way the enemy sent a single drone. Then he understood. Diversion.

"Widen the scans!" he ordered, too late.

"Drive plumes!" SitCon called out. "Drive plumes on all sides!"

"All ships, prepare for attack," the captain ordered.

Seconds before they would have rocketed past the Bakulu ships, eleven of the surviving drones flipped over and fired their powerful micro-fusion torches. Their closing speeds dropped at a shocking rate; they were all around the Bakulu, not in one area. He had been correct; the first one *had* been a decoy. "Engage at will," the captain ordered, but the drones were already firing.

The power plant on the drones would have been more than sufficient to operate a laser, but to reserve that power for propulsion the drones used chemical lasers instead. All eleven drones danced and juked as they began firing their high-frequency, chemically-pumped lasers. Each beam packed just under 10 megawatts of power.

"Drones are firing lasers," tactical told the captain. The specialist shook his eyestalks in disbelief. "They are unbelievably accurate!"

"Target?" Geshakooka asked.

"Frigate One," he replied.

"And?" he pushed. "What else?"

"Just that ship!" It was the captain's turn to shake his eyestalks in disbelief. The Human drones were not acting like drones. Frigate One was the escort which had fallen out of formation to engage the decoy. Because it was yawed sideways to the squadron's flight path, the drones targeted both its fore and aft shields. Those shields were small, thus harder to hit. They were also proportionately weaker than the side shields.

Tactical data flowed into the cruiser, updated by the SitCon on the big Tri-V in the center of CIC. Captain Geshakooka watched as his escort's fore and aft shields were knocked down, and the ship was riddled with pinpoint laser fire. Normal drones should have gone for the biggest ship, or, if targeted against the escorts, should have attacked the one closest to their location, but these drones saw a frigate out of formation, selected it as a target of opportunity, and tore it up.

"They're acting like they're piloted fighters," he said. "That's impossible." No race in the galaxy could withstand 100 gravities for more than a fraction of a second. The data on the screen indicated these had likely exceed a thousand Gs!

"Frigate One reports drive and shield damage," SitCon said. "They are unable to resume chase."

"Acknowledged," Geshakooka said, "tell the commander to go defensive." The frigate would cease powering her drive and divert all energy to shields and close-in defensive laser fire. "See what their engineers can do to get the ship back under control." He turned his attention toward tactical. "Results of the anti-drone fire?"

"Three more drones destroyed," the sensor tech reported. On the Tri-V, the eight remaining drones showed small secondary sensor echoes. At first the captain thought they were missiles, but the new contacts didn't move with their own power, and the sensor returns were shallow, or not dense enough to be weapons. He blinked in confusion, just as the drones again lit their engines and accelerated. Not toward the now disabled Frigate One, but toward the rest of the squadron.

Geshakooka looked at the Tri-V tactical display, considered the radical way these drones were acting, and made a snap decision.

"Order the squadron to alter course and take evasive action," Geshakooka ordered, "emergency thrust!" As one, the four ships still under power initiated skew turns in four different directions, and under nine Gs for almost 10 seconds. He had a glimpse of the command crew relaying orders and commanding the ship's computers to execute the maneuvers an instant before the mollusks all withdrew into their shells where they were most tolerant of the extreme thrust. He gritted his radula as the acceleration slammed down like a hammer.

* * *

Geshakooka was right, the drones were not ordinary in many ways. They were custom manufactured by the Winged Hussars from the ground up. They were more powerful than any others available and had longer-endurance micro-fusion torches. Their structure matched the performance of the fastest missile manufactured in the galaxy as the Hussars' Geek Squad, in designing them, had started with that missile and turned it into a drone.

The Winged Hussars employed three classes of drone. Standard drones were carried by nearly every ship in the mercenary company, but the other two types were only used by *Pegasus*. Of those two, one was outwardly indistinguishable from the ones used by other Hussar ships. The other was quite special. Of the 14 launched, 12 were the standard drones *Pegasus* used, and two were special. They'd held back as the other 12 took positions.

Captain Geshakooka was also right in that what the drones were doing should have been impossible. Drones didn't control other drones.

After the eight surviving drones finished their initial attack on the frigate designated by their controller, they were ordered to flush. The tiny reactors the drones carried were limited because of the small amount of F11 they held. The rare gas absorbed radiation, which was particularly important in the miniature, barely-controlled fusion plant of a drone. When the F11 became saturated, the reaction would cease, and the drone would be melted by its own power plant. As small as they were, they possessed almost no ability to dissipate surplus thermal radiation. The Hussar's drones had a trick, though; they carried extra F11.

Once they'd boosted at full power for nearly a minute, their F11 was almost saturated. They flushed their cores and immediately refilled them with the reserve. In addition to the F11, the drop tank contained extra reactive chemicals for the lasers, which was transferred concurrently. The now empty tanks were released, and the drones given new targets. Without the drop tanks, they could accelerate even faster, and they shot at the small squadron of Bakulu ships like lightning bolts.

This time the target was one of the cruisers. Only eight were left, but they fired their two-megawatt lasers at their weapons' maximum rate of fire. After a second of firing, the enemy ships ceased their direct pursuit course and began to maneuver radically. The drones fired their lasers until their chemical stores were exhausted, then adjusted their engines to full thrust as they fine-tuned their courses. Based on the enemy positions and their tactical responses to the drone attack, a last-minute decision was made.

After depleting their lasers, the drones accelerated for 3.1 seconds. In that time, they reached a speed of nearly 260,000 feet per second. All eight, plus one of the special drones, rammed their targets at precisely the same time. The kinetic energy of each impact was equal to 84 tons of TNT, or nearly 700 megawatts of energy.

* * *

"Damage report!" Captain Geshakooka yelled as the ship rang like a bell from the impacts.

"The drones concentrated on us," the SitCon reported.

"We have multiple shield generators out," the damage control coordinator said while SitCon continued to analyze. "Some minor primary hull damage, but no systems are down."

"Where in entropy did those drones go?" the captain demanded. "Helm, prepare to resume pursuit!"

"The drones rammed," SitCon finally concluded. He was struggling with the conclusion. It was nearly impossible to successfully ram. For all eight to do it was inconceivable. "Between the lasers and the impacts, more than a gigawatt of energy." The main tactical Tri-V updated with scrolling charts of data from the attacks, and Captain Geshakooka marveled at it. These Winged Hussars were dangerous and unpredictable. Why attack this way? They had to know that it wouldn't be enough to penetrate their shields. They'd faced *Yushispa* once before, after all.

"We are bearing back on the enemy," helm reported.

"Another drone contact!" sensors called out. "It's almost on top of us." Before the captain could issue an order, the drone exploded.

The drone controller, one of the ones Rick and the other marines delivered, carried a specially designed 20 megaton EMP warhead. The blast wasn't powerful enough to destroy a fully-shielded ship, but it was enough to blind anything within a few hundred miles.

"We are blind," the sensor operator reported.

"Shields further weakened," tactical added.

"How many more drones are there?" the captain demanded, his senses buzzing. The sensor tech was sifting the data repeatedly. "How many?!"

"I think that was the last one," he finally said.

"Entropy!" the captain cursed. This tactic only made sense if they were about to... "Helm, evade, evade, evade!"

* * *

"She's evading!" Glick yelled.

"Best guess, Edwards," Alexis said, then barked "Fire!" The small black man nodded. The ship was under his control, linked to his pinplants. Flying backward now, bow facing where she'd come from, he stabilized and opened the flower petal-shaped doors.

Pegasus' massive particle accelerator spinal mount fired, sending an underpowered, 10-terawatt beam flashing at the speed of light toward the pursuing Bakulu ships. Geshakooka realized at the last possible second the drone attack and blinding were to keep them from noticing that *Pegasus* was no longer racing toward the stargate—she'd spun around to engage the Bakulu. His sudden evasion saved the ship.

As the Maki had found, the *Pegasus'* main gun was a devastatingly effective weapon, more than making up for comparably weaker secondary batteries, and it would have been powerful enough, even at less than one quarter power, to penetrate *Yushispa's* forward shields and punch through the narrow cone-shaped ship from bow to stern if it had hit.

Edwards' best guess was better than most tactical officers' planned firing solutions, and it had also, unknown to him, been ever so slightly tweaked to make it even more accurate. Despite all that, the shot missed. Mostly.

The one second pulse of energy was aimed right down *Yushispa's* nose. The ship rotated on her axis, causing the first three quarters of the beam to miss entirely. However, as she rotated, the last quarter tore into the aft shields of the spinning ship. The shields blew out almost instantly, and the beam cut into the ship's hull like God's own plasma torch.

* * *

Yushispa shuddered and screamed in agony, explosions rippling through her overloaded rear shield generators as the particle beam carved into the hull. The beam cut through a reaction mass tank and penetrated her main engineering space, stopping mere feet before it would have sliced into one of the two main fusion reactor cores.

"We're hit!" the DCC yelled. "Aft shields are out!"

"Engine room decompressing," engineering reported. "Main reactor damaged. Going into safe mode. We are operating on backup power only. "

"Warn the escorts," the captain ordered.

"Radio is still out from the EMP," the reply came.

The escorts were blinded like the *Yushispa*, but didn't have the same caliber of commander. With the command cruiser no longer presenting a predictable target, Edwards picked another for his next shot.

The other cruiser was hit with a 20-terawatt particle beam, and it tore through her lengthwise. The ship was torn apart and exploded with the loss of nearly all hands. Edwards decided no more shots were warranted.

* * *

"Return to course," Alexis ordered and hung on as Chug spun *Pegasus* back toward the stargate and resumed the previous acceleration. He crunched the new course plot and reported in a few seconds.

"No way we'll make the transition window now," the helmsman said.

"Understood," Alexis said; "just get us there as close to transition time as possible. Also, inform Engineer Long that we're a go on the other plan."

"He'll be thrilled," Guylan quipped.

"Damage assessment?" Alexis asked Glick.

"Working," the Bakulu responded. The alien had several Tri-V displays up showing frame by frame images. Some were taken with *Pegasus'* visual tracking telescopes, others with radar, and a few were from the drones' gun cameras, taken moments before their destruction. The latter were, naturally, the worst quality. A moment later he spoke again. "In addition to the frigate the drones chewed up, one cruiser was destroyed. The other cruiser was hit, and is adrift. Flipper, can you get me any more data?"

"Not with the torch burning," the Selroth sensor tech replied.

"Then I can't give you much more," Glick said.

"Safe to say we at least clipped the other cruiser in their engineering section," Edwards said. Glick burbled his agreement.

"Any collateral damage?" she asked. They'd tried to be careful when firing at the pursuing Bakulu ships, but Karma Station and dozens of other starships were downrange of their shots.

"Deflection was more than enough," Glick said, "all our shots were outside the danger zone."

Alexis nodded, relieved. "Well done, everyone," she said to her command staff, "as always. Prepare for transition in…" she looked to Chug to finish.

"Forty-nine minutes." Paka took charge of the final preparations.

Forty-five minutes later, she spoke to the helm again. "How close?" she asked.

"About one minute," Chug confided.

"Damn it," Alexis said, "that's a long time."

"Best I could do," he said. "If we had both reactors…"

"No way," Guylan interjected.

"CIC, this is Engineer Long."

"Go ahead," Alexis said.

"We're ready, but this is not advised."

"Noted," the captain replied, then turned to her helmsman and navigator. "Chug, begin powering for hyperspace."

"Yes, Captain," he said. Reactor Three began to power up to 100 percent, and energy was channeled through the network of hyperspace nodes. They drew 20 of the power plant's 29 terawatts of power, and the rest of the ship's systems drew another seven. Staying in hyperspace with one power plant was tricky and incredibly dangerous; there was *no* room for errors.

"Calculations ready?" Alexis asked through her pinplants.

"*<All set>*" the answer came immediately.

"We've never done this at the kind of velocity we have right now." Alexis said.

"*<You have never understood that when it comes to multi-dimensional physics, velocity does not matter>*"

You are right about that, she thought. "Alright everyone," she said to her command staff; "tell the crew to stand by for transition!"

* * * * *

Chapter Twenty-Nine

Rick had just locked his CASPer into an armorer frame and popped the hatch when the PA chimed and the computer's voice spoke.

"All hands, prepare for transition."

He'd ridden out the ship's spinning and firing in his suit, using its powered hands and magnetic soles to lock himself to the deck of a gangway just above marine country. He'd spent several tense minutes wondering if they were about to be punched through by return fire or annihilated by a nuclear ship-killer. When no response came, he breathed again. He'd fought on a ship twice, but this was the first time he'd been on a ship in battle. The not-knowing was worse.

"Acceleration ends," the computer announced and *Pegasus'* powerful fusion torch cut. Rick sighed and enjoyed breathing for a few seconds. The earlier respite before they'd opened fire had been too brief. Plus, the ship had been spinning on her axis, and since he was in the lower decks, that maneuver had pulled several Gs. The final cessation of thrust was a welcome relief.

In blessed zero gravity, Rick flipped up and double checked his suit was properly locked before kicking off toward the lower deck where his squad would be. He found them all engaged in an animated discussion about the attack. Lynn was just finishing telling the others about how Rick had simply floated, shooting at the charging Zuul, without bothering to take cover. They all looked at Rick as he came in. Well, except for Oort who merely moved a couple eyes over to observe his arrival. She was holding a slate and reading with several others.

"Some kind of a Human badass?" Zit asked. Rick floated over and dropped into an open chair, quickly strapping in. "You trying to prove something?"

"No," Rick said, "I just wasn't scared."

"That Zuul could have burned your tiny brain out," Johansson said.

"Took guts," Jeejee said. The little Flatar was buckled into his harness on Oort's back. Rick figured since the Tortantula was locked to the deck with her seven remaining primary legs, it was as safe as any other place in the compartment. He made a mental note to ask the arachnid about the missing leg, but to do it from a distance. The truth was, the huge alien still concerned him.

"You were just up-ship, weren't you?" Lynn asked, changing the subject. Rick nodded. "You hear anything about what's going on?"

"No," he admitted, "nothing. After we delivered the weird drones to the hangar deck, I took these dead robots up to 18, and Kleena stole a ride on my back without my knowing it." He thought for a second. "Why, what's so weird? I heard the Hussars fight a lot."

"Not at Karma," Lynn said, to which all those with heads nodded in agreement.

"You don't go firing the spinal mount in the Karma system," Johansson added.

"Too many others here, and you might hit the wrong someone," Jeejee agreed, then used his little hands to make an exploding gesture, punctuated with a "Blooey!" sound. Rick could see how that made sense.

"So, we're running?" he asked.

"I'd say it's a strategic withdrawal," the sergeant said, and several of the others chuckled. "The captain never backs down from a fight," she added seriously.

"Just ask those Maki ships," Zit said, his translator managing to convey a certain grim satisfaction. Rick had heard about that fight, and how *Pegasus* had shot the shit out of several Maki ships on the way out of Sulaadar, as well as a couple of Bakulu. The scuttlebutt was the ships after them were either Bakulu or Maki.

"You see anything in drone control?" Jeejee asked out of the blue. Rick looked at the small alien. He couldn't help but think of a cartoon he'd seen once about three chipmunks always getting in trouble. He'd seen that as a kid with someone. There was yet another hole in his life. Rick shook his head and tried to answer the Flatar.

"I saw the drone controller." Once again, he had the attention of the marines who'd been aboard before he came on.

"Oh?" Zit asked. "You know what they call the drone controller?"

"Who's they?" Rick wondered.

"The crew up in that area."

"Okay," Rick said, "I'll bite. What do they call him?"

"The Ghost," Sergeant T'jto said, spoiling Zit's fun. The Goka's tiny head turned slightly, regarding his sergeant. Rick wondered if that was the cockroach equivalent of the stink eye. "Apparently, the Ghost has been on the ship since the Hussars found the vessel a hundred years ago."

The alarm sounded again; they were about to transition. "This Ghost, is it from the original crew?" Several of the marines shrugged, T'jto among them. "Is it alien? Is it Human?"

"No one knows," T'jto finally said. The final alarm sounded, and everyone prepared.

"It is one of the mysteries of life," Oort said, the first time the Tortantula had spoken. The seconds ticked away.

* * *

"Reactor Three at 100 percent," Long said from engineering; "all hyperspace nodes are functioning nominally. Reactor Two is idle and primed. Standing by."

"Here we go," Chug said as he fed the final details into the navigational computer. The Bakulu helmsman knew the ship could do what they were about to do; he'd done it many times. He just didn't know how it was capable. He would really have liked to.

On the big Tri-V display, the mile-wide ring of asteroids that made up the Karma system stargate was racing at them with incredible speed. In only seconds, it went from a tiny glowing spot to a rapidly expanding form with shape and definition. This was the second time in as many transitions that *Pegasus* was going to shoot the ring at an incredibly high speed. Alexis' face cracked into a little grin, and she shook her head slightly as she thought about how the Lords of the Rings would be annoyed by this.

They were still thousands of miles away when the stargate shimmered to life, and all the waiting starships moved through into hyperspace. Her smile compressed into a tight line as she realized how far off they were going to be.

"Stargate closing in 10 seconds," Hoot said, relaying the transmitted details from the stargate's controllers. Alexis knew that instruments on the stargate's control center would see the battlecruiser racing toward the ring at a couple hundred thousand miles per hour, and know they weren't going to make it. Seconds passed.

"Stargate in 10 seconds," Chug said, "nine, eight, seven..."

"Reactor Two to full power!" Alexis ordered.

Down in engineering, Long looked at the status board and its 70 little status lights for the containment buffers of Reactor Two. Nine of them glowed yellow, instead of green. He clicked his mandibles together and reached a delicate claw to slide the power control for the damaged reactor from "STANDBY" to "FULL POWER." Inside the machine, magnetic containment buffers surged and hydrogen poured into the hungry fusion reactor. The power status bar shot to just below its peak output, feeding another 28 terawatts of power into the warship's systems.

The master alarm sounded, and one of the nine buffer status lights flashed red, indicating failure. Long held onto the console, ground his mandibles together, and prayed they didn't lose anymore. A few feet away, a miniature star assailed the weakened containment field.

"Full power on Reactor Two!" Guylan announced. He normally only concerned himself with damage control, but since the ship was in such a sorry state, he was helping Long with engineering duties.

On the big Tri-V, the stargate shimmered and shut down as they hurtled toward the center. At that point, everything happened quickly.

Reactor Two's entire power output was channeled along the same conduits that fed the hyperspace nodes, sending more than twice the power that would have been needed to operate them. At the same instant, a command was sent to the nodes at the front of

Pegasus. Nine of them around the nose of the warship extended, and opened like flowers, all aimed ahead of the ship. For an instant, those nodes transformed into shunts and all the extra power was channeled against the barriers between dimensions. The hyperspace shunts discharged.

A few hundred feet in front of *Pegasus*, a stargate almost exactly the size of the battlecruiser snapped into life. The ship shot through the gate and disappeared into hyperspace, and the gate instantly disappeared behind it. The whole chain of events took less than a second.

As soon as the shunts had discharged, they immediately reverted to nodes, and the power level was decreased back to nominal. *Pegasus* was in hyperspace.

"Powering back Reactor Two," Guylan said.

"That worked okay," Alexis said.

Guylan looked up at her. "We lost two buffers," he said, and a small Tri-V showed the reactor status board. The 70 buffers were like a ring around the reactor, and one pie-shaped wedge had nine discolored magnetic containment buffers. Two of them were now flashing red.

"Well, we shouldn't need the reactor again," Alexis said. "However, keep it on-line while Reactor One's repairs are completed. For the next 170 hours, we need the backup." Guylan spoke to his counterpart in engineering for a moment.

"Long says that should be okay. However, he reminded the captain that if we lose three more buffers, Reactor Two could have a containment failure."

* * *

Geshakooka watched his prey disappear from Karma without comment. His cruiser was in no shape to do anything about it. They were back under nominal power, though only just, and braking as best they could. The helmsman had altered their course enough so they wouldn't slam into the stargate. That was something.

He was still stinging from the second spanking administered by the Winged Hussars in as many weeks. Quigg du Snoo was considered an elite space-based merc company. Being so handily worked over wasn't something Geshakooka took well. He was mad, and he didn't like being mad.

"One overpowered cruiser," he said as he floated in his command station, watching the Tri-V listing repairs underway and those that wouldn't be possible outside of drydock. He could easily have jetted over and stuck to the deck, but floating helped him think. Just one ancient cruiser, and he'd lost one of his own cruisers and had an escort mauled. He'd also come within a fraction of a second of meeting the same fate as the lost cruiser.

"Captain," the sensor officer said, "I have something for you to see." Geshakooka extended his third eye and turned them all toward the Tri-V. It was showing a loop of the enemy ship making its escape.

"I could do without watching it again," the captain said.

"I apologize, Captain, but I believe this is important."

"Then explain what I am seeing."

"As you order." The technician manipulated the image backward. The *Yushispa's* cameras were watching the enemy ship, though you could still see the stargate behind it. The discontinuity formed and tiny spots moved into it, the other ships. They'd no doubt hurried through, being more than keenly aware of the battle rapidly approaching. He continued to watch, the action happening incredibly fast. There was a swirling flash, and *Pegasus* was gone. "Did you see it?" the technician asked.

"I saw the enemy ship disappear, yes." The tech looked back with one eyestalk and waved it in annoyance.

"No, watch again. I will slow it." The scene replayed as the captain, quickly losing patience with the junior technician, forced himself to watch one more time. As *Pegasus* disappeared, he saw something.

"What was that?" he asked.

"You saw it?" the technician asked.

"Once again," he ordered, "even slower this time." It played for a third time. *Pegasus* approached the stargate. It shimmered, and he saw black stars for an instant, and *then* the enemy ship disappeared. "What am I seeing?" he asked the technician.

"The enemy ship has hyperspace shunts," the technician said confidently. Geshakooka shook all three eyestalks in denial. A warship, with shunts? A small warship, too? There were warships with hyperspace shunts, and they were incredibly rare. It took an immense amount of power to fire shunts, more than it took to operate nodes. Who would be crazy enough to put that much power on a ship that small? Then he thought, the same ones crazy enough to put a spinal mount on a ship that small, that's who. Suddenly the prowess of the Winged Hussars made a little more sense. It always helped to have a secret ability in a battle, and that was one hell of a secret.

"Excellent job," he complemented the technician, who nodded his eyestalks in gratitude. Geshakooka made a mental note to update the technician's file with a commendation. The moment of the enemy ship's transition into hyperspace via shunts was less than a second. Very few would have noticed it. "Damage control, estimated time to repair the reactor?"

"Five hours."

The helmsman had already plotted the course to decelerate and come around to the stargate again, which was scheduled to activate in eleven hours. He didn't have authorization from his company to make an unscheduled transition, which would have cost hundreds of thousands of credits. It was only four hours between the time they'd arrive back at the stargate and the next transition; he could wait that long. Plus, they could complete more repairs in the additional time. The 170 hours in hyperspace would likewise prove useful.

"Communications, schedule our transition for the next stargate opening. We will resume pursuit at that time." Armed with the additional information, Geshakooka had no intention of being caught off guard again.

"Are we certain of their destination?" the helmsman asked.

"We have intel from our contacts on Karma," the captain assured him; "we will proceed on that information." The captain began working on a battle plan.

* * *

Once they were safely in hyperspace, and the ship was secured from Condition One, Alexis dismissed the combat crew and shut down the CIC. Reactor watch teams would keep the ship safely in hyperspace, and the computer would monitor other conditions. If anything warranted it, the CIC could be staffed in minutes. Nothing happened in hyperspace that required the command crew.

"Everyone is off duty," she told them. "Get a meal, get a few hours' sleep, and we'll meet in my wardroom with all department heads in six hours." They acknowledged and dispersed. In a minute, it was just Alexis and her XO. "Paka, get some rest."

"Yes, Captain," the Veetanho said, but she hesitated.

"I mean it. We're heading into a shit storm, and there's a lot to get ready for." Paka nodded. "I'm going to sleep a few hours in my wardroom." Paka gave her a knowing look, then slowly floated out, leaving her commander alone

Alexis hovered there for an indeterminate period. The CIC command stations were all virtual; any one could be used for any function. Once an operator logged out, a series of colored lights indicated that station's readiness to accept input. With her crew gone, the CIC was mostly dark except for intermittent flashing indicators. She knew there would be the never-ending vibration of the ship's reactors, pumping energy to the nodes to keep them in hyperspace, and she could feel the gentle kiss of air being moved by the life support system. Unmanned, like it was at that moment, the nerve center of the powerful ancient warship was a beautiful thing. Almost a work of art, which at a simple touch could transform into an instrument of destruction. The particle accelerator spinal mount could, at full power, carve a city from the surface of a planet like a child scooping up a sandcastle on the beach.

Pegasus was more to her than a ship. Much, much more. It was the heart and soul of the Winged Hussars. Without it, they would never have survived the Alpha Contracts. Without it, they wouldn't have found their home. Without it, her sister might…

Alexis pushed off toward her stateroom to get some rest.

* * * * *

Interlude

20 Years Ago
Stargate Highguard
Theel System

The simplest missions were always the most dangerous. Alexis remembered her mother drilling that into her head. She had always considered it crazy. Until now.

"Another spread of missiles!" SitCon yelled.

"Roll her to match strong shields," Alexis ordered.

"On it," TacCom replied. Everyone in the CIC hung on as the ship spun, and the point-defense lasers blazed away.

"Communications," Alexis said, "order *Biter* to break off and try to flank. See if she can get the bastard to come about and stop concentrating its fire on us."

"Aye-aye," the comms officer replied. On the big Tri-V, her squadron was deployed in highguard, interdicting the stargate. The Zuul raiding party had snuck in weeks ago and quietly waited until the perfect moment, when the Maki fleet was rotating out, for their raid. The Izlian who controlled the Theel system were pissed. The Zuul had cleaned out two mining depots in the extensive asteroid belt and were now trying to punch their way out of the system. Alexis had her first squadron command, the cruiser *War Admiral* and three frigates who rode on her hull to fight detached, *Mercy, Biter,* and *Manx.*

"This defensive contract with the Izlian should be fairly simple and routine," her mother had said. "This is a good chance for you and your sister to have independent commands." The twins had flipped for overall command, and Alexis won. Katrina's squadron had been monitoring the emergence point, lest additional Zuul make an appearance. The raid appeared to be a stealth operation, and Alexis was prepared to stop them from getting away.

"Won't be too hard," she'd assured her sister who wanted to come and help. The other twin was angry at missing their first real fight. "Probably a couple of frigates, maybe a light cruiser. The Zuul don't like to run hot."

The Zuul didn't *normally* use large ships, as Alexis had said. They liked their ships fast and light. Shoot, hit, and get out was their favorite tactic, as was evidenced by the ships that had escorted the freighters which had cleaned out the depots. However, the Bakulu battlecruiser that came to break the highguard was a nasty surprise. It was a missile-packing beast twice the size of Alexis' *Crown*-class cruiser.

Several of the most recent wave of missiles from the enemy battlecruiser split their targeting. The ones that went for *War Admiral* were destroyed by point-defense fire, but the ones that cut away all scored. Alexis cringed.

"*Manx* has taken three direct hits from ship-killer missiles," SitCon reported.

"She's lost drive, shields are down," TacCom said. Alexis cringed. *Manx* had a crew of 29.

"Helm, move us to cover *Manx*!" The ship began a high-gravity turn to intercede between the battlecruiser and their crippled frigate.

"TacCom, give me a pinpoint particle cannon firing solution on the battlecruiser's drives!"

"Working," the tactical commander said.

"They're launching more missiles," SitCon warned. "*Biter* reports they have a flanking position."

"Have them fire all their tubes at the damned ship! Do you have that firing solution?"

"As good as we can get," TacCom replied.

"Fire to match *Biter's* barrage arrival!"

The seconds ticked by as a wave of missiles raced toward the disabled *Manx*. Alexis just managed to get in the way, but that meant they bore the full brunt of the 20 ship-killer missiles. This time their lasers only stopped fifteen. Just as the missiles exploded in a chain across *War Admiral's* hull, the battlecruiser pumped a barrage of four 500-megawatt particle beams into her.

"Forward and amidships lateral shield failure!" SitCon warned.

"Helm, rotate."

"Can't," TacCom overrode. "Firing in 10 seconds as ordered."

"We're going to eat some energy," SitCon warned.

"Noted," Alexis said and chewed her lip. The count wound down as their coordinated attack time raced against the enemy battlecruiser's particle cannon recharge rate.

"Firing!" TacCom barked.

"Rolling ship!" helm called. The battlecruiser was caught between a wave of 10 ship-killers from *Biter* and a barrage of six 250-megawatt particle cannons from *War Admiral.* Missiles impacted and particle beams splashed energy into the battlecruiser's rear shields.

"Her aft shields are down," TacCom confirmed.

"Order *Mercy* to put some missiles up her ass!" Alexis ordered, punching a fist on her command chair arm.

"New ships in our threat box," TacCom informed her. The Tri-V updated with four new ships. "Two frigates and two transports. It's the Zuul raiding party. A wave of red arrows appeared racing toward her squadron. "The frigates already launched missiles!" The Zuul love missile frigates. They were less versatile, and didn't defend as well, but they could put out a shit storm of missiles.

The battlecruiser hit *War Admiral* with another spread of particle beams, further weakening another section of shields. Alexis looked at the tactical board in growing fear. All but one of *Mercy's* missile spread were swatted from the air. The single successful missile exploded its squash-bomb slightly off target. It didn't take out the battlecruiser's engineering spaces as planned, it only disabled one of the bigger ship's torches.

The missiles from the newly arrived Zuul frigates flashed across the entire squadron, except for *Manx,* which was still shielded by *War Admiral.* Half her ship's shields were threatening to fail as the warheads exploded. Both *Biter* and *Mercy* were also hit.

I'm going to lose this, Alexis thought in despair. Then one of the Zuul frigates was torn apart in a ball of expanding gas and fire.

"I have *Whirlaway* coming in at high speed!" SitCon yelled in excitement. Katrina's cruiser tore into the Zuul ships from behind, her frigates were still docked to her hull, their shields reinforcing her own and raining missiles as she came.

"Am I in time to save your ass, little sister?" Katrina transmitted.

"Just in time," Alexis said, breathing deeply to control her emotions. "Kindly concentrate fire on the Bakulu battlecruiser."

"Gladly."

Both of the *Crown*-class cruisers turned their particle cannon on the now-bracketed battlecruiser. Shields already weakened from the early bombardment, it experienced multiple shield failures. Beams penetrated, hulling her in several places.

Whirlaway was traveling too fast to stop, having raced from the emergence point when it realized what was happening at the stargate. As it passed, the frigates detached, came about, and burned their fusion torches hot and hard to slow. The three *Legend*-class frigates, *Wallace, Joyeuse,* and *Lobera* added their fire to the energy weapons of their mother ship. The hull of the Bakulu battlecruiser was peppered with squash-bombs and, with most of her shields gone, the bombs tore great holes in her armor and blew out an entire section of hull.

"The enemy battlecruiser is signaling surrender," Alexis' communications officer announced with a grin.

"All ships, stand down attack on the battlecruiser," Alexis ordered. "Offer quarter to the surviving Zuul frigate and her transports." The fight was over.

Hours later, after *Whirlaway* had finally braked and come back to join her sister ship, Alexis and Katrina met in the captain's wardroom on *War Admiral.*

"You disobeyed my orders," Alexis said. Katrina had arrived all grins, having felt she saved the day. Alexis' obvious anger was not what she expected. As overall commander, Alexis had kept quiet in front of the rest of the ships' crews and captains.

"What was I supposed to do, stay at the emergence point and listen to all the fun over the radio?"

"All the fun. Is that all this is to you?" Alexis snapped, smacking her desk and almost floating away from it in the zero gravity. "It's not a fucking game!"

"I saved your ass," Katrina growled.

"You came for your share of the glory. You said it was fun." Katrina looked nonplused. "And what if another squadron of raiders came through while you were here?"

"I left sensors."

"There were already sensors there when the Zuul and Bakulu came through," Alexis reminded her. "You violated your fleet commander's orders, and I'm noting it in my log. Right next to how smart it was to arrive with your frigates docked. That was a brilliant move." Katrina didn't know how to respond and appeared confused. She never understood how she could be praised for a good idea at the same time as she was being scolded for a bad one. For her it was hot or cold, there was no in between.

"Between myself and the computer we discerned a 90% chance that you'd be overwhelmed," Katrina said, her jaw set.

"Next time unplug your pinplants and follow orders."

"Yes, *sir*," Katrina said, with as much scorn as possible. "Am I dismissed, *sir*?"

"Return to your ship, and go back to the emergence point. I'm detaching *Lobera* from your squadron to supplement mine while *Manx* finishes repairs."

Katrina nodded and turned to leave. "You're welcome," she said as she pushed off the desk toward the wardroom exit. Alexis watched her go without another word.

* * * * *

Chapter Thirty

EMS Pegasus

En Route to the Grkata System

Hyperspace

The command staff arrived at the appointed hour, looking much more rested than before. Of them, only engineer Long had been unable to get any meaningful downtime. It was difficult to tell what state the Jeha was in, though the lazy movements of the antennae and general listless behavior was a giveaway. He'd spent most of the intervening six hours working to get Reactor One back online. After Alexis grabbed four hours sleep and a shower on the gravity deck, she'd been informed by Paka that Reactor One was finally online. It was good news, indeed. Flying through hyperspace with barely enough power to stay there was something no spacer was ever comfortable with.

"Thanks for coming," she said to them. All the departments were present: Helm (Chug), Tactical (Edwards and Glick), Comms (Hoot), Damage Control (Guylan), Engineering (Long), Sensors (Flipper), Medical (Dr. Ramirez), Personnel (Paka), Science (Kleena), and the marines (Sergeant T'jto). They all acknowledged the captain. She was behind her wooden desk, an artifact from Earth. The rest were either strapped into chairs, clinging to a convenient grasping point, or floating. She collected her thoughts and began.

First, Alexis explained what brought them to where they were, including her theory that *Pegasus*, and perhaps all the Four Horsemen, were being attacked. She backed it up with the chain of events culminating in the Bakulu assault approaching the Karma stargate. Most of them had heard it already, but she went over it anyway for those who hadn't been in on the earlier discussion.

"As we were leaving," she added, "I got notice from Home that Commander Kowalczy took out Task Force Two, per our contractual obligation. I'd intended for Pegasus to take the task force out once we'd gotten Home and completed repairs and resupply, but their delaying tactics worked, and we didn't get back in time. Commander Kowalczy's task forced was ambushed. He was able to keep from being overwhelmed and is holding out in the Grkata system."

"Do you think that contract is part of whatever is going on?" Sergeant T'jto asked.

"Yes, Sergeant T'jto, I do." The MinSha looked on, her antennae quivering with interest.

"It's a trap," Kleena said.

"Yes," Alexis replied.

"But we're going in anyway," T'jto stated.

"Yes," Alexis repeated.

"Why?" This time it was Dr. Ramirez, the senior non-combat staff member. Of course, he had to put them back together after a fight, so he was just as important.

"Because the Winged Hussars don't leave people behind to die because we're afraid it might be a trap."

"What if they're counting on that?" the doctor pressed.

"They may be," Alexis said, "but they don't know all the tricks *Pegasus* has up her sleeve."

"It's likely they know we have hyperspace shunts now," Edwards reminded her.

"And it's likely they'll know another of our secrets before this is over with," Alexis added. She took a breath and looked around the wardroom, taking time to make eye contact with each of them. "If that were you or your loved ones on those ships, what would you hope for? Would you hope against hope for a rescue, even knowing it was a trap, and everyone's lives were in danger?" There were grumbles of assent and nods of agreement. "Whoever is doing this is betting we're going to stop at Home and pick up Task Force Three, and the reserves, and come in loaded for Jivool. We're not going to oblige them, though. Here's what I intend to do."

The captain activated her wardroom's Tri-V, and the presentation she'd prepared after her brief nap came up. Rather like an ancient PowerPoint presentation, she went through screen after screen of the plan. As the last screen played, the room went silent with thought.

"I'm asking a lot from everyone," Alexis said as the Tri-V went dark, "especially the marines." She looked at her MinSha marine commander. "Can I count on your people? A lot of them are inexperienced."

"They are," T'jto agreed, then nodded her head, "but we have some red diamonds in the rough. It takes pressure to make a diamond. They'll do their jobs. We'll make you proud."

"I expected nothing less. You have the plan; let's begin preparations." Everyone started to leave. "Oh, one more thing," Alexis said, holding up a hand. She reached into her desk and pulled out a case. She tossed it to T'jto, the box soaring gracefully in the microgravity. The MinSha caught it deftly. "When Lieutenant Skad was killed at the beginning of this cruise, Sergeant T'jto, you stepped up and led the marines with distinction. Even after your numbers were devastated by the misfortunes of war, you never backed down and helped us recruit a top-notch team on Karma." T'jto opened the box and found two silver bars. "Congratulations, Lieutenant! I've amended your pay record to go back to the beginning of the cruise, as well."

"Here, here!" Paka called, and courteous applause went around the room.

The newly-minted Lieutenant T'jto looked down at the emblems of her new rank in surprise, her antennae standing straight up. After a moment, she spoke.

"Many in my clan were displeased when they heard I was working for Humans." She looked at the captain. "There is bad blood between our races, as everyone knows. But I see much more in Humans than your darker side. We, too, have our demons. I think we have a future together, if only we can learn from each other." She deftly removed the bars one at a time, pulled off the backings, and affixed the adhesive emblems, one on each on her forward-most arms. "Thank you, Captain, I'll serve with honor." The MinSha gave her a salute, which the captain returned.

"I know you will," Alexis said.

* * *

So much had happened, Rick couldn't believe he'd been a Hussar for less than a week. Floating in the marine mess hall on Deck 30, eating a hamburger, he read from a slate affixed to the table. The captain had spun up the ship shortly after they'd transitioned to hyperspace, so the gravity decks were operational. Most of the crew spent several hours in one of the four decks, either relaxing, exercising, or just eating. Only a few races could exist for extended periods without any gravity at all, and Humans weren't one of them. But Rick liked eating in zero gravity, so he spent his time exercising on a gravity deck, choosing to forgo mess call. Besides, the marines preferred to eat together.

The slate contained details on the ship, *EMS Pegasus*. It was boring information, such as the layouts of each deck and section. However, it was stuff marines needed to know if they were to be useful in defending their ship against boarders. He wished he'd known it before the fight in engineering; it would have made him much more useful. The decision to have him hold the hatch with Lynn was obviously a wise one.

When Lieutenant T'jto came back from the senior staff meeting, she'd announced they were heading toward more combat. Rick wasn't surprised; it felt like he'd been fighting every minute since he'd joined. She also gave them file chips with information on several races' ships on them. Among the design specs were ones made by the Bakulu, Izlian, Jeha, Maki, and HecSha.

While training with Mickey Finn, he'd studied the Bakulu and Maki ships; the others were new to him. He was particularly interested in the Izlian because they were considered an exotic race. Unlike most races in the Union, they weren't a standard carbon-based species that ate, breathed, and bled. They looked like jellyfish, except they floated in air that was toxic to Humans, and they communicated with radiation pulses. Their ships were highly sought after and brought a premium price on the galactic market. The race itself was seldom seen outside their worlds, which tended to be a special variety of gas giant.

When he wasn't studying the new information, Rick helped engineering and damage control finish repairs. He logged several more hours in his new CASPer helping Long and his engineers. They'd shut down Reactor Two to inspect the pair of failed containment buffers. While Rick and Lynn, both in suits, maneuvered multi-ton composite lead/carbon fiber shielding, they got a lesson on how the containment buffers were incredibly strong electromagnets that also acted as tanks to hold the F11. That part was called a jacket.

Rick wasn't much of a science guy, though he thought he'd once known someone who might have loved this stuff. The fact that the huge donut-shaped buffers each had thousands of credits of F11 flowing through them was interesting, as well as the fact that if enough of them failed, the reactor would blow the ship to hell and gone. He was keenly interested in helping if it kept the last point from happening.

Lieutenant T'jto had informed the marines the company was about to go into battle to rescue some other Hussars' ships trapped by an ambush. Rick hadn't been part of the company long enough to feel like a member of the family, so he didn't feel the need to fight for them, but that's what he was paid for. He got his monthly retainer no matter what, and the combat bonuses were substantial. The fight against the boarding Zuul had already earned him more than he'd made in all his months as a trainee with Mickey Finn.

On the second day following the spectacular departure from Karma, he was summoned to Deck 16. It was Rick's first trip to the CIC, and he was both interested and worried about why a lowly private was being called to Officer's Country.

Since they weren't under battle conditions, he was able to take the lift, which was a novelty. The 10-foot cube moved smoothly on frictionless bearings, stopping on several decks as he moved toward the nose. Other crew got on and off as it traveled. A couple Humans exchanged greetings as he went, as did several alien crew members. Rick was glad the company was informal about ranks; in other organizations, as a private, he would have spent the trip on the lift constantly saluting.

He'd been enjoying the ride so much, he suddenly realized he'd missed his deck. Cursing, he got off at the next stop, a missile magazine, cut across the ship, and boarded the lift going down. He paid attention this time as they moved toward his destination. One level after a pair of chatty elSha exited, someone called out as the gate was closing.

"Hold, please?" He looked up to see a furry Cochkala floating toward him with a familiar zero-gravity food carrier over its narrow shoulders like a backpack. He quickly found the hold button and pressed it long enough for the badger-like alien to flip around and brake against the lift's opposite wall, bending its long body gracefully to stop. Rick had to admire the long tail which probably made zero-gravity acrobatics almost second nature. "Thanks," the new arrival said, "Deck 18, please?"

"Sure," Rick said and pushed the button. The Cochkala used its prehensile tail to snag a handhold as the cage slid closed, and the lift began moving aft. Deck 18 he thought, then remembered.

"Drone Control?" he asked.

"Yes," the other answered. Like a lot of aliens, Cochkala didn't need traditional uniforms. They had fur all over their bodies. This one wore a skimpy vest and belt, both emblazoned with the winged helmet logo of the Hussars. The color meant service group, Rick thought, which made sense for someone hauling food around. He decided to try to get some info.

"So, the Ghost eats?" The alien's black- and brown-striped furred head turned to regard him. Tiny ears twitched and intelligent black eyes stared.

"You know about the Ghost?"

"Yes," he said. "I've been in there before."

"Not many marines have," the alien said. "She likes her privacy." So, the Ghost is a female, Rick thought as the lift rolled onward. They were almost to Deck 16.

"What does she like to eat?"

"I don't know that she *likes* anything," the cook said. "We just pick whatever is available when she summons and bring it to her." The lift came to a stop at his destination, ending his questions.

Usually the lift opened from an air tight door into a hall, or right into another compartment. Here it was more like the hangar deck in that a second air tight door was immediately next to the lift. Unlike many, this one had a security interlock. Now familiar with how they worked on *Pegasus*, Rick touched his pinlink and thought about gaining access. The computer was waiting for him, and the door slid open.

It was the first time he'd ever seen the CIC of a warship. It really wasn't what he expected. There were a dozen work stations with variable-angle acceleration couches. Everything was arrayed in a semi-circle, and the room was shaped like a pie with a piece missing. At the point of the missing piece was the command chair. Even in zero gravity, someone was in it. Rick was surprised to see it was a Human dwarf. Only two of the other stations were occupied, one by a Buma who looked half-asleep, the other by an elSha clinging to an instrument panel with a dozen displays.

"Welcome, Private Culper," the man in the command seat said. "I'm Lieutenant Edwards, TacCom, or tactical commander." Rick saluted, and the small man returned it.

"Thank you, sir. I'm familiar with the title."

Edwards grinned. "Lieutenant Hoot over there is preoccupied with some comms data," he said and indicated the Buma. "And I believe you are familiar with Kleena, who is sitting in for us while we continue to work on damage." The elSha looked up at him and waved a wide-fingered hand before returning to work. Rick waved back.

The work stations were all at the same level in the CIC and faced toward the middle of the room, not in one direction. Rick didn't know what he'd expected, but this wasn't it. He spotted at least a dozen Tri-V projectors mounted around the perimeter of the CIC, all currently in standby.

"I was ordered to report to the captain's wardroom," Rick said, "but I only know it's on this deck."

"Of course," Edwards said and gestured behind his command chair to where a hatch stood. "It's through that door. Knock once and enter."

"Thank you, sir," Rick said and pushed off across the CIC, careful not to collide with anything or anyone. As he sailed by, the Buma's eyes opened slightly more, and its owl-like head turned to track him, even after he went past. Rick used his arms to arrest his momentum, then knocked once on the hatch before pulling it open.

"Come in, Mr. Culper," a woman's voice said, and he got his first look at Captain Alexis Cromwell, his boss. Also in the wardroom was a white Veetanho Rick guessed was the executive officer and Lieutenant T'jto. Rick nodded and pushed off the door frame toward the empty chair the captain indicated. "First, let me apologize. In the past, I've made it a policy to meet every new member of my ship's crew. As you no doubt know, we left Karma in a bit of a hurry, so I missed that ritual."

"Understandable," Rick said. "Is that why I'm here now?"

"Not entirely," she admitted. Rick examined the woman who led one of Earth's Four Horsemen. She had average to above-average looks, with narrow cheek bones and deep set, expressive eyes that were as blue as his own. Her hair was pure white, as if she were very old, though she was clearly no more than forty or so. She wore it in a carefully-knotted ponytail that somehow stayed down against her back. A wire, maybe? She looked over at her XO and nodded.

"We're not at liberty to explain the situation we find ourselves in," Paka said. "I'm sure you understand, Private?" Rick nodded. "After the boarding action in Karma, and a few other incidents, we decided it was best to undertake a security review of all the new members of the Winged Hussars."

"And after my strange behavior, I'm at the top of that list?" Rick asked.

"Actually," Lieutenant T'jto said, "you were at the bottom." Rick looked at the MinSha in confusion.

"We've found Humans are the least likely to cause trouble in a Human merc company," the captain said, then shook her head and added, "at least when hired off Earth." Rick would have to think about the meaning of that line later. "Though we're almost 50 percent alien, we're still owned and commanded by Humans."

"Then why am I here?" he wondered.

"We were hoping you'd have some insights," Paka said, simply. "Maybe observations? Have you seen anything unusual?"

Rick grunted, then tried to think of anything that would meet that criteria. What would a kid raised in an Indiana town, born into a moderately well-off family, who had travelled into space to become a marine in a merc company made up of dozens of races find unusual? He almost laughed at the idea.

"You mean besides the Ghost?"

The captain's head snapped up from the slate she'd been reading, and T'jto and Paka exchanged looks.

"You've met the Ghost?" Paka asked.

"Yes," Rick admitted. "I brought her some robots during the space battle."

"And you know the Ghost is a female," the captain added, shooting a less-than-thrilled look at her XO. It was interesting to see a Veetanho look visibly uncomfortable.

"You're not a very experienced merc, are you?" Paka asked.

"Only been off-world a few months," Rick admitted.

"Then how did you know the Ghost is a female?" the captain asked.

"I didn't until a Cochkala cook said she was female." The captain tapped on her slate, and Rick wondered if he'd just inadvertently tossed the cook under a tank.

"Besides the Ghost?" the captain asked. Rick shook his head. "Very well, remain alert. I've read the briefing on your actions during the boarding action in Karma. For an inexperienced marine, you did well. But as your lieutenant said, avoid unnecessary risks." Rick knew that meant the single-handed defense against the Zuul's last minute charge. He still didn't think it was unnecessary. "I'm glad we signed you and happy you're one of my marines."

"Thank you, ma'am," he said.

"Dismissed," the captain said, and Rick quickly pushed off the chair toward the exit. As he left the wardroom and floated across the CIC, Edwards nodded and gave him a wink that made Rick grin. As he made his way toward the lift, he promised himself he'd work twice as hard to become the best marine possible. The captain was an inspiring figure.

* * *

"What do you think?" Alexis asked her XO after the young Human was gone.

"He's straightforward," Paka said, "and desperate to prove himself."

"I agree," T'jto said.

"That injury," Alexis said and shook her head, "I'm surprised he survived. Are you certain he's fit for duty?"

"Dr. Ramirez says he is," T'jto said and glanced at her own slate. "There was a fair amount of damage to his brain, but nothing to his motor cortex or decision-making processes. Nemo added he thinks the damage is memory and emotions, and some function may return with therapy." Alexis shivered a little at that. The Wrogul's therapy methods were hard enough to watch on simple procedures; she couldn't imagine the alien digging around someone's brain trying to fix a difficult problem.

"I don't want the good Nemo experimenting on the private's brain," Alexis said, holding up a hand.

"You have more experience with his work than anyone else," Paka said.

"Don't remind me," she said darkly. T'jto glanced between the two, but didn't say anything. She'd only joined the Hussars a few years ago, and knew the captain and XO had served together a much longer time. "Lieutenant," she said to the MinSha, "call the next new hire, please."

* * *

Rick pulled off his armor and racked his laser carbine in the armory, reveling in the increased freedom of movement and cool air on his skin.

"That feels good," he said, glancing to where Johansson was doing the same. He tried to admire her naked form without being obvious, especially now that she'd been promoted to sergeant to fill T'jto's slot.

Dragon Squad had spent several hours helping in engineering, then working out in zero gravity to continue familiarizing themselves with the complicated Mk 8 CASPers. They'd jelled together quickly. Rick, Johansson, and Lynn were starting to feel like a team.

Once he put on a regular uniform, he floated into the squad bay. There, Oort and Lynn were having a discussion on philosophy. It had become a regular habit of theirs in the off-duty hours. *Pegasus* didn't have the best entertainment database, so once you exhausted the library, the options were limited. Apparently, Lynn had already seen most of what was there, so she'd taken to discussing existential matters with the Tortantula. He found it interesting to observe; most of the others usually ignored it. Today, the discussion seemed particularly interesting.

"…premise is questionable," Oort grumbled from where she was floating. Because of the size of the Tortantula, it was often more convenient for her to simply float free in the 20-by-20 space, where everyone could just move around her instead of always asking her to move. "After all, to quote, 'Under peaceful conditions the militant man attacks himself.'"

"You are simply in love with Nietzsche, aren't you?" Lynn asked. The floating Tortantula did not respond. "I would counter with an observation by Plato, 'The measure of a man is what he does with power.'"

"I find Plato to be more taken with himself than with his own philosophy," Oort responded, causing Lynn to visibly bristle. Johansson was already in the bay and was using the little autochef. Rick floated over to her as the other two marines exchanged another salvo.

"Don't they ever get tired of this?" he asked the corporal.

"Not that I can see," Johansson replied. "Never thought much of philosophy myself." She gave a shrug as she accepted the plastic container of food. The autochef had detected the absence of appreciable gravity and dispensed the meal in the appropriate container. "All my family are mercs, going back to first contact. Dinner table discussions tended to revolve around blowing shit up, not navel gazing crap like this," she finished, gesturing at the conversation.

"I have to admit," Rick said, "I never expected a Tortantula to know philosophy."

"She didn't used to," a high-pitched voice added. Jeejee said. He floated nearby with a slate, playing a game. "Oort had a couple of close calls with death, and it affected her."

"Looks like she's had a lot of those," Rick said and pointed at the huge alien's partially missing rear leg, and numerous scars on her black body. Looking at the alien talking, Rick even noticed a couple of her sharp interior teeth were missing.

"Oh, tons," Jeejee admitted. "She's been injured a dozen times badly enough to endanger her life since we became partners."

"Then what was different this time?" Rick asked.

"She says she should have died three times on a mission right before you joined us," Jeejee explained. Rick considered how he might be affected by surviving three near-death experiences in a row. It didn't elicit any feelings, but most things didn't anymore.

"And that's a big deal?"

"I've been trying to get more out of her," Jeejee admitted. "Tortantula aren't exactly talkative beings. However, I'm beginning to think it's religious."

"Tortantulas have religion?" Johansson asked incredulously.

"Sure," Jeejee said. "I don't understand it, though. Kind of a reluctant doomsday cult, I guess. It's why they tend to go crazy and attack tanks bare-handed. Any sort of threat that can kill them, is a chance to cheat death." He shrugged. "It's complicated."

"But she can still fight?" Rick asked.

"Sure," Jeejee said. "You saw her in engineering." The Flatar seemed to think for a second. "Actually, she probably fights better."

"How so?" the sergeant asked.

"She's not quite as crazy as she used to be. Before, she'd go in fangs first. Now, she seems to be more deliberate."

"Do you think she's scared?" Johansson asked.

"No," Jeejee laughed, "Tortantula are incapable of simple fear. It's like she's thinking it through more. She took chances in the engineering battle, like always, but she passed up a few chances where I'm certain she would have gone in screaming before."

"And she didn't eat any of the dead Zuul," Johansson said.

Jeejee suddenly looked up from his game. "I…hadn't noticed that," the Flatar said, "but you're correct." Rick had to admit he liked being part of this company, if for no other reason than the strangeness of it. "Any word on what to expect at Grkata, Sergeant?" Jeejee asked, changing the subject.

"You'll know when I know," Johansson said, tasting her food. "I think it's a rescue mission. I just hope it's not a wild goose chase."

"The captain is afraid something strange might be going on," Rick pointed out.

Johansson nodded. "The captain knows things, Private. She'll take care of it. But we need to get ready for Grkata in a couple days." She ate her food as they listened to the ongoing debate between Oort and Lynn until Jeejee spoke up again.

"What's a goose?"

* * * * *

Chapter Thirty-One

EMS Pegasus

Grkata System

Outer Asteroid Belt

"This is *Pegasus* calling Task Force Two, please respond on scrambled comms." The CIC was silent for a moment then Hoot turned to look at her captain. "Still no response, Captain."

"Continue hailing," Alexis ordered. The little red light flashing in the CIC reminded everyone they were under Condition One, as they had been since arriving in the system. "The task force has to be out here somewhere."

"What if they've been destroyed?" Paka asked. The commander shook her head. She refused to believe that. Everything pointed toward this being a trap. Why kill the bait before the trap has been sprung?

"I could broadcast in the open?" Hoot suggested.

"No," Alexis responded immediately, then added with less force, "at least not yet."

"<*They are still here*>" she heard over her pinplants.

"How are you sure?" Alexis asked in return.

"<*I just am*>"

Well that's a big help, Alexis thought to herself. "Status update on those enemy seekers?" she asked Flipper.

"One is two light seconds out at bearing 88-mark-12," the sensor tech responded, "the other's last reading was 192-mark-39, distance one light second." They were getting closer, and the second one worried her. The velocity they'd carried with them from Karma had served them well, but after emergence their course was unfavorable, forcing them to change bearings. The crew had determined the most logical place to look for the missing task force, and *Pegasus* had burned her torch at 3Gs for almost half an hour to turn onto the new heading. The advantage of their unconventional arrival had been effectively squandered when the massive fusion torch announced to everyone within several light hours a capital ship was in the system.

"Can't we just splash those seeker drones with our own?" she asked over her pinlinks.

"*<Inadvisable. I don't have anything quiet enough to avoid detection by them. You would be all but giving away our position>*"

"Don't they already know about where we are?"

"*<You would think so. However, they are not responding in the way I anticipated. It is likely they simply mean to wait us out and are unaware we possess our own hyperspace shunt>*"

"Not that it will help us evacuate our task force," Alexis said. The hyperspace shunt possessed by *Pegasus* was incapable of projecting a stargate for other ships to use. When it came to the overall tactical situation, it was likely her lost lambs were aware of *Pegasus'* arrival and were remaining silent on purpose to make it harder on the enemy. Or her source had been wrong about where the task force was hiding. Her gaze examined the big Tri-V projection of the Grkata system. An older, low sequence orange star, it had fizzled in its birth and didn't have a halo of planets around it. A single, poorly formed gas giant, a few dozen planetoids, and a pair of huge asteroid belts made up the entirety of the star system's points of interest.

There were several places they could be hiding. The upper atmosphere of the gas giant was unlikely as it was too easy to search and too difficult to hold position for weeks. The first asteroid belt was also unlikely, it was much smaller and only held a few dozen larger rocks and millions of tiny ones. It could have been thoroughly searched by now. Finally, the larger out-system belt, where they were heading now, was huge and full of hundreds of asteroids 500 miles wide, and thousands that were more than 100 miles or more in diameter. It would take all the ships the Hussars had more than a year to do even a basic search of the field. Their destination was based on proximity to the emergence point.

No, she reaffirmed to herself, they had to be out there. When *Pegasus* transitioned in, they detected only a single squadron of ships led by a battleship guarding the stargate. The system was lousy with distant radio squelches of active fusion torches, all in proximity to the out-system asteroid belt. That suggested a search underway. Task Force Two was out here; it had to be.

"I have something," Flipper said.

"Drone Control, stand by to launch," Paka ordered.

"*Standing by*," the monotone replied.

"What do you have?" Alexis asked Flipper.

"It's small," Flipper replied, listening to the data. Their species was good at this job because they could 'listen' to computerized sensor data converted into almost musical tones. Members of Flipper's race could process sensory data faster than any other living race in the Union. "And it's coming toward us."

"Shields?" Paka asked.

"No," Alexis said, "wait. Any signs it's scanning us?" she asked the sensor tech again.

"No," he replied, "I'm only getting passive emissions, probably from gyros and attitude control."

"Give it a sweep," she told him, "gently, on tight beam."

"There's still a risk," Glick reminded her.

"I'm aware," she replied. The Bakulu glanced at her with one eye then returned it to his controls.

From the forward array of sensors, a low-power directional radar pulsed outward. The radiation struck the approaching craft and some was reflected back. A fraction of a second later, Flipper knew a lot more about it.

"It's one of ours," he replied excitedly. "A message drone!"

"Drone Control," Paka called, "take control of the incoming message drone."

"*I have it,*" the reply came immediately. "*It is answering only to one-way commands. It has been set to full passive mode.*"

"They weren't taking any chances," Alexis said. "Bring it aboard. Helm, go full dark."

"Full dark, aye-aye," Chug replied, and the ship stopped all maneuvering. It would be hard for a seeker to spot them now, extremely hard with her reactors on low power.

Everyone in the CIC watched as the drone was plotted through its turn to come onto the same bearing as *Pegasus.* As the battlecruiser began to catch up to it, the drone fired its ion drive to match velocities. Within minutes, it was gently maneuvering sideways into the open hangar deck. The crew plugged a data line into the machine and downloaded its contents in short order.

"*Message file available,*" Drone Control reported. Alexis glanced down at the slate built into the arm of her command chair and touched the icon representing the message and the CIC PA so everyone could hear it.

"Commander Cromwell, I know it must be you and *Pegasus*, even though we dare not use active sensors. However, considering we picked up a ship emergence more than a light hour away from the emergence point says it all. This is Captain Kowalczy aboard *Alicorn*. Authentication follows." There was a series of encrypted keys which Edwards confirmed with a thumbs-up. "I knew you'd come, but wish you hadn't. While I can't say without a doubt this was a trap, the fact that they didn't just outright annihilate us and let a message drone through the stargate suggests a trap is exactly what this is.

"I don't know why this happened, but I can say the radioactive element extraction plant we were hired to take was not here and never was. There is an overwhelming force in the system prepared to destroy us once they find our hiding place. Data on our location and disposition is enclosed in the courier drone's secure bay, just in case."

Alexis looked up to find a crewman wearing the colors of a hangar tech at the door to the CIC, just visible to the camera looking outside. Per procedure, the CIC was sealed during Condition One. The tech saluted and put a computer chip in the pass-thru. While Kowalczy continued, Paka retrieved the chip and brought it to her.

"Commander, that's our situation. While I strongly advise you to take advantage of *Pegasus'* abilities and withdraw from the system, I also stand prepared to carry out your orders. Regards, Captain Kowalczy, *EMS Alicorn*."

Alexis inserted the chip into her command slate and examined the data. As she'd been told, Task Force Two was in the asteroid field, and almost directly ahead on their current course. Kowalczy had proved once again to be an outstanding officer; he was using a pair of M-type, high-nickel asteroids to conceal his task force and had only lost a single frigate in a diversionary action that allowed him to retreat. He had, however, sacrificed most of the drones on his carrier, *Chimera.* The carrier could make more, but he'd elected to avoid the energy signature of the carrier's manufactory. They'd started a few hundred drive units, but only finished a couple dozen.

Alexis fed the task force details and location to Chug, and he calculated their intercept. If they flipped and began braking, they would come abreast of the task force in a little under four hours. Their fusion torch would lead the enemy right to them.

Also included with the task force's data was the intelligence they'd gathered on the enemy. Three fleet elements were present in the system, one each from the HecSha, Bakulu, and Izlian. The breath hissed out between her teeth at the last. The Izlian were not a merc race, at least not by the book. They were an ancient race which had been designing and building starships since the First Republic. Within recent history (thousands of years), they had not been seen in active combat. Yet, here they were, facing her. Another validation of her fears.

"Total enemy disposition, Edwards?" she asked.

"Ma'am," the small man said, showing her the data. "Three battleships, twelve battlecruisers, 20 cruisers, 40 frigates, both regular and various escort types, and three carriers. Data indicates the possibility of three fleet logistics vessels, as well." The silence on the bridge was deafening. They all knew that Task Force Two was composed of the battlecruiser *Alicorn,* cruisers *War Admiral* and *American Pharaoh*, drone carrier *Chimera*, and five surviving escort frigates. Even with the addition of *Pegasus*, those were devastating odds.

"No one has seen a fleet like that in a century," Glick burbled.

"Or more," Alexis nodded gravely, "and the Izlian have come out of their hole to hunt us."

"What do we do?" Paka asked.

"We are the Winged Hussars," Alexis snarled, balling her hands into fists, "we are *no one's* prey*!*" None on the senior staff disagreed. The Hussars didn't leave their own to die.

"Hoot, use the coordinates provided by Captain Kowalczy," Alexis said, "establish laser comms. We're getting out of here. All of us."

* * * * *

Chapter Thirty-Two

Bakulu Merc Cruiser *Yushispa*
Grkata System
Hyperspace Emergence Point

"Report," Captain Geshakooka ordered as soon as the distortion of emergence had passed.

"Location confirmed," the helmsman reported.

"There are no ships in our threat box," SitCom reported.

"There is a combined fleet operations communication and sensor drone transmitting a correct IFF transponder code signal," comms said. The IFF, identification friend or foe, was a long-used way for friendly forces to avoid fratricide in combat situations. When mercs could be allies one day and enemies the next, they were essential in identifying who was who. Unfortunately, it wasn't a perfect system and could be counterfeited.

"Respond code in kind," the captain ordered, "and request a situation report." He turned to his TacCom. "Launch seekers, get eyes in the black. If that entropy-cursed Human ship is anywhere in our vicinity, I want to know about it before I lose any more of my command."

Captain Geshakooka knew right away that this operation, like the carefully planned blockade of Sulaadar, had somehow resulted in a cracked shell. There should have been an interdiction fleet watching the emergence point, which likely meant the Human ship had shot its way through it. "Humans," he muttered to himself. He scanned the near-space sensor data and didn't find what he'd expected to find—blown-apart and burning ships.

"Launch the escorts," he ordered, and a moment later the three remaining escort frigates detached from *Yushispa's* hull and maneuvered a short distance away. They'd come through hyperspace with very little residual delta V, the result of overshooting, then having to stop and come back to the stargate in Karma after *Yushispa* was damaged in the brief engagement there. His ship was once again combat ready and some payback sounded just fine to him.

"Transmission from the Izlian command ship," comms reported.

"On my personal channel," Geshakooka ordered. A moment later, he was listening to the high frequency screeches and pops of the Izlian language overlayed with his own, much more sensible bubbles and pops, courtesy of the comms' automatic translation system.

"This is Admiral Omega," the Izlian said. It was difficult enough for translators to handle the basic concepts of that race's language; names were all but impossible. To make dealing with the outside world more practical, most ranking Izlian adopted a moniker that translated easily enough. Geshakooka's eyestalks opened wider at the name. "Quigg du Snoo, it is a full cycle beyond your agreed upon arrival time."

"We attempted to disable the Human ship in Karma," Geshakooka told the aloof-sounding Izlian. "I lost a frigate, and my cruiser was heavily damaged." He didn't like Izlians, truth be told, despite the notoriety of this one. Like most of the races known as exotics, the non-carbon-based lifeforms often had motivations that were not fathomable by more rational beings like himself. While he often found himself at odds with non-aquatic races, they both breathed air and ate biologically similar food.

The Izlian resembled an analogous squid from his own home world, but that was where the similarities ended. The Izlian were composed primarily of silicon and had evolved in the dense atmospheres of a gas giant. They could tolerate inconceivable amounts of atmospheric pressure and very high G acceleration as long as it wasn't sudden. They communicated by emitting harmful radiation; you never met face-to-face with an Izlian.

"It is obvious you failed," Admiral Omega said.

"Just as you failed to ambush the Human ship here at the emergence point." Silence. He enjoyed a moment of pleasure knowing he'd struck a blow against the egotistical Izlian admiral.

"We do not know how they got through the sensor net," Admiral Omega admitted. "Their ship is a very old design; it is possible it has a cloaking field."

"The Winged Hussar ship is a battlecruiser over six hundred feet long," Geshakooka said; "even the Dusman never cloaked a ship that large."

"Move to the stargate and take highguard," Admiral Omega ordered.

"Our contract was to hunt the Humans," Geshakooka complained.

"They are deep in the outer asteroid belt. We finally detected them, and they are likely near their other fellows who have been hiding there for weeks. By the time you arrive, there will be nothing left for you to hunt." Geshakooka considered telling the overconfident old admiral about the Humans' battlecruiser being equipped with hyperspace shunts. But after being dismissed so casually, he wasn't inclined to be forthcoming.

"Very well," Geshakooka said, and ordered his helm to set course for the stargate. Still, he wasn't willing to place a large bet the Izlian's plans would go as they intended; in fact, he had a feeling he'd have another shot at the Humans all too soon.

* * * * *

Chapter Thirty-Three

EMS Pegasus

Grkata System

Outer Asteroid Belt

"It's good to see *Pegasus* again," Captain Kowalczy said over the short-range laser communications relay. They were impossible to intercept, and you had to be practically on top of the source to know one was in use. Alexis had used her ship's ion drives for the last few hours of braking to present a lower signature, thus denying the enemy an exact fix on their location. Thus far, there was no indication they'd been located.

"Good to see you too, Captain," Alexis said. She'd known Kowalczy since she was a young girl. The man had come up in the company academy just a few years behind her. In fact, in the strange inheritance system used by the company, he was third in line for company command. And, since Alexis had no children, that was a pretty good place to be.

Pegasus was only a couple thousand miles away and the high-resolution cameras were giving her images of the Task Force. The ships in Kowalczy's command all showed signs of battle, with his command ship, the battlecruiser *Alicorn,* being the worst off. Like any good commander, he put his own safety below that of his subordinates. "Are all your ships fit for combat?"

"Yes, ma'am," he said, "but there is no way we can blast our way out of here. They'll all swing around to the stargate as soon as we boost toward it." On the screen, Task Force Two was getting steadily closer as *Pegasus* continued to slow her approach.

"I don't plan on that just yet," Alexis said, "I think we'll just sit here for a while."

"They'll keep looking for us," he said, "and your arrival pretty much guarantees they'll find us."

"Based on the data we have, they won't be here for at least ten hours. I have the Geek Squad aboard," she said, "and they have a rather novel plan. Prepare to send over all the new drone drives and components your manufactory has recently produced."

"Certainly," he said with a curious expression on his face.

"We have a surprise for the bastards. Hunting the Winged Hussars was a bad career move."

* * *

Once *Pegasus* had come abreast of the hidden task force, the space around the ships became a flurry of activity. Shuttles, drones, and suited crew raced between the ships and nearby asteroids. Everyone worked as hard as they could, knowing the clock was running. They were finally detected nine hours later.

"I have an enemy seeker drone in our threat box!" Flipper called out. Alexis floated in from her wardroom where she'd been napping. The senior command staff had been given time to rest. The next few hours were going to be hectic.

"Burn it!" she barked. On the Tri-V one of their own drones changed course and a laser lanced out. The enemy drone was destroyed. "How much did they get?"

"Enough," Flipper said. "I'm sure it detected us and *Alicorn.* I don't think they saw the Geek Squad's project."

"Set Condition One," she ordered. The klaxon sounded, the CIC sealed, and the lights changed. "Comms, raise *Alicorn.*"

"Go ahead," Hoot told her.

"Kowalczy, how are you doing?"

"It's a little early, but I think we're good."

"Very well, we're going to begin."

"I'd like it on record that I disagree with this tactic," the other captain said; "you are taking an unnecessary risk."

"Noted, Captain. Follow the plan, and good luck."

"To you as well. See you in New Warsaw."

"Count on it," Alexis said, and signed off.

* * *

Geshakooka watched from his CIC as the operation to ambush and destroy the Humans slowly developed. No one alive remembered the last time the Izlian were involved in a combat action; however, all the races who had space navies had studied the enigmatic exotic's tactical doctrines. Designers of many of the ships used in the galaxy, and innovators of strategies the ships' owners employed, the Izlian were legends. They were also predictable and out of practice.

"Observe," he said to the TacCom, pointing with a pseudopod at the Tri-V. "They waited until all the elements were in their exact positions before beginning an advance toward the asteroids."

"Is that not wise?" asked the TacCom. "Overwhelming force is the best way to ensure victory."

"Right out of the Izlian tactical manual," Geshakooka said, realizing something the TacCom didn't; the quote was written by the same Admiral who commanded the fleet. The TacCom swiveled two of his three eyes to observe the captain, his remaining eye maintaining a watch on the tactical screen. "However, the Humans don't follow that manual."

"Then they are fools," the TacCom said.

"We shall see," Geshakooka said.

As the fleets advanced, seeker bots were sent out in force. Unlike the solitary drone which discovered the Human's approximate location, there would be far too many to easily destroy this time. Still, the always cautious Izlian once again followed their own tenants and kept the drones far enough back to avoid them being easily picked off. It reduced sensory resolution, though.

The Tri-V tank was updated with the remotely broadcast data, and Geshakooka saw the Human force details appear. As he'd been told, nine ships had survived from the original group trapped in the Grkata system. The tenth reading must be his quarry, *Pegasus.* The sensor readings indicated the power sources of 10 ships of various sizes. The readings fluctuated because the sensory resolution was incomplete, but there were 10 fusion-powered ships, all at station-keeping power around a pair of large asteroids. Geshakooka admitted it was a good tactic. In the short term, the asteroid would mask their ship's presence if they kept their emissions carefully controlled.

But they hadn't, and now the Izlian controlled fleets were closing in for the kill.

The friendly ships approached their targets, slowly coming within range of their seeker drones' sensors. Any time now they would have better data with which to decide on target selection. Within moments of reaching that range, all 10 targets began to accelerate with incredible speed.

"Give me an estimate on that," the captain told his SitCom.

"At least 20 gravities."

Geshakooka had been watching his own tactical screen with one eye to keep track of the squadron under his command. Now all three eyes swiveled to the main Tri-V to watch the Human ships accelerate far faster than they should have been able to tolerate.

"Update," SitCom said. "Twenty-two point two gravities."

Something is wrong, Geshakooka thought, and he considered sending a message to the Izlian commander. *The Humans cannot approach that acceleration. Almost no race could!* "The enemy ships are aiming for a course to pass within 100 miles of the Izlian fleet."

"Are they drones?" he asked the sensor tech who was interpreting the data.

"No," the answer came immediately, "their fusion torches are far too powerful, and they have formidable shields."

The three fleets had been deployed in the usual Izlian two-point strategy. Space combat involved thrust vectors, and it was hard for large ships to change course easily. The Izlian fleet was following the course directly along the line the Humans would follow if they had entered the asteroid field and then continued out the other side. Their role was called *Ram*. In the opposite direction, closing from behind, was the Maki fleet. Their job was often referred to as *Chase*.

The HecSha ships, generally lighter and faster than those of the other two races, was split into two formations and flanking to either side in the role of *Hedge*. All 10 targets were heading toward the Izlian fleet. Geshakooka watched with interest, curious to see how the cocky gas bags dealt with this threat.

Once again following their own book, the Izlian advanced with nine escort frigates in a ring formation directly ahead of their battleship. Three battlecruisers were arrayed around the battleship to provide overlapping defensive fields, and the six cruisers stood one before and one behind each of the battlecruisers. It looked like a Tri-V out of the Izlian training manual. As soon as they could lock onto the ships hurtling toward them, the escorts began to fire.

The Izlian used frigates as missile screens and vanguards to weaken enemy defenses. As such, their frigates used primarily lasers and sported only a solitary missile launcher. Geshakooka could see the computer image of the Izlian frigates raining laser fire. The image was constructed of battlespace data beamed by the three attacking fleets and was an abstract that lacked real world detail. Ship damage would appear as discoloration; critical damage would have flashing markers. The 10 advancing enemy ships were not yet identified and showed no indication of damage. Little flashes of light on the targets indicated weapons hits, so the Izlian gunners were hitting their targets, however it seemed most of the shots were missing.

"Why haven't they determined the enemy ship types yet?" he asked his TacCom. "And why are so many shots missing?"

"I do not know."

Something was seriously wrong. "Send Admiral Omega a message," he ordered. "We need to warn him he's in danger."

"They are several light-minutes away. The conversation will not be instantaneous."

"I know that, fool, but he must be warned!"

The minutes ticked by as the forces closed on each other.

"Sir, we just got a reply from Admiral Omega. He wants to know what you're babbling about. He says that, based on their sensor data, the Humans have nothing larger than a battlecruiser. They are formidable, but not against a prepared foe."

"No manned Human vessels are capable of more than 20 gravities," Geshakooka said. "If that were the *Pegasus,* wouldn't they have fired their spinal mount by now?"

"Enemy ship acceleration just shot to 100 gravities!" Geshakooka's SitCon said in stunned amazement. "They are performing skew turns in perfect formation."

"New heading?" the captain asked.

"Directly for the Izlian fleet."

Geshakooka watched the display, his stomach threatening to turn inside out. It was like watching a spaceship crash—he was horrified, but he couldn't look away.

On the Tri-V display, the 10 ships appeared as blazing points of light from their fusion torches, occasionally punctuated with flashes of laser hits. They were moving straight toward the Izlian fleet like missiles homing on their targets. Only missiles didn't weigh two thousand tons, have dozens of fusion plants, shield generators, fuel tanks, and nominal payloads. Even with all the conflicting sensory data, Geshakooka was horrified to see that only two ships in the entire Izlian fleet were trying to identify the enemy by visual means. One was occluded by the flashing of powerful laser batteries. The other, after his sensor tech enhanced it, clearly showed the enemy.

"You fools," Geshakooka said.

Ten hastily-carved chunks of M-type nickel iron asteroid weighing over two thousand tons each flashed at the Izlian ships at 174,000 feet per second. Their albedos were reduced to nearly zero, and dozens of overlapping shield generators, removed from the Hussar ships, had been skillfully installed to make it appear as a much larger ship to the Izlian weapons sensors. The drone micro-fusion engines were capable of pushing a drone at a thousand gravities for a minute. Combined as they were, they still managed to push their huge improvised craft at 100 gravities.

The shields were only oriented to the front, but since their albedo was zero, the other fleet's elements couldn't tell that. Between the dozens of fusion torch outputs, the energy being radiated by the fusion reactors, and the dense metallic mass of the asteroids, none of it made sense to the Izlian threat assessment specialists.

Geshakooka got a pretty good look at the enhanced image provided by Admiral Omega's sensor tech, but it was after the three asteroids slammed into the Izlian battleship. The asteroids were carefully spaced in a line, one after another. Two thousand tons of nickel-iron, reactors, and miscellaneous equipment traveling at 32 miles per second hit with the force of more than six hundred kilotons of energy, each.

The first one easily overloaded the battleship's shields, and it was the simplest in design of all the drones—it was nothing more than fusion plants, torches, and shields. Converted almost entirely to energy on impact, what remained after that was turned into lances of high velocity debris which smashed across the hull like a shotgun, tearing into the armor and penetrating the ship in hundreds of places. The second pounded into the bullet shaped battleship's nose like a rifle through a watermelon. The drone's computerized brain sensed the impending impact and a picosecond later detonated one of the Hussars infamous squash bombs. The blast nearly doubled the energy transfer, changing what remained into a dozen fiery, pin wheeling pieces of debris weighing tens of thousands of tons each. Admiral Omega never felt a thing and never knew what killed him.

The third drone didn't have a squash bomb; it didn't need one. Close on the heels of the previous asteroid, it spent its fury on an already dead ship. It passed through the debris cloud and out the rear of the battleship in a fantastic fountain of fusion fire, reaction mass, and thousands of tons of ejecta. What was left of the once great Izlian battleship didn't resemble a starship so much as disassociated junk traveling in a slowly expanding ball of debris.

The next three drones scored perfect hits on the trio of Izlian cruisers on point. Only a twentieth the size of the battleship, with shields proportionately weaker, the cruisers counted on the battleship to provide interlocking shield coverage for the formation. With the center of the formation obliterated, the drone-controlled asteroids annihilated the cruisers with most of their mass still intact, and went on to slam into the battlecruisers directly astern of the vaporized cruisers. Though they'd been fitted with squash bombs as well, none managed to detonate. It didn't matter; inertia was all they needed. Even after tearing completely through the cruisers, they delivered between two and three hundred kilotons of force to the battlecruisers behind them, knocking out their shields and causing serious damage.

The three follow-up drone asteroids hit the battlecruiser's unshielded hulls with their full force. Those three retained enough of their energy to hit the trailing cruisers as well. The impacts were insufficient to destroy the ships, but more than enough to blow their forward shields and hull them, rendering the ships combat ineffective.

The final attack was supposed to be the cherry on Alexis Cromwell's cake, and it was targeted on the Izlian drone carrier trailing 100 miles behind the battleship. Unfortunately, an Izlian escort frigate was in the way, and it was converted into a glowing ball of incandescent gas by the impact. The asteroid was deflected a tiny bit as it converted the frigate to disassociated particles, and it only managed a glancing blow against the carrier. The kinetic energy transfer blew out the shields on one side of the ship, and the last squash bomb detonated, wrecking a third of the carrier's drone launch and recovery systems while the EMP destroyed its computers.

The entire attack, from the time the first drone asteroid hit the battleship's forward shields until the drone carrier was wrecked, had lasted less than five seconds. Geshakooka noted the time in his implant-controlled clock. Less than five seconds to destroy seven Izlian capital ships, cripple three, severely damage their carrier, and wipe a single hapless escort from existence like the finger of God.

"Still a fan of Izlian tactical doctrine?" Geshakooka asked his TacCom. The officer sat glued to the deck, staring in stunned amazement at the carnage. "Asteroids for kinetic weapons," the captain remarked, "I've read about them being used against planets in the Great War, but never ship-to-ship."

"Crude, but effective," the sensor operator remarked.

"Crude?" the tactical analysist asked. "Look at the coordination, the accuracy, the raw power! Sure, they were blunt weapons, but they cost next to nothing. Drone fusion torches is my guess. Dozens of them on each rock. Weigh the results against the cost."

"As I said," the captain spoke, "the Humans don't follow any other race's tactical manual."

"No," the TacCom finally spoke. "Do they write their own? I'd like to read it!"

* * *

The remainder of the Izlian fleet, those still capable of maneuvering, did so for all they were worth. Even though the details of what had just happened were available to all the individual ship commanders should they simply access the data stream, none of them wished to risk more Human surprises. Admiral Omega had been a legend among the Union navies. He'd lived during the great war of the First Republic and honed his skills in that legendary conflagration. Alone among the races of the galaxy, the Izlian often lived thousands of years. He'd seen things most could only dream of.

During his long life, he'd compiled countless books on how to fight and command space ships. Sadly, most of his tactics were based on anecdotal evidence and second-hand accounts, because Admiral Omega had never actually fought first-hand in a space battle. Of course, no one alive knew that.

The HecSha and Maki commanders hadn't complained when they were put under Omega's leadership; for them, it was an honor. With the Izlians effectively removed from the tactical equation, a power vacuum formed. In the absence of the supposedly sage leadership of the eminently well-known Izlian, neither the HecSha nor the Maki commanders seemed interested in assuming control. With an adversary like Alexis Cromwell at their throats, that was a poor decision. Neither of the two remaining battleships detected the silently drifting craft in their midst until it was far too late.

* * * * *

Chapter Thirty-Four

"*Pegasus*, this is assault craft *Alpha*," Paka spoke into the laser communicator. Less than a watt in power, and precisely aimed, the lasercom was impossible to detect or intercept.

"*Pegasus* actual speaking," Alexis replied in kind, "go ahead, *Alpha*."

"We show good strikes on nine of 10 prime targets, I repeat, good strikes on nine of ten!" Everyone in the cramped pod could hear the explosion of cheers in the distant ship's CIC. "Final target only received a glancing hit. I think it did some damage, but can't tell how much. Splash the Izlian battleship, three battlecruisers, three cruisers, and partial kills on three more cruisers. We may have gotten an escort in there, too, as a bonus. Hard to tell through visual observations."

"Excellent news, thanks. Can you relay positions and movements on any elements in view?" Paka turned and looked at Zit who was operating the pod's visual scanning system. The boarding craft normally had minimal instrumentation; the improved suite had been cobbled together by Sato in just a few minutes. The Goka held out a hand in a passable imitation of the Human trademark thumbs-up.

"We'll have that data for you in a minute, *Pegasus*," she told her captain.

"Very good, Paka. It's all on you now. Can you make the objective?" The pod was being piloted by T'jto. The MinSha didn't look up from her controls, but did nod her head before speaking. "Thrashing the gas bags really threw the rest into disarray," the lieutenant said. "If I had to guess, I'd say the overall commander was in the battleship, and now they don't know what to do."

"Good," Alexis said. "Let us know when you reach your objective."

"Roger that, *Pegasus*," Paka said and cut the signal.

Rick watched the proceedings on the Tri-V projections inside his Mk 8 CASPer. Even though he was locked to the hull in four places, he and the other two Human troopers had the best ride on the small craft. With three armored troopers, a Tortantula with rider, a MinSha, and a Goka, the pod was cramped as hell. Throwing in their Veetanho executive officer made it almost too tight to breath.

"You two doing alright?" Johansson asked Rick and Lynn over the squadnet. Rick could tell the sergeant was keeping a close eye on them because it was the two privates' first boarding action.

"Doing great," Rick said.

"No problems," Lynn said at the same time.

"Good," the sergeant replied, "let me know if you have any issues. We're in the lead here, so I need to know if anything is going wrong before it happens."

Rick had to admit it, this was the only way to go. Orbital drops were insane by comparison. They strapped you in a HALD, a high altitude, low deploying rig and shot you out of a spaceship toward the planet. It was the most helpless he'd ever felt, and that was in training. At least here he was in a ship, though a nominal one, and his whole squad was with him. Good times.

He watched the data feeds Lt. T'jto was using to fly the craft. She was steering solely with chemical thrusters, a feature of the craft's design. Everything about it screamed stealth. Light and radar absorbing paint, angles to deflect radar, zero EM emissions thanks to a thin (and horribly expensive) F11 shroud inside the hull, and no windows. It was as black as space and as quiet as death. Navigation occurred via a tiny trio of cameras that were only opened to space once a minute. The sensors Zit was using didn't help navigation; they were as blacked out as the ship itself and only helped in examining the now disorganized enemy fleet's actions.

They'd been floating for several minutes with no changes in attitude when suddenly the Lieutenant chittered to herself, too quietly for the translator to pick up, and there was a long series of bumps from the attitude jets. Rick tensed, wondering if he was about to turn into a flash of light. Nothing happened. Then the lieutenant spoke louder.

"Two minutes," she said. "Everyone lock down. Here we go." Around the space, the other marines went about locking belts or other restraints in place. Oort simply put away the slate she'd been reading and used that arm to grab another handhold. Rick had seen the title: 'On the Freedom of the Will,' by Arthur Schopenhauer. He'd heard of Nietzsche from school, but this one was a mystery to him. If they lived, he was going to ask the Tortantula what was driving her reading list decisions.

Rick waited in his CASPer, not feeling anything other than boredom. He could have read or listened to music; a lot of CASPer drivers played tunes during a drop, and some even during combat. In training, he'd found it distracting. This was going to be his first real battle in an armored suit, and he didn't plan to mess with success. The clock ticked down to zero. They all felt a queasy sensation, and Rick knew they'd just passed through their target's shields.

"Firing main engine," Lt. T'jto said and activated the control. "Brace for impact!" The rear panel shielding the craft's pair of hydrogen powered thrusters blew away with a pop, and the engines were ignited. Ten gravities of thrust slammed into them.

The three Humans had it the worst, despite being strapped into their suits and padded on all sides, they were facing backward when the pod fired its engines. Rick gritted his teeth as his head was jerked forward from the thrust, and the special strap fitted around his forehead dug into his skin. He flexed his neck muscles, relieving a little of the pain.

The boost would be mercifully short, except for what was about to follow right on its heels. *Oh fuck,* Rick thought. *Fuck, fuck, fuck!* He felt a tiny sliver of fear. He didn't know if he should be glad he felt an emotion, or worried it was so intense he could feel it? After just a second they roared to over 300 feet per second. The engine cut out, Rick quickly pushed his head back against the rest, and... *Crrruunch!*

The boarding pod slammed into the target ship at over 300 miles per hour. The pod had a nose three times longer than the crew compartment, composed of an armor-piercing shaped charge that detonated on impact, followed by hundreds of layers of honeycombed titanium/carbon fiber alloy, each fit together with a relatively brittle epoxy. As the pod slammed into the ship, the explosive shaped charge punched a hole in the side, and the pod slid through.

As soon as the pod hit, the nose began to disintegrate layer by layer. Every crushed, collapsed layer slowed the pod a little more as it penetrated deeper into the target. Eventually the momentum would be spent, and the pod would come to a stop. Ideally it would have a little of the absorbent nose left, though probably not much. Ideally. However, if the hull was too thick, and the breaching charge didn't penetrate it, the pod could be crushed against the hull. Or if the hull was too weak, and the target ship narrow, it could go too deep and impact the armor on the opposite side, or hit a major internal structure and slice the pod in half. The list of things that could go wrong with a breaching pod was longer than what could go right. Regardless of what happened, it would all be over in less than half a second.

The nose was like a crumple zone on a car, designed to burn off inertial energy by keeping the Gs at survivable levels for the occupants. The book listed that as "less than 50 Gs," because 50 was fatal to most merc races, even for a fraction of a second. Optimally, the pod kept it below 30. To Rick, if felt like being rear ended by a bus, only slower. In reality, it was more like slamming into a brick wall at 35 mph, for almost a second.

The pod reverberated with the crushing impact, and the rending metal screamed. Or maybe it was someone in the pod. Or maybe the escaping atmosphere of the breached ship. Rick had no idea, only that it was over, and he was still alive. And he fucking *hurt*!

"Well that was fun," Johansson grunted.

"Call out," T'jto said. Rick had known the lieutenant would be okay if he was, the MinSha could take more transient Gs than a Human, if properly braced. The interior of the pod was a matrix of carefully erected and self-reinforcing padded walls designed to keep everyone from being crushed into each other. The only one not really braced was Oort, and she was so strong she simply moved her body by herself to prepare for the changes in thrust direction. Jeejee had a special saddle on the Tortantula, and rode it out there. Much of the interior bracing was trashed, but it had done its job.

"I think I have a cracked rib," Lynn moaned.

"Are you combat effective?" Paka asked.

"I'm taking meds," she replied, "I'll be fine." Lynn was the only one injured; everyone else was fine.

"Okay, prepare for insertion!" T'jto said. All those not in CASPers had already closed and locked their atmospheric locks. The squad wore the version of combat armor that allowed them to operate in space, albeit for just a few minutes. The CASPers could operate in space for much longer, if necessary. "I'm blowing the nose in five seconds."

Rick, Lynn, and Johansson activated the controls on their suits that caused the mechanical latches to release them. Their suits were clamped in place at the front of the pod because they were the most dangerous occupants. If one of the 800-pound steel behemoths broke loose, it could well kill everyone else aboard. Finally released, they carefully turned around and crouched slightly. Behind and around them, the padded panels that had braced and protected the others collapsed to the sides. With as little movement as possible, weapons were readied.

"As soon as it blows, get to either side of me," Johansson warned. "There are *no* invalid targets. Shoot anything that moves."

"If it's still moving, shoot it again," Zit said. The Goka had floated forward and grabbed onto the back of the sergeant's suit. The only member of the squad that didn't need a vacuum suit, the Goka could survive in space for almost half an hour. The alien almost looked like part of the CASPer, especially since their suits were painted jet black for this operation. Only the Winged Hussar's logo in gold stood out on their shoulders, a merc rule.

"Blowing the nose!" T'jto warned, and the front of the pod separated with a *Whump!* The air inside the pod left with a bang, and they were in vacuum.

The nose of the pod had been blown 10 feet forward, putting them inside an equipment storage bay. Everywhere boxes and crates bounced around in zero gravity, clearly damaged by their arrival and released from where they'd been stored. Johansson fired a little burst from her jumpjets, and she shot into the compartment. For this mission, their suits' jets were configured for zero gravity maneuvering, instead of ground-side jumping. Rick and Lynn followed, Rick to the right, Lynn to the left. They both held heavy laser rifles at the ready, with more powerful weapons in reserve.

In moments, the entire squad was out of the pod and in the ship. The last out was Paka, who only wore a combat environmental suit and had a slung laser carbine. She floated over to the chamber's only exit and examined the control.

"Only a maintenance panel," she said over the squad net. "The entire section was decompressed. I can't get any more information. Door's jammed."

"Oort," T'jto said and pointed at the door with her laser rifle. The Tortantula sailed over to the door, Jeejee down low in his saddle to avoid getting banged around. She examined the door with several eyes, then simply grabbed the door with two powerful forward limbs, braced with the others, and tore the door from its frame. Moving the door to the side, the big alien cleared the way.

Johansson, Rick, and Lynn sailed through into the corridor beyond. A single bloated, frozen Maki corpse floated in the center of the corridor. Its lemur-like body was contorted in death, and its large black eyes were bulging and frozen. Rick spotted another functioning computer terminal and pointed it out to the XO.

"Go with her," Johansson ordered, and Rick accompanied the Veetanho officer. She accessed the terminal's interface and tried to enter some commands, then growled at it.

"Paranoid Maki, it's encrypted."

"Even on their own ship?" Rick asked.

Paka nodded. "Lieutenant, I need your tech."

"Jeejee," T'jto called. The team had split up, moving down the corridor in both directions, disabling any sensors or cameras they found. A few seconds after he was called, Jeejee came sailing down the corridor, sans Oort.

"Where's your hairy friend?" Rick asked.

"She found an ordinance storage location," Jeejee said as he arrested his momentum using Rick's suit and flipped over to the panel. "She figured we'd give the bastards some going away presents." He examined the panel. "Encrypted?" Paka nodded. "Typical."

"Can you break it?" she asked the Flatar.

"In my sleep," he said. He grinned, showing buck teeth through the transparent helmet, and pulled out a special slate. In less than a minute, the ship's terminal was open.

"Good job, marine," Paka said.

"All in a day's work," Jeejee said and sailed off to find his partner.

"Found a connected section in atmosphere," Zit called over the squadnet, "shall I blow it?" T'jto cocked her head at Paka, who held up a delaying hand.

"Set charge, don't detonate until my order," the lieutenant said.

"Roger that," Zit replied. It was marine SOP, standard operating procedure, to expose as much of the boarded ship to vacuum as possible. It made it harder for the enemy to move around their own ship. Besides, when the shooting started, and it always did, it was better not to have any unexpected explosive decompressions to deal with.

Paka downloaded the ship's blueprints, as well as the crew roster, a table of organization and equipment, and current alert statuses. She was smiling broadly, showing pointy white teeth.

"All three pods have boarded," she told the squad. "Bonus, the ship's DC team thinks our pods were weapons damage. They don't know they've been boarded." They had a few minutes of anonymity left in which to sow anarchy and hopefully reach their objective. Paka uploaded the schematics to each of the squad members. Unfortunately, she couldn't send it to the other squads. Their radios were set to ultra-low power to avoid intercept. "That way," she said and pointed.

"Blow it, Zit," T'jto ordered. They were in vacuum, so there was no sound. However, a swirl of debris moved down the corridor as the atmosphere vented, and Zit giggled.

"There *was* a damage control team on the other side of the door," the Goka said, with heavy emphasis on the past tense. The little alien had a propensity for using too much explosive, to which his usual reply was, "There's no such thing as too much."

With a destination, the ship's schematics, and the location of much of the crew at their disposal, Dragon team made quick progress. In only a couple of minutes, they reached a heavy blast door which was sealed. Oort wouldn't be ripping this one out. Heavy breaching charges were taken from storage places on the CASPers and set strategically around the door's perimeter. Once ready, the entire squad backed up as far as they could. T'jto verified the marines were ready, turned up the power on her radio, and sent three clicks.

A moment later three clicks sounded in reply, and then two clicks. "One of the teams isn't quite set yet," T'jto told them. Had it been one click, or none, it would have meant they weren't going to be able to be ready, or were dead. In either case, the others would proceed without them. The only team with the must-take objective, was Dragon. Hence the reason they transmitted first.

Several long minutes passed as the team held their positions and waited, watching the heavily-mined blast door. With the ship at battle stations, it was no surprise no one was moving about. Finally, three clicks sounded over the radio.

"Go," T'jto said simply. Johansson, Rick, and Lynn pushed off toward the blast door 30 feet away, floating in a triangular formation. Oort, with Jeejee in his saddle, was right behind them. When they were fifteen feet from the door, the shaped charges blew.

The pressure differential caused a visually stunning effect. The blast door, torn completely free from the wall by twelve pounds of K2 explosive, was blown into the adjacent space. However, that space was under pressure, and the air exploded out the now-open doorway, almost instantly reversing the flight of the door and sending it flying toward the Hussars squad. The blast of air hit the three flying CASPers who responded by firing their jumpjets and throwing their shoulders forward. The nearly ton of alloy blast door was body-checked to the floor with a barely-heard crash in the temporary and thin atmosphere. The marines continued onward, soaring into the battleship's main engineering compartment.

Rick was immediately struck with how much less cluttered this engine room was compared to the one aboard *Pegasus.* You could play football in the free space he could see, and right now that space was a maelstrom of wildly spinning personnel, rebounding tools, and flying parts.

"Clean targets," T'jto snapped; "weapons hot." The three CASPer-suited marines used their jumpjets to stabilize against the hurricane of decompressing atmosphere, raised their lasers, and began firing. For the first few seconds it was a shooting gallery. The Maki crew was surprised and disorganized as the engine room explosively decompressed. Just like any warship, they all wore pressurized uniforms, but most didn't have helmets in place, and many more were without gloves. The small and agile Maki were quick to act, though, and many began to fight against the hurricane winds to race for the exits.

"Oort," T'jto said from the doorway, "cut off their escape routes."

The Tortantula had skittered in behind the rampaging CASPers and was clinging to a wall, firing a pair of leg-mounted laser weapons, with Jeejee in support. Upon hearing the order, the big alien used her multiple eyes to assess the retreat options and employ her heavy weapon. The multi-use rocket launcher snapped up from behind the saddle and fired almost immediately. The round hit right where she aimed, the warhead detonating against an exit from engineering and turning it into impassibly twisted metal.

"Above and behind," Lynn called, using their point and angle of entry for reference to indicate another exit. A warning went off on Rick's suit telling him the ablative coating of the suit's exterior rear was taking laser impacts.

"Rick, get that," Johansson ordered as she and Lynn continued cleaning up the engine room staff. It was tricky keeping the suit stable in the chaotic blowing winds as the ship continued to vent atmosphere. He spun around and found a squad of Maki security personnel in light combat armor. They were armed with low wattage laser pistols, and they were all blazing away at him.

Rick decided to forgo the heavy rifle. He let go of the weapon with his left hand and pointed his arm at the hatchway, triggering the built in light machinegun. The multi-barrel chain gun fired .20 caliber caseless projectiles at the rate of nearly 10,000 rounds per minute. He gave the squad a three-second burst, and they ceased to be a threat in a spray of blood and ruptured pressure suits. By the time he turned back, the Hussars controlled the space.

"Secure," T'jto called to Paka. The roaring wind of decompression had reduced to no more than a Martian breeze as the XO pulled herself into the engine room and looked around. Zit came in right behind her, and, along with the now-dismounted Jeejee, the two began to flit around looking for survivors. Occasionally, there was a pulse of laser light as they did their grisly work. Paka went immediately to the engineering control panel and began evaluating it. As this was the main control space, nothing was encrypted. She nodded with satisfaction as she examined the undamaged system.

"Good job, Lieutenant," she said to the MinSha marine commander. "Go live with comms."

"Roger," T'jto said and flicked on her full squadnet for the first time. "Raptor, Zenith Squads report."

"Raptor Squad," Sergeant Jones reported first. "We have the hangar deck secured, all approaches blocked. One casualty, Private Bacord took a laser through the chest." Rick shook his head. Bacord had been a nice guy. He'd played cards with him a couple times.

"Zenith Squad," Sergeant Leshto reported. She sounded out of breath. "We took AuxCon."

"What's your condition?"

"I'm hit," the Veetanho said. Paka glanced over but went right back to work. "Lost Corporal Meeroo and Private O'Neal." *We Humans aren't faring too well,* Rick thought. "Ifeeka has the command systems cut."

"Comms too?"

"Confirmed," the sergeant said, "CIC is isolated."

"Can you hold?"

"Klon and Dron are outside setting up heavy weapons." Rick imagined the two huge purple bears preparing for a last stand. He wouldn't want to come down a hallway with a pair of pissed off Oogar waiting for him. "Godor is going to hold the door from the inside. I'm helping Ifeeka."

"Tell them to upload the package and fall back to the hangar deck," Paka said. T'jto relayed the order.

"Negative," Leshto said, "if we give up AuxCon, they can take the ship back."

"You can't hold," the lieutenant said.

"We'll hold as long as we can. Beginning upload now." Everyone in engineering exchanged looks. They hadn't expected AuxCon to be the hardest target, which was why they'd sent Zenith, the squad with only one CASPer in its numbers.

"Start setting up the payload," the lieutenant ordered. "We're sure to get more serious company soon." A minute later, lights started flashing on the engineering status board.

"Here we go," Paka said and her hands moved on the controls. Around them, the fusion reactors began to thrum to full power.

Out in space, the Maki battleship's huge weapons came to life and pivoted, locked on targets close by, and fired. A few thousand miles away, the somewhat smaller HecSha battleship was struck several times by the Maki battleship's most powerful particle cannons. Caught completely by surprise, several of the target ship's shields failed, and energy beams tore great holes in its side. The HecSha ship searched for its attackers, and escort ships moved into new formations, confused and searching as well.

The Maki battleship changed targets and fired again. A HecSha battlecruiser was torn apart, then a cruiser and a pair of escort frigates. Finally, the HecSha commander realized the fire was coming from the Maki, who they tried desperately to reach on the radio. Fire continued to pour in on them even as they began to dodge, but the Maki battleship's gunnery was uncannily accurate, and the battleship didn't respond to hails.

"Betrayal!" the HecSha commander roared, and his flat head hooked from side to side as his thick arms pounded his command chair's arm. "Destroy those dishonorable mammals!" The entire HecSha fleet turned on the Maki en masse. The HecSha never noticed only the Maki battleship had fired at them. The Maki secondary ships demanded to know what was happening. The HecSha were no longer interested in talking. Confused and believing they had been betrayed, the rest of the Maki followed the lead of their strangely-silent command ship, and it turned into a free-for-all.

"Is it working?" T'jto asked as the battleship's system thrummed with power around them. Paka grinned widely and nodded.

"The captain's plan is working perfectly," she said. Rick smiled inside his CASPer as he watched the various exits in his sector of the engine room. When he'd first heard the plan, he thought Alexis Cromwell had lost her mind. Now he was beginning to think she might be the best tactical genius in the galaxy. Or the luckiest. Rick noticed Zit had returned from hunting stragglers. The Goka flew over to Oort and into a little airlock the Tortantula had on her saddle. There, the alien could catch a few breaths of air before going back outside for another stint in vacuum. Rick marveled at the Goka and was glad Earth's cockroaches weren't as resilient or as well-armed.

Alarm lights flashed, and they could see the engine room shudder, even though no sound reached them. The HecSha were targeting the Maki battleship. Paka examined the displays and gestured at one screen.

"The CIC is quite upset," she remarked.

"I can't imagine why," T'jto said.

"Incoming," Jeejee said and shot by, heading for Oort's saddle. Rick and Lynn both turned toward the exit previously sealed by rocket fire and saw it glowing brightly. Everyone cleared as lasers began to slice through the debris. Not light lasers either—heavy ones.

"Switch to the big stuff," the lieutenant ordered. The three CASPer-suited Humans magnetically locked their laser rifles in place on the legs of their suits and swiveled their MACs down over their shoulders and locked them in place.

"Ready," Rick said, and the other two Humans echoed his response.

"Good," Oort grumbled. Her multi-use rocket launcher was again ready for action, Jeejee having reloaded it from the saddle's stores.

"Wait for the first breach," their commander said. A moment later a big chunk of debris floated free, and the MACs fired hypersonic tungsten slugs at the same time. Minus an atmosphere, the rounds hit with 100 percent of their energy. A pair of Maki troopers in their version of heavy assault armor nearly exploded from the impacts, and armor, blood, and body parts flew off in a chunky red haze.

"That'll leave a mark," Zit giggled from the airlock on Oort's saddle, then launched himself out into vacuum and disappeared into the maze of equipment.

"He who fights with monsters should be careful lest he thereby become a monster," Oort said as she let her first missile fly into the now-exposed corridor. The missile exploded and flashed against a shield that had been set up there. A powerful laser flashed back at them, cutting Private Jordan in half, killing her instantly. "And if thou gaze long into the abyss, the abyss will gaze long into thee."

"Lynn!" Rick yelled.

"She's gone," Johansson said coldly as they both scrambled for cover. Another powerful laser blast cut across engineering, nearly catching the sergeant. The two halves of Lynn's suit spun, blood spraying out, joining the little red planets from the Maki they'd killed.

"I think I can get a shot around it," Rick said as he slid down along a huge support column.

"Too risky," the sergeant said, but he was already moving. The operator of the laser obviously had a good view, because the beam instantly pivoted toward him.

"Shit," he said as the beam slashed through his shielding support and moved up toward him. He couldn't back away fast enough, his jets weren't aligned properly. He raised his left arm, triggering the laser shield to snap open on either side of his forearm. It wasn't intended for lasers as powerful as the one trying to kill him, but it deflected most of the beam. The rest flashed through his lower arm.

"Huh," Rick grunted. There had been an instant of pain, then nothing. His suit's alarm screamed, and he sealed the arm without thinking about it, just like he'd been trained to do back in Mickey Finn. At the same time, he got the jumpjets realigned and pushed himself backward. The beam moved and would have cut him in two, just like Lynn, but he wasn't there anymore. It tried to track him only to be forced to stop or start cutting into a fusion reactor. The gunner was eager, not suicidal. "I'm hit," he announced.

"How bad?" Sergeant Johansson asked. Rick raised his left arm and saw it ended a few inches below his elbow.

"Bad enough," he said. The suit's systems had sealed below the severed joint using a special chemical gel that hardened instantly in vacuum. He looked back down and saw his arm floating there, spinning lazily. He didn't feel remorse or despair, only a mild disappointment. After all, it wasn't the first time he'd been maimed in his short merc career. He was still alive, at least. "I can fight."

"Help me get more rounds on that shield," she said, firing and moving. The gunner was increasingly unconcerned with damage as he continued to shoot at whatever moved. Oort nearly lost another leg, and Jeejee cursed creatively as he abandoned his saddle an instant before the beam took a chunk out of it. The Flatar launched several grenades which exploded harmlessly against the shield, before he retreated behind heavy machinery, the laser chasing him all the way.

"Can you cut the power to that?" the lieutenant asked the XO, who was safely out of the line of fire. "That's a direct power laser. No way it's chemical with that rate of fire and power output."

"No," Paka replied; "they've got it tapped into the main power relay." The ship shuddered badly. The perimeter of the engine room was lined with long superconducting power conduits which fed the shields and weapons. Two that fed the ship's shields suddenly turned red hot, their insulation flashing to powder, then exploded. White hot bits of metal splashed across engineering, some landing on other equipment. Fires flared in several places, roiling and pulsing like living things, moving along their oxidizer fuel sources in the otherworldly way fires did in zero gravity. "If I cut the mains, we'll be blown to shit!"

The huge laser cut again, the beam tearing through a fuel feed just over T'jto's head. The MinSha ducked away, armored hands brushing molten metal from her suit helmet before it could melt through the plastic dome. Little discolored spots were left behind, and tiny cracks that hissed atmosphere.

"We won't last for long if we don't stop that laser," the lieutenant said.

"I will dance the final dance," Oort said, and prepared to launch herself at the shield.

"Your huge hairy self won't get halfway there," a voice said over the squadnet. "I got this."

From the maze of pipes and equipment near the exit where the laser was set up came a black shape as Zit arced through the air. The enemy gunner didn't see the shape shoot into the passageway and land on the wall. Zit folded his wings and skittered along, his specially-evolved feet gripping the imperfections in the metal.

When he reached the shield, he slowed and moved with deliberate precision. The shield shimmered as the marine slid through. Shields were meant to stop the energy of an attack. If you moved slowly, you could walk or float right through.

There were a dozen Maki marines manning the massive laser cannon. One finally noticed the Goka just as he cleared the shield and yelled a warning. The enemy marine brought up his personal laser carbine and fired several times. The beams flashed against the Goka's laser-resistant carapace. Zit drew a pair of long blades and leaped.

"Damn," Jeejee said. "Look at him go!" The Goka tore into the midst of the gun crew. Zit rammed a blade through the heavy armor of one of the troops with surprising ease, sending a gout of blood spraying in a fan. He spun and smashed the faceplate of another with a blade's hilt, even as the others drew weapons. Laser beams began to crisscross the space.

It was the most intense close quarter's battle Rick had ever seen. The Goka punched, slashed, and kicked at the enemy troopers with all six limbs. When one tried to grab him in a desperate bear hug, Zit popped his wing cases open, forcing the hands away, but was hit by a laser beam that punched through the wildly-struggling alien's abdomen while the protective cases were open.

"Gah," Zit screamed, unconsciously broadcasting over the squadnet through his implants. "You mammalian fuck!" He spun and threw one of his knives hard enough to punch through the hardened plastic face shield of the Maki marine who'd fired the shot. But the damage was done, and Rick could see through his suit's visual sensors that the Goka's bodily fluids were spraying out.

The two remaining members of the gun crew, the ones operating the weapon, were crouched behind the weapon's control system, shooting at Zit with small arms. Zit clung to a badly-injured Maki, using it for a living shield. The Goka's movements looked uncoordinated.

"You did well, Private," T'jto said to Zit, "now get back here so we can fix you up." A laser beam flashed out at the lieutenant, who cursed and moved back again.

"Oh, fuck you," the Goka said, "and fuck this job." From under his carapace, Zit pulled out a pair of K2 grenades. He pulled the pins and leapt at the gun crew. An instant later, gun and crew went up in a brilliant ball of rolling flame.

"Crazy bug," Jeejee said, although Rick thought the words held a tone of respect. He wasn't sure; he was too busy telling his suit to give him more happy juice. The severed arm was really starting to hurt.

The battleship shuddered again, and a beam of pure white energy lanced through the engine room. Lightning danced along the length of the beam as it cut through the corner of one of the fusion reactors. The massive ring of magnetic containment buffers shuddered, and exploded outward.

For an instant, Rick thought they were going to die. When the containment system of a fusion reactor failed, especially one running at full power, it was a touch and go thing. This time the system worked as it should. When the buffers failed, they used the last of their energy to channel the fusing plasma out through a special section of hull into space. The containment vessel, now visible, glowed bright red in vacuum and started to deform and fall apart. Hissing jets of F11 sprayed as it failed and the last of the plasma leaked out.

"Holy shit," Johansson gasped. Rick just shook his head. They were only a few hundred feet from all that heat, but because of the vacuum, they couldn't feel it at all.

"Yeah," Paka said, "I guess it's about time to go."

Rick wondered idly how much radiation they'd just absorbed.

* * * * *

Chapter Thirty-Five

Alexis floated in her CIC, watching the big Tri-V displaying the developing battle between the HecSha and the Maki. She'd secretly considered the idea of creating this infighting as borderline insane when it was suggested to her. Too many things had to go just right for it to work. Yet, there it was; both fleets were tearing into each other with wanton abandon.

"<*I told you it would work*>"

"Yes," she replied over the pinlink, "you did. But is this going to cost me all my marines?"

"<*I cannot predict that*>"

I knew you'd say that, she thought. "TacCom," she said, "bring us about and target the HecSha drone carrier. Full power to the reactors. Prepare for battle!"

As the two fleets tore into each other in earnest, they'd nearly drifted right by *Pegasus*. When the ancient warship was practically in their midst, it came alive and spun about.

"Match bearings and fire, Edwards!"

"Match bearings and fire, aye," the small man said, and the crew held onto their seats as the 80,000-ton warship spun on her central axis. Several escorts from both fleets noticed the massive EM power spike as *Pegasus* came alive and maneuvered, but their calls to the command ships were either not received (in the case of the Maki ship), or not immediately heeded (in the case of the HecSha). "Firing!" Edwards called as the target fell within the main gun's sights.

Managing shot placement of a weapon like the spinal mount on *Pegasus* was an art form. Punching holes was useful, but causing cut damage was much more effective. When firing the spinal mount, Edwards had helm control, and he used it to maximum effect. He fired the spinal-mounted particle accelerator cannon in a 40-terawatt pulse lasting just over three seconds. It began just before coming on line with the HecSha carrier, so the first quarter-second missed the ship proper, but hit the shields. Battleship shields struggle with multi-terawatt range weapons; the carrier's shields were no match. By the time the beam reached the hull, the shields were down, and the weapon carved into the relatively delicate carrier like a chainsaw into a watermelon. Gouts of fire erupted from critical damage, and the carrier lost drive and stabilization.

"Ship-killers on the Maki carrier, five tubes." Alexis ordered, and the hull thrummed as five of the 10 launchers hurled missiles into the black. They burned like tiny suns as they accelerated away at five hundred gravities. On the Tri-V, the HecSha carrier was structurally compromised. When they'd been hit they were maneuvering, and the 40,000-ton ship folded in on itself and crumpled like a box being sat upon. Secondary explosions rippled across the crippled ship like Christmas lights as she died. Alexis nodded. "SitCom, redirect power to defenses." The spinal mount doors closed protectively. "All laser batteries, free fire. Reload tubes one thru five with anti-missiles. Helm, three Gs, get us moving."

The five ship-killers reached the Maki carrier, which fared worse than the HecSha had. Unaware of the new tactical situation, the defensive lasers were arrayed toward the HecSha fleet. The first two missiles knocked its shields down, and the next three detonated directly against the hull. The carrier was annihilated in less than a second.

On the Tri-V, the two fleets suddenly became aware of the killer in their midst. Though they were busy flailing at each other, they also began to fire at the *Pegasus*. No sooner had Alexis ordered power directed to the shields then they started to flash from raking laser fire from the two closest HecSha escorts. Edwards immediately directed 10 of the ship's offensive laser batteries at the closer of the two. One hundred megawatts each, the combined fire punished the smaller ship's shields, forcing it to maneuver to bring its other shields to bear. A single ship-killer lanced out, and the escort frigate died in a nuclear fire. The first enemy missiles began to reach out for *Pegasus*. Alexis' lips drew back from her teeth. The battle was joined.

* * *

"Sergeant Leshto," T'jto called over the squadnet as her team began moving down the service corridor. It was an extremely tight space for Oort.

"Here," the pained reply came.

"We're heading for your position. Can you disengage?"

"Negative," the Zenith Squad's sergeant replied immediately. They were fighting in atmosphere and T'jto could hear the reverberations of heavy weapons fire being transmitted through metal. "Klon and Dron are heavily engaged just outside. Their portable shield generator is about to fail. We're opening AuxCon doors to help them fight. Last stand." Johansson consulted her version of the map and sent a route to her lieutenant who glanced at the mental image before replying.

"We can be there in three minutes," she said, "those doors should hold that long. Have the Oogar pull back inside with you and hold on!" Through the link there was a resounding explosion followed by an Oogar roar. Another series of explosions, then nothing.

"They're gone," Sergeant Leshto said. There was banging against the AuxCon blast door. "Get to the hangar deck," she said. "If they're trying to get in here, that heavy weapons team can't be hunting you. We've set charges on all the systems."

"I will hold them," Godor grunted. The Lumar were not particularly bright, but they were brave, strong fighters.

"I do not know what to say," T'jto said.

"Thank you will suffice," the Veetanho replied, then gave a little laugh that turned into a strangled cough. The entire battleship rocked violently. "Main shields are out! You'd better hurry while there's a chance for any of us to survive!"

"Good luck, Sergeant," T'jto said. There was a moment of intense static, and the squadnet went silent. "Damn," she said. A moment later the ship shuddered from an internal explosion.

"Lieutenant, Raptor here."

"Go, Sergeant."

"A security detail just ran into the guards I had at the main hangar entrance. We beat them back, but I lost Private L'kto." If the lieutenant showed any more emotion at losing one of her own kind, she didn't show it.

"Acknowledged, we're almost there. Hold the entrance at all costs."

"We won't be able to launch if they're blowing the shit out of that hangar," Johansson noted.

"Suggestions?" the lieutenant asked. Rick had been using his pinplants to study the layout as they moved. It was distracting him from staring at the nasty stump of his arm. Looking at the route, he piped up.

"How about this," he said, and he transmitted the deck plans with a route in red.

"Nice," Johansson said.

"Very good," the lieutenant agreed. "Jones, we'll need an extra minute."

"We'll hold," he replied with grim determination. A short distance ahead, T'jto and her team transitioned through a maintenance lock into atmosphere and hurried onward.

The team of 20 heavily-armed and -armored marines, one of only four platoons on the battleship, were tasked with taking the hangar deck. The ship's captain knew the entropy-cursed invaders would want a way off the ship, and that was the most logical choice. The invaders may have cut off his control of the ship and turned his allies against him, but they wouldn't get away with their lives.

The Maki marines understood they faced elite troops. The team that tried to retake engineering had been lost. The one that assaulted AuxCon had finally taken it, with nearly 90 percent casualties, only to have the entire room blow up in their faces. The only other marines on board were the platoon guarding the CIC. They had to succeed, so they pressed the attack with single-minded determination. So single-minded, in fact, they didn't see the access panels above them slowly slide open.

A Tortantula could squeeze through a surprisingly small space, if it really wanted to. Oort had removed her saddle and slid through the 30-inch square access shaft and pushed off into the midst of the extremely surprised Maki marines. They were about half the size of a Human, and were even tinier compared to the monstrous Tortantula. Oort snatched the first one that came to hand and used the heavily-armored marine as a convenient club to pummel the hapless marine's teammates. Her Flatar partner flipped out of the hatch, holding onto the opening with one arm while firing his handgun with the other.

Further down the corridor, two arm-mounted miniguns fired like buzz saws, cutting their way out of the access corridor to fire at the Maki below. The arrival of the two CASPers was an even worse surprise for the already-stunned marines. Rick had to use his right hand and legs to do the rending. With their teammates mixed in with the enemy, they couldn't use their MACs. Instead they triggered their retractable arm blades and, with puffs from their jumpjets, waded into the battle.

T'jto had intended to join the battle, but as she slid through the massive gouge left by the two CASPers, she realized it would be foolhardy, so she pulled back to cover the lightly-armored XO.

Even with a Tortantula, two CASPers, and a trigger-happy Flatar on one side, the Hussars were still outgunned five to one, and the Maki marines weren't slouches. They quickly recovered from the surprise attack and concentrated fire on the biggest threat, Oort. The Tortantula's armor took several laser hits before one found a soft spot. A splash of orange-tinted blood was the only sign she'd been injured; even the second and third shots that got through didn't slow her. Above, Jeejee shot one of the marines who had injured his partner through the top of its armored head. A second later a laser beam neatly drilled through the Flatar's chest.

Jeejee jerked, his gun floating free as his life was snuffed out. With her numerous eyes, Oort saw it happen, and she went completely berserk.

"Nooooo!" she screamed, slashing at Maki marines with arm blades, grabbing one and crunching down on its head with her fangs. The marines fell back from the ferocity of her attack, hitting her a half dozen times with laser fire. She responded by using the machine gun on her manipulative arm and unloaded it into the group, mercilessly slaughtering them.

Rick and Johansson tried to help, but the grieving Tortantula was a whirling dervish of death and destruction. She didn't stop until the corridor was awash in Maki blood. It floated everywhere, covering the huge spider and turning her into a nightmare image which would have made Dante shudder.

T'jto floated into the corridor behind the squad. Oort drifted amidst the carnage, her thorax slowly pulsing with each breath. She was wounded in a dozen places, her eyes wide and staring.

"Private," the MinSha said, and Oort caught the wall and spun around. Even the CASPer-suited pair tensed. The Tortantula looked…feral. "Private, are you in there?" Rick selected his MAC, and waited. "*Private!*" T'jto barked, then spoke in a softer voice. "We'll all miss Jeejee, but we need to get back to *Pegasus;* the captain needs us."

"I'm sorry we lost him," Rick said. "Really. He was nice, for a sarcastic killing machine." For a second he thought he'd made a mistake, then the Tortantula gave a single laugh.

"Let's get out of here," Oort finally said.

* * *

"Signal from the boarding teams," Hoot said. Alexis looked away from the status board, hoping it was good news. "They are about to depart, with all objectives achieved. Lt. T'jto reports twelve lost."

Alexis' jaw muscles bunched, and she looked down at her lap. She'd known when she sent them that it might be…would probably be…bad. But some part of her had counted on the judgement of…of the entity, who had said there was an almost certainty the plan would work. She'd believed that if it worked, most of them would come back. It had worked, but most of them weren't coming back.

"Understood," she said, managing to keep the catch out of her voice. "Tell them to initiate the next stage of the plan." The Buma comms officer acknowledged the instructions and transmitted them. "Helm, prepare to come about to new course!"

* * *

Captain Geshakooka laughed long and hard while the command crew looked on, wondering if their captain had gone utterly mad. He continued to laugh, eyestalks shaking with ridiculous humor and unequaled irony. First the Humans had completely wrecked the Izlian fleet in less than a minute, and now, somehow, they'd gotten the quick-to-anger Maki and the prideful HecSha to turn on each other as if one had betrayed the other! From several light seconds away, Geshakooka watched the two battleships pound each other like raging giants.

Then the sensor technicians relayed data from the fleet—the Human ship had reappeared and was destroying both fleets. Amazingly, even though the HecSha and Maki were the ones sending Geshakooka the data, none of them seemed to realize they were being destroyed by the quarry they'd been hired to eliminate. The captain finally stopped laughing, his eyes fixing on the quarry. In quick order, it killed first one, then another carrier.

"They finally noticed!" SitCom said, indicating that several frigates were beginning to fire at the Human ship. First one, then another of those frigates were destroyed, but more of the other ships' crews began to realize what was in their midst. What he didn't understand was how the Humans had gotten the two fleets to attack each other. How? The key had to be the Maki battleship. Its behavior was the least logical in the engagement. It had fired first and switched targets more than a ship of that size should have. While that switching of targets was causing the ship to get torn up badly, it was also tearing up the other fleet's secondary ships just as badly.

"Helm," he said, "set course for the engagement zone."

"Captain," the XO spoke up, "we were ordered to stay on highguard at that stargate." Geshakooka wasn't used to the XO being back on station. He had been injured during the long pursuit back in Karma and had only this ship-day come back on duty. The XO was also a strident supporter of propriety and less willing to take risks than the captain.

"Noted," he said; "however, there is no one left to tell us how to proceed, and our contract was to see that ship destroyed." He indicated *Pegasus* on the tactical display, which was beginning to maneuver after having wrecked several more Maki ships. "We are going to see that contract fulfilled."

* * * * *

Chapter Thirty-Six

Paka took the controls of the shuttle. It was the only logical choice, considering the craft was of Maki design, and she was the only one familiar with their configuration. The craft was powered up quickly and everyone strapped in. Rick and Johansson were both out of their CASPers, which were stored in the cargo area.

Getting Rick out of his had been a chore, as the sealing spray was like concrete over the stump of his severed limb. Johansson was playing medic to both Rick and Oort. The more of the Tortantula's armor they removed, the more they realized just how badly injured she was. Between the two, Johansson had already gone through three nanite dispensers. There had been 21 marines when they'd boarded in three pods; only nine were leaving.

"Powered and ready," Paka said to T'jto, her copilot and the person holding the all-important control slate. "Arm them." T'jto entered the coded sequences and the "Initiate" icon lit.

"Ready," the lieutenant said.

"Go," Paka said, and the MinSha tapped the icon with a finger.

A program which had been inserted into the battleship's main computer evaluated the targets that were left. The HecSha fleet was in terrible shape after the extended, confusing battle. There were no clear targets there. So, the battleship locked onto the only surviving battlecruiser which happened to be Maki as well, and unleashed all its remaining weapons on it. The ship, already slightly damaged from trading fire with the HecSha, was caught flat footed by its own battleship attacking it and was almost immediately destroyed. A second later, charges left in the battleship's engine room exploded.

"Better get out of here," T'jto suggested as the battleship began its death throes. Paka nodded and used the controls located in the cockpit to open the hangar deck to space. As the battleship's surviving reactor began a critical overload, she deftly piloted them out of the bay and into space. They were less than a mile away when the engine section went up in fusion fire.

"That happened faster than I expected," Paka said as she adjusted the shuttle's course and cut the engines.

"That's Jeejee for you," T'jto said. "He loved fast, big explosions. How long to rendezvous?"

Paka consulted the instruments before answering. "Fifteen minutes."

In the back, Rick looked after himself as best he could with one arm. A ragged, chewed, burned hunk of meat marked the end of his other arm. His mom wouldn't be pleased; that is, if she were still talking to him.

"Sorry about the arm," Johannsson said. Rick shrugged.

"I fared better than Lynn." The sergeant patted him on the right shoulder and went to check on her other patient.

* * *

Pegasus accelerated from the engagement zone for several minutes before executing a turn and slowing. The remnants of the HecSha and Maki fleets exchanged desultory fire as they both withdrew in complete disarray. Either insufficient senior staff remained to remember what they'd been hired to do, or they didn't care any longer. Between the asteroid drone attacks, the two fleets attacking each other, and *Pegasus* taking advantage of the same, the three combined fleets had lost more than 27 ships, and another 10 were seriously damaged. Alexis didn't know it, but since hers was the only ship actively involved on her side of the battle, it was the most one-sided trouncing in galactic history. Admiral Omega was unavailable for comment.

"Full sensor sweeps for the boarding teams," she ordered Flipper. "They will be running quietly to keep any stragglers from taking pot shots." The Selroth sensor tech nodded, water sloshing around in the rig he wore on the bridge to breath. "Glick, any signs they can pull it together and pursue?"

"None, captain," the SitCon replied. "I don't even see indications of an organized regrouping. It's a real mess out there."

"Good," she said. She looked at the spot where Admiral Omega's battleship would have been on the plot. "Hunt me, will you?" she added, quietly. She'd only wanted to get her stranded task force home, but sending them a message was good too.

In the back of her mind she was already formulating a plan of action for when they got home. It was plain to see a huge shift in the galaxy was taking place. If it were Earth, she'd have thought it was political, but there were so little politics in the Union, at least not the kind you found on Earth. Considering the hell they'd just been through, and the extent to which someone had gone to try and kill her, she decided she'd had just about enough of being a target.

"Helm is being overridden!" Chug cried out.

"*<Hang on>*" Alexis heard. She slapped the all hands broadcast control on her chair.

"Prepare for radical maneuvers!" she yelled. Even as the last word was out of her mouth, *Pegasus'* powerful maneuvering jets spun her around and the fusion torch screamed to life with more than 10 Gs of brutal, crushing thrust. Everyone on the bridge gasped and struggled to draw breath. Alexis gritted her teeth, feeling the skin pull taut on her face and prayed the casualties would be low. But she knew something bad was coming.

"Incoming missiles," Glick managed to say. Ten gravities was intense, even for a Bakulu. "Ten missiles inbound."

"Anti…missiles…firing," Edwards groaned, crushed so far into his chair that he was nearly invisible. If it weren't for pinlinks, no one on the CIC would have been able to do a thing. "Lasers…too." He used his pinlinks to resolve the missile tracks then spoke again. "Prepare…for…impact." He triggered the collision alarm.

Pegasus rolled and yawed, thrust increasing even further as her hidden controller struggled to save the ship's life. Alexis struggled to understand what the tactical Tri-V was displaying, but a red mist was descending over everything, and she couldn't concentrate. It took every bit of strength just…to...breathe! Then the world exploded.

* * *

"Multiple hits," TacCom announced.

"Their shields are down," the sensor operator reported. "Thermal variance indicates a possible fire on several decks."

"Excellent," Geshakooka said. Finally, they'd hurt the entropy-cursed Human ship! "Commence rapid fire with the bow particle cannon. Target her engineering section! Order the escorts to reload missiles and prepare to fire."

* * *

"Shield generators two, nine, and 18 are down!" Guylan said as thrust suddenly fell off. "Radiological alarms on Decks 25 through 28. Hull stress alarms tripped amidships, but no signs of failure. There is a fire on Deck 27 in the aft shield generators. Dispatching damage control teams."

"Edwards, get a firing solution on the attackers! Flipper, what do we have?!"

"Multiple targets in our threat box," he responded, "they were coming from the stargate so we never saw them. Feeding the solutions to SitCon."

Alexis turned to the Bakulu who was sifting through the data.

"Four ships," Glick said, then added a second later, "you'll never believe this."

"Let me guess, a Bakulu cruiser?" A single eyestalk looked back at her and managed to appear incredulous. "Captain Geshakooka is back. What's the position of Task Force Two?"

"They've already completed their orbit around the gas giant and are coming at the stargate from the opposite side," Chug said. "Shall I send for Commander Kowalczy to assist?"

"Negative," she said, "They'll never get here in time, and if the other fleets get organized, they still have enough throw weight to outgun our people, especially since our ships have no drones. No, let him get through the stargate as planned."

"We don't have any drones either," Edwards reminded his captain.

"I'm all too aware of that," she replied. "Anything that will keep us from fighting?" she asked the DCC.

"Not immediately," Guylan admitted.

"Very well. Chug, bring us about to the target. One point five gravities, please. Edwards, full spread of missiles. Target *Yushispa.* Forward lasers fire on the escorts." On the Tri-V, the enemy ships were closing at a good clip. "Keep her nose toward the enemy to avoid giving them a shot through those downed shields."

"More missiles," Glick warned.

"Reload rear missile batteries with defensive missiles, fire when ready," she ordered. On the forward section of the battlecruiser, powerful lasers began to pulse and dump energy into the shields of the approaching escorts. "Raise the boarding party, tell them we'll have to pick them up later."

"I have them on speaker," Hoot said and Paka's voice instantly came on.

"We're coming up astern, *Pegasus,*" the XO said. Alexis looked, and there was the tiny shape of the Maki shuttle hurrying up from behind. "We saw the sneak attack and realized the original intercept was not going to work."

"You're taking a hell of a chance," Alexis warned; "if those Bakulu notice you, that shuttle is gone."

"They have to hit us first." There was a moment of silence. "We're going to be alongside in two minutes if you maintain thrust."

"Close approach to enemy?" Alexis asked.

"Three minutes," Glick replied. Alexis' eyes narrowed as she thought.

"Engineering, decrease power slowly. Helm, reduce thrust to one gravity at the same rate." Edwards looked at her and grinned.

"Wounded mother bird?" he said.

"Exactly," she agreed, "and it gives our chicks an extra few seconds to get aboard before the shit hits the fan. Helm, plot and prepare for hyperspace. Engineering, we're going to need Reactor Two again. Begin channeling surplus power…"

* * *

"The enemy ship is slowing," the sensor operator reported, "and EM readings indicate fluctuations in power output from their reactors." The captain weighed the odds. If they were hurt, and some shields were down, this was the moment for a bold stroke to end the battle and fulfill their contract.

"Prepare for close approach," he said, "ready all weapons. Escorts, spread formation and continue to fire as the enemy ship comes to bear."

* * *

Pegasus shuddered and alarms sounded as a laser from one of the Bakulu escort frigates slashed through an opening in a downed shield.

"Hull breach," Guylan said, "Deck 27. Damage to the water purification plant. Closing connecting air tight doors."

"Chug, keep them away from those downed shields," Alexis ordered.

"They've spread their formation," Glick said. "We can't keep all the unshielded sections away from fire."

"Spread out, are they?" she asked and that look crossed her face again. Her lips skinned back from her teeth and she let out a little laugh. "Initiate roll, vary speed, keep them guessing." The ship began to roll along its long axis, causing the unshielded sections to change bearing. As ordered, the helm operator randomly increased and decreased the rate of roll, making it impossible to predict. Guylan had been working furiously over his damage control teams' dedicated channels when he suddenly called out.

"We've having difficulty in containing the fire," he told the captain. "Several of the magnesium feed mechanisms have caught, and we're struggling to arrest the spread." The original mechanisms had been made of a hybrid alien alloy. They were replaced with a light weight but strong magnesium alloy decades ago. It was the best choice for such operations, but came with its own risks. "Aft missile feed system is offline. All you have are what's in the tubes."

"Very well," Alexis said, "get that fire under control. Update on the shuttle?"

* * *

Oort had been treated and strapped into the cargo hold; the Tortantula was riding in silence. It took four emergency nano treatment canisters to seal all her wounds. She'd never made a noise during the therapy. No one knew the alien's state of mind after having lost her longtime friend and companion in combat. It wasn't often a Flatar was killed and not its mount. The entire shuttle smelled of blood; Oort was coated in it.

Instead of staring at his teammate, or fixating on his missing arm, Rick watched the monitor next to his seat. The Maki ship was quite a bit fancier than the no-nonsense shuttles of the Winged Hussars. Each seat, while snug for a Human, was well apportioned with its own monitor slate and comfort controls. It was like a commercial suborbital shuttle back on Earth. On that display, currently, was *Pegasus*.

The battlecruiser was thrusting away from them, and their shuttle was braking as it caught up. Once away from the battle, Paka rode the engines, pushing them for stints upwards of five Gs for a minute at a time, to reach a preplanned rendezvous destination. But when the Bakulu ambushed *Pegasus*, everything changed.

"We can continue to the rendezvous area and hope *Pegasus* makes it," Paka had explained to them, "or try for an ASAP intercept. I say we go for the intercept." No one disagreed with the strategy, though if they'd known how hard the Veetanho would be pushing the shuttle, they might have reconsidered.

Several minutes of hard maneuvering later, they were coming up astern of the ancient warship, alongside her blazing fusion torch. Luckily, their shuttle was approaching aft-first, so their most shielded part faced the blazing radioactive drive of their ship. Their angle of approach had to be close; there wasn't time to maneuver laterally as they came alongside…and, if they came alongside from further out, they'd be a bigger target for the Bakulu.

"We're going to be doing an underway docking," Paka warned them. "This isn't going to be pretty. Strap down as best as you can and hang on for all you're worth."

In the cockpit Paka tightened her restraints. Her body was longer and legs shorter than the Maki, though they weren't completely dissimilar. T'jto didn't fare nearly as well. She settled for locking the copilot's chair flat and wrapping the restraints around her thorax twice before buckling them in place. Her combat armor provided a lot of protection, if she could keep from flying free during maneuvers. Oort was secured like cargo; the Humans were all crammed into the overly small seats.

"Final approach," Paka said as they came up on *Pegasus* at what appeared to be an improbably fast pace. "Prepare for last burn." She flipped on the PA again. "Six gravities for 10 seconds," she warned. "Here we go."

Outside, the flare of *Pegasus'* fusion torch was a white-hot flame hundreds of yards long, and it appeared as if they were about to fly right into it.

Paka touched the controls, and they were slammed back into their chairs or restraints as the shuttle's engines roared. Six Gs was bone crushing, even for the relatively short burst needed to bring them alongside. In the rear, Rick watched on the monitor as *Pegasus* loomed large, his arm burning in agony. He imagined this was what it felt like to have your arm eaten, slowly. Then *Pegasus* was sliding by at an astonishingly close distance, close enough to see the burn marks from the recent combat. His eyes widened—there were gouges just north of the engines that were trailing the vapor plumes of escaping fluids. The battle had not been without cost.

As he watched, the movement of the battlecruiser slowed quickly, and then stopped at the exact instant Paka cut the engines. They were drifting close to the looming hull of their home, almost perfectly adjacent to the hangar decks. Amazingly, *Pegasus* was spinning, so the hangar doors rotated by every few seconds. Outside, missiles shot away from Pegasus in the quiet of vacuum, and Rick wondered, *are they going to stop the rotation?* But then, as an open hangar door appeared, Paka pulsed the reaction thrusters, pushing the shuttle rapidly sideways.

"Holy shit!" someone hissed. In a second, they were inside the hangar deck. Paka rode the stick expertly, arresting their sideways momentum before they could crash into the opposite wall, then lowered the landing legs and pushed them down onto the deck. There was a slight jolt as magnets clamped the legs down; outside the door was already sliding closed. The hangar crew launched themselves from protective alcoves with restraining cables to lash the stolen shuttle to the deck.

"That rat can fly!" Sergeant Stan Jones whistled.

Rick rather doubted the XO would appreciate being called a rodent.

"Damned fine flying," the lieutenant said.

"Thanks," Paka replied. "Good shuttle. I think we'll keep it."

* * *

"Shuttle has been recovered and locked down," came the report from the hangar deck. "We're secure for hyperspace."

"Target deviation on the enemy cruiser has dropped to less than one percent," Edwards said. In the Tri-V display of their forward view, the enemy ship was visible for the first time. Shorter and wider than *Pegasus*, it was still evident that, like all medium-sized capital ships, they shared a similar lineage.

Particle beams lashed out at *Pegasus*, one splashing against a shield and nearly overloading it, the second one penetrating and burning a chunk out of her hull.

"Another penetration on Deck 28," Guylan warned, "I have casualties in the damage control party." He listened to the report. "The fire is mostly under control." Then a laser from one of the Bakulu escorts flashed through the same hole in the shield, and into *Pegasus'* hull. A split second later the ship shuddered and metal screamed. "Deck 28!" Guylan yelled, red flashing all over his status board. "We've had an ammo cook off!"

"How bad?" Alexis asked, looking at the main tactical board. There were only seconds before they passed dangerously close to the Bakulu cruiser.

"Section Three is gone, hull blowout. It didn't migrate to the other sections." On a Tri-V came a picture from a camera mounted on the hull showing a huge section of deck plating blown outward. Debris, stuttering fire, and gases were pouring out of the hole. "Structural integrity is intact," the elSha said with an audible sigh. The blow out panels on the hull along all the missile magazines were designed to force the explosion outward, instead of inwards. Had the blast reached an adjacent magazine, the resulting shockwave could have cut the vessel in half.

"Long, full power to all reactors!" Alexis barked.

At the rear of the warship, the Jeha engineer ground his pincers together, then he slid the controls for the reactors to maximum, and power surged through the distribution network of the great warship. Instantly, a magnetic buffer on Reactor Two failed, and the engineer cringed as two more went from green to yellow.

"Hold together, you entropy-cursed junk," he demanded of the machine. "We only need a minute or two!"

The next moments passed in a flash. The four surviving Bakulu ships unleashed everything they had on the Human warship, which suddenly turned slightly, and the protective doors opened over the glowing maw of its spinal mount. Captain Geshakooka had never seen the tiny shuttle, so he didn't know why *Pegasus* didn't fire its main gun or use its hyperspace shunts to escape. He had thought they were too damaged, but now, less than 100 miles away and passing each other at an incredible speed, *Pegasus'* spinal mount spun and lined up perfectly. He knew there wasn't a thing he could do about it.

Missiles, lasers, and other beam weapons lashed back and forth across space in a furious exchange of fire, and *Pegasus'* spinal mount discharged at nearly peak output. A full 40-terawatt particle accelerator beam lanced across space, directly in the path of the *Yushispa.* The Bakulu ship flew through the beam, and it cut the ship completely in two down its length. Missile magazines and fusion reactors exploded, turning the ship into a roiling fireball which was quickly consumed by the void.

Its tubes loaded for offensive operations, *Pegasus* fired 10 ship-killer missiles. Four had been aimed at *Yushispa*, and they spiraled away harmlessly, their target vaporized before they could reach it. The other six were tasked, two each, with hitting the three escort frigates. As the battlecruiser was spinning, *Pegasus* brought all her laser batteries to bear, and they pounded the escorts with withering, inhumanly-accurate fire, dumping thousands of megawatts of laser energy into their shields.

The frigates were many times nimbler than their now dead mothership, and they shuddered under a dozen gravities of desperate maneuvering power as they tried to avoid the Hussar's missiles, their anti-missile lasers pulsing furiously. The Winged Hussars' ship-killers performed as designed, though, and four of the six found their marks, wiping the last of the Bakulu ships from the system. However, Geshakooka's final blows were not without their own results.

"Multiple hits!" Guylan yelled as the ship rocked, bucked, and screamed. "Penetrations on Decks 9, 17, 29, 25, 31, and 32!"

"Hit on main engineering!" Long exclaimed over the intercom. "We're bleeding reaction mass!"

"Status on the reactors?" Alexis asked as Chug worked to stabilize the ship. Her eyes widened as the lights flickered.

"Main power bus damaged," Guylan said.

"Reactors!" Alexis barked. "Status?"

"Reactor One took a direct hit," Long said; "it's bad. I vented the drive plasma to space. We lost two more buffers on Reactor Two, as well. Three is fine. Earlier repairs are holding." Alexis wiped sweat from her brow and nodded.

"Set course for rendezvous with the task force at the stargate. Let's get out of here."

"Ships entering our threat box," Glick said. The SitCon was displaying multiple red triangles heading toward them. Edwards evaluated and spoke.

"Two battlecruisers and a cruiser," he said. "It's a mixture of HecSha and Maki."

"They figured it out," Paka said, flying into the CIC, the huge safety door sliding closed behind her.

"Welcome back," Alexis said. The Veetanho looked at the sea of red and yellow indicators on the Tri-V display of *Pegasus* that floated near Guylan.

"How bad?" she asked.

"Bad," Alexis said, and turned to Chug. "Can we beat them to the stargate?"

"How many Gs can you give me?" he asked Guylan, who tapped at his controls.

"Three, with minimal shields and defenses. Only one and a quarter with full shields, and three quarters with currently available offense and defense at maximum."

On the big Tri-V, the three flight solutions were displayed, as Chug had suggested. It also noted the intercept points on all three. Even with no shields and simply running, the three enemy ships would have weapons range on them almost 20 minutes before they reached the stargate. They wouldn't make it.

"What's our tactical situation, Edwards?" Alexis asked.

"Not good, Captain," he said and took temporary control of the central Tri-V. "While the blast on the rear magazine didn't spread, there's damage to the feed mechanisms. Missiles are out. Some of the thruster relays were damaged from the hit on Deck 9; and it looks like the maneuvering bridge is toast. Deck 25 took a hit that destroyed three of our five main laser generators, so the aft battery is effectively out until DC can evaluate secondary damage. We don't want to risk turning 100 megawatts loose inside the ship. We're down to forward missile and laser batteries, the main gun, and about two-thirds of our anti-missile lasers pods. Nine of 28 shield generators are out. Three look completely blown, but we need DC to evaluate further. We also can't fight at full power while running for the gate."

"I don't see a lot of options here," Alexis said, then keyed the intercom to engineering. "Long, I need that Reactor Two again for a minute. Just like back in Karma."

"You're kidding, right?"

"Long, have you ever known me to kid?"

"No, I haven't," he said. The sounds of shorting electrical connections and shouting damage control parties were clearly audible over the engineer's clicking, hissing voice. "We had 70 containment buffers. Four are toast, eight more are damaged." In the CIC, a graphic representation of the toroid-shaped reactor appeared, the donut shaped ring of buffers showed 70 slices around the reactor. Four were red, eight more were yellow. The red slices were all on the same corner, the yellow spread out. "We can lose almost half the buffers and maintain containment," Long explained, "as long as they're spread out." Adjacent to three of the four red buffers, were yellow ones. "Losing two next to each other creates stress. Lots of stress. Enough to make more of those yellows fail. Running the reactor at 100 percent, which is what we need to power the hyperspace shunt *and* the hyperspace generators at the same time, is foolhardy."

"But only long enough to get into hyperspace," she reminded him. "Then you can run off Reactor Three, which is in perfect shape, right?" Silence answered her. "Right?"

"Yes, Captain."

"Good," she said. "Then once more unto the breach, dear friend. Once more, and we can get Home."

"Yes, Captain." Long looked away from the intercom at his tired, sweaty, wounded engineering staff. He'd lost two of the reactor watch when the laser tore through the hull and destroyed Reactor One. How much more could you demand of beings before they broke? He was afraid he would find out before it was all over. "Okay," he called out over the squadnet to his crew, "we need peak output from Reactor Two for about one minute. Double the reactor watch and stand by!"

Fifteen minutes later, Reactor Three was at 100 percent power, and Two was on standby. Power coursed through the hull, energizing the hyperspace generators, and the circle of shunts was activated and ready around her nose.

"Ship reports ready," Paka said, and the intercom sounded.

"Prepare for transition in one minute."

"*<Danger>*" Alexis heard. *What now*? She thought, then spoke to her CIC crew.

"Be alert, something is wrong." They all double-checked their boards. It was the sensor operator, Flipper, who spoke up.

"I have low power signals in near space," he said.

"Drones," Glick said after running the data. "Shit, four seekers. They're all around us!"

"Chug, get us out of here!" Alexis barked.

"Power to the shunts," Chug called, and engineering spun up Reactor Two. Long chittered nervously as he slid the power control up on the already damaged reactor.

"Come on hatchling," he said, almost caressing the control, "one more time…"

"Power coming up," Chug said, "course set for Home. Energizing the shunts. Five…four…three…two…"

A two-terawatt particle beam slashed into and through *Pegasus* from almost directly astern, and it sliced into one of the three fusion torches. The energy was held in check for a fraction of a second by the reactor chamber as the hyperspace window opened, and *Pegasus* transitioned out of the normal world. Then the engine exploded, destroying Reactor Three.

*****

Chapter Thirty-Seven

EMS Pegasus

En route to Home

Hyperspace

The impact of the beam weapon against the stern of the ship didn't immediately register on the bridge. There was a singular moment of creation/uncreation as the ship moved into hyperspace, then the explosion. The entire ship lurched, as if it had been struck from behind by another, faster ship. Alarms blared, and the power fluctuated. Alexis' eyes went wide with surprise and fear. Transition to hyperspace was the most dangerous moment of space travel.

"What was that?" she demanded. Guylan turned to look at her, his mouth open in shock.

"Reactor Three is offline," he said, "we have massive damage to engineering."

"Long, report," she called. There was no immediate response. She looked back to Guylan. "Get every available hand to engineering immediately!" He nodded and started sending the all-hands call. "Engineering, do you read?" Alexis called out. Finally, Hoot turned his head around to face her.

"I have engineering on the emergency circuit. Most comms are down."

"I'm having to use radios for my teams," Guylan confirmed.

"Long here," came the scratchy, static-filled voice of their Jeha engineer. "Reactor Three was almost completely destroyed." He was forced to yell to be heard over the blaring alarms and the roar of the overloaded systems. "There are plasma fires burning in a dozen places!"

"What happened?" Alexis asked. "Reactor Three was fine!"

"We took a hit," the engineer replied. "I can't be sure, but I'd say it was a particle beam right into the fusion torch just before we transitioned."

"Oh gods," Chug said.

"I lost a dozen members of my staff," Long continued. "We're in deep shit down here." Alexis caught movement out of the corner of her eye as Guylan flipped out of his chair and flew for the exit. "The beam must have blown out the torch's reaction chamber, and then gone right into the reactor core. There's nothing left of the reactor; we have pieces of buffers and the containment vessel everywhere. Safeties failed, and the drive plasma started arcing around engineering. One of my assistants waded in and manually engaged the vent. We never found his body. He saved the ship."

"Are we stable in hyperspace?" Alexis asked Chug.

"Yes," her helm answered, "but power is fluctuating."

"We're at 89 percent," Long warned. There was a resounding bang. "And there goes another buffer! Captain, if you can't reduce the power load, we're going to lose the last reactor." The display showing the reactor was still up on the bridge. Everyone could see five red buffers now, all on the same quadrant of the reactor. The newest one was just four buffers from a previously failed one, and there were two yellows between them.

"Guylan," Alexis said over the radio. "Override and shut down everything you can."

"What do you mean, 'everything?'" the elSha asked as he raced aft.

"We need 20 terawatts to stay in hyperspace," Chug said.

"I mean everything besides the hyperspace nodes," Alexis ordered. "Put the ship on emergency life support for now. Shut it all down!"

The elSha gasped in alarm, but a second later status boards started to go red. Throughout *Pegasus,* every deck began to go dark. After a moment, Long spoke again.

"Down to 72 percent," he said. "Any more?" Chug shook his head adamantly.

"I'm afraid not," Alexis said. They waited for several long moments as the Jeha worked at the other end of the ship.

"It might be enough for now," he said. "But for 170 hours?" He didn't sound optimistic.

"One hundred seventy hours," Alexis said. She looked up. On the CIC display, now running off emergency power, was a number; *169:56:15.* It continued to count down.

* * *

Rick had been doing okay until they landed, thanks to the drugs and his altered emotional state. Paka exited the shuttle like a streak the moment they set down, and the marines stayed buckled into the shuttle to ride out the final minutes of the battle.

The seconds of radical acceleration knocked him out for a minute, and his head was swimming a bit even before they transitioned to hyperspace; but the sudden, jarring, and unusual leap into that nothingness temporarily jerked him back to reality.

"What the hell was that?" the marines asked at the same time.

"I've never felt a transition like that before," T'jto said. When the hangar deck crewmen opened the door, the look on her face confirmed it was far from normal.

"Lieutenant," she said, looking confused and unsure, "better get your marines below. Captain's orders." Confused and sore, they did as ordered.

As they moved aft, the damage to the warship was more and more evident. The blast doors on Deck 25 were sealed off and showed signs of heat damage. They had to divert to the opposite gangway on Deck 29 to avoid the missile magazine that had exploded.

"The ship really took a pounding," T'jto said, looking at the deformation of the overhead in the squad bay, the result of the magazine detonation.

"Makes you wonder who thought it was a great idea to put a missile magazine next to the marine's barracks," Eskla, one of the two Zuul in Raptor Squad, said as they split off to go to their quarters.

"The missiles are essential," Johansson said; "we aren't."

One of the marine armorers, Tina Bradshaw, was a qualified Human medic. She came in and gave Rick's arm a single look, turned green, and left to tend to the CASPers.

Several of the other marines took Oort and gently strapped her to a spot in the squad bay. She was breathing regularly, but still hadn't said a word since they'd fled the Maki battleship.

Rick helped himself to some more pain relievers from his medkit. He knew enough about a trauma like this; using nanites would be a mistake. His arm was gone, but there were other options, and spraying the stump with nanites would limit them. A few minutes later, the main lighting cut out, and they had to dig out portable, battery-powered lanterns. They were also warned that main life-support was shut down, so field oxygen recyclers were taken from the stores.

"It's bad," T'jto said, as she helped set them up. When a pair of damage control crew passed through, the marines waylaid the hapless men for information. They finally found out the ship was indeed in hyperspace, but operating on one fusion reactor—the badly damaged one. Damage control teams were still working on the wreckage in engineering, that strange impact they'd felt was a last-second hit just before they transitioned to hyperspace. It had cost them their last fully-functional fusion reactor.

It was more than three hours before the medical team arrived. They'd been in engineering, treating more severely wounded crew. Dr. Ramirez went straight to Rick, his medical equipment in a big backpack for ease of movement. The man seemed quite at home in null gravity. His assistant, Nemo, went straight to Oort and began feeling her numerous injuries with his tentacles.

"Where are the rest of the marines?" Ramirez asked as he examined Rick.

"Aside from four in Raptor Squad, we're it," Rick said. Ramirez stopped and looked up at him, shock and pain registering in his eyes.

"I'm sorry," he said as he removed a portable X-ray scanner from the backpack.

"We're mercs," Rick said; "it happens." The doctor gave him a pained expression which Rick didn't understand. He used the scanner on Rick's arm for several minutes, downloading the data into one of the most complicated slates Rick had ever seen. It had two-fold out screens and a Tri-V projector. He watched as the wound was rebuilt in high-resolution detail on the Tri-V. For once, he was glad he was without emotion; otherwise, it would have been tremendously depressing. The severed bones and tissues were detailed in crystal-clear images.

"Okay young man," the doctor said; "we have three options."

"Let me have them," Rick said.

"One, we stabilize the wound. I use a tailored nanite to clean and close, but that's it. The pain remaining will be minimal, and you'll be well-positioned for a cloned rebuild when we get to a suitable facility on Home. Two, I use some similarly-tailored nanites to begin prepping the wound for a temporary cybernetic replacement. I can have you up and going in a few hours with that, but the limb is extremely limited in ability. You'll not really be able to pilot a CASPer with it, and it won't be comfortable."

"And the third option?"

"I use nanites to integrate metallic monocarbon into your bones, debride the wound, blend your skin and muscles with synthetic, and give you a permanent cybernetic replacement."

"Why would it be permanent?" Rick asked.

"Well, strictly speaking it isn't. But the bone and muscle rework isn't compatible with a cloned replacement arm, so we'd need to cut above the modifications before attaching the new one." The doctor reached out and touched Rick's arm, just below the shoulder joint. "Right about here."

"What are the advantages to each?" The doctor ticked them off on his fingers, one at a time.

"Option one, you get your actual arm back, almost perfect, but it'll be at least 90 days once the genetic material is sequenced for cloning. It's also pricey, so likely the Hussars are going to have to charge back some of that to you. With the partial cybernetic, you'd be back in operation almost right away, but at a considerably reduced capacity. At least you'll have two hands. And the third option, a new arm, is more powerful than a Human limb, is nearly bullet proof, and feels just like the real thing to you."

"Can you put a laser in it, or something?" The doctor shook his head and chuckled. "Can't blame a guy for trying. How long for option three?"

"The treatment for your arm, about four hours. I can print the cybernetic in about the same time. Say two hours to install it, less if Nemo helps. So, five hours, tops." There was a sudden shudder from the hull and a great groaning sound reverberated the length of *Pegasus.*

"Better make it option three," Rick said.

"Are you sure, son?" Rick simply nodded. "Okay." He touched a series of controls on his slate.

"Now what?" Rick asked.

"The arm is printing right now, and I set the computer to tailor the nanites."

"I thought most of the systems were shut down," Rick said.

"Wonders of modern Hussars' technology. We have a micro-fusion reactor in medical. Similar design to the ones used in the drones. It's linked to a miniature manufactory, all designed by Taiki Sato."

"Smart man," Rick remarked.

"The smartest," Ramirez agreed. He fished out a syringe from his bag and mixed several one-shot ampules of drugs into it, then took Rick's intact arm. "These are some preliminary enzymes to get things going. Eat a half-sized meal, drink at least a liter of liquids, no alcohol, and meet me around the corner in medical no less than an hour from now."

Across the squad bay, Nemo gave Oort a monstrous injection and spoke closely to the Tortantula's hearing organs. It was too quiet for Rick to hear what was said. After a moment, Oort blinked her eyes, her race's equivalent of a nod of acknowledgment. Ramirez floated over and spoke with Nemo. He gestured back at Rick, and Nemo regarded the marine with his big blue eyes. After a second, the alien medic gave Rick an almost Human appearing thumbs-up, made all the more amazing because the race only had tentacles.

"One hour," Dr. Ramirez reminded him, and he was off to see other patients.

* * *

"What was that shudder?" Alexis asked. With her in her wardroom were Paka, Chug, Glick, Edwards, Hoot, and Flipper, with Guylan and Long joining via intercom from engineering. It was the elSha DCC that answered a second later.

"That was gravity Deck 4," he explained, "it's gone."

"So much for pushups," Edwards said darkly. Despite his somewhat overweight appearance, the dwarf spent hours working out in gravity.

"Damage from the battle," Long added, working with Guylan in engineering. "The hull was under stress, and it just broke off."

"I think we can agree that a lost gravity deck is the least of our worries," Alexis said, and those present nodded. "First, Paka, give me the casualty count." The Veetanho consulted her slate and spoke.

"Among the crew, 29 are dead or presumed dead, six injured. Among the marines, 12 dead, two injured. The injured will be back up in about 24 hours, according to Dr. Ramirez." A somber silence took over for several moments. It was the costliest cruise, in terms of lives lost, in any of their memories. "Do you want the names now?"

"Send them to my slate," Alexis ordered, "I'm sorry to say we simply don't have time to grieve." She glanced at the display on her desk which read *167:58:01*, the amount of time left in their current hyperspace trip. "Engineer Long, please give me the details."

"Certainly, Captain," he said from the rear of the ship. "As I guessed, recorded data shows we were hit the instant we transitioned to hyperspace. I estimate a yield between one and two terawatts, and the weapon was definitely a particle accelerator."

"One of the battlecruisers," Edwards offered.

"They were several light seconds away," Alexis pointed out, "how did they manage that?" Glick explained.

"It was either a lucky shot, or the seeker drones gave accurate, ideal targeting data." The Bakulu scratched an eyestalk with a pseudopod. "I'm leaning toward the latter."

"It was the extreme edge of their range," Edwards nodded. "Both the HecSha and the Maki employ five-terawatt particle accelerator cannons on their bows. Fired from that range, the attenuation table suggests a yield of no more than two terawatts remaining. We're lucky it was at extreme range."

"It would have punched halfway through the ship," Alexis said under her breath. Both Edwards and Glick nodded in agreement.

"It was also luck it hit one of the torches," Long said. "The engine chamber chewed up a lot of energy."

"What did it do to us?" she asked the engineer.

"After the beam blew through the torch, it went through the side of Reactor Three. We had a partial containment loss, which caused considerable secondary damage, and a lot of casualties. If not for the assistant who vented the plasma, we'd probably have lost Reactor Two as well."

"Put a commendation in that crewman's file," Alexis said, "and see that he gets double combat benefits." Paka nodded and made a note. "Please continue, Long."

"About eight percent of Reactor One was either blown to shit outright, or damaged when the buffers ran away and tore themselves loose from their housings. We salvaged nine buffers and a lot of the control circuits. That's better than Reactor Three."

"The big question is," Alexis started, "can you get Reactor One online before Two fails? I assume you still predict it will fail?"

"Yes," he said, "with a five percent probability per hour, increasing two percent cumulative."

"Forty-eight hours," Alexis said after running the math, "that's all we have."

"Yes, Captain. But probably less, if you play the odds. As for getting another reactor back in operation? Unlikely."

"And there's no chance of fixing any of those buffers on Reactor Two with the salvaged units?"

"No," he said. "It's the same problem we had back in Karma. The damaged and defective ones are inaccessible. Three are where we could reach them, but we'd have to shut the reactor down and open up the entire engineering section to get at the rest. A hot swap of a buffer is nearly impossible. The magnetic field is strong enough to suck the hemoglobin from your blood." He was silent for a moment. "No, Captain, in about 40 hours, we'll lose the last reactor."

"*<Let it fail>*"

"What?" Alexis was so stunned, she accidentally spoke out loud.

"I'm sorry, Captain?" Paka asked. Alexis held up a hand to silence her. Instantly the XO recognized her boss' state. Several of the other senior staff looked from their captain to the XO. Paka mouthed the word *Ghost*, and the others nodded their heads.

"*<I said let the reactor fail>*"

"I heard you, I just don't understand. Should we just give up and die?"

"*<No. I cannot explain>*"

"And I can't just give up." Her eyes refocused and she addressed her engineer. "Long, I know you said it isn't possible, but we have forty hours. Do everything you can to make Reactor One functional again." She turned to Guylan. "Conserve every ounce of power we can so the reactor has as little load as possible." The elSha DCC nodded. "All right, everyone, let's get to work."

* * *

Engineering became a beehive of activity as every hand available rushed to help. Long quickly found himself with more people than he could use and started turning others away. The marines sent two of their available micro-fusion power plants to other areas of the ship to power non-vital, but still important, systems. Oxygen candles were pulled from emergency lockers and used to keep the atmosphere breathable. Entire decks were sealed. They managed to wring another two megawatts of power from non-essential systems.

Although the failure clock stalked them like a relentless predator, Long began to think it might be possible to salvage the reaction vessel from Reactor One by overlapping parts with what remained of Reactor Three. It was far from perfect, but would probably hold long enough. The containment buffers were robust and could be turned up to hold the fusion reaction closer to the chamber center.

Alexis arrived to do what all captains have done throughout history—to see to the fate of her vessel in person. She was smart enough to stay out of the way, but she had to know. She had to see it with her own eyes. She'd never seen so many of her crew working on one project. There were even three CASPer-suited marines helping move the salvaged buffers into place to construct the improvised emergency reactor. She was also there when it all came crashing down.

"We're done," Long told her, floating over, "we can't do it."

"Why, what happened?"

"F11," he explained. "The secondary tank is empty. One of the plasma fires took out the control circuity and breached the tank. Odorless and tasteless. The chamber probably has a few hundred gallons floating around in the atmospheric processors. We could get some back out, if we had a week."

"So even if you get the improvised reactor built, you can't make it run."

"Essentially, yes," he agreed. "And I expect Reactor Two to fail within about 40 minutes at the latest. There's nothing more I can do."

"I understand," Alexis said, and turned to go.

"Captain, I'm sorry."

"It's not your fault," she said. "You gave it your best, and then some. Thanks for trying."

Alexis returned to the CIC and floated across the nerve center of the doomed warship. The numbers floated above the main Tri-V display, *150:22:11*. A countdown that would never reach zero.

She went through the door into her wardroom and stopped by the desk. *Pegasus* had been her home for nearly 40 years. She'd spent more time on the warship than anywhere else. She'd been commander of the Winged Hussars for 12 years with *Pegasus* as her command ship, a company tradition going back to the Alpha Contracts. She had a suite back on Home, and she seldom saw it. This ship was more than her home; it was her heart.

Alexis slid in behind her desk, pulling herself down into the chair with long-practiced ease. She glanced at the watch she wore, a gift from her mother when she'd graduated from the Hussars' flight academy. Ten minutes had passed since she left engineering. Twenty-eight minutes left. She stared at the ancient wooden desk for a long moment, then triggered the ship-wide channel with her pinplants.

"Attention all hands," she said, her voice echoing throughout the ship; "this is your captain speaking." She took another breath and composed her thoughts before continuing. "As I'm sure you are all aware, *Pegasus* was severely damaged in the battle in Grkata as we attempted to rescue our comrades, our family. The worst damage was caused by a weapons impact just before we transitioned into hyperspace. After sustaining damage so many times on this cruise and always managing to keep going, we've finally come up short.

"Despite the valiant efforts of our damage control teams, their leader Guylan, and our chief engineer Long, we've been unable to repair the only remaining fusion reactor. In 27 minutes, give or take, the hyperdrive will fail.

"I take personal responsibility for the chain of events that brings us here, and hope you draw some consolation knowing we saved thousands with our sacrifice. I hope you can find some peace in the minutes that remain. It's been an honor to serve with each and everyone one of you." She turned off the intercom and sighed. Then she did something she hadn't done in 12 years; she cried. Alone with her failure, she quietly sobbed in despair. "I've failed you all," she moaned. In freefall, tears don't fall, they just build up like puddles over your eyes. She wiped hers away with the sleeve of her uniform tunic.

After floating in her seat for a few minutes, she activated the special channel on her pinlink.

"Are you there?"

"*<Always>*"

"You are remarkably unconcerned, considering you'll die with us."

"*<I cannot die as you understand it>*" Alexis didn't know what to say to that. "*<If the reactor is allowed to fail, there is no hope. I must act>*" And just that quickly, she went from mourning to fear.

"What are you going to do?" An alarm blared. Alexis launched herself at the door to the CIC. "Status?" she ordered.

"Hyperdrive just initiated a shutdown," Chug said. Alexis drifted toward her command chair. "Ten seconds to failure!"

"What are you doing?" she asked over the pinlinks. There was no response.

"Five seconds," Chug said. The Tri-V showed the flashing emergency status of the hyperdrive. 'Danger – Imminent failure!'

"Damn you!" Alexis yelled over the links. "Why?" Everyone in the CIC looked around in that moment of panic before disaster struck.

"<*Fear not*>" a reply finally came, "<*this too shall pass*>" A second later, the hyperdrive failed.

* * * * *

Part III

I never really bought their line of bullshit. The Cartography Guild makes a lot of pretty excuses about how hyperspace is too unpredictable and intrudes on too many levels of quantum physics. I say, "Horse shit." Hyperspace travel has been in use in our galaxy for at least a hundred thousand years, according to the GalNet. And records in the Science Guild's archives back this up. There are no records, *none*, mind you, of a ship ever setting course for one star system, and arriving at another. So, we're faced with an obvious problem. If those little black boxes that control the hyperspace generators are so damned polished they never make a mistake, how come no one has ever figured out how to arrive someplace other than the predesignated emergence point around a star? Or have they, and that secret is carefully kept by certain people? Don't rock the boat, our world government says. Well, I say some boats need rocking.

Excerpt from "In Our Own Time – Dawning of the Horsemen"
by Jimmy Cartwright, Sr.

* * * * *

Chapter Thirty-Eight

EMS Pegasus

Location Unknown

When the hyperdrive system shut down on *Pegasus*, the transition was like nothing any of the crew had ever experienced before. To most, it felt like they were ripped from their bodies and cast violently down a screaming whirlpool of fireworks that ended in a meat grinder. That lasted for an endless second, then it was over, and they were themselves again.

Status boards flashed messages, the big Tri-V flickered and came back on at the same time as the life support fans. The CIC was filled with the sounds of rapid breathing, coughs, and moans of pain, because everyone hurt like they'd just been beaten senseless.

"Is everyone still with us?" Alexis asked her command crew. Did her voice sound…funny? One at a time they all answered in the affirmative. They were still alive, and the ship was still intact. "Chug, where are we?"

"Checking," the Bakulu replied, his eyes looking in three directions at once.

"Sensors are not responding," Flipper said. "Both radar and lidar systems have failed diagnostics. Zero returns." The sensor tech flipped through instruments. "EM sensors show nothing. Magnetometer has nothing. No hard radiation readings, not even the usual backscatter from our drives. Visual cameras are giving an error message. Normally, in hyperspace, we just see white, same as a direct view."

Alexis let go of her chair and pushed off toward her wardroom. To her complete surprise, she only made it halfway there. In just a few feet, she quickly slowed to a stop. It was as if the air was as thick as water!

"What the hell?" she wondered aloud, floating with no spin or yaw as with normal zero gravity. Then she realized she was trapped and unable to reach anything or anyone. Paka worked her way along one bulkhead of the CIC until she was within reach of her captain, whereupon she hooked a dexterous foot around a console, reached out, and pulled Alexis down to a handhold.

"You don't feel any different when you move," Paka said, waving a hand back and forth. "It isn't like the air is thicker."

"No," Alexis agreed, "it's just as if there were a retarding gravity." She moved toward her wardroom, careful this time to remain within reach of something. "I need to see outside."

Her wardroom was the nearest place with a window; there weren't many on a warship. It was offset from the CIC, so if a laser found it, the beam couldn't go right through to the command center. The only other ones were on the gravity decks. This one was an oval, five feet tall and three feet wide, made of nearly clear synthetic ruby, and unbreakable by all reasonable measures. Through it, she saw space. Only, as she inched closer, she realized it wasn't space at all.

"Oh, my," Paka said as she moved with her to float next to the window, their faces mere inches away.

"It's black," Alexis said. "Black in the same way hyperspace is white. It's…"

"<*The Nothing*>" she heard over her pinplants.

"You knew," Alexis replied.

"*<Yes>*"

"Why didn't you say something?"

"*<And how would you explain this? A nothing emptier than any other nothing?>*"

Alexis started to provide a description, and then stopped. She was right, there were no words for this. It was like describing a sunset to a blind person, or the cry of a newborn baby to the deaf. Nothing was an apt description. The blackness drank the light the way a sponge drinks water. Only, it was more than that. It seemed to drink you, as well. She felt it pulling at her consciousness like an itch you couldn't scratch. Like the thing your parents said you must not touch, and naturally touching it was all you could think of. It was indescribable, and still she had to find a way…

"Shit," she said and pulled her eyes away with an almost physical tearing. "Oh, fuck," she hissed. It left a sharp pain behind her eyes, a gently wiggling ice pick of agony that slowly faded. Paka did the same, with the same apparent effort, then put a hand to her head. "Yeah," Alexis nodded. "Ghost said it's called The Nothing."

"Good name," her XO said. "But what is it really?" Paka glanced out the window for a second, then back at her captain. "Are we dead?" Paka almost whispered the question.

"I honestly don't know what it is," Alexis admitted. "But considering what we saw looking out the window, maybe we better keep all the other view ports shuttered for now."

"Understood, Captain," Paka said. She relayed the order.

"Captain," Hoot called. "Intraship communications are being normalized."

"Good job," she said.

"Thank you. I've had to apply some novel processing to get the signals recognized by the system." There was a chirp from the comms officer's controls. "I have a priority request for you from Dr. Sato." She was surprised to hear from the scientific genius of the Geek Squad, but indicated it should be put through. The man instantly began to babble.

"Is this the most incredible thing you've ever seen? Non-Newtonian physics are at play, but we haven't ceased to exist along with many of the rules we are used to! Our instruments can't function normally, but our bodies and much of our apparatus appear fine! And have you looked outside? This is unbelievable. We aren't leaving soon, are we? I need at least a week to study this. No, a month!"

"Doctor Sato," Alexis barked, tired of waiting for the man to take a breath, "what are you talking about?"

"Why, where we have found ourselves, Captain! If we had any idea that terminating a hyperdrive would take us here, we would have done it on purpose long ago."

"Do you know where here is?"

"Well," the man hesitated, "not precisely," he said, nonplused. Alexis and Paka exchanged knowing looks.

"What can you tell us, then?"

"This is almost certainly another level of hyperspace."

"Level?"

"Yes, we've long believed there might be an infinite number of levels. After all, hyperspace happens to be nothing more than another dimension. Since our three-dimensional minds cannot comprehend it, all we see is a featureless whiteness. Strangely, this is a featureless blackness instead." She could almost hear the brilliant scientist's brain spinning in circles. "If we assume that normal hyperspace is level one, this would be level two. Maybe this is a fifth dimension?"

"Dr. Sato, this is fascinating, but what can I do for you?"

"We need to take samples," he said, just as excitedly. "We need to go outside and examine the environment!"

"Doctor, that might not be a very good idea."

"I don't see it that way," he insisted. "Unlike the first level of hyperspace, we're not being maintained here. This is a stable state. How could it hurt?"

"I have no idea," Alexis replied, "and that calls for caution."

"Discovery calls for risk!" the doctor countered. Alexis sighed and thought for a second.

"Before we go in that direction, do you know how we might get out of here and back to normal space?"

"Not at all," he admitted. "One can assume that the hyperspace nodes might well do that, but how can we be sure? The drive systems are a mystery we still haven't solved after a century of study. No one knows how they take us from one star to another once you enter hyperspace. Thanks to your friend, we at least have cracked the problem of fixed destination."

"Do what experiments you can from inside the ship," Alexis said, "and begin checking with the crewmen to see who can tolerate The Nothing without going nuts."

"The Nothing? You mean this level of hyperspace? And what do you mean about going nuts?" She explained Paka's and her reaction to staring at it. "Oh, fascinating. I found my brief exposure to it rather exhilarating." Alexis shuddered.

"Proceed with caution," she ordered, "I'll get back with you shortly." She turned to Paka. "You have the conn. I need to go see the Ghost in person." As she moved down the companionway toward drone control, she tried to forget the last time she'd been there.

* * * * *

Interlude

Twelve Years Ago

Planet Degardo

Degardo System Orbital Defensive Operation

"Maximum defensive missile spread!" Alexis barked and instantly felt the tubes unleash a hail of missiles in all directions. The missiles exploded in only seconds, filling the space around *Pegasus* with high velocity outbound metal fragments and sensor-confusing EM chaff. The Tri-V in the CIC showed that most of the incoming missiles lost their locks or prematurely detonated, filling the area with a string of high-order nuclear explosions.

In the year since she'd taken command of the Hussars after her mother died, Alexis had never been in a fight like this. Two full Hussars' task forces were in the Degardo system fighting to hold a Wathayat ore processing facility against a concerted and unrelenting effort to take it from them. Large quantities of high-grade titanium dioxide in the system's asteroid belt made the system valuable, but when they cracked open an asteroid and found several hundred tons of red diamonds, everything escalated. The Winged Hussars had been hired, along with 13 other merc units. Elements of fifteen alien merc units showed up a week after the defenses were arrayed, though, and it was game on.

Alexis' side had lost the emergence point a week ago, and the fighting had been nearly nonstop since then. The red diamond strike was considered the biggest in history. In raw value alone, it was estimated at five trillion credits; however, many of the diamonds appeared to be flawless and exceeded 100 carats in size. These were worth many times their weighted value; after all, what collector wouldn't want a red diamond, the basis of currency valuation in the Union, larger than a MinSha's head?

"Try and get me a firing solution on that damned *Pookur*-class missile cruiser!" Alexis ordered Pat Viebey, her TacCom.

"I'm trying, ma'am," he said. The man was down one arm; his other was immobilized from taking a metal fragment. A kinetic missile had penetrated the hull and hit the armored CIC two days ago. It didn't further penetrate the CIC, but some of the armor spalled, sending pieces hurtling across the CIC. Three of her command staff were killed, and Viebey's left arm was so badly damaged that nanites couldn't fix it. There hadn't been time to get him into surgery, either.

The tactical display flashed; more missiles were incoming. The last of her drones was trying to get around the enemy's defensive formation to lay a nuke on the command battleship. It was already damaged, a victim of a Night Bird attack which cost the Japanese mercs a frigate. Alexis should have transferred the flag to another ship; it was a foolish move on her part to keep it, but now she had a clear target which might well break the assault's back.

Just as Alexis ordered another course change, the computer interfaces on the CIC flickered. It took a full second to clear; the same hit to the CIC had badly damaged their computers.

"Katrina!" Alexis called to her sister, and XO, over the intercom.

"I'm working on it!" she yelled back from the computer room. Their computer specialists had died in the attack, so Katrina had gone down to the computer core to make manual repairs. With the ship under multiple nuke attacks, the last thing Alexis wanted her sister doing was plugging her substantial pinplants into the system. EMP in space could be just as deadly as on a planet, especially in a big metal can. The computers flickered out entirely for a moment, before coming back online.

"Update?" she asked her sister, bucking sideways in her command couch as the helmsman made several radical direction changes.

"The connections for the primary and backup cores are severed," Katrina said. "That missile really fucked things up down here. I think the primary is completely shot."

"Without the connection, how is the secondary even running?"

"No clue," Katrina responded. "I think it's managing to feed through the dedicated engineering trunk and then back up the command lines."

"No wonder everything is lagging and overclocking," Alexis said.

"Incoming missiles have locks," tactical said. Lasers were lashing out at the previous wave, finishing off the last of them.

"How many?"

"More than last time," the man grunted. Alexis could see his arm bleeding again. Fuck, if she lost him, there were no more tactical officers to take his place. "Mixed nuclear, high explosive, and kinetic!"

"Anti-missile spread," she ordered.

"That will clean us out," Viebey warned.

"I know," Alexis said through clenched teeth. The missiles launched, and she watched the Tri-V, but her gaze was drawn away from near space to the distance where the command battleship skulked. The last of the Hussar drones had just gotten lucky; a screening frigate went up in a growing ball of death. The jamming cleared, and there was the command ship, clear and unobstructed.

"Only half the incoming missiles have been destroyed," Viebey reported, "firing lasers.... damn!" A second later *Pegasus'* shields were bombarded. One of the missiles was nuclear, exploding in a hydrogen fireball against the battlecruiser's shields, causing several to fail. Two kinetic missiles penetrated, punching into *Pegasus'* aft sections near engineering. The last was a high explosive, and it hit amidships, just behind the CIC. The explosion tore a 20-foot hole in the side of the ship, breaching the aft water tanks which helped shield the CIC. Part of the blast punched into the already weakened armor, penetrating and exposing the space to vacuum.

Everyone in the CIC already wore armor and helmets, which closed automatically in response to the pressure drop, but the hole was almost five feet across, and the decompression was explosive. Alexis watched in horror as a hurricane-force wind tore at her remaining command staff and flying chunks of armor killed indiscriminately.

The comms officer was pulled halfway across the compartment and impaled on a jutting lance of torn armor. Two engineering assistants who had been working on the electrical system, both elSha, were sucked into space. Viebey was torn from his couch. He hadn't been able to properly latch his safety harness with only one hand and never asked anyone for help. She saw the horrified, pleading look on his face as he was sucked toward the hole. The jagged hole raked his suit like a Besquith's claws, breaching it in several places, before he was taken by the black.

"*Glambring*, *Hrunting*!" she called out over their fleet's tactical channel. They were the closest escort frigates.

"Go ahead, *Pegasus*," they replied.

"We're hit. I need you to screen for us!"

"That'll leave the *Manticore* in dire straits," the captain of the *Hrunting* warned. The carriers were a priority for the escorts, because they were less able to defend against missile swarms; normally, Alexis would never have done this to protect herself.

"Understood, *Hrunting*, assist as ordered." Both frigates acknowledged and under their much higher thrust, quickly moved to bracket *Pegasus* and bring their defensive laser batteries into play.

"*Pegasus*," the captain of *Glambring* called, "be aware you are venting fire just forward of engineering. Looks like your missile magazines are ablaze." Alexis looked at the DCC station, but the operator was slumped over her console; part of her head was gone. Alexis accessed the damage control on her pinplants and saw there was fire reported on Decks 28 and 29, Section Three, in a missile magazine and launcher. A second later her interface failed, and the computer flickered yet again.

"Thanks, *Glambring*. Try and keep them off us for a few minutes, and we'll see if we can end this fight." With a sinking sensation, she realized she was the only one alive in the CIC. Alexis tried the redundant controls in her command station and found them nonresponsive. Her pinlinks would connect with the computer, fail, then try to reconnect again with the same results. The big tactical Tri-V showed the enemy missile cruiser maneuvering to fire again, and *Pegasus*, unable to maneuver, was a sitting duck.

"Katrina, I need those computers!" she said as she unbuckled and pushed toward the tactical station. Vacuum-boiled, black blood stained the controls, and the couch was bent slightly on its mounting. Alexis pulled herself onto the couch and clipped on the waist restraint. There wasn't any reason for the heavy three-point harness; no atmosphere was left and no one was piloting the ship. She configured the controls as quickly as she could; it had been years since she'd run a tactical station. Her hands remembered, though, and she found what she wanted. It also appeared to still be functioning. The problem was, she'd need helm to use it.

"Katrina, I need to get the ship repositioned."

"I'm not stopping you," her sister replied over their pinlinks.

"I'm the only one left alive here; that last hit hulled us and penetrated the CIC. The ship is in bad shape." Silence for a moment as Alexis' hands worked almost without thought, redirecting power from the two functioning reactors to get the shields back. "Kat, I need you to figure this out or we're dead."

"Okay," the other woman replied; "I got this, Alex." The two sisters hadn't called each other by their childhood names since before their mother died. "It's just like old times, right?"

Alexis worked frantically, getting the defensive lasers functioning to sweep away a few errant missiles, all the while praying her sister could make good on her promise. The seconds ticked away as the enemy escorts tried to close the box. A pair of heavy cruisers were also trying to come around her starboard flank, where a squadron of Zuul ships had been badly mauled by a drone attack. The status board reported the weapon ready.

"Now or never," she whispered to her sister as the computers continued to flicker.

And then, all the systems came alive. The computers were acting like the CIC hadn't just been blown to shit, or the computer room half-trashed from secondary explosions hours ago. *Atta girl,* Alexis thought as she brought a secondary control alive and worked it with her pinplants. *Pegasus* groaned as she spun, and her torch burned anew. The bow of the ancient battlecruiser swung rapidly, the shield doors opening. Alexis fired the spinal mount.

"Surprise, asshole!" she snarled as forty terawatts of particle energy lashed into the enemy's command battleship. *Pegasus* continued its turn during the two second beam pulse, and the weapon punched through the battleship's superstructure, and sliced out its side. The engine room was hulled, three of its nine reactors completely destroyed, and the ship exploded like a supernova.

The power drain of firing the particle accelerator was usually compensated for with capacitors to allow secondary systems to continue functioning, but one of the enemy's kinetic missiles had damaged the capacitors, halving the ship's backup power. Her screen showed more missiles incoming, but only half the defensive lasers had power to fire. It wasn't a big wave of missiles, but it was enough, and one of the ship-killers detonated its nuclear warhead within 100 meters of *Pegasus'* already severely weakened shields.

The EMP washed over *Pegasus*, creating a power spike through the entire ship. Alexis yelled as the ship was rocked by the impact, and the tactical console exploded in her face, pelting her armor with shrapnel and cracking the visor on her helmet.

"Damn it!" she cried as her armor's life support system cried an alarm. She felt a pain in her gut and looked down to see the plume of escaping air. It was tinged red. She grabbed at her patch kit, and as she slapped the goopy thing on the leak, she saw several more. Her suit said 10 minutes of life support remaining. Time to get out of the CIC. While she worked to extract herself, she made a last radio call.

"*Sleipnir*, this is *Pegasus* actual," she called to the other Winged Hussar battlecruiser in the system, hoping it was still there.

"*Pegasus*, this is *Sleipnir* actual. What's your situation?"

"We're screwed," Alexis said. "I think we just took an EMP. Can you give me a status update on the enemy? Am I about to get turned into atoms?"

"Negative," the other commander replied. "You kicked them in the balls, Commander Cromwell. They are retreating toward the stargate. Shall we pursue?"

"How are my escorts, *Hrunting* and *Glambril*?"

"They ate that last wave, Commander. They're gone." She exhaled and shook her head.

"Understood. Do not pursue in force. Send a cruiser, *Seattle Slew* or *American Pharaoh*, whichever is in better shape, and four frigates to harry them until they transition out. Notify me if they decide to rally."

"Understood, Commander. Do you need assistance? You appear adrift."

"Yes," Alexis admitted. "Send over all the available damage control teams from the fleet support vessel ASAP. We'll also need the medical teams." She switched to a local channel. "Good job, Katrina. You saved us and the fleet. The enemy is bugging out." There was no reply. "Katrina?"

Alexis had reached the CIC secondary exit, a small, one-person air lock. It was manual, a contingency for this sort of event. She spun the controls with a growing sense of dread. "Captain to any damage control teams!"

"DC Team Nine," a beleaguered elSha answered.

"Get to Deck 18, auxiliary and drone control computer room, on the double!"

It took her several minutes to get out of the CIC; even the emergency exit had damage. It was a miracle she was alive at all. The entire armored CIC was only held in place by a pair of reinforcing beams. Cut them, and the room would have floated into space. She managed to move down to Deck 17 via the spinal service way and then crawled through the access shaft onto the nearest gangway. There she encountered a pair of medics seeing to an injured MinSha gunner.

"Is she stable?" Alexis demanded. The medic looked up in annoyance, then surprise as he realized it was his captain addressing him.

"Oh, yes sir," he replied.

"Then come with me!" With the medics in tow, she left the surprised gunner behind. When they got to the next deck, they found the damage control team already there, with the doors to AuxCon open to reveal the trashed interior. The room was full of smoke and flame suppressant. Normally the backup command crew would be there, in case the CIC was taken out. Most had been in the CIC with her as replacements from earlier attacks. It was clear the EMP had roasted most of these controls too. *Pegasus* was a wreck. The DC team was just opening the access to the computer room, at the back of the AuxCon.

The door pulled open slowly. There was no light inside, only the headlamps of the elSha damage control team illuminating the interior. Her sister, Katrina Cromwell, floated in the center of the room. A dozen wires led from her pinplants to the various computers in the room. She'd been using her implants to run the computers and provide control at the critical moment of the battle. All the leads were smoking and blackened. Her sister's eyes were open and staring as she slowly spun in the web of ruined, smoking wires.

* * * * *

Chapter Thirty-Nine

The access door at the back of AuxCon opened as she floated toward it. Moving in this new water-like medium was taking some getting used to. As the door opened, and she pulled herself inside, she realized it was the first time she'd been there in many, many years.

A food container was stuck to the wall magnetically, waiting for a crewman to pick it up. The room held the slightly sour smell of unwashed bodies and ozone. It was dark except for a few displays glowing on a work bench. That light revealed electronics and parts of robots and drones strewn haphazardly.

"Hello, Ghost," the captain said.

"*I knew you would come,*" the voice said. It sounded just as inhuman as it did through her pinplants.

"I can't see anything," Alexis said.

"*The light hurts.*"

"Maybe turn it up a little bit?" After a moment, a series of inset lights began to glow slightly, revealing a figure strapped into a reclining chair, held in place with a single belt. The head slowly turned toward her and Alexis saw herself. Only this vision looked much older, with skin stretched taut over bones, and hair floating in wispy threads. Eyes regarded her, the same brown eyes, the same white hair. Alexis cringed and swallowed.

"*Does the sight of me disturb you that much?*"

"No," Alexis lied, then changed the subject. "How do you know about this place, and why didn't you say we could get here and keep me from scaring my crew to death?"

"*I said nothing because arriving here intact after a drive failure is not an assured outcome. I know about it because it was explored eons ago,*" Ghost said. "*As you have no doubt surmised, it is a place well beyond our normal universe's rules and understanding.*"

"Your people explored it?" Alexis asked.

"*For our masters, yes.*" A skeletal hand rose and made a sweeping gesture. "*The Nothing led to the discovery of the rules of hyperspace travel. Before that, travel in regular hyperspace was risky, even dangerous. Coming here allowed for the development of the hyperspace navigation system. This level of hyperspace was kept a careful secret.*" A robot skittered, and Alexis jerked slightly. It moved along the work bench, across the floor, and up the chair to Ghost's chest. A tube came out and she drank. It was an almost mechanical action. The robot looked like a spider with long delicate legs; its abdomen was a water bladder. After a moment, it skittered away. With her eyes becoming accustomed to the dim light, Alexis could see the place was crawling with all manner of little robots. She could also see the array of pinlinks and the gossamer cables connecting the woman to the banks of computers.

"Is this place dangerous?"

"*In the short term, no. However, there are dangers.*"

"It hurts to look at it," Alexis said.

"*The effects can be unpredictable. It's one of the reasons it was never utilized as a regular form of transportation.*"

"Regular? That means it was used?"

"*Yes, by many races, in many galaxies, over all of time.*"

"You said dangers, plural."

"Other races have used this place, some continue to do so. There are things that live here; it is where they are from. Nightmare things even my kind fear. Things everyone fears."

"Then we should get out of here as soon as possible?" The head nodded on a neck no thicker than Alexis' wrist. "Can we get out? If so, how?"

"*Yes, you can leave,*" Ghost said, "*and it is far easier to leave than to get here. I can give your engineers the data they need to power the hyperspace nodes to work here.*"

"I hear a 'but' coming," she mumbled.

"*Because you are intuitive, for a Human.*" Alexis felt the irony of that statement wash over her like a wave. "*It will take more power than we have. Your people must get another one of the fusion reactors operating.*"

"I don't know if that is possible. Reactor Two still works, but Long never finished building the other one."

"*It is possible,*" Ghost said confidently. "*I have been monitoring Long's computer access. He will explain. There are great risks, and I advise you take them quickly.*"

"Then I better get to work," she said. "If anything comes up I need to know…"

"*I will not hesitate to tell you,*" Ghost finished for her. Alexis nodded and moved toward the door, then stopped and spoke without looking back.

"I don't hate you," she said, "I hope you understand that?" She closed her eyes tight, trying to forget how her sister looked floating there, her brain burned out. Trying to forget the horror when she realized the body wasn't dead, and something new had moved in. Something that had been hidden in the ship for untold eons. The person who used to be Katrina Cromwell looked at her with expressionless eyes. "I just hate Katrina had to die so you could live." Ghost watched her go without comment.

* * *

An hour later Alexis had briefed the department heads on the ship's current condition and had them disseminate the details to the crew. She hadn't told them everything Ghost told her; that didn't seem prudent. No need to scare them with stories of boojums or unknown monsters in the mind-rending dark of The Nothing. What she did explain was that there was a way out, and they were working on it. She needed to give them a reason to work, some hope there was a future. Further fear wasn't useful.

Next, she went to engineering and talked with Long. Just like Ghost had said, her Jeha chief engineer verified it was possible to get another reactor going.

"Possible, but not easy," he said. "Reactor Two is unstable, but serviceable. At least for a short time. We have forty of the buffers salvaged from the other reactors, and the vessel from Reactor One."

"You said before it was wasted," Paka said.

"The shot that took it out hit the inside buffers and caused an overload. However, the breakers kicked in and not all of them were blown. The 30 buffers along the hull side were saved. Because the safety functioned, and the drive plasma vented, the vessel is fine. I've already had a drone inside examining it. It's had a lot of hours, but no damage. We can put together a reactor. In fact, I've started work already."

"That's excellent news," Alexis said. He held up a pincher to forestall any celebration.

"That just leaves the F11," he said. "We scrubbed some from the atmosphere, but not enough. We need another 50 gallons, minimum, to have any hope of generating enough power to do what your Ghost says needs to be done."

"Where in entropy are we supposed to find 50 gallons of F11?" Paka asked.

Alexis' pinlink chirped, letting her know someone was trying to reach her. She checked and saw it was Dr. Sato, and ignored it. They talked about ways of solving the problem, including filtering the atmosphere for more of the lost F11. Possible, but not practical. Her pinlinks went off again. Sato was persistent.

"Excuse me a moment," she said to the others and answered the call. "Dr. Sato, I'm really quite busy."

"I thought you'd want to hear the results of the first EVA experiments and sensor modifications."

"What?" she said. "You went EVA already?"

"Well, yes," he said, and sounded pleased with himself. She suddenly remembered why they never took the Geek Squad on cruise.

* * *

Rick was jarred into consciousness as *Pegasus'* hyperspace generator cut out. It was immediately his least favorite way of being woken up. Period. Bar none.

"What the fuck!" he screamed and looked around in shock, afraid he'd been murdered in his sleep…or worse. He was alone in his little cubicle. A zero-gravity IV was hooked into his right wrist, and a small bio monitor beeped quickly in time with his racing heart rate. It indicated medical staff had been summoned, but none showed up.

Rick examined the IV in his wrist and, after a minute, figured out how to pull it out without injuring himself. He shut off the machine and tied a knot in the tube to keep it from leaking all over his cubicle, then realized he'd used both hands to tie the knot.

Remembering his injury, Rick studied his left arm. His new arm was similar to his natural one, but not exact; it was a bit thinner and colored a strange metallic blue. There were ripples for the cybernetic muscles, and it made a tiny scritching sound when he moved it. The limb felt and responded just like his own had before it was burned off, though, and he reached out and touched it with his right hand. It was cooler than skin, but not cold, and he felt the touch from his right hand on the left's skin just like normal.

"Amazing," he said. It felt great.

No one responded to the monitor's summons. Recalling the strange, reality-rending sensation he'd felt, he decided something might be seriously wrong and decided to go investigate. His pinplants said he'd only been asleep for six hours after the cybernetic grafting; that would have to be enough. He slid open the partition and quickly discovered physics didn't work like they used to. He coasted to a stop only halfway down the corridor.

"Woah," he said, and tried to push off into a spin. The spin quickly slowed and stopped. "That's not normal."

"You think?" asked Johansson as she came into the corridor.

"What's going on?" he asked her.

"Hyperdrive failed." Rick blinked. "Yeah."

"Shouldn't we be dead?"

"Don't know what we should be," she said, "only that no one has ever admitted to coming back from a hyperdrive failure." They went to the squad bay where the rest of the surviving marines were relaying their experiences.

"We're not dead," he said, obviously.

"So it would seem," Oort agreed. Did she sound disappointed?

Everyone was experimenting with the not-quite zero gravity.

"It's almost like water," Johansson laughed, now stuck floating in the middle of the room with the same movements you'd expect from someone in freefall. "But you can't feel any resistance slowing you down!" They were all trying to understand the new reality when the lieutenant received a summons on her pinlink. She listened for a moment then spoke.

"That was Dr. Sato. He wants the marines to report to the hangar deck immediately." They all exchanged looks of uncertainty. The Geek Squad had a reputation. It was Rick who spoke up.

"Courage is being scared to death…and saddling up anyway." Nods went around the assembled marines, and in a second, they were all heading forward.

"That is an interesting bit of philosophy," Oort said to Rick. "Which philosopher said it?"

"John Wayne," Rick said.

"I will need to read his material."

Dr. Sato, along with Kleena, Thing 1, and Thing 2, had conducted a systematic test of the ship's various races and had determined which ones could be exposed to what they called "Level Two Hyperspace" for more than a few minutes. Humans were generally tolerant, though that tolerance varied greatly. The Selroth had no tolerance at all. One Selroth, a laser gunner, almost had a psychotic episode from just a few seconds' exposure. The Veetanho and the Jeha responded similarly to Humans. The MinSha seemed a bit less tolerant, and the elSha became disturbed after only a few minutes.

The most resistant proved to be the Vaga laborers and Oort. Rick mentioned to Dr. Sato that Oort noticed something was different shortly after they arrived.

"Has to be a peculiarity of their neural makeup," the scientist said. Rick proved, by far, the most resistant Human tested, but all the Human marines tested high on the tolerance spectrum. It was Rick and Oort who were floating outside in pressure suits when the captain discovered the unauthorized experiments.

"Why did you take it upon yourself to authorize this?" she demanded shortly after arriving. "Was it that important to get someone out in the black?"

"After your blasted sensor officer refused to allow me to modify any of the ship's instruments, I was forced to conduct hands-on experiments." The scientist gestured toward the airlock and shrugged. "Your marines graciously volunteered to help."

"Flipper did the right thing stopping you," she said, making the doctor scowl.

"I don't recall volunteering," Rick said outside in 'space.' Sato grumbled something about ungrateful people. Rick didn't feel any different. It was a strange version of space, with no visible stars, but not disturbing.

"I find it rather compelling," was all Oort had to say.

"You can have it," Captain Cromwell said. She grudgingly gave them permission to continue.

Rick and Oort spent over an hour running tests under the close supervision of the Geek Squad. Once Dr. Sato had the data, he became even more excited.

"It turns out we can see over distances here, unlike Level One hyperspace." He told Flipper how to adjust the sensory input filters. Instantly data began to flow into the ship's sensors to be interpreted by the computers. A picture of the space around them began to take shape.

"Wow," Edwards said from his tactical station.

"I'm picking up large returns," Flipper said. Every second there were more returns, ever further away. "The lidar and radar bounces were not returning at the normal speed." He looked at Dr. Sato who was floating in the CIC, watching with a huge, satisfied grin on his face.

"The rules are different," he said.

"Selectively different," Alexis agreed. "If the speed of light isn't a constant here, though, why do our electronics still function? Or even our nervous systems?" The doctor looked at her, and his grin faltered. "Can you determine what those readings are?"

"I'm not sure if I can trust the returns," Flipper said. "They're not big, in the cosmic scheme of things. I'd say ships."

"Ships?!" Paka asked, surprised. "Are any moving?" Both Glick and Edwards were suddenly more alert.

"I don't think so," he said. Rick and Oort confirmed the same phenomenon that kept crew from floating any distance in the ship seemed to hold true outside the ship. It was also still a vacuum. "The returns are so slow, it will take a few sensor-sweeps to find out."

"Our number one priority is F11," Alexis said, and turned to Paka. "Assemble a team of those with the highest tolerance. Have a shuttle prepped and standing by." She looked at the Tri-V display and chewed her lower lip absently. If those ships, if they were ships, were castaways like the crew of the *Pegasus*, there was a good chance they'd have some F11. She didn't need a lot, just 50 gallons. Long's report said he'd have it ready in five hours.

* * * * *

Chapter Forty

Alexis pulled herself back into the CIC after sleeping for three hours in her wardroom. She tried jumping for the door, and was almost marooned in the middle of the compartment, having forgotten the new rules. She hoped they could get out before too long, otherwise a lot of Hussars were going to get injured when they returned to normal space and started crashing into walls.

Her primary command crew arrived at the same time. Alexis wondered, and not for the first time, if they'd bugged her wardroom and knew when she was returning to the bridge so they could all arrive at the same time. Flipper was just slipping on the special headset that let him breathe and receive sensory data through his sonar receptors when Alexis spoke.

"Updates?" It took the Selroth a moment to finish scanning his screens before he reported.

"We have confirmed 111 ships within five light minutes of our location," he reported.

"Did you say over 100?" Paka asked, joining them.

"Correct," Flipper said. "Sizes are extrapolated based on radar profiles, but we can't confirm because the modifications to the lidar aren't as accurate as those made to the radar."

"I've been running simulations on small craft flight," Chug said, "based on data from the marines who've been messing around in that soup out there." Data appeared on the main Tri-V. "Our shuttle's maximum range is going to be about four light minutes."

"Why so short?" Paka asked.

"The strange resistance?" Alexis asked.

"Exactly," Chug agreed. "Though it isn't really resistance. We used a couple Vaga with maneuvering packs to test this universe's flight characteristics. The thrust needed to reach a certain speed is identical to normal vacuum. But the instant you cut thrust below a certain threshold, you start to experience drag." A graph appeared. "The test with the Vaga subject produced this curve." Alexis examined the data.

"According to the curve, when you reach five hundred feet per second you'd come to a complete stop in five hundred feet?" The Bakulu helmsman nodded. "How were the G forces?"

"There were none."

"None?" Alexis asked incredulously.

"None," Chug agreed. "Dr. Sato was manic, wanting to take out a ship to see if that held true at a few thousand feet per second. I convinced him you wouldn't approve."

"You are correct, of course."

"Regardless," Chug continued, "we found that if thrust remained at least 10 percent of the current velocity, you wouldn't experience drag."

"That means you have to keep increasing power indefinitely?" Alexis asked.

"We don't know, having not tested the theory. The endurance of the shuttle is based on this assumption. We don't want to take it above a speed where the potential Gs would be dangerous, if our assumptions are incorrect."

"Good plan," she agreed. "Where does that leave us, then?" The helmsman manipulated the display and it shrunk to the distance mentioned.

"There are 29 ships within the operational range of the shuttle. If we allow for maneuvering at the individual targets, or moving between targets," the display changed again, "we end up with 19 ships within range. They appear to range in size from frigates to at least one possible behemoth."

"Is there any record of a behemoth lost in hyperspace?" Paka asked.

"None that we could find," Chug replied. On the display, there were several dozen courses plotted to the ships in range. Each one went by at least three ships before returning to *Pegasus*.

"Let's rule out the behemoth," she said, and four of the courses disappeared. "Same for the frigates." Another five popped out. "Try to keep it to ships of cruiser or battlecruiser size." Only four routes were left. "Very good, please consult with Dr. Sato and pick the most probable one. The away team is to include a light squad of marines, engineering staff, and any of the Geek Squad who elect to go. Is the shuttle ready?" she asked her XO.

"Yes, Captain, fueled and equipped with F11-rated tankage. Pilot Southard has volunteered to fly the mission."

"He's a good choice," Alexis said. "Better have the marines go out in CASPers."

"<*That is a good idea*>" Ghost spoke to her.

"I'm heading to engineering to check on repairs. Notify me when the shuttle is ready to depart. Paka, you have the conn."

* * *

Eventually T'jto forced Dr. Sato to stop conducting science experiments on her marines and brought Rick and Oort back aboard. The two had returned to their respective quarters to rest. Between the physical work of the experiments and the mental gymnastics involved in understanding how this strange version of hyperspace worked, Rick was physically and mentally exhausted. Just before he fell asleep, his pinplants informed him he needed to prepare for a mission in three hours. He had just enough forethought to set an alarm before passing out.

When the alarm sounded, and he struggled back to wakefulness, he realized he didn't dream. He'd never been much of a dreamer, but since the laser injury, nothing. *What's left of me?* he wondered as he dressed. In the squad bay, the lieutenant was waiting to brief him. He listened as he ate a couple of ration bars high in protein and nutrients. They weren't sparing power for things like the autochef yet.

The marines were tasked with investigating nearby derelict ships for possible sources of F11. Besides Oort, only Humans in CASPers were going on the shuttle, as there could be some risk. They weren't told what the risk was. Sergeant Stan Jones of Raptor Squad would command the marine detachment.

Naturally, the marines were incredibly curious about where they were. The captain's briefing hadn't been very detailed, and they tried to grill the lieutenant for details.

"Culper and Oort are the only two who've been in the black here," T'jto said.

"And it's really, really black," Rick said. He told them about his experiences while he finished another protein bar and an energy drink. Oort added occasional color as she slurped something that looked like motor oil from a zero-G tube. Then it was time, and the

Humans went to their respective armories to suit up. The armorers had repaired Rick's CASPer by replacing the arm he'd gotten sliced off. Oort's armor was likewise fixed up. Rick felt a little spoiled. Training with Mickey Finn, he'd had to do most of his own repair and maintenance work.

As he was finishing his suit check, he wasn't surprised to see a familiar elSha clinging to the wall nearby, making notes on a slate.

"Hello Kleena," Rick said.

"Rick," the scientist said.

"Can I ask what you are doing to my suit?" Rick could have sworn the little reptile grinned.

"Sato had a few algorithm updates for your suits. They should make the jumpjets respond properly to the drag this place induces on movement. Likewise, I've recalibrated the radar, lidar, and thermal imagers. You won't be blind, at least."

"Thanks," he said. "That should help a lot." Rick considered something. "What about weapons?"

"We didn't have time to check," the scientist admitted. "Ballistics should work at short range, and energy at long. I left off the MAC shoulder mount and gave you a heavy laser rifle instead."

"Better than nothing," Rick said as he started to wiggle into his CASPer.

"Listen," the little alien said. "Be careful out there. We're off the map. I've read some of your Human fiction. Here, there be dragons." Rick chuckled and nodded.

"I will. Thanks."

* * * * *

Chapter Forty-One

"Everyone strapped in?" Southard asked from the cockpit. In the rear of the shuttle were four 50-gallon portable tanks designed to be worn on the backs of combat suits to hold any F11 they found. Four CASPer-suited Human marines and one Tortantula were locked down. Latched to the wall were four specially-made drones, modified for this mission. A single engineer, a woman named Bonnie Cole, was included almost as an afterthought. She wore a light combat space suit and was obviously uncomfortable amidst the squad of hulking eight-and-a-half-foot-tall combat suits and a ten-foot-wide spider.

"Good to go," Corporal Johansson told him and used her suit's powerful arm to flash a thumbs-up. Cole finally finished getting the straps on her seat settled and looked peevishly at the four marines standing clamped magnetically to the floor, holding to a brace with one hand.

"We'll take care of you," Alvarado told her as she checked the buckles on the backward-facing fold-down rumble seat at the front of the cargo hold.

"I don't understand why I couldn't get one of those combat suits," she said. All four Human marines chuckled, even Rick. "What? Don't think I could handle one?"

"No," Sgt. Jones said; "we don't just *think* you couldn't handle a CASPer. We *know* you couldn't." She glared at the suit, but was obviously uncertain where to glare since the suits didn't have heads, and, unlike the older Mk 7, no visible cameras.

"Might have been amusing to watch," Oort noted. That elicited even more laughter, and the engineer decided the floor was interesting.

"Launching," Southard said, and they felt sideways acceleration.

* * *

Alexis had come up from engineering in time to watch the shuttle launch. Long, good to his word, had nearly finished the new, improvised reactor. They were behind schedule, but only because of manpower shortages. He was confident they'd be able to begin running containment tests in three hours.

She watched through the window as the shuttle cautiously left. Beyond was the hideous blackness. She turned away before she got another headache and returned to the CIC. Everything hinged on what the marines would find. It was down to one big roll of the dice.

* * *

When the shuttle was only a couple minutes out, the pilot tried to check in with *Pegasus* and got the first nasty surprise.

"Comms are out," he told the passengers.

"Our radios work between suits," Sgt. Jones said.

"Must be something to do with *space* here," Bonnie said, holding up fingers to make quotation marks when she said space. It was as good a theory as anything else. They flew on.

The shuttle flight took longer than Rick thought it would. He didn't understand the strange effects of hyperspace here, only that it seemed they were flying much slower than he was used to, considering the distances they'd mentioned. The furthest they were supposed to go was only two light minutes out, or around 22 million miles. Even at one gravity constant, they could do that in an hour or so. But because of the weird physics, Southard had to carefully balance a thrust/deceleration curve and override the ship's automatic maneuvering subroutines because they kept trying to compensate for a roll that was automatically cancelling itself. They could hear him in the cockpit, mumbling to himself unhappily.

"Everything okay, pilot?" Sgt. Jones asked after fifteen minutes.

"Okay for this fucked up place," Southard answered.

"We flipping over to slow soon?"

"No," he growled back.

"Huh?"

"We don't have to," Rick said, and explained the drag Oort and he had experienced. The scientists were calling it counter-gravity.

"How many Gs we gonna pull?" the sergeant wondered. "We have to be really moving by now."

"We're not even going a thousand feet per second," Southard called back, and Rick nodded. That was why he kept pulsing the engines. No doubt the cursing was because they kept slowing down, but didn't feel it. The pilot didn't like the fact that physics had a different playbook here. Several hours passed until he finally announced, "We're approaching the first ship."

Southard routed the camera feed through the displays mounted on the forward bulkhead of the shuttle's cargo hold, just behind the cockpit. The visual projection inside Rick's CASPer was wonky, and had been since Kleena had modified the input filters. It gave everything a hazy fishbowl appearance which he hoped would clear up when they were in space.

The image on the shuttle monitor looked perfect to him, the modifications Kleena had made were doing their job. The ship, on the other hand, looked unlike anything he'd ever seen before.

"Looks like a snowflake," Johansson said.

"Or a crazy old Earth sci-fi movie space ship," Alvarado said.

"I didn't know you were into old stuff like that," Rick said. He'd watched a lot of those shows with someone he couldn't remember now. Come to think of it, the memories of those old films were hit and miss too.

"Whoever set up the video library on *Pegasus* certainly was," Alvarado said, "there have to be two thousand old Earth movies and TV shows."

"More like 10,000," Johansson said. "You can blame or thank Edwards, the TacCom."

"The little black man?" Rick asked.

"That's him," she said. "He was born with the diastrophic dysplasia form of dwarfism. Couldn't walk for most of his childhood. His older brother joined a merc unit and sent almost every credit home to be used for nanotherapy. It got him as far as he is now, otherwise he'd probably never have lived this long."

Rick was more than a little amazed Corporal Johansson knew that much medical terminology. Mercs tended toward the smarter side of the scale, the VOWS pushed that number up, but she seemed even smarter than average.

"You know a lot about the little dude," Jones said. "You sweet on him?"

"Fuck off, sergeant," she said coldly. The sergeant laughed uproariously, but he was the only one.

"If you people are done fucking around back there?" Southard barked from the cockpit. Rick thought his voice had an edge to it. "We gonna board that snowflake, or not?"

Bonnie was studying the image on her slate, which had likewise been modified by Kleena to interpret images in this space. She was frowning and shaking her head.

"There isn't anything like this in the Union, not even close." She pointed at various parts of the ship. "I can't see any obvious form of propulsion, and it looks like more than one gravity would tear it apart! But I'd love to get a look inside."

"No time," Sgt. Jones said, shaking his head. "Our orders are to find some F11 and get our asses back to *Pegasus* ASAP."

"Why the hurry?" Rick asked. "We're not going anywhere fast." The sergeant shook his head and shrugged.

"Don't know," he said; "don't care. Southard, push on to the next one."

"Fly close by," Bonnie asked, "I want to record as much as I can!" They moved on with the same surging on-again off-again acceleration. Bonnie was given views of the snowflake from only a few hundred yards away. "Looks like it's disintegrating," she said. Sure enough, parts of the structure were clouds of debris. Rick wondered if someone, or something had done it on purpose. Seemed a shame to destroy something so beautiful.

Another hour passed in silence as they flew to the next ship, which would be the furthest they went from *Pegasus*. Southard's grumbles grew less vocal as he became accustomed to the altered physics. The passengers watched the video screen as they drew closer to their objective. Engineer Bonnie recognized it before long.

"That's a Maki battleship," she said, running her finger along the blunt, bullet-shaped ship's outline on her slate. "No doubt about it. Long range sensors didn't think it was this big. Calibration must be off." Even the marine's uneducated eye could catch the weapons damage and scorch marks on the hull as their pilot played the telescopic view along the hull.

"So, it's a Union ship," Sgt. Jones said. "You sure?" The engineer nodded her head emphatically. "Then they should have F11."

"Yes," Bonnie said, "unless engineering is wrecked. Pilot, can you take us around to the rear of the ship?"

"Sure," he said, but his voice sounded strained.

Rick began to wonder about Southard. "How are you doing up there?" Rick asked, realizing Southard had a window.

"My head hurts," he admitted. "I'm trying to fly with the cameras as much as possible, but that's not how I was trained. Fucking space here is like ants digging into your head."

"Shutter the windscreen," the engineer suggested.

"I'll do that after approach."

The shuttle flew in along the length of the massive battleship. As they passed the bow, they could see the ship's merc registry information. The engineer keyed in the alien writing for a translation.

"*Ardent Grove*," she said, using the English translation. "Registered to the merc company Guardian Forest." She read a moment. "No notation of it being lost."

"Didn't we just fight some Maki?" Rick asked.

"Both in the last system and before you signed on," Johansson confirmed. Rick had vivid memories of fighting on a Maki battleship. The engineer tapped her slate.

"One of the ships we fought in Grkata was the *Illustrious Meadow*," she said, "and that ship was torn to shit, from what I heard. Chief Engineer Long was talking about it yesterday; he wants to do a failure analysis on it. I don't know about this one. The Maki are big into space; they have a lot of ships."

"But this one isn't listed as missing," Southard said from the cockpit. "Losing a battleship isn't a casual thing. Surely they filed a claim, or notice of loss in action."

"Any signs of life?" the sergeant asked.

"Nothing," Southard said, "but I don't know if the modified sensors are working well. We lost comms with *Pegasus* only a mile out, after all. Your call, marines."

Jones was silent for a minute as they slowly flew on intermittent engine thrusts along the nearly half-mile-long length of the warship. He knew the captain had set their search route intending to find only cruisers. This was way bigger than a cruiser. Finally, they reached the rear of the ship where they saw a great rent in the hull. It didn't look like something done by any weapon they'd ever seen, it looked like someone took a huge pair of pliers and ripped open the superstructure, bending a chunk of the hull outwards. The shuttle flew slowly through a cloud of debris. Metal, piping, odd flotsam, and bodies.

"Maki all right," Southard confirmed, and they had an all too vivid look at a Maki's furry body distended and contorted from exposure to vacuum, its eyes wide in death. Now they knew another law of physics that applied here. "But what caused that damage to the ship?"

"Nothing friendly," Johansson concluded. "Does the damage affect engineering?"

"I don't have a lot of information on that type of ship," Bonnie said, "but the damage is pretty far forward. A battleship should have multiple reserve tanks of F11."

"We're approaching our minimum fuel," Southard said. "We'll have to return soon."

"Okay," Jones said. "Southard, see if you can find access to the engineering section." The pilot only grunted in response.

The shuttle took a course around the rear of the ship where they found a standard airlock. It only took a minute to match and dock.

"No response from the battleship's docking mechanism," Southard said. "Initiating external dock. Better button up, I don't know if there is any atmosphere in there." The CASPer-suited marines were already air tight; the engineer slid her visor closed.

"We're ready," the sergeant said, and there was a clang followed by the shuttle's interior door swinging inward to reveal the other ship's lock door. As the most qualified, Bonnie unbuckled and moved over to examine the door.

"Atmosphere?" Jones asked.

"No," she said, "it's in vacuum."

"That makes it easier," he said, "open her up."

She nodded, opened the access panel set next to the lock, and removed a crank stored there. "Depressurize the hold," she told the pilot.

"Roger that," he said, and the door separating the cockpit from the hold slid closed. Atmosphere was pumped out as the suited marines each picked up one of the F11 tanks.

"Alvarado take point," Sgt. Jones said. "Ms. Cole, please follow behind Alvarado with Johansson and myself. Culper, take the rear." The pressure equalized, and the engineer used the crank to slowly pump the door open.

"We're in," Jones told the pilot.

"Roger that," Southard said, "I'm closing the cockpit shutters. Oh, fuck, my head hurts." The boarding party moved into the ship and left Southard to nurse his abused brain.

* * * * *

Chapter Forty-Two

Progress down the companionway was slow because the ship was made to Maki proportions. The furry arboreal mammals were half the size of Humans, so the CASPers were behemoths in comparison.

At the first connecting corridor, the engineer used her diagnostic slate on a control panel to see if anything worked. To her surprise, the ship's computer and communications system was still functioning.

"Does that mean there are survivors?" Sgt. Jones asked.

"No way of telling," she said. "I can try and hack the computer, but that would take a while, with no guarantees of success."

"No," Jones said; "just get us to the F11 storage." She nodded her helmeted head and worked on the access panel. The layout of the ship was located and downloaded.

"This way," she said, pointing.

Alvarado pulled himself down the corridor. "I hope we don't get hit here," the point marine said. "I feel like I'm crawling down a mole hole." Rick and his team hadn't used the crew access corridor on the other battleship they'd boarded; they'd stuck to the larger service ways which were used to move equipment.

The data proved accurate. They reached a huge blast door, which stood open, and on the other side was the expansive open spaces of one of the ship's engine rooms. Rick nodded; it looked like the one he'd been in before.

"Score!" the engineer said. It was a long way across the space to where she pointed. "Take forever to crawl along the walls."

"Not necessary," Alvarado said. He gripped her armor and launched with his jumpjets.

"Shiiiit!" she squealed as they soared. Rick had to grin; Alvarado had obviously done that on purpose. After Bonnie's crack about handling a CASPer, it was expected.

A moment later, the team was boosting across the open spaces of engineering with puffs of their jumpjets. It was strange, not having to flip over and reverse.

Their destination was a series of armored tanks arrayed next to one of the massive fusion reactors. The engineer shot Alvarado a dirty look once they landed, then began examining the connections and piping.

"This will take a few minutes," she said as she took out her slate and started taking images for translation.

"Understood," Jones said. "Everyone keep an eye out," he told the other marines.

Rick used his jets to fly over to a platform full of displays and acceleration couches. A work area, he guessed. He examined some of the controls and thought they indicated the reactor was in shutdown mode. The workstation seemed orderly, with no signs of anything amiss. It was as if the crew had shut down the reactor and left. No flashing lights or alarms were going off.

"Everything seems too calm," he said over the squad net. "If they ended up here the way we did, you'd think they would have tried everything to get out."

"Too much to assume," the sergeant said. "Stay alert."

Time passed and eventually the engineer figured out the system. She inserted a connector and used her instruments to test the tanks.

"They're full!" she exclaimed. "Pure, unused F11. Hundreds of gallons."

"Fill 'er up!" Alvarado said, removing the tank from his suit and letting it float next to her. Everyone else flew over and four tanks were set near the engineer. She used a flexible line she'd brought and connected the first one.

"How long?" the sergeant asked.

"The system is pressurized, so I don't have to use the portable pump I brought. Say five minutes per tank?"

"We only need one, right?" the sergeant asked.

"Redundancy," she replied.

"Yeah, and money," Johansson pointed out. "That stuff is 10,000 credits a gallon!" Rick looked at the four containers they'd brought. Half a million credits each when full. He let out a long slow whistle. "No sign of the locals," she told the sergeant, "I think we can afford an extra 15 minutes."

"Fine," he said. They could tell by the sound of his voice he liked the idea. "Do it." As a salvage party, they'd each get a percentage of the value. The precious gas was transferred. As they were filling the last tank, the sergeant called the shuttle. The sergeant accessed their other channel. "Shuttle, status check?"

"Trying to get rid of this skull-bursting headache," Southard replied. "Jesus, this place is a living hell."

"You can't shutter?"

"I have to keep opening up. Can't rely on the sensors," he said. Then there was a loud *thump* clearly transmitted over the radio. "Wait one."

"Shuttle, what was that?" Jones demanded.

"Something hit the hull," Southard said. "It was back by the cargo bay. Probably drifting debris." Rick was about to remind him that nothing drifted in this strange place when Southard suddenly spoke up. "Shit, something is on the hull! I can hear it moving!"

"Detach," the sergeant ordered, "Get clear, you can pick us up at another lock."

"Roger, beginning undocking-" he stopped and there was a sharp intake of breath. "It's on the window," he whispered. "Oh, oh god…it looks like a-" There was an explosive crash and a scream, followed by a hurricane sound. In a second, the channel was quiet.

"Southard!" Jones yelled. "Southard, report!"

"Well, hell," Alvarado said, summing it up. "There went our ride."

* * * * *

Chapter Forty-Three

"There is movement," Flipper said and pointed to the big Tri-V display. Alexis looked up from the engineering report to the indicated display. Even though they'd lost contact with the shuttle shortly after it departed, they' been able to watch its progress through a rather-delayed sensor picture. For the last half hour, the shuttle had been as far away as they could track.

The greatly hampered ship's sensors had picked up a signal near the ship the shuttle was investigating. She watched a little radar return that was past the derelict ship steadily moving toward it.

"Any idea what that is?" Alexis asked.

"No clue," the Selroth said. "It's not very big though. Probably smaller than a frigate."

"*<Your team is in danger>*" Ghost said to her.

"Are you sure?" Alexis asked.

"*<Yes>*"

"Engineering, this is the captain."

"Go ahead, Captain," Long replied.

"Can you give me propulsion?"

"Without a fully functional fusion reactor?"

"Yes." There was a slight pause.

"The maneuvering ion drive," he finally said. "But not too much or too long. If we lose another buffer before we start the other reactor…"

"Understood, give us what you can. Chug, set course for the shuttle's last location. Best speed engineering can give us."

Pegasus rotated on her maneuvering jets, too slowly and not far enough. Chug burbled and cursed, and maneuvered again, finally bringing them onto course. The modest thrust of the ion drive engaged and began to move them toward the distant ship.

* * *

The last tank was detached, full of F11. The only problem was getting back to the *Pegasus*. Each of the CASPer-suited troopers secured a tank to their back, ready to go.

"What's the plan, Sarge?" Johansson asked.

"There have to be shuttles on this ship, right?" He looked at the engineer who thought for a moment then nodded. "So, lead us to their hangar deck, and we'll steal one."

"Sounds like a plan," Johansson agreed. The engineer consulted the downloaded deck plans on her slate.

"We can use this main maintenance corridor," she said, pointing to a huge exit. Sergeant Jones approved, and they moved out.

With their objective in hand, the team proceeded as quickly as they could. They fairly flew down the much larger corridor, learning to move in leaps because of the strange drag. Engineer Cole was riding on the back of Alvarado's suit because she couldn't keep up.

"Another four cross passages," Cole said, hanging desperately onto Alvarado.

"Their shuttles are pretty nice," Rick commented.

"That one we stole sure did the job," Alvarado agreed. "We're starting a collec—" Alvarado's CASPer exploded. It was so sudden, he didn't even have time to scream.

Whatever hit him nearly tore the suit in half. The kinetic energy blew Cole off the back of the suit where she spun once and came to a sudden, stunned stop a few feet away in the middle of the corridor.

"Heads up!" Jones yelled, grabbing ahold of the wall and lowering his shoulder-mounted laser.

"What the fuck did that?" Johansson barked. Blood, gore, and chunks of armor were scattered all over the intersection; the view in the direction of the attack was like looking through a charnel house window. Rick reached out and snatched Cole by the leg, pulling her to the side as an energy beam passed through where she'd been. The beam looked like a laser, but it crackled like a particle accelerator. That was impossible—there were no portable particle accelerators! Particle accelerators were ship-based weapons because of their massive power draw.

Both Jones and Johansson's heavy lasers sent beams down the hall past their dead companion. Rick, guarding the engineer, tried to convince his unreliable sensors to tell him what they were facing. He got a thermal outline of something hot. It looked insectile, with six limbs, and was twice the size of a CASPer. He saw the red line of a laser beam hit and do absolutely nothing. No flash, no reflection, no shield absorption, nothing.

"We better run," he suggested as another beam flashed by, barely missing him.

"Good call!" Jones said. "Go!" He fired several more times as Rick took the still-stunned engineer and went back the way they'd come.

"Get out of this corridor!" Johansson said, turning and firing her jumpjets. Jones fired once more and began to turn but never finished. An energy bolt blew him and his suit to bits.

"Fuck!" Johansson cried as she pushed her jets to catch up to Rick.

The next cross corridor loomed, and Rick cut his jets. The crazy drag effect brought him quickly to a stop, allowing him to grab a handhold and turn the corner. A beam lanced past his suit. As he pulled the engineer around the corner, he realized he was only holding a bloody arm.

"Fuck," he said, tossing it aside. Another beam crackled past the intersection, and he was afraid the sergeant had been hit, but an instant later, she careened into the intersection without even slowing. The CASPer crushed the metal of the corridor wall, and she scrambled clear of the cross corridor.

"Move, move, move!" Johansson yelled. "Where's Cole?"

"Gone," Rick said. Rick took a second to remove a string of K-bombs. The powerful grenades were designed to work in sequence, if you had time. He didn't have much, so he thumbed three to "Gang Fire" mode and pushed them against the wall.

"Fucking hurry," Johansson said.

"I am!" Rick snatched a multi-function detonator, spun it to 'proximity – 5 seconds', and thumbed the 'link' button. The green light on the detonator turned red and flashed, and the three grenades flashed in unison. Rick let the detonator hover in the center of the side corridor. "Where to?" he asked the corporal.

"Away from that damn thing." she said, and they pushed away a dozen yards before firing jumpjets.

"What is it?" Rick asked. Johansson was panting, trying to catch her breath. "Did you see it?"

"It looks like a robot," she said, "or a CASPer for something as big as a Tortantula! Whatever it is, I don't want to be near it." They turned another corridor and Rick's ordinance interface control flashed red. The booby trap he'd left behind went off. He hoped it had done something, but didn't have a lot of faith. Anything that could ignore half a megawatt of tightly-focused laser energy might not be impressed with high explosives, either.

They raced down a series of corridors in full flight. Rick saw his jumpjet fuel falling at a precipitous rate and found that he cared. Was it fear he was feeling? In his mind's eye, he kept seeing Alvarado explode. Who had portable weapons that powerful? His mouth was dry, and he couldn't swallow. He didn't know where they were going and didn't really care.

And then they were at the end. The corridor stopped at a hatchway which looked like the lock they'd come through originally. Remembering how the engineer operated the lock, Rick jerked open the access panel and spun the spindle with his powered suit fingers, not needing the handle. The lock started to creep open.

"Is there a ship out there?" Johansson asked.

"No clue," Rick said. "Don't care."

"Yeah," she agreed as the door crept open. Johansson had her back to the door as Rick worked, her heavy laser rifle pointed down the corridor the way they'd come, the light mini-gun also aimed. It took an eternity of cranking to make it wide enough to slip through, and another eternity for Rick to close it from the inside. The lock was crowded with the two huge CASPers inside, and all the time he worked the spindle, he kept expecting to take an energy beam to the head.

The inside door closed, and to his surprise the outer one swung open automatically, completely catching them by surprise.

"Look out!" Johansson yelled, and spun toward the opening door.

* * *

"Range down to under a light second," Chug said.

"Movement on the target," Glick warned. On the status board, another object had separated from the ship and was moving toward them. They'd finally identified the derelict a few minutes earlier. They were all surprised to find it was a ship they'd faced before, the Maki battleship *Ardent Grove.*

"What do we have, Flipper?" Alexis asked.

"Small target," she said. "Shuttle size."

"Ours?" Edwards asked, bringing his weapons alive. The small man had a scowl on his face, knowing the lack of fusion power meant he had very little offensive capabilities and almost no defensive.

"I don't think so," Flipper said.

"Any sign of that frigate sized target?" Alexis asked. They'd watch it come up to and merge with the derelict, increasing her anxiety for the boarding teams.

"Nothing yet," Flipper said. "That shuttle-sized target is making directly for us."

"TacCom, target that shuttle," Alexis said, "but hold your fire until ordered."

"Forward laser batteries are charged, I have one shot each," Edwards said. *Eight shots,* Alexis thought. That wasn't much. Flipper focused on the approaching shutter with a telescope, and they looked at it through filtered images. The craft wasn't theirs; that much was obvious. It looked more like a huge manta ray than a spacecraft.

"I've never seen a ship like that," Paka said.

"Me neither," Alexis agreed. "Stand by, Edwards." The TacCom nodded, his weapons armed and aimed. Only moments before Alexis was going to let him go hot, the strange looking shuttle did the unexpected. It slewed from side to side. "Is that a wing waggle?" It did it again.

"Sure seems that way," Chug said. Alexis laughed and shook her head. "It appears our boarding team acquired another vehicle. Inform the hangar deck to prepare for arrival."

"New target," Glick said. Another vehicle had moved from behind the derelict battleship.

"There's the frigate," Flipper said.

The strange alien shuttle was closing in rapidly, and the radio started to work again.

"*Pegasus, Pegasus,* this is Corporal Johansson in the alien shuttle."

"We saw your wing waggle," Hoot confirmed. "There is a ship behind you which just left the derelict ship. Is that more of your team?"

"Negative, *Pegasus,*" Johansson said. "We were attacked, and lost two marines as well as the engineer to some strange armored alien."

"Acknowledged," Hoot said.

"Orders?" Edwards asked.

"Target the alien frigate and fire at will," Alexis told Edwards. "Lasers only please, we don't know what nukes will do here."

"Ranging shot," Edwards announced and the weapons station chimed as a pulse fired. On the telescope, the distant frigate only looked like a lumpy stick. But the laser could clearly be seen impacting it with a bright flash. "Good hit," Edwards said. "Firing for effect." Three more lasers pulsed in quick succession. Flash, flash, flash. "It can take some damage," he said.

"The unidentified enemy was resistant to laser fire," Johansson said over the radio.

"Edwards," Alexis said, "combined fire please."

The TacCom waited while the four discharged lasers recharged. A second later, all eight fired at the enemy ship. It seemed to glow on the screen, then exploded. Everyone breathed again.

"Clean kill," Flipper confirmed.

"No other targets," Glick said.

"Recover the shuttle," Alexis said. "Helm, move us away from the Maki ship, just in case." *Pegasus* began to maneuver in the opposite direction.

* * *

An hour later, Rick floated in the engineering control center and watched as the much-reduced staff finished transferring the hard won F11 into *Pegasus'* repaired storage tanks. He'd had a short debriefing with Paka and Lt. T'jto, telling them all Johansson and he knew about the new enemy they'd encountered.

When they'd landed the shuttle, the Geek Squad had shown up almost immediately and begun taking it apart. Dr. Sato and his team were ecstatic as they assailed the strange machine. Johansson had been a little annoyed. It had taken her quite some time to make the thing fly, after all.

"Pressurize the F11 manifold," Long ordered. Rick should have been in his quarters resting, but he wanted to see the end of this. A marine would never be welcome if he just showed up in the CIC, but no one minded him here.

"Pressurized at optimal," someone said. Long's wide insectile head moved from side to side, examining readouts.

"Agreed, prepare for power transfer from capacitors. CIC, we're about to start the new reactor."

"Understood," the captain's voice came through the intercom. "Good luck."

"To all of us," Long said, making a final check of the system. "Stand by. Energize buffers." The engine room began to vibrate with a deep, comforting thrum. "Inject hydrogen and commence compression in three…two…one…go!" The lights flickered, and the reactor performed its magic. It was almost quiet for a moment, then the hum gradually got louder and throatier. The engine room began to vibrate with a familiar feeling, and the power meters on the board started to climb.

"Self-sustaining!" a technician crowed. "One terawatt, two, five, ten!"

"Power levels climbing to optimal," Long said. If it were possible for a ten-foot-long centipede to smile, Rick guessed this one had an ear-to-ear grin. "Command, we have good power-up."

"Excellent job," the captain said. "We all owe you a debt of gratitude."

"Get us back home and consider it paid."

"That was incredible," Rick said. Long's eyestalks swung to him, apparently noticing the marine for the first time.

"It is exciting, isn't it?"

Rick nodded. "Now what?" he asked.

"Now, we see if our commander has any magic left."

* * *

"Now what?" Alexis asked Ghost. "Even with a reactor at full power, we can't run the hyperspace shunts and nodes."

"*<Have your helmsman engage the hyperspace nodes>*" Ghost replied.

"That's it?"

"*<Yes>*"

"Chug," Alexis said, "power to the hyperspace nodes." All three eyes turned to regard her in a Bakulu version of incredulity. "You heard me."

"Very well, Captain. Engaging hyperspace node generators."

The fusion reactor spun up to nearly full power, and the energy was transmitted through the ship's web of hyperspace nodes. Instantly *Pegasus* was surrounded with a crackling nimbus of multicolored energy. The cameras and sensors began to go crazy.

"*<This might feel strange>*" Ghost said. A second later, they were pulled taut like a rubber band. It felt like they were bugs in water, swirling around the drain. Then it was over.

"Oh, hell," Alexis said, trying not to vomit. All over the ship, others were less successful. Flipper seemed completely unaffected.

"I have good sensor data again!" he said.

"Are we in hyperspace?" Alexis asked, still feeling nauseous.

"No," Flipper said, turning to look at her. "We're in normal space!"

"Can you get a position?" the captain asked.

"Easily. We're Home."

* * * * *

Epilogue

Winged Hussars' Prime Base
New Warsaw System

Alexis stood in the familiar three-quarters gravity of her office on Prime Base watching the slowly spinning view of *Pegasus* in the near distance. The drydock that enveloped her ship was a swarm of activity as the entire engineering section had been removed and was being rebuilt from the keel out. That problem of not being able to reach all the reactor buffers was being fixed, permanently. Since the ship had been so badly damaged, it hadn't been much extra work.

A dozen other sections of the ship were open to space, and a multitude of components were being replaced, repaired, or upgraded. *Pegasus* looked like a patient on life support, undergoing multiple organ transplants.

The return of her surviving marines after the mission to secure the F11 brought both relief and further heartache. Still more casualties. Yet it was the shuttle they returned in which proved the most amazing part of the mission. Johansson and Culper reported finding the shuttle docked to the alien ship, it's systems on and engines warmed up. While they found the controls unusual, they accessed their pinplants and found an interface that worked. The systems were similar to a race known as the C'Natt, which was now extinct. There'd been no sign of who'd left the shuttle there, or why. According to the marines, it was much too small to have held the alien which attacked them.

As soon as the shuttle was on board, Dr. Sato had descended on it with a glee she'd seldom seen. On her desk were the first preliminary reports from the Geek Squad. Shortly after coming Home, they'd taken the disassembled shuttle and retreated to their labs in Prime Base.

The report didn't give a lot of details, although it confirmed the belief the shuttle was made by the C'Natt and indicated the shuttle operated on a micro-fusion power plant more efficient than anything the Union used. It also used very little F11. The rest of the shuttle was being investigated in a 'logical progression of importance,' according to Dr. Sato. Kleena confirmed she was carefully working to channel the brilliant doctor's efforts. Sato promised the captain more details when they were available, but she hadn't heard anything since. When Sato and Kleena were quiet, it usually meant they'd found something interesting. Alexis wondered what other tidbits the shuttle had yielded, but she'd learned to let the geniuses work without bugging them too much.

Parked a few miles to the other side of *Pegasus*, Task Force Two was disembarking personnel. They'd arrived yesterday, more than a little surprised to find *Pegasus* had not only survived, but beaten them Home.

"I should be working on the reports," she said to the empty office. The problem was she couldn't concentrate. Too much had happened, too many had died, and too much was at stake. Someone, or something had tried their damnedest to see her and her ship dead. That effort had cost thousands of lives on the enemy side, and by last count, over two hundred Hussars. She burned with the desire to go back out and find whoever had done this. After ripping the reasons from them, she'd kill them slowly. Only, she had tens of thousands of lives depending on her, so a vendetta wasn't something in which she could indulge.

Out the other window of her office, on the other side of the station ring, the planet they simply called Home lay. Five times the size of Earth, it received just 10 percent of the light. Only the equators were habitable most of the year, and that was still twice the land area available on Humanity's home world, because Home had no massive oceans.

New Warsaw's ancient red giant star cast its baleful glow on the planet, allowing life to eke out a minimal existence. For 100 years, the Winged Hussars had lived here, slowly engineering life that not only survived on the cold, dark world, but thrived there.

Elsewhere in the system, the F11 extraction mine on the remnants of an ancient gas giant was producing more than a gallon a day, and that would only increase. Research on Jupiter had paid off. The massive asteroid belt was now yielding vast amounts of minerals and rare earth elements. Finally, there was Prime Base, the ancient space station she stood on. Set to orbit Home before the First Republic was formed, it provided more room than they would ever need. Prime Base was four times the size of Karma Station.

"Why leave?" she asked the universe. "We have everything we need here." A glint caught her eye, and she knew it was the stargate at the LaGrange point. An unmapped stargate, just like this station. Forgotten by the galaxy before humanity learned to make fire. "You gave us this for a reason."

"<*I led you here because it was the only safe place for me*>" Ghost replied. "<*But it will only remain safe if you stay here. If we stay here*>"

"You were right," Alexis said. "Leaving was a mistake. Let them have their conflicts, I'm done with it."

"<*What about Earth? Aren't the Four Horsemen pledged to defend your home world?*>"

"The other Horsemen know where to find us," Alexis said. "Some of the Golden Horde are still here. We'll continue to work with them until the defenses are finished. But we're not going out there anymore, not after that."

"<*There could be more of my kind*>" Ghost reminded her. "<*The Dusman made thousands of us to run their war machines. Some could even be in The Nothing*>"

"We'll have to consider that," Alexis said. "Later."

One of the Hussar's many transports was loading next to the station. While she'd decided no more missions would be run, they had relationships outside that couldn't be severed without dire repercussions. She didn't worry that the location of the system could be stolen from these ships. Their computers were programmed by Ghost. Hacking an AI was a task no one in the Union would be capable of.

There were personnel out there who would want to come home, just as the transport held some who wanted to leave. Several hundred had elected to depart when it was announced that no more missions would be run. All aliens. Several thousand remained, most of those had families and lives here now. They were all welcome to stay.

One of those leaving was the Tortantula, Oort. She hadn't taken the loss of Jeejee very well. Alexis couldn't exactly blame her; their kind shared a deep, symbiotic relationship. Oort was going to Lycosa, her race's home world. Oort had thanked her for the ride home when she accepted her severance pay. She also thanked Alexis for the books on philosophy. The captain had been feeding her the texts since she discovered the former killing machine was having a crisis of conscience.

"What are you going to do when you get home?" Alexis had asked her.

"I intend to share what I've learned," she'd replied. Alexis wondered what she'd turned loose on the galaxy. Considering how the galaxy had treated her lately, she considered turnabout fair play.

"For now, the galaxy can go to entropy."

* * *

Rick stood in the huge promenade as dozens of people and aliens moved about. It was like the main promenade on the station around Earth, only much, much bigger. The window was spectacular. Easily 100 feet tall, it extended 1,000 feet in either direction. He'd been told the window was a single piece of perfectly clear quartz, something that no one had been able to make for thousands of years.

New Warsaw was an amazing system where a red giant had flared eons ago, scouring all the inner worlds. Somehow the Dusman had shielded the world the Hussars now called Home, maintaining a minimal ecosphere. The Hussars had added to the biosphere, and now it was a vibrant, if cold, world. More than 10,000 lived there, and seven times that in space.

"A dead-end system," they called it. The stargate wasn't in the Cartography Guild's database. No one would come here. Eons ago it had been mined out. That was before the sun flared, destroying several worlds and releasing gigatons of valuable elements into the solar system. It had also blasted off most of the gas giant's atmosphere, making the F11 accessible. Someone, long ago, had hacked the Cartography Guild's database and taken it off the records. For all intents and purposes, New Warsaw didn't exist. "Brilliant," he said to himself.

"I guess this is home," he said. The word had come down that no more missions would be taking place for the foreseeable future. For now, Alexis Cromwell would allow any who wanted to leave to do so. Only after whatever was happening played itself out would they resume merc operations. A vast plot to kill the Winged Hussars was the rumor. The powerful woman who led the Hussars wanted no part of it. He wasn't sure if he'd leave or not. He'd bled and died with a lot of these people.

On his slate was an invitation from Nemo, the Wrogul physician, and Dr. Ramirez to attempt surgery to repair the damage to his brain and maybe restore both his memory and his emotional balance. He'd decided he would take them up on it. It felt like he was living a half-life, and that wasn't right. There was also an invitation to dinner from Sergeant Johansson, and that interested him too. Maybe he'd be even more interested after the surgery, if it worked.

"Excuse me, Corporal?" a voice asked. He almost didn't respond, still not accustomed to his new rank. Corporal of the reformed Zenith Squad. He turned to see Paka standing there.

"Yes, sir!" he said and stood at attention. The Veetanho waved casually.

"We don't go in for that formality," she said. "I just wanted to say hello and ask if you had gotten settled in."

"Yes, sir. I mean, yes, Paka. I got an apartment here on the station."

"Not down on Home? I thought Humans preferred it dirtside."

"I'm from Texas originally," Rick said. "It's too darned cold down there for me."

"I see," she said. "So, you've decided not to leave?"

He shook his head. "No, I don't think I will. Maybe someday. We'll see." Paka nodded and turned to go. "What about you?" he asked. "There are only a handful of Veetanho here."

"I like my job," she said. "It suits me." And with that, she strolled away. On the promenade, scores of Humans moved about their business, interspersed with a good number of aliens. It was an interesting world they were building here. Maybe it was the future? Rick decided he'd like to find out.

# # # # #

ABOUT THE AUTHOR

Located in rural Tennessee, Mark Wandrey has been creating new worlds since he was old enough to write. After penning countless short stories, he realized novels were his real calling and hasn't looked back since. A lifetime of diverse jobs, extensive travels, and living in most areas of the country have uniquely equipped him with experiences to color his stories in ways many find engaging and thought provoking. Now a bestselling author, he has no intention of slowing down anytime soon.

Sign up on his mailing list and get free stuff and updates! http://www.worldmaker.us/news-flash-sign-up-page/

Caution – Worlds Under Construction

Titles by Mark Wandrey

Cartwright's Cavaliers

A Fistful of Credits

A Time to Die

Earth Song: Twilight Serenade

Earth Song: Etude to War

Earth Song: The Lost Aria

Earth Song: Sonata in Orionis

Earth Song: Overture

*****

The following is an

Excerpt from Book Four of the Revelations Cycle:

The Golden Horde

Chris Kennedy

Available from Seventh Seal Press

August 4, 2017

eBook, Paperback, and Audio Book

Excerpt from "The Golden Horde:"

25 Miles East of Tashkent, Uzbekistan, Earth

The Tortantulas covered the hills at the edge of First Sergeant Muunokhoi 'Mun' Enkh's vision like a black blanket. If Mun looked hard, she could see the hillside moving, crawling with the giant spiders. She had never seen Tortantulas wait before, and it was disconcerting; normally, they threw themselves into combat recklessly and attacked at the first chance. In fact, they usually only took contracts that offered maximum carnage, which didn't bode well for the waiting Humans.

They should have charged, but they hadn't. Obviously, there was someone from another race in charge of them. Based on that observation alone, Mun suspected a Veetanho lurked somewhere in their command structure, holding their chains until the exact moment the time was right. Tactical experts, the Veetanho rarely lost; Mun knew the attack would commence at the worst possible time…for her.

The spiders continued to mill just outside the effective range of the Human mercenaries' weapons, almost daring them to waste some of the ammunition she knew they would need once the attack commenced. With that many Tortantulas, she wasn't sure there was enough ammo on the entire planet to stop their assault, much less here with her battalion. It looked like someone had taken an entire Tortantula world, emptied it, and sent them here.

She scanned behind her; the last of the noncombatants had emerged from the escape tunnel and were running as fast as they could to where the shuttles waited two miles down the ravine. As noncombatants, they were more used to sitting on their butts in the rear echelons and less accustomed to physical exertion; 'running as fast as they could' was barely more than a quick walk for many of them. Her job was to hold off the spiders until the shuttles were safely away, but she could already see that was going to be like holding back the tide. This was the worst possible time for an attack.

The enemy commander must have realized it, too, for at some unseen signal, the Tortantulas moved forward as one, the blanket flowing forward smoothly. Mun shook her head inside her Combat Assault System, Personnel, or CASPer. Tortantulas never flowed forward smoothly. There was definitely a Veetanho nearby.

"*Here they come!*" Lieutenant Colonel James Laverno transmitted. Not really necessary, Mun thought; the spiders had been the sole focus of the battalion's combined attention ever since they had formed up.

"*Mark your targets!*" Mun added. "*Even though they look like a solid mass, they aren't. Stay in your sectors and pick a target for every shot.*"

She activated the battalion's targeting program, and symbology appeared on each of the trooper's displays showing the area each was assigned to defend. When the spiders got closer, it would change to a defensive arc; right now, their targets were far enough away that the lines extended nearly straight out.

With a thought, she armed all of her suit's weapons. The eight-foot-tall powered armor currently mounted a heavy magnetic accelerator cannon, or MAC, on her left arm, a 15mm autocannon on the right arm, and a missile pack on the right shoulder. The Tortantulas wore armor on most of their exposed surfaces; lasers were usually a waste of time against them.

Although it looked like a wall of spiders, there were places in the line where some of the spiders were slightly slower. Missiles arced out from across the battle line as the Humans tried to break the cohesion of the Tortantulas' advance. She targeted three, and missiles leapt from her shoulder to detonate on the targeted aliens, killing them and wounding a number of other spiders in the area. The missiles also left a gap in the lines…until spiders from the following ranks sprinted forward to fill them.

Unlike many races who wouldn't attack without their comrades on both sides of them to provide support, the Tortantulas didn't care. The spiders in the lead, who suddenly found themselves without their supporting squad mates, only raced faster to get among the hated enemy who had killed them.

A lone Tortantula is killable, though, and the battalion's MACs, autocannons, chain guns, and heavy machineguns opened up across the front to pick them off. Unfortunately, killing huge numbers of the five-foot-wide Tortantulas rarely stopped their advances; no matter how many you killed, they just kept coming. At least the dead aliens were big enough their corpses provided obstacles that slowed the following ranks as they had to go around.

The firepower of the 170 CASPers was enormous, but they were spread out over a mile-wide front, with huge cliffs on both side of the ravine; each trooper had to cover over 30 feet of battlespace. Mun knew the ravine widened behind them; they would get even more spread out if they retreated.

Despite horrific casualties, the Tortantulas continued to flow forward. The Humans couldn't kill them fast enough, and it was quickly apparent the Humans *would* need to give ground or they would be overrun. Mun had once read a historical report that said the worst thing in all of warfare was to be on the receiving end of a cavalry charge. Whoever had written that had never seen Tortantulas. The ground shook like a minor earthquake, and they seemed all but unstoppable. Worse, they hadn't even fired a round at the Humans yet. It was overwhelming to see them ignore the devastation they were receiving and keep coming, and Mun had experienced it before. For the newbies, it was suit-wetting time.

"*Battalion, stand by to conduct a fighting withdrawal up the canyon,*" Lieutenant Colonel Laverno ordered. Good, Mun thought; the officer had seen it, too. She checked her rear screens; the noncombatants were at least a half mile away. "*Execute the fighting withdrawal.*"

Along with the rest of the battalion, she activated her jumpjets, and the suit flew into the air to land 50 feet back from her original position. At the height of her jump, she marked two new targets and launched missiles at them upon landing.

The icon for Private Esendai Enkh went red in her display. He was dead.

"I've got hypervelocity rounds incoming!" one of the sensor operators called. "The spiders have riders!"

Gichii. Of course the lead Tortantulas would have Flatar riders. The Humans might have stopped the advance otherwise. Aliens that looked like foot-long chipmunks, the Flatar used hypervelocity pistols that fired a really small projectile at an incredible velocity. The bullet didn't have much mass, but the kinetic energy it carried from the velocity was enormous. The dead private's body, and the nearly half-ton suit he wore, were knocked backward by the impact.

"*Continue moving,*" Mun ordered. "*Even when you aren't withdrawing, keep moving to make yourselves harder targets.*"

The battalion continued to withdraw, and more troopers were hit. When one of the CASPers went down, the ones on either side shifted to fill in the gap, with the rest of the battalion shifting slightly to cover the resulting gaps.

"Damn it, Berke," Sergeant Stan Jones, one of the squad leaders, radioed, *"get back in formation!"*

Mun shifted her heads-up display to show the whole battlefront while she continued to pick off Tortantulas, and she immediately saw the problem. Private Berkelun Enkh was out of place. Way out of place. She had jumped to the right, probably to avoid terrain, but had gone almost all the way over to the next CASPer in line, leaving a huge gap in the line. Since she was still alive, the trooper to her left, her squad leader, Sergeant Jones, hadn't moved over to fill in the gap.

The spiders had seen the gap and were rushing toward it.

Mun activated her jets and jumped toward the opening as Sergeant Jones and Private Enkh both jumped toward each other to fill in the gap. Unfortunately, both soldiers chose the same landing spot and Private Enkh landed on top of Sergeant Jones half a second after he had touched down. Both soldiers went down in a tangle of metal.

Mun jumped again, trying to position herself to cover them, but the two soldiers were overrun by the Tortantulas, and both suits showed red within half a heartbeat. She touched down in the center of the gap and bounced back into the air, firing the last of her missiles to break up the mass of spiders skittering into the gap. If she didn't slow their advance, the spiders would be in a position to flank the rest of the battalion.

Her missiles were effective, blowing huge holes in the ranks of the spiders, but the rest kept coming and were nearly upon her. Mun bounced back from the throng, but could see she was now the focus of all the nearby Flatar. She hit her right jet to throw off their aim, but a round hit her left boot, destroying its jumpjet. Unable to control her descent, she hit nearly horizontally, crashing onto her left side to roll to a stop. A variety of yellow and red lights appeared in front of her blurred vision.

Mun shook her head, and her sight cleared. One of the Tortantulas was already on top of her, its Flatar rider aiming his pistol down at her. The last thing she saw was her tactical display. The spiders had broken through the gap in the line. While some of them fired down the Human line in enfilade, others raced off to chase down the fleeing noncombatants. She had a second to realize they had failed, again.

Then the Flatar fired, killing Mun instantly.

*****

*****

The following is an

Excerpt from Book One of The Kin Wars Saga:

Wraithkin

Jason Cordova

Available Now from Theogony Books

eBook, Paperback, and (soon) Audio Book

Excerpt from "Wraithkin:"

Prologue

The lifeless body of his fellow agent on the bed confirmed the undercover operation was thoroughly busted.

"Crap," Agent Andrew Espinoza, Dominion Intelligence Bureau, said as he stepped fully into the dimly lit room and carefully made his way to the filthy bed in which his fellow agent lay. He turned away from the ruined body of his friend and scanned the room for any sign of danger. Seeing none, he quickly walked back out of the room to where the slaves he had rescued earlier were waiting.

"Okay, let's keep quiet now," he reminded them. "I'll go first, and you follow me. I don't think there are any more slavers in the warehouse. Understand?"

They all nodded. He offered them a smile of confidence, though he had lied. He knew there was one more slaver in the warehouse, hiding near the side exit they were about to use. He had a plan to deal with that person, however. First he had to get the slaves to safety.

He led the way, his pistol up and ready as he guided the women through the dank and musty halls of the old, rundown building. It had been abandoned years before, and the slaver ring had managed to get it for a song. In fact, they had even qualified for a tax-exempt purchase due to the condition of the neighborhood around it. The local constable had wanted the property sold, and the slaver ring had stepped in and offered him a cut if he gave it to them. The constable had readily agreed, and the slavers had turned the warehouse into the processing plant for the sex slaves they sold throughout the Dominion. Andrew knew all this because he had been the one to help set up the purchase in the first place.

Now, though, he wished he had chosen another locale.

He stopped the following slaves as he came to the opening which led into one of the warehouse's spacious storage areas. Beyond that lay their final destination, and he was dreading the confrontation with the last slaver. He checked his gun and grunted in surprise as he saw he had two fewer rounds left than he had thought. He shook his head and charged the pistol.

"Stay here and wait for my signal," he told the rescued slaves. They nodded in unison.

He took a deep, calming breath. No matter what happened, he had to get the slaves to safety. He owed them that much. His sworn duty was to protect the Dominion from people like the slavers, and someone along the way had failed these poor women. He exhaled slowly, crossed himself and prayed to God, the Emperor and any other person who might have been paying attention.

He charged into the room, his footsteps loud on the concrete flooring. He had his gun up as he ducked behind a small, empty crate. He peeked over the top and snarled; he had been hoping against hope the slaver was facing the other direction.

Apparently Murphy is still a stronger presence in my life than God, he thought as he locked eyes with the last slaver. The woman's eyes widened in recognition and shock, and he knew he would only have one chance before she killed them all.

He dove to the right of the crate and rolled, letting his momentum drag him out of the slaver's immediate line of fire. He struggled to his feet as her gun swung up and began to track him, but he was already moving, sprinting back to the left while closing in on her. She fired twice, both shots ricocheting off the floor and embedding themselves in the wall behind him.

Andrew skid to a stop and took careful aim. It was a race, the slaver bringing her gun around as his own came to bear upon her. The muzzles of both guns flashed simultaneously, and Andrew grunted as pain flared in his shoulder.

A second shot punched him in the gut and he fell, shocked the woman had managed to get him. He lifted his head and saw that while he had hit her, her wound wasn't nearly as bad as his. He had merely clipped her collarbone and, while it would smart, it was in no way fatal. She took aim on him and smiled coldly.

Andrew swiftly brought his gun up with his working arm and fired one final time. The round struck true, burrowing itself right between the slaver's eyes. She fell backwards and lay still, dead. He groaned and dropped the gun, pain blossoming in his stomach. He rolled onto his back and stared at the old warehouse's ceiling.

That sucked, he grousd. He closed his eyes and let out a long, painful breath.

*****

Find out more about Jason Cordova and "Wraithkin" at:
http://chriskennedypublishing.com/imprints-authors/jason-cordova/

*****

18776719R00298

Printed in Poland
by Amazon Fulfillment
Poland Sp. z o.o., Wrocław